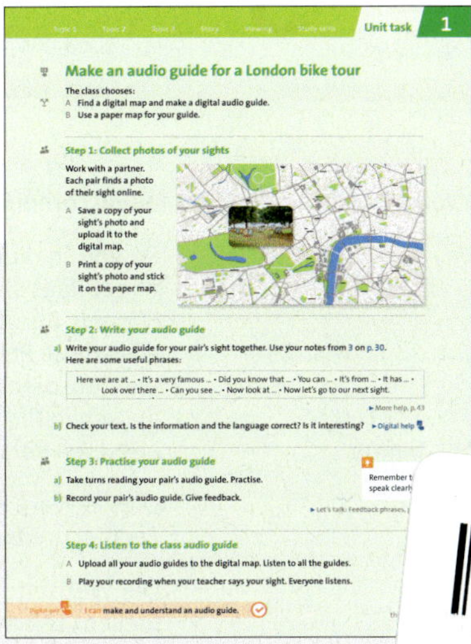

Lern- und Arbeitstechniken

Auf der *Study skills*-Seite übst du wichtige Lern- und Arbeitstechniken, z. B. wie du deine Meinung ausdrücken kannst.

Eine Aufgabe am Unit-Ende

In der *Unit task* erstellst du ein größeres Produkt, z. B. einen Audioguide. Dabei wendest du das Gelernte aus der Unit an.

Im *Checkpoint* wi… …ist du

Hier überprüfst du, wie gut du die Lernziele der Unit schon erreicht hast.

Nach Units 1 und 3 findest du ein *Text file* mit interessanten Texten zum Thema der Unit.

Diese Verweise führen dich in die *Diff bank* am Ende der Unit

► More help	► Parallel exercise	► More practice
Hilfen zu den Aufgaben	einfachere Variante einer Übung	weitere Übungen

Diese Lernangebote findest du im hinteren Teil des Buches

► Skills file	► Language file	► Wordbank
eine Übersicht über die Lern- und Arbeitstechniken	die wichtigsten Sprachregeln	zusätzliche Wörter zu bestimmten Themen
Let's talk	**Vocabulary**	**Dictionary**
Redewendungen nach wichtigen Themen und Situationen geordnet	eine Liste der neuen Vokabeln einer Unit mit hilfreichen Tipps	eine alphabetische Wörterliste zum Nachschlagen (Englisch – Deutsch)

BASIC lighthouse 3

Im Auftrag des Verlages herausgegeben von
Ulrike Rath, Aachen
sowie
Martin Bastkowski, Schellerten;
Sonja Mahne, Basel;
Berit Schaarschmidt, Aschaffenburg

Erarbeitet von
Olivia Wintgens, Würselen; Rebecca Robb Benne, Kopenhagen; Zoe Thorne, Royston
sowie
Jennifer O'Hagan, Bristol und Chris Maxwell, Berlin (*Checkpoints*);
Ursula Fleischhauer, Hannover (*Vocabulary*)

In Zusammenarbeit mit der Englischredaktion
Klaus Unger (Projektleitung),
Silvia Wiedemann, Kathrin Spiegelberg (koordinierende Redakteurinnen),
Franziska Gräbe sowie Josephine Bienert-Köhler, Chiara Castellano, Sandhya Gupta, Chelsea Ledvinka-Heß, Mara Leibowitz, Elizabeth Pancake-Steeg, Julian Theo Wacker, Karin Wedepohl
Ingrid Raspe, Düsseldorf (*Vocabulary*, *Dictionary*)

Beratende Mitwirkung
Sabine Bay, Cloppenburg; Armin Düpmeier, Warendorf; Lina Hein-Gehrmann, Wuppertal; Daniel Henn, Frankfurt/Main; Tobias Pfeifer, Dossenheim
sowie
Vertr.-Prof. Dr. Christian Ludwig, Berlin;
Prof. Dr. Michaela Sambanis, Berlin

Medienmanagement
Silke Kirchhoff

Illustrationen
Harald Ardeias, Schelklingen; Irina Zinner, Hamburg

Fotos
Chocolate Films, London

Umschlaggestaltung
Rosendahl, Berlin

Layoutkonzept
Klein & Halm, Berlin

Layout und technische Umsetzung
designcollective, Berlin

Druck
Mohn Media Mohndruck, Gütersloh

PEFC-zertifiziert
Dieses Produkt stammt aus nachhaltig bewirtschafteten Wäldern und kontrollierten Quellen
PEFC/04-31-1033
www.pefc.de

www.cornelsen.de

Soweit in diesem Lehrwerk Personen fotografisch abgebildet sind und ihnen von der Redaktion fiktive Namen, Berufe, Dialoge und Ähnliches zugeordnet oder diese Personen in bestimmte Kontexte gesetzt werden, dienen diese Zuordnungen und Darstellungen ausschließlich der Veranschaulichung und dem besseren Verständnis des Buchinhaltes.

Dieses Werk berücksichtigt die Regeln der reformierten Rechtschreibung und Zeichensetzung.

Die Webseiten Dritter, deren Internetadressen in diesem Lehrwerk angegeben sind, wurden vor Drucklegung sorgfältig geprüft. Der Verlag übernimmt keine Gewähr für die Aktualität und den Inhalt dieser Seiten oder solcher, die mit ihnen verlinkt sind.

Die ***Cornelsen Lernen App*** ist eine fakultative Ergänzung *zu Lighthouse*, die die inhaltliche Arbeit begleitet und unterstützt. Als solche unterliegt sie nicht der Genehmigungspflicht.

© 2024 Cornelsen Verlag GmbH, Berlin

Das Werk und seine Teile sind urheberrechtlich geschützt. Jede Nutzung in anderen als den gesetzlich zugelassenen Fällen bedarf der vorherigen schriftlichen Einwilligung des Verlages.

Hinweis zu §§ 60 a, 60 b UrhG: Weder das Werk noch seine Teile dürfen ohne eine solche Einwilligung an Schulen oder in Unterrichts- und Lehrmedien (§ 60 b Abs. 3 UrhG) vervielfältigt, insbesondere kopiert oder eingescannt, verbreitet oder in ein Netzwerk eingestellt oder sonst öffentlich zugänglich gemacht oder wiedergegeben werden.
Dies gilt auch für Intranets von Schulen und anderen Bildungseinrichtungen.

Alle Drucke dieser Auflage sind inhaltlich unverändert und können im Unterricht nebeneinander verwendet werden.

ISBN 9783060358274 broschiert
1. Auflage, 1. Druck 2024

ISBN 9783060358281 gebunden
1. Auflage, 1. Druck 2024

Produktnummer 1100028095 E-Book

BASIC
lighthouse 3

Cornelsen

Unit 2
Manchester: Who we are

Unit 3 Scotland: Adventure

Unit 4 Wales: Digital life

L Listening · **R** Reading · **S** Speaking · **W** Writing · **M** Mediation · **V** Viewing · **IC** Intercultural competence · **MK** Medienkompetenz · **LS** Life skills · **GG** Global goals · **Voc** Vocabulary · **G** Grammar

Unit 5 OPTIONAL Two Irelands: Together

L Listening · **R** Reading · **S** Speaking · **W** Writing · **M** Mediation · **V** Viewing · **IC** Intercultural competence · **MK** Medienkompetenz · **LS** Life skills · **GG** Global goals · **Voc** Vocabulary · **G** Grammar

Anhang

Die Angebote des Schulbuchs sind nicht obligatorisch abzuarbeiten. Die Auswahl der Übungen und Übungsteile richtet sich nach den Schwerpunkten des schulinternen Curriculums.

Hello!

Where we're from

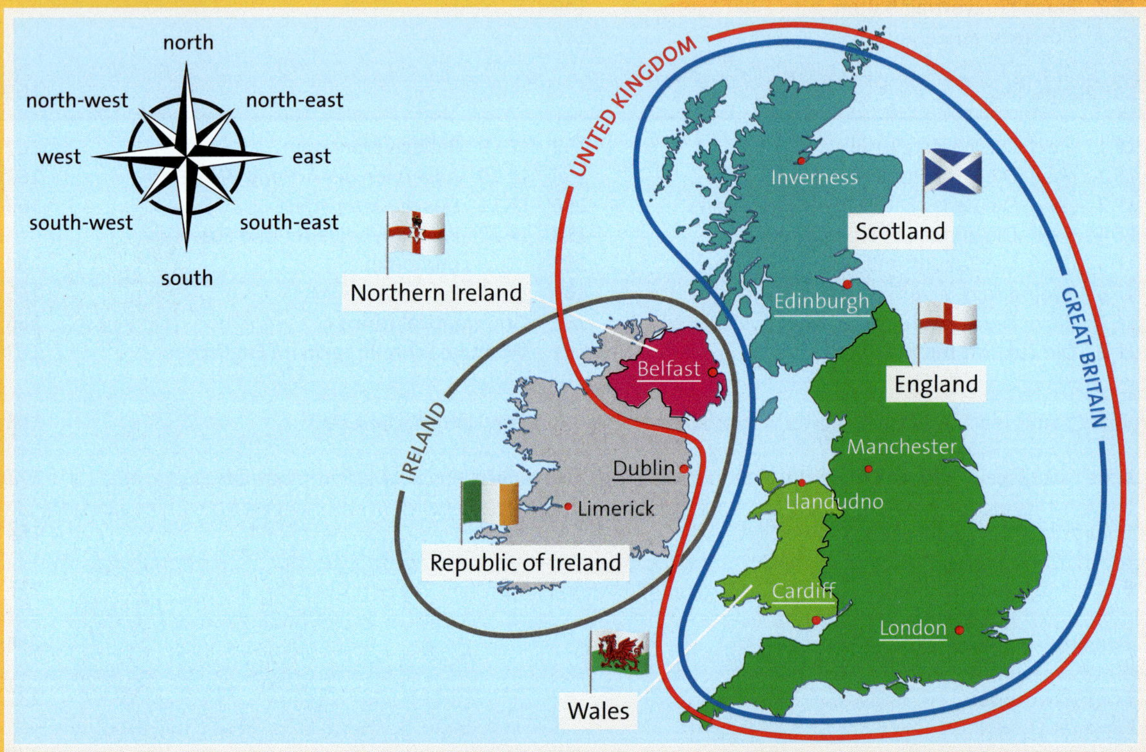

1 VIEWING The United Kingdom and Ireland

a) BEFORE YOU WATCH **Look at the map and answer the questions. Which countries make up ...**

1 Great Britain (GB)? – England, ... and ...
2 the island of Ireland? – The Republic of Ireland and ...
3 the United Kingdom (UK)? – England, ..., ... and ...

b) **Watch part 1 of the video. Check your answers from a).**
Then watch both parts of the video. True or false? ☒ Correct the false sentences.

1 England is the biggest country in GB.
2 Northern Ireland has over 790 islands.
3 Edinburgh is the second largest city in Wales.
4 Each country has its own national team.

2 SPEAKING **Hello!**

a) Listen and read what the students say.

b) Find the students' hometowns on the map on **p. 10****.**
Point to the places:

London is here on the map.

c) Three greetings on this page are not in English.
Find them. What do you think they mean?

1 How are things? 2 Hello! 3 God be with you!

Good to know

Some people in the British Isles speak English and an old Celtic language too: Scottish Gaelic in Scotland, Welsh in Wales, and Irish Gaelic on the island of Ireland.

A

This place has it all – big businesses, old castles and friendly people.

B

Listen to bagpipes near a loch or in town.

C

See skyscrapers and other amazing modern buildings in this city.

3 LISTENING **Where we live**

a) BEFORE YOU LISTEN **Look at the photos (A–F). What can you see?**

In the foreground I can see ... A musician is ... In the background there's ...

b) **Write the names of the students from** p. 11 **(Pearl, Omar, Grace, Dylan, Jack, Orla) in your exercise book. Listen and match the photos to the students.**

Pearl: C, Omar: ...

▶ More practice 1, p. 38

c) **Listen again and check.**

D

Look at street art and murals, like this one of the Titanic.

E

Visit Conwy Castle, one of many castles in this area.

F

Experience the city on a boat trip on the canals.

4 The best place

Which photo looks interesting to you? Why?

I think that	photo A, B, ...	looks interesting • boring • ...
I like I don't like	street art • big cities • castles • old buildings • music • boat trips • ...	

▸ Workbook: Check-up, pp. 6–15; ▸ Workbook, pp. 16 17

Digital quiz I can talk about the UK and Ireland.

Unit 1
London: City life

Go shopping and eat amazing food here.

See this popular tower at the Houses of Parliament and hear the famous sound.

1 LISTENING **Your London, my London**

Lily has just moved to London. She's talking to her new friend Ali about London sights.

a) BEFORE YOU LISTEN **Look at the photos and read the captions. Then guess. Match the names in the box to photos A–E.**

Big Ben • Buckingham Palace • Camden Market • The London Eye • The Tower of London

b) **Listen and check.**

c) **Listen again. Where are Ali and Lily going this weekend?**

► More practice 2, p. 39
► Skills file 8, p. 147

Nach dieser Unit kann ich ...

- Informationen über London verstehen und wiedergeben
- über Verkehrsmittel in London reden
- eine Tour planen
- das Leben in der Großstadt und in meiner Gegend beschreiben
- online recherchieren

Unit task

- einen Audioguide für London erstellen

C

Visit the home of the royal family.

D

Learn about history in this old castle.

E

Ride this wheel and take great photos.

2 SPEAKING Visiting London

Talk to your partner about the places in 1.

I think that	Big Ben • Buckingham Palace • Camden Market • the London Eye • the Tower of London	looks	cool • interesting • fun • exciting • ...
I like to	take photos • see famous sights • learn about history • go shopping • eat amazing food • ...		

► Workbook, p. 18

Digital quiz **I can understand and share information about London.**

Travelling in London

1 Reading London's public transport

a) Before you read **What kinds of public transport do you know? Tell a partner.**

Our town has ...

Big cities have an underground.

b) **Read the travel guide and complete the sentences below.**

No car? No problem!

There are many ways to travel in London and they're all green.

The underground, also called "the tube", is a great way to travel in London. Tip: Look at the tube map before you start your journey and remember the names of the tube lines and stations that you will need.

Try London's famous red buses. They often have two levels. If you can, go up the stairs and sit at the big windows at the front – it's fun!

You can also find and hire bikes all over London with different apps. There are bike lanes, but there's also a lot of traffic, so be careful. Wear a helmet if you can.

Walking is a great way to see London and it's very green too! But don't forget that people drive on the left in the UK. When you walk or cycle, you must look right first for cars, taxis, bikes and buses before you cross the road!

1 London has different kinds of ...
2 When you're on the bus, it's fun to go up the stairs and ...
3 "The tube" is the name for ...
4 When you cycle in London, it's a good idea to wear ...
5 If you're walking across the road, remember that you first look ...

2 Words Transport

Match the words to make phrases.

1 buy	A on the left
2 cross	B lines
3 take	C bikes
4 drive	D a ticket
5 change	E the road
6 hire	F the tube / bus / train

► More practice 3 + 4, p. 39
► Workbook, p. 19

3 Listening A trip

a) Before you listen **It's Saturday. Do you remember where Lily and Ali want to go?**

b) **Listen. How will they get there?**

c) **Listen again. True or false?**

1 There's only one way to get there.
2 It takes 25 minutes to walk.
3 The bus will be slow because there's too much traffic.
4 They'll change lines on the tube.
5 A ticket for the tube costs £1.60.
6 Lily wants to go by bus.

► Skills file 8, p. 147

4 On the way

Complete the conversation. Use the will-future: *'ll* or *won't*.

Ali We... (1) go to all the best stalls! You... (2) love the market, Lily.
Lily I don't have a lot of money, so I ... (3) buy much. I... (4) just look at the shops.
Pearl Me too! But it... (5) be fun. There's so much to see – we ... (6) get bored!

► More practice 5–7, p. 40 ► Language file 5, p. 159

Remember

Du verwendest das *will-future* für zukünftige Ereignisse: *The train will be here soon. I'll take the stairs.*
Du verwendest die Kurzform nach Pronomen *(I, we, you, they, he, she, it)*: *She'll go home.*
Du verwendest *won't* (= *will not*) um zu sagen, was nicht geschehen wird: *It won't be quiet.*

My task

5 What's the best transport?

a) **You're at Camden Market and you want to go to Oxford Street.**
Partner B: Look at p. 38.
Partner A: Copy and complete the table. Ask each other questions to find the missing information:

Camden Market to Oxford Street (3 km)					
	bus	tube	taxi	bike	walk
time	17 min.	7 min.	?	?	?
price	free for kids	90p	?	?	free

Partner A: *How long does it take if we walk / go by taxi / bike?* – **Partner B:** *It takes ...*
Partner A: *How much does it cost?* – **Partner B:** *It costs ...*

b) **Now decide and tell your partner: How will you get there? What won't you do?**

I'll	walk • hire a bike • take a taxi • go by bus • go by tube	because	it's cheap • it's fast • it's green.
I won't			there's too much traffic • it's slow • it's expensive.

► Workbook, p. 20

Digital quiz **I can talk about transport in London.**

A different kind of tour

1 Reading Which tour?

a) Before you read **Pearl's family is going to visit London next week. Pearl has found three tours for her family. Look at the photos and find the right tour name for each.**

1 Ghost Bus Tour
2 Classic London Segway Tour
3 Rock Walking Tour

A

Calling all music fans! Join our Rock Walking Tour to discover important places in London's music history. You'll visit Denmark Street, where many top rock bands and singers recorded their albums. We'll go to the best music shops in the Golden Mile. Then we'll have lunch at Hard Rock Cafe!

WEEKENDS ONLY

B

If you're scared of the dark, you won't like this tour! Join our Ghost Bus for a tour of the scariest and oldest places in London. Will you see ghosts in the Tower of London? Are you brave enough to go into the London Dungeon? There's only one way to find out ...

MEET US EVERY DAY AT 9 P.M. AT THE GHOST BUS STOP

C

Discover traditional London sights! Ride your own Segway as we show you the classic sights: See Buckingham Palace, where the royal family lives. Cross the River Thames on the beautiful Tower Bridge. And visit the home of the prime minister at 10 Downing Street!

2 P.M. EVERY DAY EXCEPT MONDAYS

b) **Read the descriptions of the tours. Choose the correct tour (A, B or C).**

1 This tour is in the evening.
2 You can buy something on this tour.
3 You can see famous homes on this tour.
4 This tour is only on Saturdays and Sundays.
5 You must be brave to do this tour.
6 You can eat on this tour.

c) **Tell your partner which tour you want to do and why.**

I want to do the	Ghost Bus Tour London Segway Tour Rock Walking Tour	because I like	riding Segways • music • scary stories • traditional sights • walking • ...

▶ More practice 8, p. 41
▶ Workbook, p. 21

2 Looking at language Conditional sentences type 1

Erklär-film

a) Read what the tour guide said. Which tour from 1 did Pearl's family choose?

1 "If you look to your left, you'll see the most beautiful building in London."
2 "If the King is at home today, there'll be a special flag on top of the building."
3 "If we're lucky, it won't rain today."
4 "If we have time after the tour, we'll visit that shop."

b) Read the rule and choose the correct answer A or B.

Mit *conditional sentences type 1* sagst du, was unter bestimmten Bedingungen geschehen wird.
Sie bestehen aus zwei Teilen:
Einer Voraussetzung (*if*-Satz im *simple present*) und der Folge (Hauptsatz im *will-future*).
If you look to your left, you'll see the most beautiful building in London.
If the King is at home today, there'll be a special flag on top of the building.

1 *If the King is* ... beschreibt A die Folge B die Voraussetzung.
2 *there'll be* ... beschreibt A die Folge B die Voraussetzung.

▸ Digital help

▸ Language file 6, p. 160

3 What will we do if ...?

Pearl is planning activities with her family after the tour.
Match the correct sentence parts.

Der *if*-Satz kann vorne oder hinten stehen.

1 If Aunt Vera sees a famous person,
2 If it rains,
3 If my cousins go to Hamleys toy shop,
4 We'll get there faster
5 If Uncle Roy smells good food
6 We won't go to the London Dungeon

A they'll buy too many toys.
B if we take the tube.
C I'll take them to a museum.
D if the tickets are too expensive.
E she'll be so excited!
F he'll want to stop and eat.

4 Pearl's family's visit

Complete the conditional sentences. Use the correct form of the simple present.

1 If Pearl's cousins ... (be) late, they'll miss the train.
2 If they ... (see) some musicians on the street, they'll listen to the music.
3 If Aunt Vera ... (find) a nice book, she'll buy it.
4 If the weather ... (be) good, Pearl's family will have a picnic in the park.
5 If Uncle Roy ... (forget) his hat, he won't be happy!
6 If Aunt Vera ... (remember) Uncle Roy's hat, he'll say, "You're the best!"

▸ More practice 9, p. 41

▸ Workbook, p. 22

5 Speaking Quiz-quiz-swap

a) What will you do if you go to London? Make notes on a card. Use the ideas in the box to help.

b) Find a partner. Say:

If I go to London, I'll ...

buy	a T-shirt • an umbrella • a phone case • sunglasses • ...
eat	burgers • pizza • fish and chips • curry • ...
travel by	bus • underground • bike • ...
visit	Big Ben • the London Eye • Buckingham Palace • ...

Then it's your partner's turn.

c) Swap cards. Find new partners and make new sentences.

6 Mediation St James's Park

You're on a walking tour in St James's Park.
A German tourist needs your help.
Have a conversation with two partners. Then swap roles.

Good to know

London has lots of parks and gardens – over 40% of London is green space!

Guide Here we are in St James's Park. It's not the biggest park in London, but I think it's the most beautiful.
Tourist Was hat er gerade über den Park gesagt?
You St James's Park ist nicht ...
Guide The biggest park in central London is Hyde Park.
Tourist Was hat er zum Hyde Park gesagt?
You Der Hyde Park ist ...
Guide Now, if you look over the Blue Bridge, you'll see Buckingham Palace. And the other way, you can see the London Eye and the tallest building in London, the Shard.
Tourist Was hat er über die Gebäude gesagt?
You Dort siehst du ...
Guide Look! We're very lucky to see those birds! Aren't they beautiful?
You ...

▸ Skills file 10, p. 149

7 VIEWING A virtual tour of London

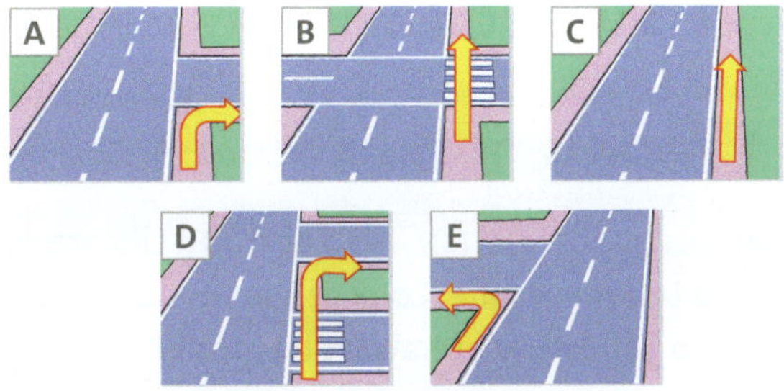

a) BEFORE YOU WATCH **Match the pictures A–E to the directions.**

1 Go straight on.
2 Turn left.
3 Turn right.
4 Go across the road.
5 Take the second road on the right.

b) VIEWING **Watch the video and complete the directions.**

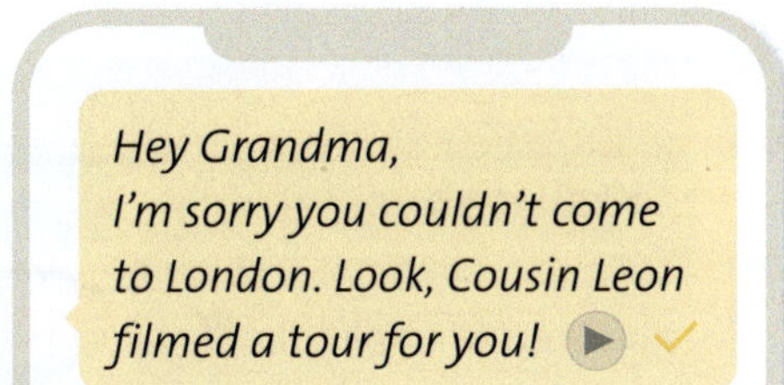

At Trafalgar Square, turn right at / go across (1) the roundabout and the road. Go straight on down / Walk past (2) Whitehall and take the second / third (3) street on the left / right (4). At the river turn left / right (5) and go straight on / across the bridge (6).

c) VIEWING **Watch the video again and choose A, B or C.**

1 Nelson's Column has A two B three C four lions.
2 You can see the Changing of the Horse Guards at A 10 o'clock B 12 o'clock C 2 o'clock.
3 Tattershall Castle is now a A castle B restaurant C shop.
4 The London Eye has A 32 B 30 C 23 capsules.
5 The tour ends at A Trafalgar Theatre B the London Eye C Big Ben.

My task

8 A tour of London

▸ Digital help

a) **Plan a tour in London. Pick one place to start and one place to finish the tour. Write directions with the words from 7.**

▸ Wordbank 1, p. 168 ▸ More help, p. 42

b) **Swap with a partner and follow their directions. Tell your partner where you finished the tour. Were you right?**

▸ Digital help

▸ Workbook, p. 23

Digital quiz I can plan a tour.

Living in London

1 Listening In a cafe

a) Before you listen **Ali, Pearl and Lily are at a Lebanese cafe. Look at the menu. What dishes do you know or have you eaten?**

I know ... I've eaten ...

Menu

Small dishes		
Hummus (chickpea dip) 🍃		£5.75
Halloumi cheese with cucumber and tomatoes 🍃		£6.25
Spicy sausages with lemon		£6.50
Falafel with sesame sauce 🍃		£6.25
Spicy potatoes 🍃		£6.50
Chicken and potatoes with lemon		£7.50

Drinks		
Apple juice		£2.50
Orange juice		£2.50
Cola		£2.50
Lemonade		£2.95
Bottomless tea or coffee		£2.50
Bread		90p

Dishes with 🍃 are vegetarian

b) **The kids order food and drinks. Copy the waiter's notes. Then listen and complete them.**

Drinks: ________ *(2x)*, ________

Small dishes: *spicy sausages*, ________

________ , ________ , *bread*

c) **Complete the phrases. Write one word for each ✱. Then listen again and check.**

Can • I'd • I'll • like • please • some

1 Could I have ✱ tea, please?
2 I'd ✱ a cola, please.
3 ✱ like the spicy sausages, please.
4 ✱ have the falafel, please.
5 ✱ you tell me what halloumi cheese is?
6 Could we have some bread too, ✱?

2 Word building **Everything looks wonderful!**

The waiter has come with the food. Read and choose the right answers.

1 *Wonderful* bedeutet A wundervoll B furchtbar.
2 *Careful* bedeutet A vorsichtig B unvorsichtig.
3 *Careless* bedeutet A vorsichtig B unvorsichtig.
4 *Bottomless* bedeutet A übervoll B bodenlos, d. h. du kannst so viel trinken, wie du möchtest.

► More practice 10, p. 42

Die Endung *-ful* bedeutet „voll von", *-less* bedeutet „ohne". Damit kannst du viele Wörter erschließen.

3 Speaking **Let's order!**

a) Who says what? Write "waitress" and "customer" in your exercise book. Read the speech bubbles and write the numbers under the correct person.

1 I'll have / I'd like ..., please.

2 Are you ready to order?

3 Would you like anything else?

4 What would you like to drink / eat?

5 Could I have ..., please?

6 Yes, we're ready to order.

b) Role-play One student is the waiter, and the others are the customers. Have a conversation using the phrases in a).

c) Give each other feedback.

Good job. You were a great waiter!

You spoke loudly and clearly.

Next time say "please" and "thank you".

► Workbook, p. 24

4 Song My London

After they finish their food, Pearl takes Ali and Lily to Rap Club to listen to some music.

a) Before you listen **What's good or bad about a big city like London? Copy and complete the table. You can add your own ideas.**

👍	👎
sights	*traffic*
...	...

sport teams, museums, public transport, noise, rubbish, ...

b) **Listen to the song.**
Tick the ideas in your table that are in the song too.

c) **Listen again and read the text.**
Can you add more ideas to your table? 👍 *people help the homeless*

My London

My London, it's not about the Tower or the Dungeon
or the big wheel – my London's real, it's something that you feel.
It's here I was born, with all the traffic and the car horns.
Capital L, with all the noises and the smells
and Big Ben's bell goes bong, *can't stay away too long.*
Don't get me wrong, we are strong, that's why I wrote this song.

My London – sing it loud, I'm so proud.
My London – I don't care about the crowds
or the grey clouds.
My London, my London!

London is my city and it's always pretty busy.
On the walls we have graffiti and the city's never sleepy.
We have to help the homeless, I know this.
Yeah, we have people on the street,
but we also have hip-hop beats and good things to eat.
I know it's not perfect,
but it's my favourite place on earth, it's worth it.

My London ...

d) **Do you think the singer likes London? Which line in the text has told you?**

► Workbook, p. 25

5 GLOBAL GOALS Green cities

There are 17 global goals to make the world a better place. 'Green cities' is one goal.

a) LISTENING Lily and her friends talk at Rap Club. Listen. What did Lily think before she moved to London?

b) LISTENING What things do you find in green cities? What things aren't in green cities? Copy the table. Listen again and complete the table. You can add your own ideas too.

👍	👎
bike lanes	*fast fashion*
...	...

c) What about the place where you live – is it green? Why or why not? Tell each other. Give examples.

We live in a ... There's lots of ... There's not a lot of ... I think ... is very / not very green.

My task

6 A blog post about city life

a) Look at a blog post about city life. Does Baz like living in a city? Why?

www.example.com/city-life

My life in the city by Baz

City life is amazing, but in my opinion, there are good and bad things about big cities.

There are lots of activities and interesting places in my city. You can eat great food, like at my favourite Lebanese cafe. I love my sport teams – game days are the best!

Sometimes it takes a long time to travel in the city. The buses and underground are often very full. But public transport is very green. It's much better for the planet than cars!

I don't like villages in the country very much. I went on holiday to the country last year, and it was really boring! There was only one restaurant, and the food wasn't very good.

b) What about you – do you like big cities? What's good, bad or green about them? Write a post. You can use the blue words in Baz's post.

► Wordbank 2, p. 169
► More help, p. 42

c) Hang the posts on the wall. Read the posts and leave "likes" or comments.

► Digital help

You gave interesting reasons. Good job!

Cool post!

I disagree. Villages are great!

► Let's talk: Feedback phrases, p. 182

► Workbook, p. 26

Digital quiz I can describe life in cities and in my area.

Where is Lily?

1 Before you read Places in London

Look at the photos on pages 26–27. Find them on the map.

2 Reading Let's find Lily

► Skills file 9, p. 148

Pearl and Ali are hanging out after school. Read the story and follow Ali and Pearl's route on the map with your finger.

Pearl looked at Ali. 'That was Lily's dad on the phone. She didn't come home after school, and she isn't answering her phone. Her dad asked if she was with us.'

'Hmm,' said Ali. 'She sent me some photos from Harrods right after school.'

'Harrods? The department store? Why was she there? Everything is super expensive!' said Pearl.

'She wanted to buy some special chocolates for her mum's birthday. Look!' said Ali. 'Yeah, good photos! So maybe her phone is dead now? Or maybe she's lost. She doesn't know London very well. We should look for her.'

Harrods

Pearl and Ali took the tube to Knightsbridge and walked to Harrods.

'If we ask the doorkeeper, maybe he'll help us,' said Pearl. She showed the doorkeeper a photo of Lily on her phone. 'Excuse me? Did you see this girl earlier?'

The doorkeeper looked at the photo. 'Yes, I did. When she came out, she asked me for directions to Hyde Park.'

Pearl and Ali walked to Hyde Park.

'Why did Lily go to Hyde Park?' asked Pearl.

'I don't know,' answered Ali. 'Maybe she wanted to swim in the lake? I know Lily misses the sea and beach in Brighton.'

They asked at the Lido about Lily.

Lido Cafe

'No sorry,' said the woman behind the desk. 'I haven't seen her.'

Suddenly Pearl saw something. 'Those red sunglasses over there – they're Lily's! So she was here. But where is she now? Oh no, I hope she's OK.'

'Let's walk across the grass,' said Ali. 'Maybe we'll see her.'

Suddenly Pearl remembered something. 'Look, here's the Princess Diana Memorial Fountain. Lily's mum loved Princess Diana – you know, King Charles's first wife. Diana died a long time ago. Maybe Lily wanted to take photos of the fountain for her mum. Let's ask people.'

Princess Diana Memorial Fountain

'Yes, I remember her,' said a woman. 'She asked me the way to the nearest tube station, so I gave her directions to Lancaster Gate. It's easy, just follow The Long Water that way until you come to a big road.'

Pearl and Ali said thank you and started to run.

'If we hurry, we'll catch her at the tube station!' said Ali.

The kids were fast, but when they got to the Peter Pan Statue, Pearl stopped. 'I can't run any more,' she said. 'If you wait for me, we'll miss Lily. I'll come after you.'

Peter Pan Statue

3 The route

a) **Describe Ali and Pearl's route to find Lily. The map can help you.**

1 First they went to ...
2 Then they went to the ... in Hyde Park.
3 After that, they checked the ... in Hyde Park.
4 Then Pearl stopped at the ...

b) **How did Ali and Pearl know to go there? What were the clues? Who helped them?**

1 The first clue was the photos from ...
2 Then ... helped them.
3 Then they saw Lily's ...
4 Then ... helped them.

c) LISTENING **Listen to the end of the story. What happened?**

... found Lily. She was at the ...

4 Why?

a) **Read the story again and complete the sentences.**

1 Lily's dad called Pearl because ...
2 Lily went to Harrods because ...
3 Pearl and Ali wanted to find Lily because ...
4 They went to the lake in Hyde Park because ...
5 Ali and Pearl started to run because ...
6 Pearl stopped at the Peter Pan statue because ...

► Parallel exercise, p. 42

b) LISTENING **Listen to the end of the story again and complete the sentences.**

1 Lily wants to get the train because ...
2 Lily can't call or text her dad because ...
3 Lily's dad won't be worried because ...

► Skills file 8, p. 147
► Parallel exercise, p. 43 ► More practice 11, p. 43

5 What do you think?

Answer the questions. Then tell your partner your opinion.

Did you like the story? Why?	No, I didn't like it very much. / Yes, I liked it a little / a lot. I thought it was boring / interesting / exciting / realistic / ...
Which part did you like most?	I liked the end / the part about ... the most.
Have you ever been lost? When and where?	I've been lost once! It happened in ... / I've never been lost.

Digital quiz **I can follow and discuss the events in a story.**

On the streets of London

1 Before you watch What does it mean?

Match the sentence parts.

1 A hairdresser
2 A homeless person doesn't
3 A community is
4 To volunteer means to
5 To get involved means to
6 To make a difference means to

A work for free to help someone or something.
B have a flat or a house to live.
C join something.
D change the world for the better.
E gives people haircuts.
F people who live in the same place.

2 Viewing Josh and Jade

a) **Copy the notes about Josh and Jade. Watch the video and complete them.**

Name	Jade
Job	...
How she helps	...

Name	Josh
Job	...
How he helps	...

b) **Watch the video again. Are the sentences true or false?**

1 Josh started cutting hair for people on the street two years ago.
2 He puts photos online to show other people that they can get involved too.
3 Jade got the idea to volunteer from one of Josh's posts.
4 If you don't have money, you can't make people smile.
5 Josh feels happiest when he volunteers.

3 Life skills Make a difference!

a) Think **What could you do to help your neighbours, community or school? Or have you done something already? Your ideas can be big or small.** ▶ More help, p. 43

b) Pair **Compare ideas with a partner. Which idea do you like best?**

c) Share **Tell the class.**

▶ Workbook, p. 27

Do online research

1 Choose a London sight

You're going to make an audio guide for a bike tour of London. Each pair is going to present a different sight. Choose your sight. Here are some ideas:

Big Ben • Buckingham Palace • Camden Market • Harrods • the London Dungeon • the London Eye • the Tower of London

2 Use good keywords and websites

a) Use good keywords to find information on your sight, for example:

Big Ben fun facts, Buckingham Palace history for kids

b) Be careful: Not everything that you read online is correct.
Always check your information on at least two websites.
Look at these websites. Which one would you use? ☒ Why?

A

TravelKid12 Look at my amazing photo of London Bridge! ♥ 1,611

B

Fun facts about
Tower Bridge

- It opens for big boats.
- You can walk across it at the top.
- Tourists often think that it's called *London Bridge*, but that's wrong.

c) Make bookmarks of the most useful websites.

3 Collect information and make notes

Collect interesting information about your sight. These questions can help you.

- What is it?
- Why is it interesting?
- What can you do there?
- How old is it?

Make notes. Don't just copy the text – use your own words.

► Skills file 4, 12, p. 142, 151

Digital quiz I can do online research.

Make an audio guide for a London bike tour

The class chooses:

A Find a digital map and make a digital audio guide.

B Use a paper map for your guide.

Step 1: Collect photos of your sights

Work with a partner. Each pair finds a photo of their sight online.

A Save a copy of your sight's photo and upload it to the digital map.

B Print a copy of your sight's photo and stick it on the paper map.

Step 2: Write your audio guide

a) Write your audio guide for your pair's sight together. Use your notes from 3 on p. 30. Here are some useful phrases:

> Here we are at ... • It's a very famous ... • Did you know that ... • You can ... • It's from ... • It has ... • Look over there ... • Can you see ... • Now look at ... • Now let's go to our next sight.

▶ More help, p. 43

b) Check your text. Is the information and the language correct? Is it interesting? ▶ Digital help

---

Step 3: Practise your audio guide

a) Take turns reading your pair's audio guide. Practise.

b) Record your pair's audio guide. Give feedback.

> Remember to speak clearly.

▶ Let's talk: Feedback phrases, p.182

Step 4: Listen to the class audio guide

A Upload all your audio guides to the digital map. Listen to all the guides.

B Play your recording when your teacher says your sight. Everyone listens.

Digital quiz — I can make and understand an audio guide.

1 LISTENING Rock walking tour

I can understand and share information about London.

a) You're on a rock walking tour with your dad. Listen to the tour guide. Put the pictures (A–E) in the correct order.

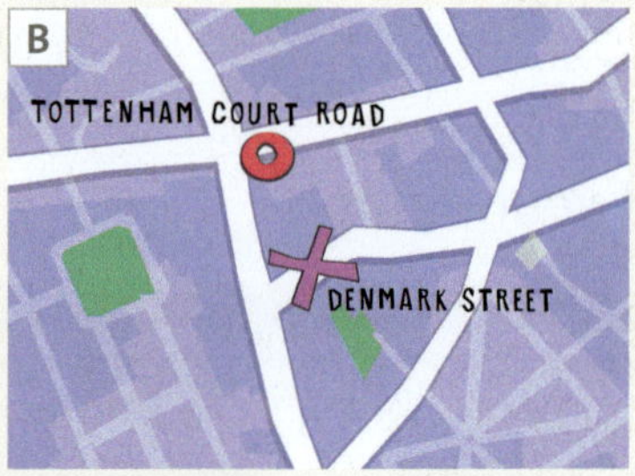

b) Listen again. True or false?

1 On the tour, they will see five London sights.
2 Tottenham Court Road Station is half an hour away from Denmark Street.
3 300 years ago, Denmark Street wasn't an important place for music.
4 The magazine company is still on Denmark Street.
5 Today, people still buy guitars on Denmark Street.

2 MEDIATION On the rock walking tour

On the next part of the tour, your dad needs your help because he doesn't speak English very well. Complete the sentences.

Guide So, this is Berwick Street. It's a very famous street in London. A photo of Berwick Street was on a famous album by the band Oasis.
Dad Was hat sie über Oasis gesagt?
You Ein Foto von Berwick Street war ... (1).
Guide This market is very old. We think that it started around 1770! You can buy fruit and vegetables here.
Dad Wie alt ist der Markt?
You Sie denken, dass er ... (2).
Guide Or if you are hungry, there are lots of great food stalls in the market. My favourites are the falafel, curry and burgers.
Dad Was kann man hier essen?
You Wir können ... (3).
Guide Before the internet, there were lots of music shops on this street! There are still a few today. These are good places to buy CDs or band T-shirts.
Dad Was gab es vor dem Internet?
You Es gab mehr ... (4).

Check

3 WORDS Let's go to the South Bank

I can talk about transport in London.

a) **Complete the conversation with words from the box.**

change • hire • line • ticket • traffic • tube

Lily Do you want to go to the South Bank? You said there are often dancers and musicians there!

Ali Sure! Let's take the ... (1) to Waterloo Station. We can take the Piccadilly ... (2) from here. We'll need to ... (3) at Leicester Square.

Lily But then I'll have to buy an extra ... (4) for the tube. Can we walk there?

Ali Walk? That takes so long! Why don't we cycle?

Pearl We can't ... (5) bikes because we're only 13. Come on, Ali! It's only about half an hour. You can do it!

Lily Also, the ... (6) on the roads is terrible!

Ali OK, let's walk!

b) SPEAKING **You and your friend want to travel from Camden Town to St James's Park.**
Partner A: You want to take the tube.
Partner B: You want to walk.
Act out the dialogue. Partner A starts.
Then swap roles.

Camden Town to St James's Park

take the tube	walk
22 minutes	55 minutes

It's a nice day.
Do you want to go to ...?

Sure, let's ...
It takes ... and it's ...

I don't really want to ...
Why don't we ...? It takes ...

That's a good idea.

Great, let's go!

Check

4 LANGUAGE Ideas for a day in London

I can plan a tour (conditional sentences type 1).

Darja and Theo want to visit London and are planning what to do there.

a) **Read Darja's ideas. Match the correct sentence parts.**

1 *We'll see lots of the city*
2 *If we want to go shopping,*
3 *If we get tired,*
4 *Maybe we'll see the King*
5 *If we aren't too scared,*
6 *And if we visit the Dungeon,*

A *we'll go to Camden Market.*
B *maybe we'll see a ghost!*
C *if we go to Buckingham Palace.*
D *we'll visit the London Dungeon.*
E *we'll sit in Hyde Park and relax.*
F *if we go on the London Eye.*

b) **Read Theo's ideas. Copy and complete the sentences.**
Use the correct form of the simple present.

1 *If you … (go) to the Dungeon, I'll stay outside!*
2 *If we … (stop) at Hyde Park, we'll see the Princess Diana Memorial.*
3 *If it … (not be) sunny, we'll find a nice cafe.*
4 *If we … (not go) on the London Eye, we'll have more money for presents.*
5 *We'll see some street art if we … (visit) Leake Street Tunnel.*
6 *We won't get tired if we … (travel) by tube.*

5 WRITING Hanna's blog

I can describe life in cities and in my area.

Hanna wants to tell her English friends about life in Dortmund.
Look at her notes and write her blog.

I want to tell you about …
We have …
And we have … too.
I love our …
I don't like our …
That's great!
That's terrible.

Life in Dortmund

🙂
- famous football team
- big park
- nice zoo

🙁
- traffic
- cold winters
- rubbish

Check

6 Reading At Leake Street Tunnel

I can follow and discuss the events in a story.

'Hey, Ali, sorry I'm late,' said Lily.

'No problem! That's a big bag – did you go shopping?'

Lily laughed. 'No, these are my art things. Look, I have some paper and lots of pencils.'

'Cool! But you know this is a graffiti wall?' asked Ali. 'People don't use pencils and paper here!'

'Oh yeah, I know. But maybe it will give me some ideas for my own art.'

'True!' said Ali. 'Let's go in.'

'Wow, this place is amazing,' said Lily. She couldn't see any walls at all, just art!

'Lily, I need to go outside to call my mum. I'll find you in five to ten minutes, OK?' asked Ali.

'Sure!' said Lily.

When Ali went back into the tunnel, he was surprised. On Lily's paper there was a beautiful picture of a beach.

'Lily, this is so good!' said Ali.

'Do you think so? I'm not sure,' said Lily.

Suddenly someone said, 'It's a very good picture!' A boy stood next to Lily and Ali. He smiled at them.

'Hi, I'm Zach. I come here every weekend. So do you want to put your picture on the tunnel?'

'Erm, I don't know how,' said Lily.

'I'll show you!' said Zach.

Read the story. Put the events in the correct order.

A Lily draws a great picture.
B Ali leaves the tunnel for a phone call.
C Lily and Ali meet outside the tunnel.
D Two people like Lily's picture.
E Lily shows Ali the things in her bag.
F Zach asks about Lily's plan for the picture.

7 Study skills London taxis

I can do online research.

Read the sentences (1–3) and choose the best answer.

1 You're writing about London taxis, and you want to know their history. You look for information online and use the keywords ...

A *London old cars*
B *London taxis*
C *London history taxis*

2 You should always check your information ...

A on at least two different websites.
B with your teacher.
C with your partner.

3 You can find the most useful websites again if you ...

A remember what you did.
B make bookmarks.
C write the name of the website.

Check

United[1]

A magazine for young[2] people across the UK

Multicultural London

by Pearl Cole

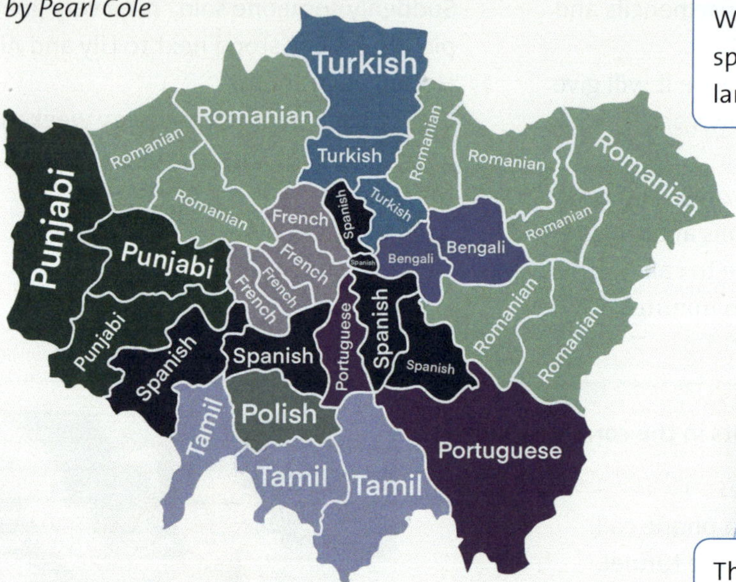

Datenquelle: Office for National Statistics in London: https://www.ons.gov.uk/datasets/TS024/editions/2021/versions/1#version-history

I love that people in my city come from all over the world! Check out this map of London: It shows the main second languages that people speak (after English). Did you know that kids in London schools speak over 300 languages? Which languages do people speak in your area? In how many languages can you say 'Hello'?

This is my favourite poem about London. It's called "All in this together," by Zaina. She was twelve when she wrote[3] it.

***All in this together** by Zaina (12)*

Once I walked down the lane
and I heard[4] somebody say
I am Chinese, Japanese, German,
Spanish, French
but it doesn't matter[5] who you are,
or what language you speak ...
(...)

Everybody can speak this language
Old or young or smart or not.
If we smile and laugh and love each other
It's clear what we're going to say.

We are all in this together
doesn't matter who you are
doesn't matter what you speak or say
if you laugh or cry[6] or love or play ...
(...)

[1] **united** *vereinigt* [2] **young** *jung* [3] (to) **write, wrote** *schreiben* [4] (to) **hear, heard** *hören*
[5] **it doesn't matter** *es spielt keine Rolle* [6] (to) **cry** *weinen, schreien*

Let me tell you more about …

London's multicultural communities

Over the years, Britain has needed workers for many different jobs. That's one reason why there are so many multicultural communities in London.
My great-grandparents[1] came from Jamaica in the 1950s to work as a nurse and train driver. My dad says that they had hard lives. We're so proud of them! In this picture my family is eating my great-grandmother's famous jerk chicken[2].

Brick Lane is a street in London famous for its large Bangladeshi community. My friend Fahra's grand-parents were doctors who lived near Brick Lane. They and many other British Bangladeshi worked very hard so that their children could have a better life. Fahra and I go to Brick Lane to enjoy the best curry in Britain.

The Chinese community has been in London for a very long time. At first, most Chinese people only lived in Chinatown, but today's Chinese Londoners live and work all over the city. I love to go to Chinatown with my family and eat dim sum. There are more than 80 Chinese restaurants! Look at my amazing picture.

My neighbour Zuzia is from Poland. She came to London with her family. Her dad is a builder[3], and he has started his own business. This is her mum's Polish food shop. You can buy really good pierogi[4] here! Zuzia says that many Polish people have left London after Brexit, but she and her family want to stay.

---

[1] **great-grandparents** *die Urgroßeltern* [2] **jerk chicken** *gewürztes, gegrilltes Huhn* [3] **builder** *der Bauunternehmer*
[4] **pierog** *die Pirogge (Teigtasche)*

Partner page

▸ Page 17

5 What's the best transport?

Partner B:

a) **You're at Camden Market and want to go to Oxford Street. Copy and complete the table. Ask each other questions to find the missing information. Partner A starts. Answer the questions. Then it's your turn:**

Partner B: *How long does it take by bus / tube?*
Partner A: *It takes ... minutes.*
Partner B: *How much does it cost?*
Partner A: *It costs ...*

Camden Market to Oxford Street (3 km)	bus	tube	taxi	bike	walk
time	?	?	6 min.	13–17 min.	36 min.
price	?	?	£10	£1.65 for 30 min.	?

b) **Now decide and tell your partner: How will you get there? What won't you do?**

I'll	walk • hire a bike • take a taxi • go by bus • go by tube	because	it's cheap • fast • green.
I won't			there's too much traffic • it's slow • it's expensive.

Diff bank

▸ Page 12

More practice 1 **What home is like**

Listen again and choose A or B.

1 Interesting buildings in London are A old and new B only new.
2 In the past, Manchester had a lot of A industry B skyscrapers.
3 Nessie is the name of a A lake B monster in Scotland.
4 Wales has about A 60 B 600 castles.
5 In Belfast you can see large A murals B lakes.
6 Ireland has earned money from A street art B big businesses.

▸ Page 14

More practice 2 Your London, my London

Before you listen, look at the topic.
What do you think you will hear?

Listen again and choose A, B, or C.

1. Big Ben is really the name of
   A Parliament B the bell C the tower.
2. At Buckingham Palace you can't take pictures A outside B inside C at all.
3. The Tower of London is interesting if you like A old buildings B stairs
   C modern towers.
4. The London Eye is a tall A tower B church C wheel.
5. Ali's favourite thing to do at Camden Market is to A eat food B shop C take pictures.

▸ Page 16

More practice 3 London transport

buy • change • cross • drive • hire • take

Ali's friend Mo from Canada is visiting London.
Complete their conversation with the correct verbs.

Ali	At the weekend we can ... (1) bikes and see the real London!
Mo	Great! But I'm really tired now. Can we take a taxi?
Ali	Well, it's expensive, and it's not very green. Let's ... (2) the tube.
Mo	OK. But I need to ... (3) a ticket.
Ali	No problem. The station is over there, we need to ... (4) the road here. Careful – cars ... (5) on the left here, remember?
Mo	Oh yeah, thanks! So do we have to ... (6) lines?
Ali	No, we don't.

More practice 4 WORDS A transport mind map

a) **Make a mind map in your VOCAB FILE with transport words and phrases.**
Use the words from p. 16.

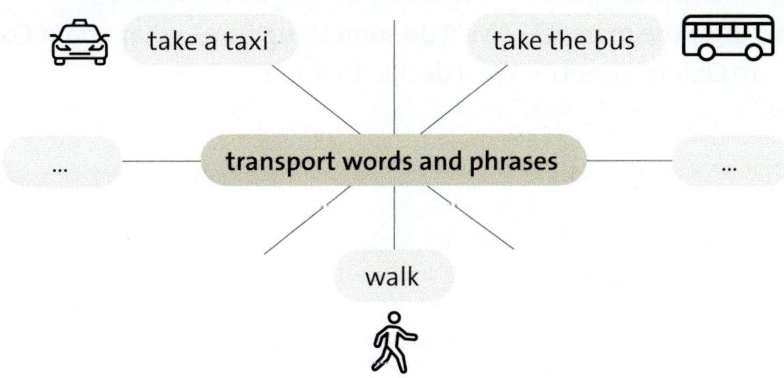

b) **Mark words that are similar in German or other languages you know.**

▸ Skills file 1, p. 139

▸ Page 17

More practice 5 What will you do?

Read sentences 1–8. What will you do? Match A–H to the correct sentence.

1 Someone is knocking at the door.
2 You're sitting in a very hot room.
3 You're feeling very hungry.
4 You don't understand your English teacher.
5 It's snowing outside.
6 You get an invitation to a birthday party.
7 Your dad is cleaning the kitchen.
8 You're feeling very tired.

A 'I'll get something to eat.'
B 'I'll ask her to repeat the question.'
C 'I'll help him.'
D 'I'll go to bed now.'
E 'I'll buy a present for my friend.'
F 'I'll open a window.'
G 'I'll see who it is.'
H 'I'll wear warm clothes.'

More practice 6 What will happen?

What do you think will happen? Look at the ideas and write six sentences.

Maybe I think Perhaps	Lily will / won't Pearl will / won't she'll / she won't Ali will / won't he'll / he won't they'll / they won't	be early. take pictures. bring a bottle of water. buy a T-shirt. eat good food. get lost.

More practice 7 Lily's questions

Write Lily's questions for Ali and Pearl.
Use *will* and the verbs in the box.

be • buy • do • go • stay • travel

1 Where ... we ... first? – We'll go to the food stalls first.
2 ... there ... a lot of people? – Yes, there will be a lot of people!
3 ... you ... something, Pearl? – No, I won't buy anything today.
4 How long ... we ... at the market? – We'll stay as long as we want to!
5 What ... we ... after the market? – We'll do something fun – what about Oxford Street?
6 How ... we ... to Oxford Street? – We'll decide that later.

▸ Page 18

More practice 8 London sights

a) **Match the places to the photos (A–D). Then read the descriptions and check your answers.**

Buckingham Palace • London Dungeon • Tower Bridge • Tower of London

A

This is a museum about the scary history of London. There are shows, rides and actors to scare the visitors – it's very frightening.

B

This is a very old castle from 1708. Some people think there are ghosts here. The royal family keeps its crowns and jewels safe here.

C

This is the King's biggest home and it's where he meets the Prime Minister and other guests. The guards wear uniforms and special tall black hats.

D

This is maybe the most beautiful bridge in London. You can walk, cycle or drive across it, and it can open when big ships need to go down the River Thames.

b) WORDS **Work out the meanings of the words in blue and add them to your VOCAB FILE.**

Look at the pictures or think of words that are similar in German or other languages you know.

▸ Skills file 2, p. 140

▸ Page 19

More practice 9 My friend's visit to London

Complete the conditional sentences about a future visit to London. Use the will-future.

1 If my friend goes to London, she ... (travel) on the underground.
2 If she travels on the underground, she ... (buy) a ticket.
3 If she buys a ticket, she ... (not have) much money to buy a nice souvenir.
4 She ... (be) sad if she doesn't buy a T-shirt.
5 So I think if she goes to London, she ... (walk) – because it's free!

▸ Page 21

More help 8 A tour of London

a) Plan a tour in London. Pick one place to start and one place to finish the tour. Write directions with the words from 7.

Start at	Big Ben • the London Eye • Trafalgar Square • ...
Go along Turn left / right into	... Street • ... Road • ... Place • ...
Go across	Westminster Bridge • the road • ...
Now stop. You have arrived! Where are you?	

▸ Page 23

More practice 10 Word building -less and -ful

Complete the sentences. Add -ful (+) or -less (–) to the words in brackets.

1 When you cross the street in London, be ... (care +) because cars drive on the left.
2 London is great! The number of things to do is ... (end –).
3 There's interesting and ... (colour +) street art all over the city.
4 If you're lost, you can ask people for directions. They're usually very ... (help +).
5 The Lion King is my favourite show in London. I think it's very ... (power +).
6 If the train is leaving soon, don't run for it – it's ... (hope –)! Just wait for the next one.

▸ Page 25

More help 6 A blog post about city life

b) What about you – do you like big cities? What's good, bad or green about them? Write a post.

I think / In my opinion ...	There is / There are ...
I like / I love ...	Sometimes / Often / Usually / ...
I don't like ...	I think small towns are better / worse than ...
You can ...	I like / I don't like villages in the country / ...

▸ Page 28

Parallel exercise 4 Why?

a) **Read the story again and match the correct sentence parts.**

1 Lily's dad called Pearl because ...
2 Lily went to Harrods because ...
3 Pearl and Ali want to find Lily because ...
4 They go to the lake in Hyde Park because ...
5 Ali and Pearl started to run because ...
6 Pearl stopped at the Peter Pan statue because ...

A Lily misses the sea and beach.
B they wanted to catch Lily at the station.
C she wanted to buy chocolates.
D Lily didn't come home after school.
E she couldn't run any more.
F she doesn't know London very well.

Parallel exercise **4 Why?**

b) Listen to the end of the story again and match the correct sentence parts.

1 Lily wants to get the train because ...
2 Lily can't call or text her dad because ...
3 Lily's dad won't be worried because ...

A Lily can use Ali's phone to call him.
B her phone is dead.
C her dad will be worried and she wants to hurry home.

More practice 11 **Words in the story**

Choose the correct meaning for the words in blue.

1 A department store sells ...
A cars B different things like food, clothes and bags.
2 A doorkeeper ...
A opens the door for people B makes doors for buildings.
3 A memorial is a ...
A trophy B way to remember people or past events.
4 A fountain is ...
A a place with moving water B a place where you can swim.
5 When you catch somebody, you ... A meet them B hold them.
6 When you miss somebody, you ... A hug them B don't see them.

Find the words in blue in the story. Look at the words and sentences around that word and at the pictures. Similar words in German and other languages can also help you. You can check in the Dictionary (pages 215–235).

▸ Page 29

More help **3** LIFE SKILLS **Make a difference!**

a) What can you do to help your neighbours, community or school? Your ideas can be big or small.

- plan and do a clean-up day
- volunteer at a charity
- help neighbours with chores
- find books, clothes, shoes or other things to give to a charity shop
- make money for a charity

▸ Page 31

More help UNIT TASK **Make an audio guide for a London bike tour**

You can use the blue phrases for your guide.

Here we are at Tower Bridge. It's a very famous bridge on the River Thames. Did you know that lots of people think it's called London Bridge? But look over there, that's the real London Bridge! It's modern, but Tower Bridge is old. It's from 1894. It has two tall towers. The bottom part of Tower Bridge opens for ships to go through. Now look at the top of the bridge. Can you see people? You can still cross the bridge up there, even if the bottom part is open! Now let's go to our next sight.

Unit 2
Manchester: Who we are

Hey! *The online magazine of Trafford Secondary School in Manchester*

Welcome, Rosie and Omar, to our team! Read to learn what's important to them.

Hi everyone! I'm Rosie. I'm 13, and I'm in year 9. Our planet is important to me. ❤️

My favourite thing is my phone. My friends and I text each other every day. 😇

I have a disability and some people only see my disability. That's annoying! 🙄 *But my family and friends are amazing.* 🥰 *They see me:* Rosie!

1 Reading What's important to Rosie and Omar

a) Before you read **Rosie and Omar share information about themselves in the magazine. Look at the pictures. What can you see?**

b) **Read the speech bubbles. What do we learn about Rosie and Omar? Make a profile (name, age, ...). One of you chooses Rosie, and the other one Omar.** ► More help, p. 66

c) **Now tell each other about your person.**

Rosie is ... and in year 9. ... is important to her. Her ... and ... are important too. Her favourite ...
Omar is ... and he's in year ... too. His ... is important to him because ... His favourite ...

Nach dieser Unit kann ich ...

- erklären, was mir wichtig ist
- über Mode reden
- Ratschläge geben
- über Selbstbewusstsein sprechen
- einen Konflikt besprechen
- meine Meinung ausdrücken

Unit task

- an einer Diskussion teilnehmen

2 Speaking What's important to you

a) What is important to you? Make a list of four to six people or things.

b) Tell a partner what people or things are important to you. Explain why.

... is important to me.

▸ More help, p. 66

c) Compare your lists. What is the same or different?

Music is important to me. — *I have that too.* — *I don't have that.*

▸ More practice 1, p. 67
▸ Workbook, p. 34

Digital quiz — I can explain what's important to me.

Manchester fashion

1 LISTENING Omar's interviews

a) BEFORE YOU LISTEN **Look at the pictures. Tell each other what clothes you can see.**

b) **Omar is doing interviews about street fashion for the school magazine. Listen and match the names in the box to the teenagers A–D.**

Eliza • Maya • Neil • Richard

c) **Listen again. Who says it: Omar, Eliza, Maya, Neil or Richard?**

1 I think ripped jeans look really cool.
2 I sometimes borrow clothes from my sister.
3 This is one of my favourite outfits.
4 A cool brand at a good price is the best.
5 It's cold today! But my sweater is warm.
6 I think skirts and socks look cool together.
7 Fast fashion is a big problem.
8 They're the most comfortable trousers ever.

► Skills file 8, p. 147 ► Wordbank 3, p. 170 ► Workbook, p. 35

2 Compare the outfits

Erklär-film

a) **Look at the pictures in 1 again. Which outfit is better?**

1 Nice black shoes look ... (smart) than trainers.
2 Ripped jeans are ... (popular) than normal jeans.
3 The sweater in picture B is ... (warm) than the sweater in picture C.

b) **Look at the pictures in 1 again. Which outfit is the best?**

1 Picture B is the ... (colourful) outfit.
2 Picture C is the ... (cool) outfit.
3 Picture D is the ... (comfortable) outfit.

Remember

cool
cooler than
the coolest

popular
more popular than
the most popular

► Language file 7, p. 160 ► More practice 2, p. 68

3 Words Describing clothes

a) Make a mind map in your Vocab file with words to describe clothes.
Use words from p. 46 and any words that you know.

► Skills file 1, p. 139

b) Mark words that are similar in German or othe languages you know.

► Skills file 1, p. 139

My task

4 My fashion

You Choose Do task A or B.

A Describe your favourite outfit to a partner.
Then say where you buy your clothes. What's important to you?

My favourite outfit is ... I like it because it's ...
I go to the shops / buy my clothes online / ...
I do clothes swaps with friends / I don't buy lots of new clothes ...

► Wordbank 3, p. 170

B You need a new outfit for a special event,
but you don't have a lot of money to spend.
What are you going to do? Talk to a partner.

► More help, p. 68

I'm going to wear ...
I'm going to borrow ...

► Digital help

► Workbook, p. 36

Digital quiz I can talk about fashion.

Family, friendship and love

1 Reading I need some advice!

a) Before you read Talk to a partner.

- What kinds of problems do teenagers have?
- Where can they get advice?

b) Students at Rosie and Omar's school can write to their school magazine to get advice. Read the messages (1–4) and match them to the correct headings (A–D). *1 ...; 2 ...; ...*

A Problems with parents

B Worried about a friend

C Trouble with school

D Student in love

www. hey-trafford-school.example.net/advice

1

Dear *Hey!* Magazine
I'm not doing well at school. I'm often really tired during the day, and I don't understand everything in my lessons. Do you have any advice for me? I'm going to join the homework club next week, but I don't know if it will be enough. What else should I do?

Worried student

2

Dear *Hey!* Magazine
My parents have so many rules, and it's so frustrating. I'm not allowed to do anything! We fight about this all the time. They always ask me, 'Am I going to get a text when you leave? Is your phone going to be on? Are you going to be home on time?' I'm not a child!

Angry student

3

Dear *Hey!* Magazine
I have a crush on a girl in my class. I'm very shy and I sometimes find it hard to talk to other people. But with her, I can just be me. I'm going to go to the cinema with her and some friends this Friday. Should I tell her how I feel? What if she doesn't like me back?

Shy student

4

Dear *Hey!* Magazine
My friend's dad is going to get married in a few months. I know she doesn't like her dad's girlfriend. My friend was always happy, and now she's quiet and sad. I asked how I can help her, but she said I should forget it, and that she's fine. I know that's not true. What can I do?

Best friend

► Workbook, p. 37

2 Mediation Lots of problems

You and your partner are going to choose two messages each. Tell each other about the problems in German. Only say the most important information. You can start like this:

In meiner ersten Nachricht sucht jemand Hilfe, weil ...
In meiner zweiten Nachricht hat jemand ein Problem mit ...

In meiner ersten Nachricht bittet jemand um Rat, weil ...
In meiner zweiten Nachricht macht sich jemand Sorgen um ...

► Skills file 10, p. 149

3 What about you?

Answer the questions with a partner.

1 What can you do to stop fighting with your parents?
2 If a friend has a serious problem, what do you think is the best thing to do?
3 How does a good friend make you feel?
4 How does a crush make you feel?
5 If you're not doing well in maths, who can you talk to?

► Parallel exercise, p. 69

4 Looking at language The going to-future

Erklär-film

a) Look at the examples from the emails. Complete the rule.

I'm going to join the homework club.
I'm going to go to the cinema with her.
My friend's dad is going to get married.

Mit dem *going to-future* sprechen wir über Pläne für die

A Vergangenheit. B Gegenwart. C Zukunft.

Wir bilden das *going to-future* mit einer Form von to be + ... + Verb.

b) Now look at these questions. Complete the rule.

Am I going to get a text when you leave?
Is your phone going to be on?
Are you going to be home on time?

Going to-Fragen, auf die man mit Yes, ... / No, ... antwortet, beginnen mit einer Form von ...

► More practice 3, p. 69 ► Language file 8, p. 161

5 Talking about the problems

Rosie and Omar are talking about the problems. Complete the sentences with *'m / is / 're*.

Omar What do you think about the first message? The person … (1) going to join the homework club. That's a start!

Rosie Sure, but they really should try to get more sleep.

Omar That's hard! I always tell myself, 'Tonight, you … (2) going to go to bed early!' And then I stay up on my phone.

Rosie I feel really bad for the girl in the fourth message. She … (3) going to have a new stepmother soon.

Omar Yeah. I don't know what to tell her friend to do. Giving advice is hard!

Rosie It's good that Ms Hall … (4) going to write the answers with us. She'll know what to say.

Omar That's true. We … (5) going to talk to her tomorrow. Let's write down our ideas so far.

Rosie OK. And later I … (6) going to spend some time online. Maybe I can find more ideas.

▶ More practice 4, p. 70

6 LISTENING Crushes

a) BEFORE YOU LISTEN **Rosie is talking to Alex, who wrote the third message on p. 48. Can you remember: What's a 'crush'? What was the problem?**

b) **Listen. True or false?**

1 Rosie has a crush on somebody.
2 Alex wants Lisa to tell his crush the truth.
3 Rosie thinks that Alex has to talk with his crush.
4 There's only one option for Alex.
5 The safe option is not to take a chance and just be friends.
6 If Alex tells his crush how he feels, he could be successful.

c) **Write the sentences and questions in the right order. Then listen again and check.**

1 tell her / going to / how you feel? / Are you
2 the truth? / going to / Is Lisa / tell your crush
3 going to / Are you / watch a film / with her?
4 for his birthday. / She's / visit her uncle / going to
5 am I / going to / What / do?

d) **Imagine you're Alex's crush. What are you going to do when he tells you how he feels?**

I'm going to …

▶ Workbook, pp. 38–39

7 Reading Giving advice

a) **The school magazine is trying a new chat program to give students advice more quickly. Read the chat. What is SadGirl's problem?**

SadGirl	I don't feel comfortable in my body. Why does everyone else look better than me?
Hey!	I'm sorry that you feel bad. We often compare ourselves to other people, but that's not helpful. Everyone is different! What can you do to feel better?
SadGirl	Well, I already run every day and I only eat healthy food. But I still feel bad.
Hey!	Sport is a great idea! But you should rest too. You shouldn't run every day. You should eat healthy food, but you are allowed to eat chips and sweets sometimes too.
SadGirl	OK, I'm going to run three times a week. And I'm going to eat food that I like more often.
Hey!	And this is the most important thing: You should be kind to yourself! You shouldn't compare yourself to other people.
SadGirl	I have an idea. When I look at myself in a mirror, I'm going to think about what I like.
Hey!	I really like that idea. That's wonderful!

b) **What advice does *Hey!* give? Read the box and find three more examples in the text. Do you agree with the advice?**

– *You should ...* – *You shouldn't ...*

We use *should* and *shouldn't* to give advice. *You should rest too. You shouldn't run every day.*

▸ More practice 5, p. 70

My task

8 Make a plan

a) **When you have a problem, it can help to make a plan. Read this plan and complete the sentences. Use the going to-future.**

I have to give a presentation, and I'm scared of talking in front of the class.

1. First, I'm going to be kind to myself. I... tell myself that it's OK to be scared. I can be scared and still do hard things!
2. I... practise my presentation in front of a mirror.
3. I... ask my friends or family to watch my presentation.
4. I... tell my teacher and a friend in my class that I'm nervous.
5. During my presentation, they... smile at me.
6. They... clap and cheer for me at the end.

b) **Think of a problem. Make a plan how to deal with it. Write the steps in the going to-future.**

▸ More help, p. 70 ▸ Digital help

Digital quiz I can make plans.

Confidence

1 LISTENING Mei's school radio podcast

a) BEFORE YOU LISTEN **Do you listen to podcasts or radio shows? If you do, which ones? If you don't, why not? Tell a partner.**

b) **Listen to Mei's podcast and choose the correct answers.**

1 Today Mei is talking about
A school B music C confidence on her podcast.
2 When she was younger, Mei
A had lots of friends B felt different C was very confident.
3 So she A joined a football team B asked her dad for help C joined a new band.
4 Rosie says we're often A mean to our friends B nice to our friends
C nice to our mothers.
5 Mei asks her listeners to A look after themselves B share more tips C choose a song.

Mei is in year 12 at Rosie and Omar's school.

2 LOOKING AT LANGUAGE Reflexive pronouns

a) **Listen to Mei's podcast in 1 b) again. Complete the phrases with the reflexive pronouns in the box.**

herself • himself • myself • ourselves • themselves • ~~yourself~~ • yourselves

1 If you don't believe in *yourself* it can be a big problem.
2 A lot of people don't like ... at some time in their lives.
3 That's how she taught ... to be more confident.
4 We often say really mean things to ...
5 This is what I tell ...
6 He listens to it when he doesn't believe in ...
7 I want you all to look after ...!

b) **Copy and complete the table with the reflexive pronouns in a).**

I	*myself*	it	itself
you	...	we	ourselves
he	...	you (all)	...
she	herself	they	...

► Language file 9, p. 162

They are looking at themselves in the mirror.

► Workbook, p. 40

3 Feel more confident

Read the sentences and choose the correct pronouns.

1 Mei wants her listeners to believe in himself / themselves.
2 When she was younger, she taught herself / myself to be more confident.
3 If *you* don't like ourselves / yourself, it makes you feel bad.
4 That's why Mei says, 'It's important to me that I like itself / myself.'
5 'And we have to take care of ourselves / themselves!'

▸ More practice 6, p. 71

4 READING A confidence role model

a) BEFORE YOU READ **Brainstorm confident people with your class. They could be famous or people from your personal life.**

b) **Read the article and find three things that Marcus Rashford is famous for.**

Marcus Rashford: Champion of confidence

Marcus Rashford is a champion footballer, *and* he's a champion of the people too. He's a very successful player for Manchester United and as an activist, he has helped poor children all over the UK to get free meals. He believes that we all need to support each other – just like a football team.

Rashford is very busy! He's also written two books about confidence: *You are a champion* and *You can do it*. In these books, he helps young people to believe in themselves.

Rashford has experienced problems with his confidence in the past. When he missed a penalty in an important match, some people sent him racist messages. But he had a lot of support too, and now he's more confident than ever. He says, 'Whenever I hear *no*, I ask myself: *why not?*'

Marcus, all your fans here in Manchester hope that you're proud of yourself – because we're proud of you!

c) **Read the article again. Are the statements true (T) or false (F)?**

1 Marcus Rashford is only interested in sport.
2 He plays for Manchester City.
3 He fights for free food for poor children.
4 He's also a writer.
5 People were horrible when he missed a penalty.
6 His fans in Manchester believe in him.

▸ Workbook, p. 41

5 Song *Brave*

a) Before you listen **Omar loves *Brave* by Sara Bareilles. Find the video on the internet and watch the first minute with no sound. How do the dancers in the video feel? Discuss ideas with the class.**

I think they feel ...

bored • brave • confident • excited • happy • shy • ...

Sara Bareilles

b) **Now listen to the song. What is its message?**

A I don't feel very confident.
B We should all be the same.
C You should believe in yourself.

c) **Tell your partner what you think of the song and video. How do they make you feel?**

▶ Wordbank 4, p. 171

6 Viewing Ways to appear confident

a) Before you watch **Later in the podcast, Mei recommends a video with confidence tips. Think of some endings to this sentence with your partner.**

I feel more confident when ...
- *I wear my favourite clothes /*
- *I'm with my best friend /*
- *I do yoga / ...*
- ...

Often if you try to appear confident, you actually feel more confident too!

b) **Watch the video. Do you think Sammy is shy?**

c) **Watch again and complete the tips.**

- stand up ...
- speak clearly and ...
- repeat ...
- don't interrupt ...
- wear ... that make you feel good
- smile

d) **Look at the tips in c) again and try some of them. How useful are the tips for you? (1 = not at all useful 2 = some are useful, some aren't 3 = quite useful 4 = very useful)**

e) **Sammy says you should stand up straight to feel more confident. As a class, stand in a power pose or superhero pose for 30 seconds. Do you feel more confident?**

▶ Workbook, pp. 41–42

7 Speaking Compliments

Mei always ends her podcast with 'Classmate compliments'. Her listeners send her anonymous compliments for other students at school.

a) Think Make a list of five kind words or phrases to describe someone.

I think you're ... You're amazing at ...

b) Pair Tell your partner your ideas. Choose some of their ideas and add them to your list.

c) Share Walk around and give each other compliments. Remember to say 'thank you' and 'you're welcome'!

Hi, Suki. I think you're very clever. – *Thanks, Atalay! I want to tell you that you're very kind.*
Thank you, that's nice of you. – *You're welcome!*

▸ Workbook, p. 42

My task

8 Being confident

a) In groups of three, think of three to five tips for being more confident. The ideas in 6 c) can help you.

b) Role-play Write a short role-play about meeting for the first time. It should have three parts:

1. Student A meets student B. Student B is nervous and not very confident.
2. Student C gives student B some tips for being confident. (Use *You should / shouldn't ...*)
3. Students A and B repeat the first part of the role-play. This time, student B uses the tips and is more confident.

▸ More help, p. 71

c) Make cards with keywords to help you remember what you want to say.

d) Do your role-play for another group. Give the other group a compliment about their role-play. Give them some advice too.

You acted really well. / You said some very useful tips. / You spoke clearly.
Next time, you should speak more loudly / add some extra tips / remember the words better.

Digital quiz I can talk about confidence.

A Manchester match

1 Before you read Sports and games

Tell a partner about your favourite sports or games and why you like them. Is winning important to you?

My favourite sport / game is ... because it's ...
Winning is / isn't important to me.

▸ Wordbank 6, p. 173

2 Reading Omar's favourite team

Do you remember the name of Omar's football team? Look at the pictures and read the first paragraph to check. Then read the story.

Omar was so excited. Today was the football match of the year between Manchester City and Manchester United. Omar, his dad and his sister had tickets for the match. He put on his blue Manchester City football shirt and his scarf and looked at himself in the mirror.

'Omar,' said his sister. 'We're going to be late!' Omar didn't answer, he just smiled and picked up his jacket. They took the bus to the stadium and waited to get in with hundreds of other Manchester City fans.

'We are City, super City, from Maine Road,' sang the fans and Omar sang with them. 'City, City, the best team in the land, in all the world.'
The players came onto the pitch and the fans went crazy.

Omar got a text from Trent:

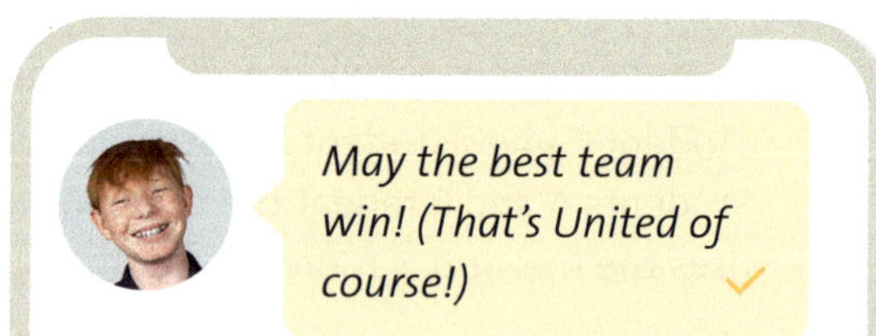

Trent's older cousin Ollie was a Manchester United supporter, and they were at the match too. Omar read the message and laughed. 'In your dreams, Trent!' he thought.

At half-time there were no goals. 'I can't believe they missed those two chances,' Omar's dad said as they waited for a hot dog.

'They were unlucky,' said Omar's sister. 'Just wait! The Boys in Blue will show them who are the best players.'

The next half was fast and exciting. The fans sang and Omar was full of love for his team. But suddenly the United players were near the goal and the City goalkeeper came out too far. Then the ball was in the goal.

'Yes!' cheered the Manchester United fans. Omar felt terrible. Then he got a new text from Trent:

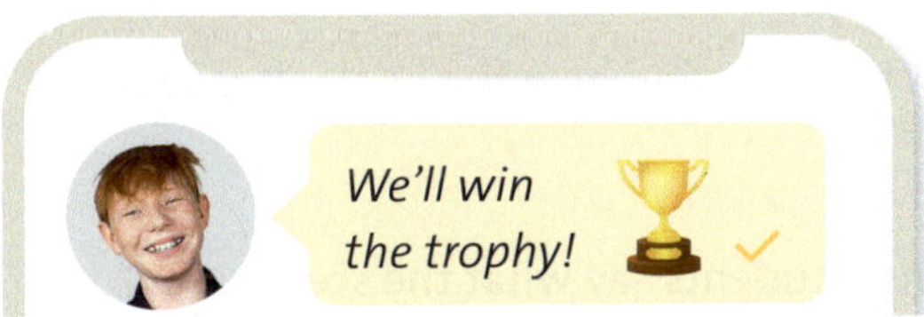

Omar looked at the message, but then put his phone back in his pocket and felt angry with Trent. A few minutes later, Manchester City's best player scored a goal.

Omar cheered and texted Trent back:

After 90 minutes the score was still 1-1, but there were three minutes of additional time. Omar crossed his fingers in his pockets. Two minutes later Manchester City scored! Omar, his dad and his sister hugged each other. All round the stadium, City fans clapped and sang.

Later, outside the stadium, there were people everywhere. Some unhappy Manchester United fans called the Manchester City fans horrible names and took their scarves. Omar's dad said, 'Just keep walking,' and went ahead with Omar's sister.

Omar saw Trent and waved to him, but Trent looked down. At first, Omar didn't understand why.

But then Ollie, who was next to Trent, saw Omar. Ollie had a mean smile on his face and called Omar racist names.

Omar felt hot all over. He was angry and hurt. He stood in front of Trent and looked at him. Omar asked, 'Are you my friend or not?'

3 What happened

Copy the timeline. Put the events in the story (A–F) in the correct place on the timeline.

Before the match	At the beginning of the match	At half-time	At the end of 90 minutes	In additional time	After the match
?	?	?	?	?	?

A Trent's cousin Ollie was horrible to Omar.

B Trent sent Omar a message that United is the best team.

C Omar put on his Manchester City clothes.

D Manchester City scored.

E there were no goals.

F the game was 1-1.

4 Are you my friend?

Decide what Omar's last words to Trent mean. Choose A, B or C.

A I don't want to be your friend because your cousin is a bully.
B You aren't a good friend because you aren't helping me.
C Good friends call bullies names.

5 Freeze!

a) **Choose a scene from the story. Talk about what happens and how the characters feel.**

Let's take the scene when ... I think Omar feels ...

b) **Show your group's scene as a freeze-frame. Other students say what the scene is, what is happening and how the characters feel.**

6 The ending

a) **What do you think happened next? Talk to a partner.**

Maybe I think	Trent Ollie Omar	told ... to stop. said sorry to ... walked away. called ... names. went home with ...

b) **Listen to what happened. Compare your stories.**

c) **What would you do in this situation? Discuss.**

▶ Workbook, p. 43

Digital quiz I can **discuss a conflict in a story.**

Coach

1 Football fans

BEFORE YOU WATCH **Are you a football fan? Why (not)?**

- *I like / don't like football because it's exciting / boring / the best sport / ...*
- *In my opinion, football fans are / aren't cool, funny, friendly, helpful, loud, mean, nice, quiet, polite, ...*

2 VIEWING What happens

a) **Watch the film. What are the football fans in the film like at first? What about later?**

b) **Put the events in the right order. Then watch the video again and check.**

A David and his dad are on the way to a football match in Paris, but there's a problem with the car.
B David sees the fight and helps his dad.
C David gets back on the coach alone, and his dad and one of the fans start to fight.
D The police come and stop the fight.
E The coach stops at a service station, everyone gets out, and David's dad wants to leave.
F They get on a coach with lots of loud football fans.
G The police drive all of them back to Calais, so they can't watch the game in the stadium.

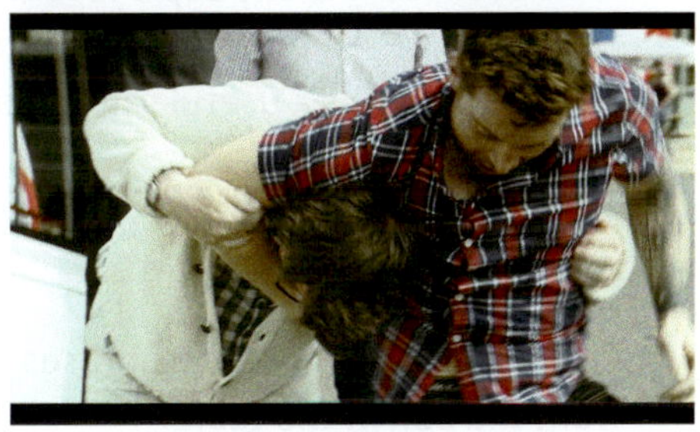

3 What do you think?

a) **How does David feel? You can match more than one feeling to each sentence.**

- At the start of the film in the car with his dad.
- When he and his dad start singing.
- When there's a problem with the car.
- When they get into the coach and all the fans are singing.
- When he fights the football fan.
- At the end of the film when they are back on the coach.

angry • annoyed • bored • excited • happy • tired • unhappy • worried • ...

b) **What did you think of the film? Which part did you like? Which part didn't you like?**

I liked the part when ... / I didn't like the part when ...

Giving opinions

1 Give your opinion

a) Tell your partner which of the opinions 1–5 you agree with. How many opinions do you have in common?

b) Opinion phrases can help you to give your opinion more clearly. Find the five opinion phrases on the right. Add them to your VOCAB FILE.

I think …

1 *I think football is the best sport.*

2 *In my opinion, ketchup on pasta is delicious.*

3 *If you ask me, snakes are scary.*

4 *I believe that we should learn coding at school.*

5 *I would say that fashion is stupid.*

2 Give reasons

Match the reasons A–E below to the opinions 1–5 in 1.

A … because they move very fast and can be dangerous.
B … because I like tomatoes and I enjoy it on everything.
C … because lots of people love it and it's exciting when the players score goals.
D … because it's too expensive and clothes aren't important.
E … because it's a useful skill for the future and I like technology.

3 Agree or disagree

Copy the table. Write the phrases from the box in the table. ► Skills file 5, p. 144

agree	disagree
Maybe you're right	*Sorry, I think you're wrong …*
…	

Phrases

- ~~Maybe you're right.~~
- ~~Sorry, I think you're wrong …~~
- I don't agree with you at all.
- I completely agree.
- That's a good point.
- I see it a little differently.

4 WALK AROUND Quick opinions

Your teacher says two things, for example 'cats and dogs'. Use the opinion phrases in 1 and tell different partners which you like better and why.
Your partner agrees or disagrees and gives their opinion. Remember to be polite!

In my opinion, dogs are better than cats because they're kind and friendly.
– I completely agree! / I don't agree with you at all. I would say that cats are better than dogs because you don't have to take them outside.

► More help, p. 71

Digital quiz   I can give and explain my opinion.

Have a discussion

Step 1: Collect ideas on your topic

a) You're going to have a discussion about school uniforms. Find a partner. Read these arguments and decide: Are they for or against school uniforms?

1 It's easier to get dressed in the mornings.
2 Clothes are part of my personality.
3 You feel like you're part of the school.
4 It's difficult to buy school uniforms second-hand.
5 You don't have to worry about the newest fashion.
6 They can be uncomfortable or difficult to move in.

I think number ... is for school uniforms.

Right. And number ... is against them.

b) Think of more arguments for and against uniforms. Make notes.

► Skills file 12, p.151 ► Digital help

Step 2: Practise your discussion

a) Partner A is going to argue for and partner B is going to argue against school uniforms. Choose arguments from Step 1.

b) Discuss with your partner. Use the phrases from p. 60.

A *School uniforms are good because ...*
B *I don't agree with you at all. I think that ...*
A *Well, I see it a little differently. In my opinion, ...*
B *I think you'll find that school uniforms are bad because ...*

► Digital help

Step 3: Give your opinion

a) Now what's your opinion? Say what you think and why.

b) OPINION LINE Are school uniforms a great or a terrible idea for your school? Stand in a line. Then count the students.

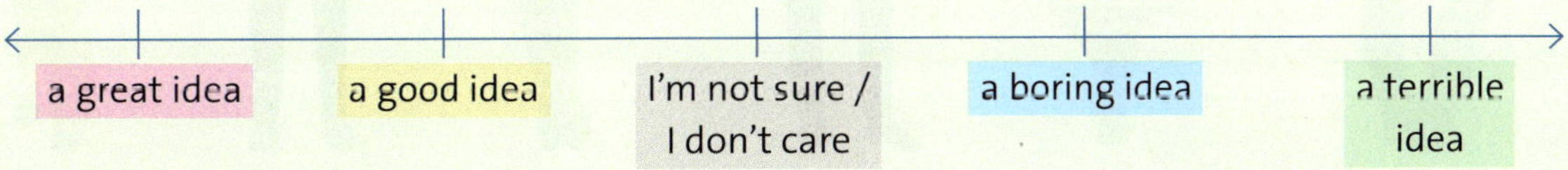

c) Talk about your results.

Three students think that school uniforms are a great idea.

Digital quiz **I can have a discussion.**

1 Listening Mei's podcast

I can explain what's important to me.

a) What's important to you? Put the pictures (A–F) in order. Then tell a partner. Say why.

A

B

C

D

E

F

b) Listen to the podcast and choose the correct picture (A–F) for each person: Ethan, Hafsa, Ryan and Laura. There are two extra pictures.

c) Listen again. Match the reasons to the students.

1 I can talk to them about anything.
2 I learn so much and it's never boring.
3 They always listen to me.
4 I feel safe and happy there.

2 Words What are they wearing?

I can talk about fashion.

Look at the pictures and describe the clothing.

1 2 3 4 5 6

1 *This person is wearing a purple headscarf, a blue sweater, grey trousers and black boots.*
2 ...

Check

3 LANGUAGE Aya's problem

I can make plans.

Complete Zoe and Aya's messages. Use the going-to future.

Zoe Hey Aya, are you OK? I heard that Josh was mean mean to you again.
Aya Hey Zoe. He was horrible.
Zoe Oh no, I'm so sorry. He's such a bully!
Aya He is. I don't know what I ... (1) do.
Zoe He ... (2) keep doing this, you know. I think you have to talk to someone. What about Ms Thomas? She's nice.
Aya You're right, she is. But I don't know what to say ...
Zoe You ... (3) say, 'Ms Thomas, I have a problem.' And then you ... (4) tell her what he did.
Aya What if I can't remember everything?
Zoe You can check our old messages. You wrote me every time he was mean.
Aya That's a good idea! I ... (5) read our old messages and then tomorrow I ... (6) show them to her.
Zoe And then you ... (7) tell me what she said. We ... (8) stop this!
Aya OK. Thanks, Zoe! I feel better now. You're a great friend!

4 MEDIATION Ole's problem

SadBoy has written an email to the *Hey!* advice column about a problem with his best friend. Read the answer and tell your German friend Ole about it – he has the same problem.

Dear SadBoy
Thank you for your letter. We understand that you're feeling sad about your friend. It's difficult when your best friend has a new girlfriend and you can't spend so much time together. We think you should explain to your friend how you're feeling. Try to stay calm when you talk to him. We're sure he didn't want to make you feel bad. Maybe you can agree on a special activity every week that's just for the two of you?
The *Hey!* Advice Column

Hi Ole,
ich habe gerade in einer englischen Schulzeitung über einen Jungen gelesen, der das gleiche Problem hat wie du: Er ist traurig, weil ... Das Zeitungsteam rät ihm, ... Er soll ...
Vielleicht ...
Schöne Grüße

Check

5 Speaking Looking and feeling confident

I can talk about confidence.

a) Look at the pictures. What do you think: Who is confident? Who isn't confident? Why? Make notes. You can use the ideas in the box.

... looks angry / happy / nervous / sad / ... • ... is/isn't looking up / smiling / standing up straight / ... • ...

The boy in picture 1 doesn't look confident. He isn't looking up.
The girl in picture 2 looks ... She's ...

1

2

3

4

b) Use your notes to talk about the people in a) with a partner. Are your opinions the same or different?

6 Study skills An online profile

I can give and explain my opinion.

a) Jack is giving his opinions on his online profile. Do you agree or disagree with Jack's opinions? Use these opinion phrases in your answer.

Maybe he's right.
Sorry, I think he's wrong.
I completely agree.
That's a good point.
I see it a little differently.

I don't agree with Jack at all. I think that ...

b) Give your opinion on these four questions.

Cars or bikes?
Books or TV shows?
Saturdays or Sundays?
Comfortable clothes or smart outfits?

Tell us what you prefer!

1. Cats or dogs?
   I think that dogs are the best because you can play games with them!
2. Football or basketball?
   If you ask me, football is better because you can play it anywhere.
3. The sun or snow?
   I would say that snow is really fun because you can go skiing.

Check

7 READING The school fashion show

I can discuss a conflict in a story.

1 It's Monday, and Omar and Rosie are working on their project. On the table in front of them is a piece of paper with lots of notes. In the middle of the paper it says: **Trafford School Green Fashion Show!** Rosie and Omar are excited and have lots of ideas.

2 'So I think I will be the presenter. I can give a short speech at the start of the show. And you could sit at the front and take notes for the newspaper,' says Omar, smiling.
'Why?' asks Rosie.
'Oh, well, I thought it might be easier for you. Because then you can sit down,' says Omar, looking at Rosie's legs. Rosie looks at Omar. 'I need to go to my next lesson now. Bye.'

3 After school, Omar gets a message from Rosie. Omar can't believe it. That night, he doesn't sleep at all.

Hi, Omar. I have thought about the show, and I don't want to be part of it any more. Good luck with it. Rosie

4 The next day, Omar sees Rosie before school.
'Rosie, wait,' he says. 'What's wrong? Are you angry with me?'
'Yes, I am,' says Rosie. 'You didn't ask me what I wanted to do in the show. You only saw my disability. You didn't see me!'

5 After a long pause, Omar starts to speak. 'I'm so sorry, Rosie. You're right, I didn't ask for your opinion. Can we meet at lunchtime to make a new plan? I can't do the show alone!'
'We can,' says Rosie, 'but this time we should *both* say what we want to do. And I'm going to be part of the show!'
'Sounds like a much better plan!' smiles Omar.

a) **Read the story. Match the correct headings (A–F) to the paragraphs (1–5). There's one extra heading.**

A Rosie tells Omar how she feels
B Rosie's mistake
C An exciting new project
D Omar's plan
E A different plan
F Omar is shocked

b) **Correct the sentences. The mistakes are underlined.**

1 Omar and Rosie are planning a <u>fast fashion show</u>.
2 Omar thinks Rosie should <u>be the presenter</u>.
3 Rosie's text message shows that <u>she likes Omar's idea</u>.
4 Rosie was angry because Omar only thought about her <u>skills</u>.
5 Rosie <u>wants to watch</u> the fashion show.

Check

Diff bank

▸ Page 44

More help 1 What's important to Rosie and Omar

b) Read the speech bubbles. What do you learn about Rosie and Omar? Make a profile. One of you chooses Rosie, and the other one Omar.

Name:	Rosie
Age:	...
School year:	...
What's important?	
Favourite thing?	
What else?	

Name:	Omar
Age:	...
School year:	...
What's important?	
Favourite city?	
What else?	

▸ Page 45

More help 2 What's important to you

b) Tell a partner what people or things are important to you.

My bike is really important to me.

computer • pet • hobby • watching/playing football • youth centre • dance group • band • school club • ...

Explain why.

My bike / skateboard / ... My pet My computer / phone / ... Watching/Playing football / ... My hobby / dance group / band / youth centre / school club / ...	is	important to me because	it's fun to ride / ... it's my best friend / it's cute / ... I can text friends / take photos / ... I love sports / ... I can relax / I meet my friends / it's where I spend my free time / ...
My friends / parents / ...	are		they support me / we have fun together / ...

▸ Page 44

More practice 1 In and around Manchester

a) **Omar loves Manchester! In the magazine he writes about four places. Read the descriptions and match them to the photos.**

1 I love the National Football Museum in Manchester. You can see famous football shirts. The building is cool too. It's really big and has lots of windows.
2 I love the Trafford Centre. It's good for shopping but also for bowling and watching films at the cinema.
3 Blackpool is a great day trip from Manchester. You all know Blackpool Tower, right? It looks like the Eiffel Tower in Paris. I love the beach and the pier there too.
4 Another great day trip from Manchester is the Peak District National Park. We went on a tour of a cave there once. It was so scary to be underground in the dark!

A

B

C

D

b) **Which of these places would you like to see? Tell a partner.**

I want to go to ....

▸ Page 46

More practice 2 Three teens

a) **Compare the teens in the picture.**

1 Adam is ... (small) than Nia.
2 Nia is the ... (tall) of the three teens.
3 Adam's trousers are ... (long) than Nia's trousers.
4 Nia has the ... (short) trousers of the three teens.
5 Leo's hair is ... (short) than Nia's hair.
6 Adam has the ... (long) hair.
7 Nia's clothes are ... (colourful) than Leo's clothes.
8 Adam has the ... (colourful) clothes of the three teens.

b) **Now say what you think. Write four sentences.**

Nia's trousers are cooler than Adam's trousers.
But Leo's trousers are the coolest.

boring • cool • interesting • nice • uncool • colourful • ...

▸ Page 47

More help 4 My task My fashion

B **You need a new outfit for a special event, but you don't have a lot of money to spend. What are you going to do? Talk to a partner.**

I'm going to ...	borrow something from ...
	clean / fix ...
	go to a charity shop
	make ... cooler with a ...

▸ Page 49

Parallel exercise **3 What about you?**

Read the questions and answers with a partner. Find the best answers for each question. There can be more than one right answer. Can you think of more answers?

1 What can you do to stop fighting with your parents?
  A Don't talk at all. B Clean the kitchen so they forget the fight.
  C Be honest with them.
2 If a friend has a serious problem, what do you think is the best thing to do?
  A Ask about the problem in class. B Wait for a quiet moment to talk.
  C Never talk about it.
3 How does a good friend make you feel?
  A Happy and safe. B Nervous and unhappy. C Uncool and stupid.
4 How does a crush make you feel?
  A Bored. B Really excited and happy. C So nervous that you feel sick.
5 If you're not doing well in maths, who can you talk to?
  A Your maths teacher. B Your dance teacher. C Your friend who is good at maths.

▸ Page 49

More practice 3 **What are you going to do this weekend?**

a) **Plan your perfect weekend. Use the going to-future.**

This weekend On Saturday On Sunday In the morning In the afternoon In the evening	I'm going to I'm not going to	be busy / lazy. tidy my room. go shopping / on a trip. do homework. practise football. play video games. ...

b) **Now ask each other questions.**

What are you going to do on Saturday morning?

I'm going to be lazy!

▸ Page 50

More practice 4 Rosie's day

Rosie has a busy day! Complete the sentences with the going to-future.

In the morning Rosie ... (1 take) an early bus to school because she ... (2 finish) her maths homework before class. Then she ... (3 go) to her first class, but she ... (4 not be) late because her teacher is strict. At lunch Rosie ... (5 meet) Omar to talk about the messages for the school magazine. But they ... (6 not write) the answers yet, because they want to talk to a teacher about the messages first.

▸ Page 51

More practice 5 Help!

Take turns to read out a problem or give advice with *should / shouldn't*. Use the ideas below or your own ideas.

1 Help! My cat can talk.
2 Help! My mum is an alien.
3 Help! There's a lion in my garden.
4 Help! I have four legs.
5 Help! My ears have fallen off.
6 Help! My neighbours are vampires.

You should You shouldn't	go on TV. call a vet / a doctor / the police. try to run really fast. go to a hospital. ask your friend ... for help. take pictures and sell them to a magazine.

More help 8 My task Make a plan

Problem	I'm going to ...			
My friend is sad.	*ask if she/he wants to talk.*	*say that I want to support her/him.*	*do fun things with her/him.*	*talk about it with my parents / an adult.*
My parents have too many rules.	*ask them to talk.*	*tell them how I feel.*	*stay calm and listen to their points.*	*ask for new rules because I am older now.*
I'm not doing well at school.	*talk to a teacher about it.*	*find out where my problems are.*	*ask my parents for support.*	*do all of my homework.*

▸ Page 53

More practice 6 Looking after yourself

Complete the advice. Use the words in the box.

himself • myself • ourselves • yourself • yourselves

It's important that you all look after ... (1). We can't be really happy if we don't love ... (2). Of course, friends are important too, and good friends look after each other, but you should be just as kind to ... (3) as you are to your friends. My brother says something nice to ... (4) in the mirror every morning. And I take care of ... (5) by running after school, getting enough sleep and eating healthy food. Healthy body, healthy mind!

▸ Page 55

More help 8 MY TASK Being confident

I think you	look	shy. nervous.
	don't look	very confident.
	should	stand up straight. speak clearly and loudly. smile. look at the other person.
	shouldn't	speak too quietly. look down at the ground.

▸ Page 60

More help 4 Quick opinions

	I agree	I disagree
Döner is better than pizza.	– tastes great and is usually cheaper	– you can put anything on pizza
Ice hockey is better than football.	– football is too slow – hockey is faster	– ice hockey players fight too much
Big cities are better than small towns.	– lots of things to do	– too expensive
School should start later in the morning.	– teenagers need lots of sleep	– less free time after school

Unit 3
Scotland: Adventure

A
Inverness: The capital of the Highlands

B
Kayaking on the west coast

C
Visiting Eilean Donan Castle

1 LISTENING A school trip in Scotland

a) BEFORE YOU LISTEN **Look at the pictures. What do they tell you about Scotland?**

b) **Grace and her friend Rhona are talking about their school trip. Listen and put the photos A–F in the order that you hear about them.**

c) **Listen again and complete the sentences with one word.**

1 Grace says that their school trip sounds ...
2 A lot of shops in Edinburgh are for ...
3 Eilean Donan Castle has a ...
4 Rhona says that kayaking looks ...

▸ Parallel exercise, p. 96

Nach dieser Unit kann ich ...

- über Schottland reden
- Geschichten und Sagen verstehen
- über Aktivitäten und Abenteuer sprechen
- über die Natur sprechen
- Entscheidungen in einer Geschichte besprechen
- Ideen für eine Geschichte gliedern

Unit task

- eine kurze Abenteuergeschichte schreiben

D

Shopping in Edinburgh

E

Hiking on Ben Nevis (the highest mountain in the UK!)

F

Visiting Loch Ness

2 Speaking Pictures of Scotland

a) **Look at the pictures again and answer the questions. Take notes.** ► Skills file 11, p. 150

What can you see? Where are the people? What are they doing? What is the weather like?

b) **Ask each other the questions about the photos. Each partner talks about three photos.**

c) **Ask and answer these questions with a partner. Give reasons for your answers.**

1 Which place or activity looks the most interesting?
2 Do you like to go on trips or do you like to stay at home?

► More help, p. 97 ► More practice 1, p. 97
► Workbook, p. 50

Digital quiz I can **talk about Scotland.**

Scary Scotland

1 Reading The legend of the Loch Ness monster

a) Before you read **Grace and Rhona were at Loch Ness today and learned about Nessie. Do you remember: What is Nessie?**

Nessie is a … *It lives in …*

b) **Rhona and Grace have written short texts on what they have learned.**
Partner B: Look at **p. 96.**
Partner A: Read Rhona's text on Nessie. What's the main idea?

A The legend of Nessie is very popular.
B The loch is too small for a monster.
C People don't believe that Nessie is real.

Nessie: The legend *Rhona*

Today we learned about Loch Ness and its monster, Nessie. Loch, of course, means lake, and Loch Ness is the second biggest loch in Scotland. It's 23 miles long and 88 feet deep. But it is famous for a different reason!

In 1934, Loch Ness quickly became famous when a tourist took a photo of something with a long neck and a small head in the lake. People all over the world saw the photo and believed that a monster lives in the loch.
Since then, lots of people have taken photos or videos of something in the water. Some people believe that Nessie is real because the loch is so big that there has to be something big in it.

I think that Nessie is real because it's fun and exciting to believe in monsters.

c) **Answer partner B's questions.**

d) **Now ask partner B these questions:**

1 Why do tourists come to Loch Ness?
2 What have scientists found in Loch Ness?
3 Does Grace think Nessie is real? Why or why not?

2 Speaking **My opinion about Nessie**

a) Think **Think about the information in 1 from both texts. Do you think Nessie is real or not? Why? Write one sentence.**

In my opinion, it's just a story for tourists because ...
Yes, I think Nessie is real because ...

b) Pair **Tell your partner your opinion.**

c) Share **What does the class think? How many students think Nessie is real?**

3 Mediation **A tour of Loch Ness**

a) **You're in Edinburgh with your family. You want to go on this tour. Read the advert and answer your family's questions in German.**

1 Was kosten denn die Karten für Erwachsene? Und für Kinder?
2 Wann und wo fängt die Tour an?
3 Wie lange dauert die Tour?
4 Müssen wir Mittagessen mitbringen oder können wir da etwas kaufen?
5 Ist der Audioguide nur auf Englisch?
6 Wie lange dauert die Bootsfahrt?
7 Wie viel kostet die Bootsfahrt für Erwachsene? Und für Kinder?

Edinburgh to Loch Ness
One-Day Tour

Our most popular tour. Explore beautiful Scotland with us.

Maybe you'll see Nessie too!

- *Adults: £65, children under 14: £45, babies under 1: free.*
- *We leave at 8.00 a.m. from platform 11 at the bus station in the centre of Edinburgh. Please don't be late! The tour takes about 12 hours.*
- *Bring your own lunch or buy one from us: Sandwich, coffee or juice and traditional Scottish biscuits: £5*
- *Audio guide with over 20 languages and headphones: £3.50.*
- *One-hour boat trip of Loch Ness: £18 for adults, children under 14: £15, babies under 1: free.*

b) **Now you're buying the tickets. Your dad tells you what to buy. Talk to the tour guide in English.**

Tour guide How can I help you?
You We would like to buy ...
We would also like ...
We don't want to go ...

Wir möchten zwei Eintrittskarten für Erwachsene und zwei für Kinder für den Tagesausflug nach Loch Ness kaufen. Dazu vier Mittagessen und zwei Audioguides, aber wir wollen nicht mit auf die Bootsfahrt gehen.

▶ Parallel exercise, p. 98 ▶ Skills file 10, p. 149

▶ Workbook, p. 51

4 LISTENING Scottish ghosts

a) BEFORE YOU LISTEN **Tell your partner what scary stories, books, films or series you know.**

I know a scary story / film / ... It's called ...
It's about ...

► Wordbank 5, p. 172

b) **Next, Grace and Rhona visit Eilean Donan Castle and go on a tour. Read the sentences. Then listen. Are the sentences true or false?**

1 Everyone wanted the same person to be the King.
2 British soldiers went to Spain.
3 The King found out about the secret plan.
4 The castle we see today is one hundred years old.
5 They call the ghost Carmen.

c) **Is it a good story? Why or why not? Tell the class.**

It's a good story but it isn't really scary. / I like the story because it's about soldiers and history.

d) **Read the questions. Then listen again and answer the questions with 1–5 words.**

What does the ghost wear? How does it walk?
What's special about its head? What's its name?

► More practice 2, p. 98

5 LOOKING AT LANGUAGE Adverbs of manner

Erklär-film

a) **Look at this example from the story about the castle ghost and read the explanation.**

I'm a quiet ghost. I'm walking quietly behind you.

- **quiet ist ein Adjektiv. Es beschreibt, wie eine Person oder Sache ‚ist'.**
- **quietly ist ein Adverb. Es beschreibt, wie jemand etwas tut oder wie etwas passiert.**

b) **Read the sentences 1–4. Write the adverbs for the adjectives in the table on the right.**

1 I'm going to tell you a story, so listen carefully.
2 They made their plans secretly.
3 He walks slowly around the castle.
4 He carries his head safely under his arm.

adjective	adverb
careful	...
secret	...
slow	...
safe	...

c) **Complete the rule.**

Um die meisten Adverbien zu bilden, hängen wir die Endung ... an das Adjektiv an.

Good to know

Ausnahmen: *good → well, fast → fast*
It's a good story. He told the story well.

► Language file 10, p. 162
► Workbook, p. 52

6 The Edinburgh Castle ghost

Write the story in the pictures. Make adverbs from the adjectives.

1 A long time ago, people found tunnels under Edinburgh Castle. But they got lost ... (quick), so they decided to make a map.

2 They asked a small boy to help because he played the bagpipes ... (good).

3 The boy walked down the tunnels and played his bagpipes ... (loud), so people could hear him.

4 Above ground, people listened ... (careful) and followed the music of the piper.

5 But then the bagpipes stopped ... (sudden). Nobody ever saw the boy again.

6 Today tourists often hear music from underground. Somebody is playing the bagpipes ... (sad).

▶ More practice 3, p. 98 ▶ More practice 4, p. 99 ▶ Workbook, p. 53

My task

7 My scary monster

a) **Think of a ghost or another scary monster.**
– **Give it a good name.**
– **Describe it. How does it walk / talk / eat / scare people / ...? Use adverbs.**

▶ More help, p. 99 ▶ Wordbank 5, p. 172
▶ Digital help

b) **Make a poster of your monster. You can draw it or find a picture online.**

c) GALLERY WALK **Walk around and look at the posters. Write comments on sticky notes.**

That's a scary monster.

Cool name!

My monster is the Homework Ogre.
He's very tall and strong and scares students easily. He walks and talks slowly, but he eats homework quickly.
Students have to do their homework carefully and quietly ... or the Homework Ogre will take it from them and eat it!

Digital quiz I can understand stories and legends.

Outdoor activities

1 Listening An adventure trip

a) Before you listen **Look at the pictures and the activities in the box. What can you do at the Adventure Centre? Talk with a partner.**

You can ... / That's in picture ...

drive a go-kart • hike up a mountain • jump off a cliff • ride a horse • ski down a mountain • sleep outside in a tent

1

2

3

4

5

6

b) **Grace and Rhona are on the bus to the Adventure Centre. Listen and say why Rhona is worried.**

c) **Listen again. Who says what? Write G (Grace) or R (Rhona).**

1 I've slept outside in a tent before.
2 I haven't hiked up a mountain.
3 I haven't jumped off a cliff before.
4 I haven't ridden a horse before.
5 I've skied down a mountain.
6 I have driven a go-kart before.

▶ Skills file 8, p. 146

2 Now you

Tell a partner which activities you want to do.

I want to drive a go-kart. / ...
I don't want to hike up a mountain. / ...

▶ Workbook, p. 54

Erklär-
film

3 Looking at language The present perfect

Read what Grace says. Then copy and complete the rule in the box.

I've just **read** the programme and **I've looked** at all the activities again. **I've** never **been** to an adventure centre before. I'm really excited.

You've already **done** one activity!

I've gone up lots of mountains, but **I haven't jumped** off a cliff before. **Have you** already **done** that?

My sister has tried so many scary things.

Wir bilden das *present perfect* mit *has / have* oder den Kurzformen *'s / 've* und der dritten Form des Verbs *(past participle)*.
Worauf enden regelmäßige *past participles* wie *looked, jumped, tried?* – ...
Manche *past participles* haben eine unregelmäßige Form *(read, been, done, gone)*.
Diese musst du lernen!

Wir verwenden das *present perfect* für etwas, das irgendwann oder noch nie geschehen ist.
Der Zeitpunkt der Handlung ist unwichtig, aber sie hat oft Folgen in der Gegenwart.

PAST → PRESENT

I've gone up lots of mountains, but I haven't jumped off a cliff before. Have you already done that? → *No, I haven't, and I don't want to try it! It sounds really scary!*

▸ Language file 11, p. 163 ▸ Irregular verbs, p. 238

4 Are you ready?

Grace and Rhona are getting ready for a hiking trip. Complete the sentences with *'ve / have* or *haven't*.

Grace Let's see. I *haven't* (1 not) packed my water bottle yet. I'll do that now.
Rhona But I ... (2) remembered my warm sweater.
Grace And I ... (3) already put that in my rucksack too. Is that everything?
Rhona I'm sure that we ... (4) forgotten something!
Grace I know what I ... (5 not) done yet. The website! We ... (6 not) looked at it yet.
Rhona That's right! Let's do that now.

▸ More practice 5, p. 99

▸ Workbook, p. 55

5 READING The Adventure Centre's website

a) BEFORE YOU READ **Rhona and Grace are looking at the website and reading about one of the instructors, Kirsten. Look at the pictures.**
- **What is Kirsten doing?** *She's doing different (outdoor) activities. She's taking photos / ...*
- **What do you think her job is like?** *I think her job looks fun / ...*

www.example.com/adventure-team-instructors

Meet our newest team member: *This is Kirsten*

Tell us your name, job and favourite activities.	My name is Kirsten and I'm 21. I'm a new instructor. My favourite activities are taking photos, hiking and camping. And I love animals, especially horses.
Have you ever ridden a horse?	Yes, I have! I've ridden lots of horses.
Have you ever slept in a tent?	Yes, I have. And I've cooked so many meals outside that I'm really good at it now.
Have you ever swum with dolphins?	No, I haven't, but I've swum in really cold water.
Have you ever hurt yourself?	Yes, I've broken my arm and I've hurt my ankle.
Tell us your motto.	I think that life should be an adventure. Come and have adventures with us!

b) **Read the text. What has Kirsten done? What hasn't she done? Make a list.** ► Skills file 9, p. 148

c) **Kirsten answers four questions. Ask each other the questions.** ► More practice 6, p. 100

Have you ever ridden a horse?

Yes, I have / No, I haven't.

6 What about you?

Rhona and Grace are talking about the website.
Write the questions in the right order.

Grace Kirsten thinks that life should be an adventure! That sounds amazing.
Rhona Sure, but Kirsten has broken her arm! That sounds horrible.
Grace Maybe you're right. ... (1 broken / you / Have / ever / your arm?)
Rhona No, I haven't.
Grace Some of these activities sound easier, right? Like camping, for example. ... (2 been camping? / you / ever / Have)
Rhona Yes, I have. You're right, it was fun.
Grace Or horse riding. ... (3 you / ever / Have / ridden a horse?)
Rhona No, I haven't. But my cousin has. She's very brave, like Kirsten. And like you. ... (4 ever / Have / been scared? / you)
Grace Yes, of course I've been scared before.
Rhona What about Kirsten? ... (5 ever / Has / been scared? Kirsten)
Grace Yes, I'm sure she has been scared before! Everybody is scared sometimes.

▶ Workbook, p. 56

My task

7 Have you ever ...?

a) THINK **What adventures has your partner had? Write at least six interview questions. Use *Have you ever ...?***

Have you ever travelled to a different country?

Yes, I have. / No, I haven't.

▶ More help, p. 100 ▶ Wordbank 6, p. 173 ▶ Irregular verbs, p. 238 ▶ Digital help

b) PAIR **Ask your partner your questions and take notes. Answer your partner's questions.**

▶ Digital help

c) PAIR **Write what your partner has done. Remember to use *has / hasn't*.**

d) SHARE **Listen to the class share what their partners have done. Who has had the most interesting adventure?**

I think ... has had the most interesting adventure because ...

Digital quiz I can talk about activities and adventures.

In nature

1 GLOBAL GOALS Protect nature

a) The instructors tell Grace and Rhona's class how to protect nature. Look at the pictures and make sentences.

You should	close the ... • leave ... alone • use the ...
You shouldn't	give food to ... • leave ... • make ...

1 farm animals

2 paths

3 rubbish

4 gates

5 a fire

6 flowers and plants

b) WORDS Make a mind map with words about nature in your VOCAB FILE.
Start like this:

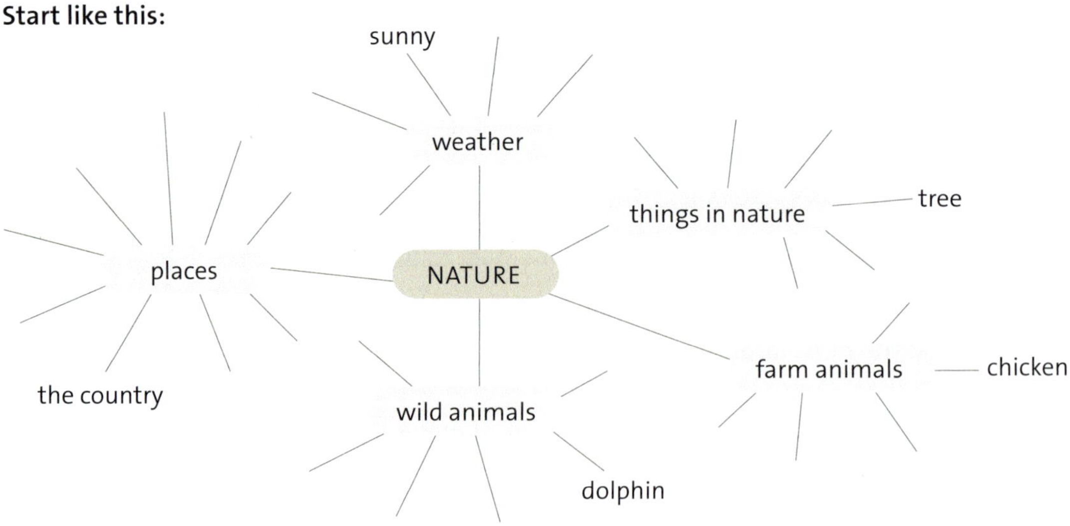

▶ Skills file 1, p. 139 ▶ Wordbank 7, p. 174
▶ Workbook, p. 57

2 What can we do?

a) **Say what you can do to help protect nature. Match the words to make phrases.**

1	recycle	A	public transport more often
2	collect	B	more often
3	save	C	less meat
4	eat	D	paper and plastic
5	use	E	rubbish in the neighbourhood
6	cycle	F	energy

b) **Do you do any of the things in a)? Talk to a partner.**

I eat less meat.

In my family we save energy.

c) **What else have you done or can you do to help protect nature? Write at least four sentences.**

I often / always walk or go by bus. / ...
I have / haven't been to climate protests. / ...
We can try to buy less stuff. / ...
Let's do a clean-up day. / ...

▶ Workbook, p. 58

My task

3 Nature and me

a) THINK **Is nature important to you? Make notes. You can use the ideas in the box or your own ideas.** ▶ Skills file 12, p. 151

I like / I love to It's fun to	be in nature • walk in a forest • climb a mountain • swim in a lake • go camping • go to a park • sit on grass • watch birds • see wild animals • ...
I don't like to go outside because	there are a lot of insects • it's too hot/cold/rainy/... • I think it's boring • ...
Nature is important because	it gives us food / clean air / clean water / ... I feel great when I'm in a forest / on a mountain / ...

b) PAIR **Talk to a partner. Say what you think.**

c) SHARE **Find out: How many students in the class like to be in nature? How many students think that nature is important and why?**

Digital quiz

I can talk about nature.

A mountain adventure

1 Reading Preparing for an adventure

a) Before you read **What should you do to prepare for hiking or mountain climbing? Brainstorm ideas as a class. Look at Grace's bag to help you.**

You should bring / check / remember / wear ...

b) **What do you think will happen on the mountain? Read the title and look at the pictures.**

Maybe Rhona / Grace will ... *I think they will / won't ...*

c) **Read the story and find out if you were right.**

Rhona and Grace were on the bus on their way to Ben Nevis. Mr McAlister, one of the teachers, saw Rhona's shoes. 'Rhona, where are your walking boots? You can't wear trainers today.' 'Oh ...' Rhona's face was red. 'It's OK, Mr McAlister – my walking boots are in my bag. I'll put them on when we get there.'

Mr McAlister walked away. Grace looked at Rhona. 'You didn't put boots in your bag this morning.'

'I know ... I don't have walking boots,' said Rhona. 'Walking boots are so expensive. I'm not going to buy walking boots for one trip!'

A few hours later, they were on the mountain. It wasn't as bad as Rhona thought, but Grace was bored. 'Ugh, there are too many people on this path and it's too easy! Come on, I know a better path. It's a little more difficult but the views are amazing and there aren't as many tourists.'

Rhona was worried but she agreed to go on the new path. 'I'm nervous, but I want to try it,' she said. Grace and Rhona moved quickly when Mr McAlister was busy. Grace was right – it was very beautiful, and they were alone.

Rhona stopped suddenly. The path was really small, and they were right next to the cliff. She could see all the way down to the valley at the bottom of the mountain. One wrong step ...

'I can't do it,' she started to cry. 'It's too high. I'm really scared!'
Grace took Rhona's hands and looked into her eyes. 'Breathe slowly, like me. In ... out ... in ...'

After a few minutes, Rhona felt better. The path got bigger again. It was easy for Grace, and she walked quickly, but it was hard for Rhona because her trainers weren't good enough. Then a rock moved under her foot and she fell.

'Ow!' said Rhona. 'Oh Grace, I've hurt my ankle. I can't walk any more.'
'Oh no! OK, I'll call Mr McAlister,' said Grace.
Grace called Mr McAlister and explained what happened.
'Mountain Rescue are sending a helicopter now, so don't move,' he said. 'We'll find you.'

As they waited, they felt more and more scared, and they started to argue.
'Why did you want to go on this dangerous path?' asked Rhona.
'Well, why did you wear trainers for climbing a mountain?'
'Hey, I didn't even want to climb this mountain!'

Finally, after what felt like hours, they heard a loud noise – it was the helicopter!

Rhona climbed into the helicopter first. She felt sick and her ankle hurt, but she remembered how it helped to breathe slowly.
She thought, 'In ... out ... in ...,' and felt a little better.

Soon they were safely in the helicopter. Grace and Rhona didn't say anything at first while the people from Mountain Rescue looked at Rhona's ankle. They both felt tired, angry and embarrassed.

Suddenly, the girls looked at each other and spoke at the same time:
'Grace ...'
'Rhona ...'

They both laughed. 'You go first, Grace,' said Rhona. 'What did you want to say?'

2 Good and bad choices

a) Read the sentences and decide if they are true or false.

1 Rhona had walking boots in her bag.
2 Mr McAlister didn't see them leave the group.
3 Rhona got hurt and had to stop.
4 Grace called Mr McAlister. He told them to come to him.
5 Rhona and Grace felt bad and blamed each other.
6 They didn't talk at all in the helicopter.

b) What good and bad choices did each character make?

1 Grace helped ..., but she ...
2 Rhona tried ..., but she ...

► Parallel exercise, p. 100 ► More practice 7, p. 100

3 Linking words

a) There are eight blue linking words on p. 85. Find them. Write a list.

b) Choose the correct linking word.

1 Rhona didn't buy walking boots because / while they're too expensive.
2 Grace was bored then / so she wanted to walk on a different path.
3 Grace liked the new path but / finally it was too high for Rhona.
4 They started to argue soon / while they waited for the helicopter.

► More practice 8, p. 101

4 Saying sorry

a) Write what you think Grace and Rhona say to each other at the end of the story.

I'm sorry, it was a bad idea to ...
I don't know why I ...
Thank you for saying sorry.
I feel better now.

b) Read your partner's conversation. Then choose one and read it out.

5 LIFE SKILLS Learn from your mistakes

Look at the bad choices in 2b). What should the characters do next time?

Next time, Grace should ...

► More help, p. 101

Digital quiz I can discuss good and bad choices in a story.

A road trip

1 Before you watch The best way to travel

a) What's your favourite way to travel and why? Tell your partner.

b) What's a road trip? Compare your answer with a partner.

2 Viewing Sightseeing

a) Watch the video. Which of these things do Mon and Jorge see on their road trip?

A a bridge
B a valley
C a fire
D a boat
E a horse
F a cat
G a castle
H a city
I a lake
J a cave

b) Watch the video again and answer the questions with one word.

1 What is Scotland famous for?
2 Which city do they stop in?
3 What haven't they seen today?
4 What do they have a lot of for the next vlog?

3 Scottish activities

a) Complete the sentences with the activities.

1 On the Isle of Skye, they don't ...

2 At Loch Ness, they go ...

3 At Dunrobin, they listen to ...

b) Which place in the video would you most like to visit and why? Tell your partner.

▸ Workbook, p. 59

Structuring your ideas

1 Choose a topic and a title

You are going to write an adventure story. Look at the pictures for ideas and read the titles. Choose one or think of your own idea.

A big surprise

A mountain rescue

A dark, scary forest

An exciting sea trip

Lost in the city

2 Answer the wh-questions

a) Make a mind map with your title and answer these questions:

- Who were you with?
- When did it happen?
- Where were you?
- What did you see?

b) Think of more ideas. Answer these questions:

- What happened next?
- What happened after that
- How did you feel?

3 Add more information

Look at your partner's mind map. Do you have more ideas? Tell your partner so that they can add more information.

Remember to use adjectives and adverbs to make your text more interesting.

► Skills file 6, p. 145

Digital quiz I can structure ideas for a story.

Write a short adventure story

Step 1: Use your mind map to write your story

a) **Begin to write your story. Use the first three wh-questions: Who, When, Where?**

Last summer ...:
... my family and I ...
... went to Scotland ...
... visited Loch Ness ...
It was a ... afternoon ...

b) **Think about what happened. This is the most interesting part of your story. What happened first, what happened next? How did you feel?**

Suddenly, we saw ...
It was ...
... was scared, so ...
Then it ...
We felt ...

► More help, p. 101 ► Digital help

Step 2: Check your story

a) **Read the checklist. Have you answered all the questions?**

b) **Write your story again.**

► Skills file 13, p. 152

► Digital help

Checklist
- Does your story have a beginning, middle and end?
- Have you used the simple past? *(saw, visited, went to)*
- Have you used linking words? *(and, but, because, so)*
- Have you used adjectives and adverbs? *(it was a rainy afternoon, she shouted loudly)*
- Have you spelled everything correctly? *(~~schouted~~ – shouted)*
- If you write your story digitally, you can use the spellchecker to make sure your spelling is correct.

Step 3: Share your story

Read your partner's story or listen as they read it out loud. Give feedback.

Your story was exciting!

You used lots of interesting vocabulary and linking words.

► Let's talk: Feedback, p. 182

Digital quiz I can write a short adventure story.

1 SPEAKING A day in Edinburgh

I can talk about Scotland.

You're planning a trip to Edinburgh. Look at this website and tell your partner which place you want to visit. Use the phrases below.

www.discover-Edinburgh.example.net

Edinburgh Castle

The perfect place to discover Scottish history and to enjoy amazing views of the city.

Open every day from 9.30 a.m.
Ticket: £19.50
Child ticket (age 7–15): £11.40

Edinburgh Zoo

Our zoo is home to over 2,500 animals from around the world.

Open every day from 10 a.m.
Ticket: £24.25
Child ticket (age 3–15): £15.70

I'd like to see / go to ... • I'm really interested in ... • I want to know more about ... • It's cheaper than ... • I don't want to go to ... • I think the ... is boring / ...

2 LISTENING Grace's story

I can understand stories and legends (adverbs of manner).

a) **Listen to Grace's story. Which picture matches the story, A or B?**

b) **Listen again. Choose the correct answer.**

1 Culloden is a small village / big city.
2 People fought there almost 3 / 300 years ago.
3 They fought for one hour / days.
4 The ghosts come back every month / year.
5 One Scottish soldier / piper walks alone.
6 The ghosts come to Culloden on 15th / 16th April.

c) LANGUAGE **Read what Grace's uncle said. Make the adjectives 1–6 into adverbs.**

I went to Culloden last April. At first it was calm, but the ghosts appeared (1) sudden. They shouted (2) loud. One ghost was alone. He walked around (3) slow and (4) sad. I went back to my car (5) careful and (6) quiet because I didn't want the ghosts to see me!

Check

3 The adventure centre website

I can talk about activities and adventures.

a) LANGUAGE **Read the website. Complete the sentences with *have, haven't, has* or *hasn't*.**

www.adventure-centre-who-is-who.example.net

We'd like to introduce everyone to two new instructors: Gemma and Ron.
They ... (1) just joined the team.
Gemma is 25 and she's from Inverness.
She ... (2) been an instructor for two years at another centre.
She ... (3) always loved adventure, but she ... (4 not) ever jumped off a cliff before. Do you think she will? We'll see!

Ron is 21. He's from Glasgow, and this is his first job. We know that he'll be great! He ... (5 not) been an instructor before, but he ... (6) always spent time outdoors and he wants to share his love of nature with other people.

For the last few weeks, we ... (7) travelled with Gemma and Ron around this beautiful part of Scotland. They ... (8 not) seen such a beautiful place before! It already seems like they ... (9) been with us forever. Welcome to the team, Gemma and Ron.

b) WORDS **Look at these pictures from the website and complete the sentences with the correct words.**

Have you ever jumped off a 1 f l f c i before? It's amazing!

You haven't been camping before? Click here to learn how to put up your 2 t t n e.

You never know what will happen in 3 a n t u e r. Bring rain clothes.

Click here for a full list of what things you need to 4 k p c a.

We've planned lots of cool 5 d o u o t o r activities for you.

Listen to our instructors. They will 6 t p o t e r c you from danger.

Check

4 Writing A message to a friend

I can talk about nature.

Imagine you are on a camping holiday in Scotland and you're staying near place A or B.

A

B

Write a message to your friend Michelle. Tell her:

- about the area.
- what you can see and hear.
- if you like it there and why.

The phrases in the box can help you.

area	beautiful • cold • wild • ...
see	flowers • a mountain • a valley • ...
hear	birds • the rain • the river • the wind • ...
like	clean air • feels good to be outdoors • ...
don't like	miss my friends • bored • too quiet • ...

Dear Michelle,
I'm camping in Scotland at the moment. ...
...

Take care!
(Name)

5 Study skills Ahmed's story

I can structure ideas for a story.

Read Ahmed's notes for his story. Draw a mind map and add his notes to it.

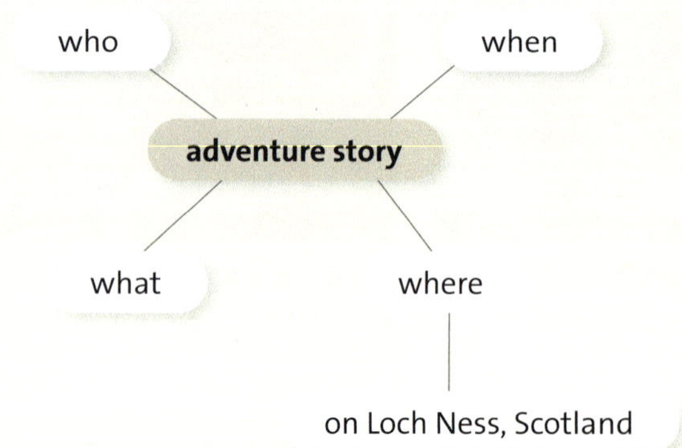

Adventure story: my ideas
- ~~*on Loch Ness, Scotland*~~
- *one month ago*
- *two boys – James and Hussein*
- *school trip*
- *want to see the monster*
- *big thunderstorm*
- *next, James – nervous*
- *but Hussein – brave!*

Check

6 READING Kayaking on the river

I can discuss good and bad choices in a story.

Right, everyone,' said the instructor, 'Now you know how to use the boats safely. The last thing I want to talk about is the dry bag. This is where you put things to protect them from water. Great, everyone looks ready now. Let's get onto the river. Just remember the number one rule: Any problems, call me!'

a dry bag

Grace and Rhona got into their kayak excitedly. 'This is amazing,' said Grace. 'Let's go faster!' Rhona laughed. She was surprised – this was fun! 'Let's take some photos,' said Grace. 'I'm not sure,' answered Rhona. 'My phone is in the dry bag. The instructor said we should leave our things in there.' 'That's true. But we can take it out for a minute,' said Grace.

Rhona opened the bag very carefully and took out her phone. Then the kayak stopped suddenly. 'Woah!', called Grace, 'I think there are some big rocks under our boat! Are you ok?' 'Erm, yes, I'm OK ...,' said Rhona. 'But my phone isn't. It's in the water!' 'Oh no, I'm so sorry,' said Grace. 'The water isn't very deep here. I'll get out and find your phone.'

'No, you stay in the boat,' said Rhona. 'I'm a stronger swimmer than you are. I'll get out and find the phone.'

Rhona climbed into the water confidently. 'I can see it,' she called, 'it's not far from the boat. I'll just ...,' Rhona suddenly looked worried.

'Rhona? Are you OK?' asked Grace. 'I – I can't move my foot!' said Rhona. 'I think it's stuck.'

'Stay there, and don't try to move,' said Grace. 'I can see the instructor. I'll ask him to come and help us.

a) Read the story. What's it about? Choose the best main idea.

Grace and Rhona ...

A had a perfect kayaking adventure.
B found kayaking really difficult and didn't like it.
C made some mistakes while kayaking.

b) Complete the sentences with the correct name.

1 ... wanted to take photos.
2 ... took her phone out of the bag.
3 ... got out of the boat.
4 ... asked the instructor for help.

c) Read each of the sentences from b) again. Decide if it was a good choice or a bad choice. Say why.

Check

United

A magazine for young people across the UK

Scottish traditions *by Rhona Murray*

We have wonderful traditions in Scotland. You can try some of them at home or in class!

Hogmanay

Hogmanay means *New Year's Eve* and we celebrate it from 31 December to 2 January. There are street parties, fireworks, music and concerts. It's amazing!

At midnight[1], people sing the famous song *Auld Lang Syne*[2]. The Scottish poet[3] Robert Burns wrote the words.

Auld Lang Syne

Have you heard it before?

Burns Night

Do you know what Burns Night is? It's on 25 January, the birthday of Robert Burns.

On Burns Night people eat a special food called haggis. Today you can buy vegetarian haggis, but traditional haggis is made from[4] different parts of a sheep mixed with oatmeal[5], onions and spices.

Before dinner, people listen to bagpipes and read a special poem from Robert Burns. After dinner, people read out more poems, play music and dance. At the end of the evening, everyone sings *Auld Lang Syne*.

Would you like to try haggis?

---

[1] **midnight** *Mitternacht* [2] **auld lang syne (Scots) = old long since** etwa: *vor langer Zeit* [3] **poet** *der Dichter, die Dichterin*
[4] **is made from** *wird gemacht aus* [5] **oatmeal** *das Hafermehl*

Try this in class. It's great fun !

Let's dance!

This traditional Scottish dance is called *Stripping the willow*. Look at the pictures and read the instructions or watch a video on the internet.

Girls and boys stand across[1] from each other.

Boy 1 and Girl 1 link[2] **right** arms and turn.

Girl 1 goes to Boy 2. Boy 1 goes to Girl 2. Both pairs link **left** arms and turn.

Boy 1 and Girl 1 link **right** arms again and turn.

Repeat all the way down to the end of the line: Girl 1 turns with all the boys and Boy 1 turns with all the girls.

Shortbread: a Scottish biscuit recipe

You need: 200 g butter, 100 g sugar, 300 g flour

Heat[3] the oven to 160° C.

Put baking paper in a tin[4].

Mix the butter and sugar.

Add the flour and mix.

Press the shortbread into the tin.

Make small holes[5] with a fork[6].

Bake for 25 minutes.

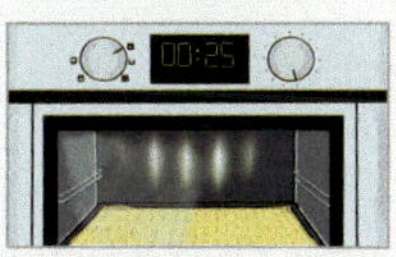

Cut the shortbread into 'fingers' in the tin.

Leave the shortbread to cool[7] in the tin. Enjoy!

[1] **across from** *gegenüber* [2] (to) **link arms** *sich einhaken* [3] (to) **heat** *vorheizen* [4] **tin** *das Backblech*
[5] **hole** *das Loch* [6] **fork** *die Gabel* [7] (to) **cool** *abkühlen*

Partner page

▸ Page 74

1 READING The legend of the Loch Ness monster

b) Partner B: Read Grace's text on Nessie. What's the main idea?

A Scottish people don't like Nessie.
B Scientists haven't found anything in the loch.
C There are lots of pictures of Nessie, but they aren't real.

Nessie: The science *Grace*

Today we went to Loch Ness (*loch* means *lake*). It's famous because people believe that Nessie, a monster, lives there. It's an important Scottish legend, and every year lots of tourists spend money in the area because they want to see Nessie.

But I want to know: Is Nessie real? There are many photos and videos of something with a long neck and a small head. But all the pictures of Nessie are fake!

Scientists have even used special technology to find out what animals lived in the lake. They haven't found a monster – but they have found lots of different animals and fish, especially eels. That's why some scientists think that Nessie could be a big eel.

I don't think that Nessie is real because all the pictures are fake. But I still loved my visit to Loch Ness. It was a real Scottish adventure!

c) Ask partner A these questions about Rhona's text.

1 How big is Loch Ness?
2 What happened in 1934?
3 Does Rhona think Nessie is real? Why or why not?

d) Now answer partner A's questions.

Diff bank

▸ Page 72

Parallel exercise **1 A school trip in Scotland**

c) Listen again and complete the sentences with the right word.

1 Grace says that their school trip sounds exciting / amazing.
2 A lot of shops in Edinburgh are for students / tourists.
3 Eilean Donan Castle has a ghost / monster.
4 Rhona says that kayaking looks easy / fun.

▸ Page 73

More help 2 SPEAKING Pictures of Scotland

c) Ask and answer the questions with a partner. Give reasons for your answers.

1 Which activity looks the most interesting?

I think	visiting Inverness kayaking on the west coast visiting Eilean Donan Castle shopping in Edinburgh hiking on Ben Nevis visiting Loch Ness	looks the most interesting because	I like lakes / old buildings / the sea / shopping / small towns / doing sports / being outside / ...
			I'd like to see a ghost / the Loch Ness Monster / ...

2 Do you like to go on trips or do you like to stay at home?

I like to go on trips I like to stay to stay at home	because	I like seeing new places / being outside / ...
		I don't like travelling / it's nice to stay at home / ...

More practice 1 Glasgow and Edinburgh

Look at the photos of Glasgow and Edinburgh, the two biggest cities in Scotland. Read the information. Which city would you like to visit and why? Tell your partner.

I'd like to visit Edinburgh because I like scary tours. / I'd like to visit Glasgow because I like to shop.

Activities for kids and teens in Edinburgh

- Climb Arthur's Seat for great views of the city.
- Tour the famous Edinburgh Castle and learn about its history.
- Go on a scary tour through Edinburgh's tunnels.
- On December 31st, visit the famous street party for music, fireworks and fun.

Activities for kids and teens in Glasgow

- Go to Buchanan Street for its great shops, cafes, and street musicians.
- Visit the Science Centre and learn more about our planet and our bodies.

- The Riverside Museum of Transport and Travel shows you how people in Glasgow travelled a long time ago.
- At the Museum of Piping, try playing the bagpipes yourself!

▸ Page 75

Parallel exercise 3 A tour of Loch Ness

b) **Now you are buying the tickets. Read what your family wants to do and say it in English.**

Tour guide	How can I help you?
Dad	Wir möchten zwei Eintrittskarten für Erwachsene und zwei für Kinder für den Tagesausflug nach Loch Ness kaufen.
You	We would like to buy …
Tour guide	OK, four tickets to Loch Ness. Would you like to buy lunch?
Dad	Ja, wir hätten gerne vier Mittagessen.
You	Yes, we would also like to buy …
Tour guide	And would you like to buy audio guides?
Dad	Ja, zwei Audioguides, bitte.
You	Yes, we would also like …
Tour guide	OK. And would you like to go on the boat trip of Loch Ness?
Dad	Nein danke, wir wollen nicht mit auf die Bootsfahrt gehen.
You	No thank you, we don't want to …
Tour guide	OK, so four tickets, four lunches and two audio guides. That will be £247, please.

▸ Page 76

More practice 2 Scottish ghosts

Draw the ghost. Then show your picture to a partner. What are the differences between your two pictures?

My ghost has a … but your ghost has … *My / Your ghost is much scarier / nicer / …*

▸ Page 77

More practice 3 The perfect minute

a) **Work in groups. Your teacher says a sentence. Say as many adverbs as you can in one minute. The adverbs must fit the sentence! One student counts the adverbs.**

b) **Your teacher says a different sentence. Say more adverbs. You can use words from the boxes.**

Teacher: I dance … *Student 1: happily / Student 2: slowly / Student 3: …*

dance • do my homework • eat • go down the stairs • read • run • talk • walk • write • …	careful • happy • loud • nervous • proud • quiet • quick • sad • slow • …	-ly

c) **Which group said the most correct adverbs altogether?**

☒ More practice 4 **The Blue Men of the Minch**

Complete the legend about mermen. Use the adverb form of the adjectives in the box.

correct • easy • fast • loud • quiet • ~~secret~~

Off the coast of Scotland, there is a sea called the Minch. People say that's where the Blue Men of the Minch live *secretly* (1) under the water. They have blue faces and bodies, and they usually sleep ... (2) below the water. The Blue Men of the Minch are amazing swimmers. They can swim ... (3) and jump ... (4) like dolphins. But when they see a boat, they shout part of a poem at the sailors. If the sailors can't finish the poem ... (5), then the Blue Men attack their boat. When the boat sinks, they're happy and they laugh ... (6).

▸ Page 77

More help **7** My task **My scary monster**

My monster ...	walks • talks • eats • listens • plays • runs • sings • sleeps • smiles • speaks • ...	angrily • bravely • calmly • carefully • crazily • easily • happily • loudly • noisily • quietly • quickly • sadly • slowly • weirdly • ...

▸ Page 79

More practice 5 **The Highland Games**

Complete the conversation with *has* or *have*.

Rhona My mum ... (1) just sent me some pictures from the Highland Games. Look!

Grace I ... (2) never liked Scottish dancing. We ... (3) tried it at school, remember?

Rhona That's right! I think Scottish dancing is great fun.

Grace Well, that's because you're a good dancer! And you ... (4) had lessons. That helps too.

Rhona That's right. I like the photo of the four guys in kilts. I think that they ... (5) already thrown the caber.

Grace I think you're right. Maybe they ... (6) already won and now they're just holding it up for a photo. It looks very heavy!

▸ Page 80

More practice 6 Spot the difference

a) Look carefully around the classroom. Look where people are sitting and where things are in the classroom.

b) Two or three students leave the classroom. One student in the classroom moves something or asks students to move.

c) The other students come back and ask questions about changes.

Have you moved the blue rucksack? – No, we haven't.
Have Lukas and Mateo swapped chairs? – Yes, they have.

d) Play again: This time different students go out and a different student changes something.

▸ Page 81

More help 7 MY TASK Have you ever?

Write at least six interview questions. Use *Have you ever ...?*

Have you ever	tried	cliff jumping / climbing / hiking / paddleboarding / rafting / skateboarding / skiing / snowboarding / surfing / windsurfing / ...
	climbed	a mountain / a tree ...
	ridden	a horse / a pony / ...
	travelled	by yourself / by plane / by boat / to a different country / ...
	swum	in really cold water / with dolphins / with fish / ...
	broken	your leg / your arm / ...

▸ Page 86

Parallel exercise 2 Good and bad choices

b) What good and bad choices did Rhona and Grace make? Look at the table and decide which character did what.

+	–
helped her friend to breathe	*didn't wear the right shoes*
tried something new	*wanted to go on a difficult path alone*

More practice 7 *When, where* or *why?*

Choose the correct word to complete the sentences.

1 When you go hiking, make sure someone knows when / where you are.
2 There were tourists everywhere / because the girls looked!
3 Grace takes notes on because / where she has hiked.
4 It's important to look at the path, so / when you don't fall over.

More practice 8 Linking words

Choose the correct linking word.

1 I had plans to go hiking then / and I was so excited.
2 I checked my phone while / finally I got ready.
3 I put on a scarf because / so it was cold.
4 It was sunny in the morning, because / but in the afternoon, there was a big thunderstorm.
5 While / Finally after a few hours, the rain stopped.
6 It was late, so / soon I walked quickly down the mountain.

More help 5 LIFE SKILLS Learn from your mistakes

Look at the bad choices in exercise 2b) on page 86. What should the characters do next time?

Next time,	Grace Rhona	should	stay with the group
			tell her teacher the truth
			wear the right shoes
		shouldn't	tell her friend to do something dangerous
			say yes if she doesn't want to do something

▸ Page 89

More help UNIT TASK Write a short adventure story, Step 1

Complete the sentences.

Last summer • went to Scotland • family • on holiday • visited Loch Ness • rainy afternoon

Suddenly • saw something • the water • was really big • everyone pointed • took photos

little sister • scared • shouted loudly • everyone scared • monster scared too

swam away quickly • felt excited • talked about it • looked at photos • best holiday ever

Unit 4
Wales: Digital life

A

Donkeys on Llandudno beach

B

Wales uses green energy.

C

Our national sport

D

There are more sheep than people in Wales!

1 READING An online quiz about Wales

a) BEFORE YOU READ Dylan and Owen's class is preparing for a visit of a German exchange class. They have made a website about Wales. Look at the pictures and tell each other what you see.

b) Dylan and Owen have made a quiz about Wales for the website. Look at the quiz on page 103. Can you guess the answers?

c) Compare your answers with your partner.

Nach dieser Unit kann ich ...

- ein Quiz über Wales durchführen
- eine einfache Anleitung geben
- meine Gegend mit Wales vergleichen
- über soziale Medien sprechen
- flüssig vortragen

Unit task

- einen kurzen Vortrag über soziale Medien halten

Dylan and Owen's quiz about Wales

1 What are the two official languages of Wales?
A English and Welsh
B English and Scottish
C English and Irish

2 Look at this map. What colour is Wales?

3 Llandudno is the name for ...
A a pet donkey
B our town
C the flag

4 What is on the Welsh flag? A red ...
A lion B dragon C sheep

5 What is the national sport in Wales?
A rugby B football C judo

6 There are three million people in Wales. How many million sheep are there?
A one B two C ten

2 Listening Dylan and Owen's message

a) Listen to the message for the German exchange class. Check your answers from 1b.

b) Read these sentences, then listen again. Are they true or false?

1 Dylan and Owen are in class 8A.
2 They go to Prince of Wales School.
3 Owen speaks Welsh at home.
4 They both play rugby.
5 Owen sings in a choir.
6 Dylan loves to use social media.

► More practice 1, p. 125

c) Talk about what places in your area you would show exchange students.

► Wordbank 8, p. 175
► Workbook, p. 66

Digital quiz — I can understand information about Wales.

Welcome to Wales

1 READING Talking about the class videos

Dylan and Owen's classmates are making videos for the German exchange class. Read the conversation. Which places do they talk about? Say which place you want to visit.

Gwen Hey, Flynn, I've just finished my video! 😊 I'm really happy with it. I filmed mine at Cardiff Castle. What about your video? Did you finally decide where to film yours?

Flynn Yes, I decided on the ski centre. I'm going to go there tomorrow. Promit has already finished his video. He made his about GreenWood adventure park.

Dylan Cool! Owen and I have almost finished our video.

Owen Yeah, Dylan is writing a song for ours. It's going to be so good. 😊 After that we still need to edit it.

Gwen Samara and Louise have just finished their video. They filmed the pier and the beach in Llandudno. I think theirs will be popular because of the donkeys.

Dylan That's true. Everyone loves the donkeys!

Good to know

Wales has one of the longest place names in the world.
🔈 Listen. Can you repeat it?
Llanfairpwllgwyngyllgogerychwyrn drobwllllantysiliogogogoch

2 LOOKING AT LANGUAGE Mine and yours

a) **Copy and complete the table with the blue possessive pronouns in 1.**

I	you	he	she	it	we	they
my (video)	your (video)	his (video)	her (video)	its (video)	our (video)	their (video)
...	...	...	*hers*	*its*	...	...

b) **Read the conversation from the next day. Look at the underlined words and complete 1–5 with possessive prounouns from the table so you don't have to repeat the noun.**

Flynn Megan just sent me her video. Sorry everyone, ... (1) is my new favourite video!

Gwen I don't have a favourite, I think all our videos are amazing! In fact, I think ... (2) are better than the ads on TV. 😊

Flynn I've almost finished my video. I'm really happy I chose the ski centre for ... (3).

Gwen Can I help you with your video? What do you still need to do for ... (4)?

Flynn I'm trying to find the right music for it.

Gwen Have you heard the new song for Dylan and Owen's video? I think ... (5) is going to be so good!

▸ Language file 12, p. 164 ▸ More practice 2, p. 126
▸ Workbook, pp. 67–68

3 Song Dylan's song

a) Before you listen **Talk to a partner. What do you think Dylan will say about Wales in his song?**

1 It's boring.
2 It's a mixture of old and new.
3 The old parts are the best.

b) **Listen to the song. Were you right?**

c) **Listen to the song again and complete it with the words in the box.**

beautiful • Cardiff • green • love • new • place • sea

d) **What do you think about the song?**

I like the music / text / ...
It makes me feel ...

► Wordbank 4, p. 171

A valley in the Brecon Beacons

My Cymru

Drop the beat, turn up the bass.
Let me tell you about a special ... (1)
where everybody has the space to breathe.

My Cymru where the fields are ... (2),
the music's cool, the air is clean.
I ... (3) it and I never mean to leave.

Come see where the old meets ... (4)
and the valleys meet the ... (5).
Come with me
to my beautiful Cymru.

Mae hen wlad fy nhadau
yn annwyl i mi.
O dwi'n dy garu di
*fy Nghymru i!**

We've got tech and the Brecon Beacons,
... (6) in every season.
That's why my Cymru cannot be beaten.

From the music clubs of ... (7)
to the hills of Aberystwyth –
*everybody sing: Cymru am byth!***

* *The land of my fathers is dear to me.*
Oh I love you, my Wales!
** *Wales forever!*

► Skills file 8, p. 147

My task

4 Record a voice message

a) **You're in the exchange class. You're going to record a voice message for Dylan and tell him what you want to do and see when you visit Wales. First write your message.** ► Digital help

Hi Dylan, I can't wait for the trip! It's going to be so much fun. Here's what I want to do in Wales.

I really want to	visit	an adventure park • the beach • a castle • the mountains • Cardiff • ...
I would like to	go	shopping • hiking • swimming • on a tour • ...
Also, can we	buy	a toy dragon • a hat • a T-shirt • some souvenirs • some chocolate • ...

b) **Now record your message for Dylan.**

Digital quiz   I can talk about Wales.

Life with and without technology

1 Viewing Life in a Welsh village in 1927

a) **Before you watch** **Dylan found a video online about life in a Welsh village in 1927. What do you think life was like then? You can use the notes in the box for your answers.**

1 What did they wear?
2 How did they travel?
3 How did they get food?
4 What did they do in their free time?
5 What did they use for light?

They
- made their own clothes / food / light
- walked / rode horses / ...
- read books / sang together / ...

► Parallel exercise, p. 126

b) **Watch part 1 of the video and answer the questions.**

1 Why are the people in the video going to live in the past? *It's for a ...*
2 What is the boy going to miss the most? *He is going to ...*
3 What would you miss the most? *I'd miss ...*

c) **Now watch all the video (parts 1 and 2) and add to your answers in a).**

1 Women and girls wore skirts and dresses.
Men and boys wore caps, trousers and jackets.

d) **What do you think: Does technology bring people together? Why or why not?**

Yes, it does, because ... / No, it doesn't, because ...

► More help, p. 126

2 A letter from 1927

a) Someone found an old letter in one of the houses in the Welsh village. Read the letter. Why did Jonathon go to Cardiff?

Remember

Mit dem *simple past* sprichst du über Dinge, die in der Vergangenheit geschehen sind.

Dear Mother,

It is evening here in Cardiff. Everyone else is already asleep, but I must write you a letter and tell you everything that has happened so far.

We ... (1 arrive) in Cardiff several days ago. It ... (2 be) a difficult journey because the rain ... (3 not stop) all day. We ... (4 be) very tired, but we ... (5 know) that we ... (6 have) to get here fast.

We ... (7 ask) to see the doctor right away, but he ... (8 not have) time until yesterday because he is so busy. Many people in Cardiff are ill too. But he ... (9 say) that he can give us the medicine on Friday.

I hope that it will help father. I'll write again soon.

Yours, Jonathon

b) Complete the sentences. Use the *simple past*.

▶ More practice 3, p. 127

3 Speaking An evening with or without technology?

a) Brainstorm free-time activities.

b) Walk around Tell different partners what you did yesterday evening. Use the simple past. Listen to them and take notes.

Yesterday evening I went / did / listened to / made / texted / played / watched / ...
My family ...
My friends and I ...

▶ More help, p. 127

c) Tell the class about one partner.

Amira played football. / Jonas texted his friends.

d) How many students used technology or social media yesterday evening?

▶ Language file 4, p. 158

▶ Workbook, pp. 69–70

4 On the phone

a) **Owen calls Dylan. Read their conversation. What do they want to do? Where and when are they going to meet? Don't worry about the missing words.**

Owen Hi Dylan. How ... (1)? What did you do yesterday?
Dylan Great, thanks. I watched a video about life in 1927. It was interesting – I'll send you the link.
Owen Oh, yes – videos. We still need to finish ours. Are you free later after dinner?
Dylan No, sorry, I have to help my mum with her new smartwatch. What about tomorrow?
Owen What? Sorry, I can't ... (2).
Dylan Can you hear me now? I said: Let's finish our video tomorrow.
Owen Yeah, that's cool. How about at your house after school?
Dylan What? Can you ... (3), please?
Owen How about at your house after school?
Dylan Yes, that's fine.
Owen Oh, ... (4), Dylan. Can we use your computer? Mine is broken.
Dylan Sure, no problem. Sorry, I have to ... (5). See you tomorrow!
Owen ... (6).

b) **Complete the phone call with the missing words from the box.** 1E, ...

A say that again	D Bye
B one more thing	E are things
C hear you	F go now

c) **Listen and check.**

d) **Read the complete phone call with a partner.**

► More practice 4, p. 127 ► Workbook, p. 70

5 WORDS Instructions

a) **Match the pictures (A–E) to the instructions (1–6).**

1 charge the phone
2 swipe to the right
3 tap to open the app
4 download the app
5 switch off / switch on the phone
6 switch off the sound

A 
B 
C 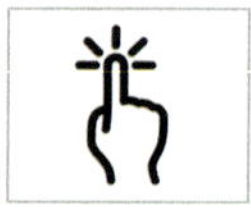
D 
E 
F 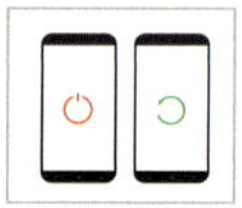

b) **Add the words and phrases from a) that you think are important to your VOCAB FILE.**

► Skills file 1+2, p. 139, 140 ► Wordbank 9, p. 176

6 MEDIATION Explaining instructions

a) **Partner B:** Look at p. 124.
Partner A: Your parent (partner B) needs help with a new smartwatch.
Explain instructions 1–4 in German.

1 First, charge your smartwatch fully.
2 Go to 'Settings' on your phone.
3 Make sure Bluetooth is on.
4 Next, download the app on your phone.

1 Zuerst musst du die Uhr voll ...

▶ Skills file 10, p. 149

b) Now you're the parent. Listen to partner B's instructions. Ask what you do next and ask questions if you don't understand.

▶ Workbook, p. 71

My task

7 Commands for a digital assistant

a) Read these commands for a digital assistant. Agree on the top five most useful commands with a partner and write them in your exercise book.

- *Switch on the lights.*
- *Play a song.*
- *Tell me what the weather is like today.*
- *Play a game with me.*
- *Switch on the TV.*
- *Tell me the score.*
- *Play the news.*
- *Say something in a different language.*
- *Tell me a recipe.*
- *Tell me a joke.*
- ...

b) **Partner A:** Now you're the digital assistant. Act out your partner's commands.
Partner B: Give your digital assistant commands.
☒ Can you think of new commands for your digital assistant?

Paula, tell us what the weather is like today!

It's sunny and warm today.

That's wrong. It's raining!

Digital quiz I can give simple instructions.

Social media

1 LISTENING Online life

a) BEFORE YOU LISTEN **Find out: What are the most popular social media apps in the class?**

I use ...
What about you?

I really like ...
Have you heard of it?

b) **Dylan and Owen asked their friends about social media. Listen and decide if each person thinks social media is good (🙂), bad (☹) or both (🙂☹).**

1 Samara 2 Promit 3 Gwen 4 Flynn

DEBATE CLUB
Tuesday at 12:30 in Room 42

This week, our question is: "Is social media a good or a bad thing for teens?"

Dylan Jones
versus
Owen Thomas

c) **Read the phrases, then listen again. Which two phrases are not in the interview? Write the numbers.**

1 follow people online
2 watch streamers
3 post photos or videos
4 subscribe to new channels
5 get a lot of likes
6 delete an account

d) **Tell a partner what you do or don't do on social media. Use the phrases in c).**

I often / sometimes / never ... *I'm not allowed to / I'm allowed to ...*

► More practice 5, p. 128

2 LIFE SKILLS Can an app make people feel better?

a) **Look at the ad for Flynn's favourite app. What do you think the app is for?**

b) **Listen to the second part of the interview. Name at least two things you can do with the app.**

c) **Listen again and complete the sentences.**

1 Flynn uses it when he has a ...
2 Or when he's angry or ...
3 You can relax your whole ...
4 He writes down his thoughts and ...

d) **Do you want to use the app? What else can you do when you have a problem?**

talk to a friend / teacher / parent • hit a cushion • draw or sing • go for a walk • hug my pet • ...

► Workbook, pp. 72–73

3 Speaking Could you help me, please?

a) **Listen to or read the conversation. Who is helping who? With what?**

... is helping ... to ...

b) **Copy and complete the table with the phrases in blue.**

asking for help	*giving help*
...	...

c) Walk around **Make notes about things that you are good at and things that you need help with. Then walk around and ask for or offer help. Use phrases from b).**

Shall I help you with your Maths homework?

Yes, please. / No thanks, I'm OK. Would you like me to ...?

Owen I want to try the Zenn app, but I don't know where to start.
Dylan I can help you if you like.
Owen Yes, please. Could you please help me to make an account?
Dylan No problem. You need a profile photo. Shall I upload one for you, or do you want to do it?
Owen Can you do it, please? Look, this one is good.
Dylan Sure. There you go. Your account is private. Would you like me to make it public?
Owen No, thanks. And what should I put in my bio?
Dylan Just some information about yourself and maybe a few emojis.

► More help, p. 128

4 Writing A bio

a) **Match the emojis (A–F) to the information in Owen's bio (1–6). What does each emoji mean? Use the words in the box.**

my birthday • my friends • my hobbies • my home • my languages • my favourite music

1 B = my birthday, 2 ...

OwenT

1 12th June
2 Llandudno
3 Dylan, Samara and Flynn
4 English and Welsh (and a bit of German!)
5 singing, table tennis, going to the beach
6 pop, rock, rap – everything!

b) **Write your own bio. Then collect all the bios in the class. Pick one, read it out and guess who wrote it.**

This one is Pratik!

I don't think so. Pratik's birthday is on August 20th. I think it's Maik.

5 READING Fact and opinion

a) BEFORE YOU READ **What social media do you get news or information from? Why?**

b) **Read the two texts. Which one has opinions, and which has facts?**

A

www.example.com/llandudno-times

Research shows cyberbullying is a big problem

The charity *Ditch The Label* has researched how teenagers use social media. The people that work for *Ditch the Label* have found a worrying statistic: One in five teenagers has experienced bullying online. One in four did not tell anyone about the messages that they got.

More and more people are using social media, so the problem is getting bigger. Research shows that 97% of teenagers use at least one social media app or website.

However, there is positive news: 58% of teenagers who became victims of bullying said their teachers helped them to solve the problem.

B

I HATE SOCIAL MEDIA!!!

We must stop social media! All the teens are using it and they're all bullying each other. Some boys who go to my daughter's school sent horrible messages to her. It happens to everyone, my daughter says. I can't believe this! The person that made social media wanted all teens to be mean and fight each other all the time. Social media is the worst thing EVER and we shouldn't let teens use it. Like and share if you agree!!!

Datenquellen zu A: cybercrew.uk und mayoclinic.org (siehe Quellenverzeichnis)

c) **Match the sentences to text A or B.** ▶ Skills file 4, p. 142

1 It says where the information is from.
2 It only talks about the writer's opinions.
3 It presents statistics.
4 It uses very emotional language.
5 It says things that aren't true.
6 It looks at both sides of the problem.

6 LOOKING AT LANGUAGE Relative clauses

Erklär-film

a) **Read these examples from text A and complete the rules.**

1 The people that work for *Ditch the Label* ...
2 the messages that they got
3 58% of teenagers who became victims of bullying

Wir benutzen Relativsätze, um zusätzliche Informationen über Personen oder Dinge zu geben.
Wenn du über **Personen** sprichst, verwendest du ... oder ...
Wenn du über **Dinge** sprichst, verwendest du ...

▶ Language file 13, p. 165

b) **Now look at these examples from text B and complete them with *who* or *that*.**

1 some boys ... go to my daughter's school
2 the person ... made social media

▶ Workbook, p. 73

7 What is it?

a) **Match the beginnings and endings of the definitions.**

1 Social media is something ...
2 An influencer is a person ...
3 Cyberbullying is a type of bullying ...
4 A follower is someone ...
5 A fact is information ...

A ... that is true.
B ... who subscribes to your page or channel.
C ... who has lots of followers on social media.
D ... that you use to talk to people online.
E ... that happens online.

b) **Complete the definitions for these words with *who* or *that*.**

1 A bio is a text ... explains all about you on social media.
2 A bully is someone ... is mean to other people.
3 A victim is someone ... experiences bullying.
4 A charity is an organization ... helps people.

In English, we don't need a comma before who or that in this type of relative clause.

► More practice 6, p. 128 ► More practice 7, p. 129 ► Workbook, p. 74

My task

8 The debate

a) **Help Dylan and Owen write their short talks for the debate.**
Partner B: Go to p. 124.
Partner A: Help Dylan. Think of reasons why social media is a good thing for teens. Write at least three good things about social media.

I believe that social media is a good thing for teens because ...
Social media also helps people ...

► Study skills, p. 118 ► Digital help
► More help, p. 129

b) **Check your writing. Then read and check your partner's sentences. Have they given reasons for each of their points? Give feedback.**

Those are great reasons.
I don't agree with that one.

► Skills file 13, p. 152

Digital quiz I can talk about the good and bad sides of social media.

Looking good

1 Reading The camera never lies, right?

a) Before you read **Skim the story and make short notes. What do you think is going to happen?**

I think that Dylan / Owen is going to ...

b) **Now read the story. Were your ideas in 1a) correct?**

When you **skim** a text, you just want to get the main ideas. Make sure you look at the title and the photos, but don't read every word.

► Skills file 9, p. 148

'Thanks for helping me with my bio, Dylan!' wrote Owen. 'I almost like to use social media now!'
'You're welcome!' replied Dylan. 'It's great that we can talk to our German exchange partners on the website before they come to Llandudno. My partner Saskia is sooo cool!'

Later that day, Owen saw a new post from Dylan. He was confused.

'Dylan's family doesn't have a new car,' he thought. 'That's a photo from when we went to the Llandudno Transport Festival last week.'

The next day at school, Dylan was really excited. 'You know that photo I posted of me playing my new song? It got a HUNDRED likes!'

At the weekend, Owen and Dylan went to the beach. Dylan just wanted to take photos the whole time.
'This is boring!' said Owen. 'Let's go swimming now.'

'Just one more,' said Dylan. 'The light is really good now. And I've got lots of followers who need to see how cool I look.'
'You mean you want Saskia to see how cool you look,' said Owen.

On Monday, Owen saw a new photo of Dylan. Under the photo, it said: 'Me at the beach'. Dylan looked different.
'I took that photo of him last weekend, but he's changed it!' Owen thought.
He was annoyed.

Later, the German exchange students arrived. Dylan finally met Saskia. 'It's great to meet you, Saskia!' he said. 'Hi, Dylan?" She looked confused. 'You look different in your photos.' 'Er ... well, it's me,' said Dylan. Owen watched them and felt annoyed again. That evening, Owen looked at Dylan's photos again and again.

'He thinks he's so cool. I'm going to show everyone how cool he really is,' he thought. He posted a photo of Dylan. In this photo, Dylan didn't look great. Under the photo, Owen wrote: 'The real Dylan is scared of water.'

People quickly started to leave comments on Owen's post. They made jokes about Dylan and said he looked stupid. At first Owen thought it was funny ... but a few hours later there were hundreds of mean comments!

Owen deleted the photo. He felt terrible.

The next day, Owen saw Dylan and Saskia in the canteen. Dylan looked unhappy. Owen took a deep breath and sat down. 'I'm really sorry, Dylan,' said Owen. 'I shouldn't have posted that photo. That was mean. I guess I was jealous of you.' 'Hey Owen. You know, at first I was really angry. You had no right to post a picture of me on the internet! But then I thought about it. It was also weird of me to post things that weren't real. I know I shouldn't care about what other people think, but I wanted to get a lot of likes.'

Saskia turned and smiled at Dylan. 'You know, I like the second photo better. It's funny – and it's real.' Dylan smiled back at Saskia. Suddenly, he didn't care about how he looked.

2 What happened in the story?

Are the sentences true or false? Correct the false sentences.

1 Owen still doesn't use social media.
2 Dylan likes his exchange partner, Saskia.
3 Dylan's mum has a new fast car.
4 Dylan doesn't have many followers.
5 Dylan edits the photo that Owen took.
6 Owen has the right to post a photo of Dylan.

3 DOUBLE CIRCLE Social media opinions

Look at the questions and make notes. Talk to a partner and ask question 1. Then ask new partners questions 2–4.

► Skills file 5, p. 144

1 Do you use social media? Why (not)?
2 Which influencers do you know? What do you think about them?
3 Is it a good idea to edit photos to make them look better? Why (not)?
4 How do you feel when you see photos of people who look perfect online?

► More help, p. 129

4 LIFE SKILLS Recognizing fake photos

a) **Influencers use different tools to make themselves look good in their photos. Which of these tools (A–F) have you used to take a better photo?**

I have used special poses / …

A filters
B lighting
C digital editing software
D poses
E clothes
F make-up

b) **Look at the two beach photos of Dylan on p. 115 again. Which things in 4a) do you think he used in the first photo?**

c) **Find a photo from an influencer that you know. Talk about how you think they have changed the photo.**

The influencer used a filter / … to look prettier. Her eyes are bigger now and …

► More help, p. 129

► Workbook, p. 75

Digital quiz I can talk about truth and lies on social media.

Sophie's cosplay costume

1 Before you watch Cosplay

Which character would you choose to cosplay and why? Tell your partner.

I'd choose Batman because he looks cool.

Good to know

Cosplay is a hobby. Fans dress and act like their favourite characters from video games, films or TV. They often post pictures and videos of themselves online and meet at events and competitions.

I'd choose Wonder Woman because she's strong.

2 Viewing Sophie's costume

a) **Sophie is a German vlogger. Watch the first part of the video and find out:**

1 who designed Sophie's costume and what it is
2 how long it took to make the costume
3 why she made the costume
4 what the problem was in Stuttgart

b) **Put the instructions for Sophie's costume in the right order. Then watch the first part of the video again and check.**

A Sew the costume.
B Design the costume.
C Put pink paint on your skin.
D Make the headpiece.
E Choose a character that you like.

3 Viewing In Cologne

Watch the second part of the video. True or false?

1 Sophie went to a games event.
2 People took photos of Sophie.
3 Sophie forgot to make a video.
4 She won a costume competition.
5 She met people who have the same interests.
6 It was an embarrassing experience.

4 Life skills Don't give up!

Tell a partner or a group about the time when you did or made something:
1 What did you try to do or make? What was the problem?
2 How did you do it differently the next time? What did you change?

1 One time I tried ... but I didn't have / know ... The problem was that ...
2 So the next time that I tried ..., I did it differently. I changed ...

Make a talk flow

Remember
- First collect ideas for your talk and put them in order.
- Make cards with short notes (keywords and tips).

1 Order ideas

a) **After the exchange, Saskia is giving a talk about social media in her English class in Germany. Look at her cards with notes. What do you think is the right order?** *1 ..., 2, ..., ...*

What I do online
– chat with friends
– upload photos and videos
– account is private

Intro
Say:
1 What I do online
2 Social media: ☺ & ☹

End
Say:
thank you
Ask:
Questions?

Social media, ☺ & ☹:
☺ friends, vloggers
☹ posts aren't realistic, trolls

b) **Decide where Saskia could use these phrases to show the order of her talk:**

That's the end of my talk ...
Next I'd like to tell you about ...
First I'd like to tell you ...
Today I'm going to talk about ...

► Skills file 12, p. 151

c) **Now listen to Saskia's talk and check your answers to a) and b).**

2 Explain words

a) **Saskia has forgotten the word *habit*. How can she explain it? Choose A, B or C.**

A It's somebody who lives in a mountain.
B It's something that you do very often.
C It's something that you never do.

I can't find the word that I'm looking for. ... Oh, I think it's 'habit', right?

When you want to explain a word, you can use a relative clause:
A video is something that you can watch.

b) **Use the tip in the box and explain these words.**

1 vlogger 2 comment 3 troll

3 Keep talking!

When you need a moment to think, you can use these phrases:

A You know, ..., • B Let me see, ..., • C I mean, ..., • D Just a minute, ..., • E Well, ...

Listen to Saskia's talk again. Which phrases does she use? Write the letters.

Digital quiz I can **make a talk flow.**

Give a short talk about social media

Step 1: Make notes for your talk

▸ Digital help

You are going to give a short talk (two to three minutes) about your online and social media habits. Answer the questions with short notes.

1 What do you do online?
2 What are your favourite apps?
3 What do you think is good or bad about social media?

Step 2: Make cards and order them

a) Think of a short introduction and an ending.

b) Make cards with your ideas. Only write the most important information. Put your ideas in order. Use phrases from p. 118.

Step 3: Use pictures

Find pictures for your talk. Make slides or print out pictures that you can show.

Achte darauf, dass die Verwendung der Bilder erlaubt ist, nutze daher z. B. *creative commons*-Bilder.

Step 4: Practise your talk

Practise your talk silently in class. Then practise it at home and record yourself.

▸ Study skills 2 + 3, p. 118

Step 5: Give your talk to a group

a) Give your talk to a group. The others listen and write three things:

▸ Skills file 7, p. 146

1 one good thing about the talk: *I really liked the picture that you showed.*
2 one thing that could be better: *Next time, you should talk a bit more slowly.*
3 one question: *How often do you use social media?*

b) The students in your group give feedback and ask their questions.

Digital quiz — I can give a short talk.

1 Reading A poster about Wales

I can understand information about Wales.

a) Owen and Dylan have made a poster for the exchange students. Skim the texts and look at the photos. Choose the correct title (A–C) for their poster.

A Three free places to visit in Wales
B Three cool places for history fans
C The three best places for kids in Wales

Conwy Castle

This castle is over 700 years old. It has eight towers and only took four years to build. You can walk around the top of the walls and enjoy the great view. A family ticket costs £37.70. In summer it's open till 6 p.m. You should bring something to eat because there isn't a cafe in the castle.

Penrhyn Castle

This castle is only about 200 years old and has a beautiful garden with views of Snowdonia national park. There are two cafes, shops and a train museum. A family ticket costs £35 and the castle is open from 10 a.m. to 4 p.m. in summer.

Castell Dinas Brân

You can't drive up to this castle – you can only get there on foot. It's high on a mountain so you will have amazing views. The castle is almost 800 years old. You'll need walking boots and a jacket because it's usually windy. You don't have to pay to visit this castle, but there are no shops, cafes or toilets.

b) Read the texts again. Are the sentences true (T) or false (F)?

1 You can only walk to Castell Dinas Brân.
2 All the castles have a cafe.
3 You get a good view from all of the castles.
4 Conwy Castle is the cheapest for families.
5 Two castles are over 700 years old.
6 You should visit Conwy Castle if you like trains.

Check

2 Mediation An email from Saskia

I can talk about Wales.

Saskia is writing an email to her cousin Marie in Germany.
Dylan is very curious and asks Saskia questions. What does the email say?

Hi, Marie, ich bin gerade mit meiner Schulklasse in Wales. Wir sind in Llandudno – das ist eine kleine Stadt in Wales. Es ist wirklich schön. Mein Austauschpartner heißt Dylan. Wir werden uns Samstag ein Rugbyspiel anschauen, weil seine Eltern beide große Rugbyfans sind. Ich freue mich sehr auf das Spiel! 🙂
Gestern waren wir am Strand und haben mit Dylans Hund gespielt.

Bin Sonntag wieder zu Hause.
Bis dahin!

Dylan	I see our town's name: 'Llandudno'! What do those sentences say?
Saskia	It's a small ... It's very ... (1).
Dylan	And what does it say about rugby?
Saskia	We are going to ... (2).
Dylan	And what's the smiley emoji for?
Saskia	I'm ... (3).
Dylan	Gestern ... that means 'yesterday'. What do those sentences say?
Saskia	Yesterday, we went to the ... (4).

3 Words Helping a neighbour

I can give simple instructions.

Your neighbour has a new smartphone and he doesn't speak German.
He asks you to help him take a photo and send it to his daughter.

Choose the correct words in the instructions.

1 Open / Edit the camera app and take a photo.
2 Write / Open your messaging app.
3 Edit / Tap 'write new message'.
4 Tap / Edit the plus (+) and find your daughter's number.
5 Charge / Tap the camera.
6 Swipe / Tap the photo that you want to send.
7 Write / Open your message.
8 Tap / Edit send. Finished! 🙂

Check

4 LANGUAGE Life online – positive or negative?

I can talk about the good and bad sides of social media.

a) Complete the sentences with *that / who*.

1 Cyberbullying is a problem ... many people have experienced.
2 Older people ... can't leave their houses can use social media to talk with friends.
3 Shops ... use social media can sell their products to more people.
4 Lots of teenagers ... use social media find friends with the same interests.
5 There are lots of news stories on social media ... are not true.
6 If you use social media, you can find friends ... live in different countries.

b) Which sentences are positive? Which are negative? Draw smileys (☺ or ☹).

5 LISTENING Fake or real?

I can talk about truth and lies on social media.

a) Look at the photos and listen to four people talking about lies on social media. What do they talk about? Match the people (1–4) to the photos (A–E). There's one extra photo.

1 Elsa 2 Hadi 3 Marie 4 Oskar

A

B

C

D

E

b) Complete the sentences. Then listen again and check.

1 Elsa's grandma fell in love with a man who only wanted her ...
2 The 'lion' near Berlin really was a wild ...
3 Marie went to a restaurant that was ...
4 Oskar's dad bought some things that never ...

c) Match the advice (1–4) to each person from a).

1 Don't give your money to people you meet online.
2 Only buy things from websites that you know.
3 Don't believe all the reviews.
4 Be careful – some videos are fake too!

d) SPEAKING Think of a story about truth and lies on social media. It doesn't have to be real! Tell a partner.

Someone A man / woman / child ...	posted a video online. bought an app. answered an email. clicked on a link. ...	Then After that ...	the police arrived! the person lost a lot of money. it was a big problem! nothing happened. ...

Check

6 Study skills Describing a word that you forgot

I can make a talk flow.

a) **If you forget a word in your talk, you can explain it to make your talk flow. Match words A–F to explanations 1–6.**

1 It's something that you take when you are ill.
2 It's somebody who is an online bully.
3 It's a short text that tells you about somebody.
4 It's when someone says something that isn't true.
5 It's like a letter that you send on your phone.
6 They are something that you use if you want to listen to music.

A message
B troll
C medicine
D headphones
E bio
F lie

b) Speaking **Now choose three words that you already know from the Dictionary (pages 215–235). Explain the words to your partner. Can your partner guess the words?**

It's somebody who ... *It's something that ...* *It's like / when ...*

▸ Skills file 3, p. 141

7 Study skills Learning Welsh online

a) **Cody wants to give a short talk about learning Welsh. Where in the talk (1–5) should he put the phrases A–E?**

... (1)

First, about the course: It's an online course. It's not very expensive. ... (2)

It's ten weeks long and it's great if you want to visit Wales and understand a little bit of Welsh.

You get some exercises by email and there is an app you can use on your phone or tablet too. ... (3)

Next, I'm going to tell you some things that I learned.

... (4) 'Good morning' is 'bore da' and 'thank you very much' is 'diolch yn fawr iawn'

I think the course was good – it wasn't too easy, and it wasn't too difficult. And in ten weeks you can learn quite a lot of Welsh.

... (5)

A *You know, it's amazing what you can do with a smartphone!*

B *Just a minute, I need to find my vocabulary list.*

C *That's the end of my talk. Are there any questions?*

D *Today I'm going to talk to you about my online Welsh course.*

E *Let me see ..., it costs 26 pounds.*

b) **Listen to Cody's talk and check your answers.**

c) **Listen carefully to sentences A–E and repeat them.**

Check

Partner page

▸ Page 109

6 Mediation Explaining instructions

a) **Partner B:** You are a parent and you need help with a new smartwatch. Listen to partner A's instructions. Ask what you do next and ask questions if you don't understand.

b) Now partner A is the parent. Explain instructions 5–8 in German.

5 Switch the smartwatch on.
6 Next, choose a language on the watch.
7 After that, tap the name of the watch on your phone.
8 Finally, tap 'pair' on your phone.

5 Schalte …

▸ Page 113

8 My task The debate

a) Help Dylan and Owen write their short talks for the debate.
Partner B: Help Owen. Think of reasons why social media is a bad thing for teens. Write at least three bad things about social media.

I believe that social media is a bad thing for teens because …
I think one of the problems with social media is that …

▸ More help, p. 129 ▸ Digital help ▸ Study skills, p. 118

b) Check your writing. Then read and check your partner's sentences. Have they given reasons for each of their points? Give feedback.

Those are great reasons.
I don't agree with that one.

▸ Skills file 13, p. 152

Diff bank

▸ Page 103

More practice 1 READING **Three Welsh cities**

a) BEFORE YOU READ **Copy the table. Find the three cities on the map on the last page of your book.**

City	Where	Sights: What you can do there
Cardiff	south Wales	...
Swansea	south-west Wales	...
Wrexham	north-east Wales	...

b) **Read about the three cities and complete the table.**

Cardiff is the biggest city in Wales and its capital. In the city centre Cardiff Castle is popular. Watch rugby matches in the Principality Stadium and go to concerts in the amazing modern Millennium Centre by the water. Cardiff is also famous for TV shows and films.

Swansea is the second biggest Welsh city. It's a modern city with many parks. If it's rainy, get some great food at Swansea Indoor Market, and if it's sunny, have a picnic on one of the beautiful beaches just outside the city. Don't miss the amazing Carreg Cennen Castle.

Wrexham is a very old city with lots of history. Its most famous sight is the Pontcysyllte Aqueduct, a large bridge for water. You can go across it in a boat. Watch Wrexham's football club play in one of the oldest football stadiums in the world, Racecourse Ground.

▸ Page 104

More practice 2 Is this phone yours?

Complete the conversation with the possessive pronouns in the box.

hers • his • mine 2x • ours • yours

Mr Price Somebody has forgotten their phone. It's on the desk over there. Owen, is it ... (1)?

Owen No, I've got ... (2) here. I'll ask Samara if it's ... (3).

Dylan I think Samara has a white phone and this one is black. But Promit has a black phone, I think. Maybe it's ... (4).

Louise No, Promit and I have the same kind of phone – ... (5) are smaller than that one.

Mr Price Well, somebody must have forgotten it. I'll look at the screen photo to see if that helps ... Oh, that's a picture of my family. Oops! It's actually ... (6)!

▸ Page 106

Parallel exercise 1 Life in a Welsh village in 1927

a) BEFORE YOU WATCH **Dylan found a video online about life in a Welsh village in 1927. What do you think it was like then? There can be more than one correct answer to each question.**

1 What did they wear?
A Clothes that they bought online. B Nothing. C Clothes that they made.
2 How did they travel?
A People walked a lot. B Some people rode horses. C Everyone drove cars.
3 How did they get food?
A From fast food restaurants. B They bought it. C From their gardens.
4 What did they do for fun? A They sang. B They played video games. C They read books.
5 What did they use for light? A Candles. B Electric lamps. C Fire.

More help 1 Life in a Welsh village in 1927

d) **What do you think: Does technology bring people together? Why?**

Yes, it does because ... Yes

- *you can talk to friends online.*
- *some technology, for example washing machines, saves us time.*
- *it's easy to find people that like the same things that you like.*

No, it doesn't because ... No

- *it's easy to bully people online.*
- *people spend too much time in front of screens.*
- *people compare their lives on social media and get unhappy.*

▸ Page 107

More practice 3 A dangerous job

Complete the sentences. Use the *simple past*.

What … (1 be) life like for children in the past?
A long time ago, most children in the UK … (2 not go) to school because they … (3 have) to work. In Wales, many children … (4 work) in coal mines and … (5 do) different kinds of jobs. Small children … (6 open) and … (7 close) doors in the mines.
Older children … (8 move) wagons of coal out of the mines. They … (9 not have) many breaks and they … (10 not see) the sun all day because they … (11 have) to work long days. Today you can go into old coal mines as a tourist, for example the Big Pit National Coal Museum in Blaenavon.

More help 3 SPEAKING An evening with or without technology?

b) WALK AROUND **Tell different partners what you did yesterday evening. Use the simple past. Listen to them and take notes.**

Yesterday evening …	I my family my friends and I	did homework / … went shopping / to a club / a friend's house / … listened to music online / a playlist / … made a cake / jewellery / a model / a video / … texted friends / an online friend / … played football / basketball / online games / video games / … watched TV / online programmes / videos / …

▸ Page 108

More practice 4 Your phone call

a) **With a partner, write a short phone call about your plans for the weekend. Use as many phrases from the box as you can.**

b) **Practise your phone call.**

c) **Read out your phone call to another pair.**

Phrases

- (Hello / Hi, it's …) • How are things?
- Are you free on Saturday afternoon / …?
- No, sorry, I have to …
- What about Sunday afternoon / …?
- Yeah / Sure / OK / Sounds good …
- Oh, one more thing: …
- Sorry, I can't hear you.
- Can you say that again, please?
- Sorry, I have to go now. • Bye! / See you later!

▸ Page 110

More practice 5 What do you do on social media?

Dylan is telling Owen how he uses social media. Choose the right word.

My mum's family lives in Kenya, so it's nice to see what they're doing. We often watch / send (1) messages to each other, and my cousins always post / subscribe (2) photos of themselves. I really like to leave / watch (3) the videos that my uncle posts of his life in Nairobi. In fact, you should send / subscribe (4) to his channel, because the videos are great. He always gets / posts (5) a lot of likes! I always make sure to get / leave (6) a comment on his videos.

▸ Page 111

More help 3 SPEAKING Could you help me, please?

c) WALK AROUND **Make notes about things that you are good at and things that you need help with. Then walk around and ask for or offer help. Use phrases from** p. 111, ex. 3b).

I can help you with Could you please help me with	homework / spelling / a tech problem / an email / a problem / ...
I can show / teach you Can you show / teach me	how to use an app / edit a video / do a trick / ... how to bake / draw / dance / sing / make something / ...

▸ Page 113

More practice 6 Tech definitions

Partner A: Choose one of the items and think of a definition for partner B – but don't say the name of the item! Partner B: Guess what it is. Then swap roles and choose another item.

This is a thing that	you can use to	go online • call people • check the time • listen to music / podcasts • ...
This is a person who	makes websites / apps / games • takes photos / videos of themselves • streams themselves • plays video games for lots of people • ...	

A

B

C

D

E

F

▸ Page 113

More practice 7 More definitions

a) Complete the definitions with *who* or *that*.

1 This is an animal ... you often see in Wales.
2 This is a symbol of a country ... is important to many people.
3 This is a language ... people speak in Wales.
4 This is a person ... can help you when you're ill and give you medicine.
5 This is a little symbol ... you use to show how you feel.
6 This is a text ... tells you how to use something.

b) Match the words to the definitions in a).

doctor • emoji • flag • instructions • sheep • Welsh

▸ Page 113 & 124

More help 8 The debate

good	bad
• you can talk to your friends • it feels good to get a lot of likes • it's fun to follow people online • some apps help people with their problems	• people only show the good parts of their lives • it is hard to delete things online • it can be dangerous • sometimes people are mean

▸ Page 116

More help 3 DOUBLE CIRCLE Social media opinions

1 I (often / sometimes / never) use social media because I like / don't like ...
2 ... is a famous influencer who ... . I like / don't like him / her because ...
3 I think it is / isn't a good idea to edit photos because it makes you feel better / they look cool / it makes other people feel worse / it's not real.
4 When I see these photos, I feel bad / jealous / sad / happy / like I want to be like the people in them.

More help 4 LIFE SKILLS Recognizing fake photos

c)

The influencer used	a filter • lighting	to look	prettier • skinnier • stronger • taller • ...
They wore	special clothes • make-up		
They	posed like this • edited the photo		

Unit 5
Two Irelands: Together

*Hi, I'm Jack.
I'm from Belfast,
Northern Ireland.*

A

The Titanic Belfast museum

B

The Giant's Causeway

C

Belfast's Peace Walls

1 Listening North & South Together

a) BEFORE YOU LISTEN ***The North & South Together*** **project wants to keep peace in Northern Ireland and Ireland. Look at the photos and read the captions. Who is from Ireland? Who is from Northern Ireland?**

b) **Jack and Orla sent each other messages. Listen and put photos A–F in the correct order.**

Good to know

'The Troubles' is the name for thirty years of violence in Northern Ireland.

Nach dieser Unit kann ich ...

- über Irland und Nordirland sprechen
- eine Reise planen und darüber reden

D
King John's Castle in Limerick

F
Live music in Dublin

E
Dublin's St Patrick's Day Parade

c) Listen again. Are the sentences true or false?

1 Jack thinks that peace is important.
2 His parents weren't scared.
3 He likes the Titanic Belfast museum.
4 Orla has been to Northern Ireland before.
5 King John's Castle is 800 years old.
6 The best St Patrick's Day Parade is in Limerick.

d) Correct the wrong sentences with a partner.

e) What would you like to see or do? Tell each other.

I want to see the Giant's Causeway. *– I want to listen to live music in Dublin.*

▶ More practice 1, p. 136

▶ Workbook, p. 82

Digital quiz I can **talk about Ireland and Northern Ireland.**

In Belfast

1 Reading Sights in Belfast

a) Before you read **Jack has sent Orla a website with information on Belfast sights. Match the names in the box to the photos A–D.**

Belfast Castle • St George's Market • the Murals • the Titanic Belfast museum

www.example.com/belfast-sights

A
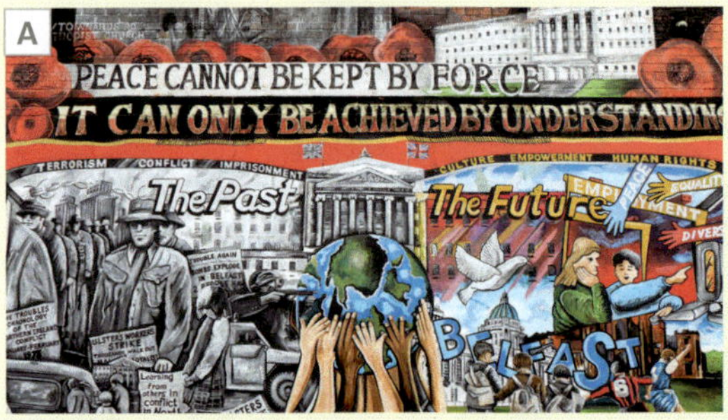

You have to see Belfast's amazing street art! They show Belfast's history as well as things that are happening today.

B

Do you want to have the best view of Belfast? Check out this famous old building. Why don't you take a break and relax in the beautiful green park?

C

Are you hungry? From Friday to Sunday you can enjoy the food, shop for special gifts, and listen to local musicians.

D

Have you heard of the Titanic? It was built in Belfast, so it's an important part of our history here. Sadly, this famous ship never finished its journey.

b) **Scan the website. Where can you do these things? There can be more than one place.**

1 relax in a park
2 learn about a sad journey
3 go shopping
4 discover Belfast's history

When you **scan** a text, you just want to find specific information. Look for keywords, but don't read every word.

► Skills file 9, p. 148
► More help, p. 137

c) **Write four sentences about interesting sights in your area.**

► Workbook, p. 83

2 Speaking Staying in Belfast

a) **Partner B:** Look at p. 136.

Orla is looking online at B&Bs for their trip. First read this note from Orla's mum:

- *How much is it?*
- *Do we have our own bathroom?*
- *Can we get a hot breakfast?*

Partner A: Read about *The Beyond B&B* and answer partner B's questions.

b) **Partner A:** Ask partner B the three questions from a) about *Ivy House B&B* and take notes.

c) Which B&B do you think will Orla and her mum choose?

The Beyond B&B

The Beyond B&B is in the centre of Belfast. Our comfortable rooms (£85) share a bathroom with two other rooms on each floor. Each room also has a TV and a kettle.

Every morning we have a hot breakfast of eggs, sausages and tomatoes. We have vegetarian options for our guests as well.

3 Listening At the competition

a) Before you listen Orla and Jack are in a dance competition. Where and when do you dance?

b) Listen and complete the sentences with one or two words.

1 At the start, Orla is nervous about ...
2 She arrived in Belfast ... ago.
3 Declan is from ...
4 He thinks the winner will be from ...
5 Orla thinks people like Declan are ...
6 At the end, Orla is nervous about ...

► Parallel exercise, p. 137

c) Listen again. Why is Jack angry with Declan?

d) What do you think will happen next? Write three sentences. Then compare with a partner. Do you have the same ideas?

I think Jack will ...
What about you?

I (don't) agree.
Maybe ...

► More help, p. 137

► Workbook, p. 84

Digital quiz I can plan and talk about a trip.

OPTIONAL

Tina times two

1 A wish

BEFORE YOU WATCH **Tina closes her eyes and makes a wish in the video. What would you wish for? Tell the class.**

I would wish for ...

2 VIEWING 'I'm Tina too'

Watch the first part of the video and say if each sentence is true or false.

1 Tina doesn't like dancing.
2 Tina's parents don't listen to her.
3 Tina has a dance partner in her class.
4 Tina's parents forget her birthday.
5 Tina 2 is a secret.
6 Tina 2 is more confident than Tina.

3 VIEWING 'I had the most absolutely amazing day today'

a) **What do you think Tina 2 is going to do?**

I think Tina 2 is going to ...

go to the dance class • speak to Tina's parents • dance in the street • eat a cake • do something funny • ...

b) **Watch the second part of the video. Were you right?**

4 'Don't be scared – be spectacular!'

How does Tina feel? You can match more than one feeling to each sentence.

1 When she dances alone at the start.
2 When she first meets the boy.
3 When she first meets Tina 2.
4 When Tina 2 locks her in the wardrobe.
5 When she runs after Tina 2.
6 When she dances with her class at the end.

angry • brave • confident • happy • proud • scared • spectacular • shy • worried

► Workbook, p. 85

1 Reading Two countries

I can talk about Ireland and Northern Ireland.

Your dad wants to know about some differences between Ireland and Northern Ireland. You find this information online. Scan the text and answer his questions.

1 What are the official languages?
2 Which country is part of the UK?
3 What are the capital cities?
4 What kind of money do you need?

www.example.com/twoirelands

Ireland and Northern Ireland

- Irish and English are official languages in both countries. More people speak Irish in Ireland than in Northern Ireland. In Ireland, most road signs show both languages, and some signs only show Irish. Signs in Northern Ireland only show English.
- Northern Ireland is part of the UK, but it isn't a member of the EU. Ireland isn't part of the UK, but it is a member of the EU.
- Both countries have their own capital city. Dublin is the capital city of Ireland, and Belfast is the capital city of Northern Ireland.
- Money is different in both countries. If you want to buy something in Ireland, you pay in euros, like in Germany. In Northern Ireland you pay with pounds, like in England. You can pay by card in both countries, but it's a good idea to bring some cash with you.

2 Listening Phoning a hotel

I can plan and talk about a trip.

a) **Joe wants to book a hotel room. He phones a hotel. Listen and put the pictures in the correct order.**

A 
B 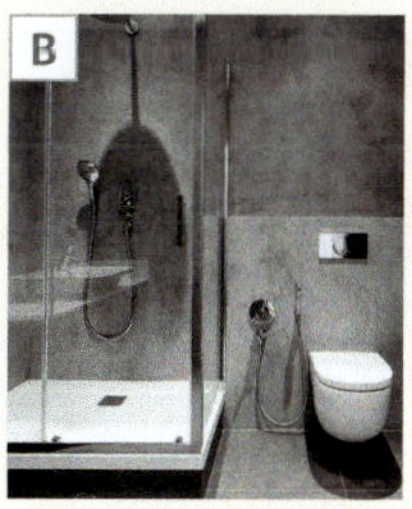
C 
D 
E 

b) **Listen again. Are the sentences true or false?**

1 Joe wants a room for tomorrow.
2 The hotel has a room free.
3 The room Joe wants costs 65 pounds.
4 Breakfast is already in the price.
5 The room has a kettle.
6 They will get to the hotel in the evening.

c) **Correct the wrong sentences.**

Check

Partner page

▸ Page 133

2 SPEAKING Staying in Belfast

a) Orla is looking online at B&Bs for their trip. First read this note from Orla's mum:

- *How much is it?*
- *Do we have our own bathroom?*
- *Can we get a hot breakfast?*

Partner B: Ask your partner the three questions about *The Beyond B&B* and take notes.

b) Now read about *Ivy House B&B* and answer partner A's question.

c) Which B&B do you think will Orla and her mum choose?

Ivy House B&B

Our large rooms have their own bathroom with a shower. There are free bottles of water in every room as well as a kettle. Rooms are £95 with breakfast.

Guests can use our free internet and relax in the garden. Enjoy a delicious breakfast of muesli, fruit, yoghurt, cheese and cold meats, and bread.

Diff bank

▸ Page 131

More practice 1 Words

Match the definitions A–H to the words 1–8.

1 peace	3 Peace Walls	5 parade	7 competition
2 violence	4 murals	6 castle	8 live music

A a big, old building with high walls, often where a king lived a long time ago	B when people fight, usually to hurt or kill other people	C when people celebrate outside and walk together, often with music and costumes	D when people play music or sing songs in public
E high walls in Northern Ireland that separate people from each other	F pictures that people paint on walls	G when there is no fighting	H an event where people try to be the best at something and win

▸ Page 132

More help 1 READING Sights in Belfast

c) Write four sentences about interesting sights in your area.

In our village / town / city, ...

my favourite sight is a we have a we don't have a you have to see a you can go to a	famous big / small cool / boring modern / traditional beautiful	canal. • castle. • fountain. • lake. • market. • museum. • palace. • park. • river. • square. • stadium. • statue. • tower. • ...

▸ Page 133

Parallel exercise 3 LISTENING At the competition

b) Listen and complete the sentences.

1	At the start, Orla is nervous about ...	A Declan	B Jack	C her dance.
2	She arrived in Belfast ...	A yesterday	B two days ago	C three days ago.
3	Declan is from ...	A Ireland	B Belfast	C Limerick.
4	He thinks the winner will be from ...	A Ireland	B Limerick	C Northern Ireland.
5	Orla thinks people like Declan are ...	A everywhere	B nowhere	C only in Northern Ireland.
6	At the end, Orla is nervous about ...	A Declan	B Jack	C her dance.

More help 3 LISTENING At the competition

d) What do you think will happen next?

I think Maybe Perhaps	Orla Jack Declan	will won't	be mean to ... • have a problem with ... • see ... again. • win the ... • lose the ... • have a great day tomorrow ... • ...

Auf den ***Skills file***-Seiten findest du Methoden und Tipps, die dir helfen, z. B. Wortschatz zu lernen, Informationen zu sammeln, Texte zu überprüfen oder kleine Vorträge zu halten.

Inhalt

MK Die mit diesem Symbol gekennzeichneten Abschnitte enthalten Hinweise und Tipps, die dir dabei helfen, elektronische Medien beim Englischlernen einzusetzen.

Erklär-film Dieses Symbol zeigt dir, dass du einen Erklärfilm zu diesem Thema in der App findest.

Lösungen der Merkaufgaben

SF 2, Merkaufgabe:
a) *ähnliches Wort im Deutschen: Pyjama stammt aus dem Dari-Persischen (پایجامه pāy-jāmeh), wortwörtlich „Beinkleidung"*
b) *Wortfamilie und Wortbildungsgesetze: taste + Nachsilbe -ful: tasteful*
c) *Wortfamilie und Wortbildungsgesetze: (to) care + Nachsilbe -er: carer*

SF 3, Merkaufgabe:
a) Säule
b) Spalte

SF 4, Merkaufgabe:
Nein: Dann musst du die Urheberinnen und Urheber der Bilder um Erlaubnis fragen oder eigene Bilder machen, wenn es keine creative commons-Bilder sind.

SF 5, Merkaufgabe:
Zehen: They're part of my foot.
Küche: It's a room where you can cook and eat.

SF 6, Merkaufgabe:
Weitere Bindewörter (linking words), die du schon kennst, sind z. B. after that, and, because, but, or, so, soon, ...

SF 7, Merkaufgabe:
Mögliche Satzanfänge könnten z. B. sein: I mean, ...; Just a minute, ...; Let me see, ...; You know, ...; Well, ...

SF 8, Merkaufgabe:
a) *allgemeine Dinge* b) *Details*

SF 9, Merkaufgabe:
Edinburgh Castle: £19.50, child ticket £11.40; Edinburgh Zoo: £24.25, child ticket £15.70

SF 10, Merkaufgabe:
b)

SF 11, Merkaufgabe:
a) *The person is playing the guitar.*

Erklärfilm

SF 1

Vokabeln lernen

► Unit 1 | p. 16, 39 ► Unit 2 | p. 60 ► Unit 3 | p. 82 ► Unit 4 | p. 108

Führe dein VOCAB FILE aus Klasse 5 und 6 weiter. Ergänze eine Spalte für Wörter aus anderen Sprachen, die du sprichst.

English	*Deutsch*	*Türkçe*
biscuit	*Plätzchen*	*bisküvi*

Neue Vokabeln lernst du am besten an einem ruhigen und aufgeräumten Platz, an dem du nicht abgelenkt wirst.

Wiederholen kannst du sie immer und überall. Für unterwegs kannst du sie dir aufs Handy sprechen oder per Vokabeltrainer-App üben. Je öfter du die Vokabeln wiederholst, desto besser wirst du sie dir merken können.

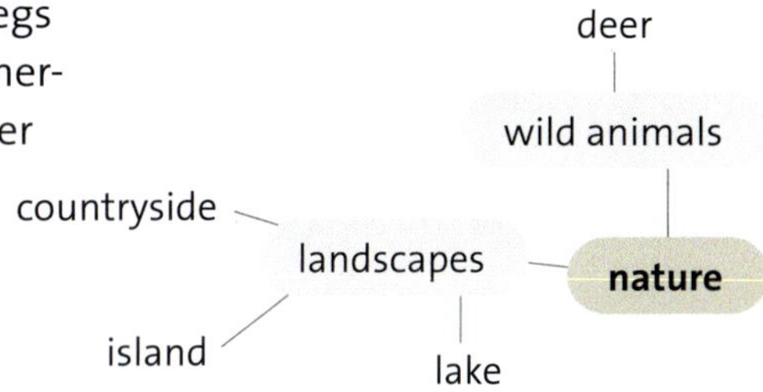

Wie merke ich mir neue Wörter besser?

Erstelle Wortfelder

- Ordne die Wörter unter einem Oberbegriff *(umbrella word)*. Du kannst eine Liste machen oder eine Mindmap anlegen, die du immer weiter ergänzt.
- Oder du arbeitest mit Karteikarten. Schreibe den Oberbegriff in Großbuchstaben auf die Vorderseite einer Karteikarte und die dazu passenden Wörter auf die Rückseite. Später kannst du neue Wörter ergänzen.
- Wenn Informationen sich in verschiedene Teile ordnen lassen, kannst du gut auch eine Tabelle anlegen, z. B. wenn du darüber reden möchtest, wann du etwas machst.

activity	*Monday*	*Tuesday*	*Wedr*
what	*piano*	–	*footb*
time	...	...	
place	...	...	

Sammle Gegensatzpaare und Wörter mit der gleichen Bedeutung

Sammle gegensätzliche Wörter und Wörter mit der gleichen Bedeutung, z. B. auf der letzten Seite deines VOCAB FILE.

friend ◄► enemy
young ◄► old
(to) remain ►► (to) stay

Lerne *phrases* statt Einzelwörter

Phrases sind Ausdrücke, die aus mehreren Wörtern bestehen, z. B. *a bottle of water = eine Flasche Wasser.* Lerne also nicht *bottle* und *water* als Einzelwörter, sondern den ganzen Ausdruck: *a bottle of water.*

Merkaufgabe 1

Gehe dein VOCAB FILE aus Klasse 5 und 6 durch und erstelle eine Liste mit zwanzig bedeutungsgleichen Wörtern.

Checkliste Vokabeln lernen

✓ Lerne nur 5–10 Vokabeln auf einmal.
✓ Lerne jeden Tag 10 Minuten.
✓ Lerne zusammen mit Freunden.
✓ Lerne unterwegs mit einer Vokabeltrainer-App.
✓ Schreibe schwierige Wörter mehrmals auf.
✓ Sprich die Wörter und nimm dich mit dem Handy auf.

SF 2

Unbekannte Wörter erschließen

▶ Unit 1 | p. 18, 41 ▶ Unit 4 | p. 108

Du kannst englische Texte verstehen – auch wenn du nicht alle Wörter kennst. Diese Tipps helfen dir, die Bedeutung von Wörtern ohne Wörterbuch herauszufinden.

Bilder

Bilder zeigen oft Dinge in einem Text, für die du das englische Wort noch nicht kennst. Schaue sie deshalb genau an.

Till has left his key ring on the park bench at the end of the path.

Ähnliche Wörter im Deutschen oder in anderen Sprachen

Viele englische Wörter klingen ähnlich wie im Deutschen oder sie werden ähnlich geschrieben. Manche kennst du vielleicht aus anderen Sprachen und kannst sie auch daher verstehen.

- 🇬🇧 garage
- 🇩🇪 die Garage
- 🇫🇷 le garage
- 🇷🇺 гараж
- 🇹🇷 garaj

Wortfamilien und Wortbildungsregeln

Ein Wort gehört immer zu einer Wortfamilie, z. B. *friend*, *friendly*, *friendship*. Kennst du ein Wort aus der Wortfamilie und ein paar Regeln zur Wortbildung, kannst du die Bedeutung ableiten:

Vorsilben		
un-	Aus einem positiven Adjektiv wird ein negatives.	friendly → unfriendly
Nachsilben		
-er	Aus einem Tätigkeitsverb wird eine Person.	(to) support → supporter
-ful	Aus einem Nomen wird ein Adjektiv.	care → careful
-less	Aus einem Nomen wird ein Adjektiv.	cloud → cloudless
-ness	Aus einem Adjektiv wird ein Nomen.	fit → fitness

Kontext

Manchmal helfen dir die Wörter oder Sätze vor und nach dem neuen Wort dabei, es zu verstehen.

We made it to the station on time! The train departs in ten minutes from platform 3.

Merkaufgabe 2

Schaue dir die Wörter an. Mit welcher Strategie kannst du ihre Bedeutung herausfinden?

a) pyjama **b)** tasteful **c)** carer

(Die Lösung findest du auf Seite 138.)

SF 3

Erklärfilm

Im Wörterbuch nachschlagen

▶ Unit 1 | p. 41 ▶ Unit 4 | p. 123

Wie finde ich Wörter und Ausdrücke im englisch-deutschen *Dictionary*?

Dein *Dictionary* hinten im Buch (S. 215–235) hilft dir, wenn du ein unbekanntes Wort nicht erschließen kannst. Du kannst aber auch ein (Online-)Wörterbuch verwenden. Beachte dabei folgende wichtige Dinge:

Die Wörter im Wörterbuch sind alphabetisch aufgelistet (j kommt vor k, ka vor ke, keb vor kee).

June [dʒuːn] der Juni 1
just [dʒʌst]:
1. nur, bloß; einfach 1
2. gerade (eben) 2: 4 (109)

K

karaoke [kæriˈəʊki] das Karaoke 1
karate [kəˈrɑːti] das Karate 2: 3 (74)
kebab [kɪˈbæb] der Kebab 1
keep [kiːp], **kept, kept:**
1. halten; behalten; aufbewahren 2: 2 (55)

Der Haupteintrag (z. B. *name*) steht farbig und **fett** am Anfang. Daneben oder darunter findest du oft zusammengesetzte Wörter oder Redewendungen (z. B. *first name*).

name [neɪm] der Name 1 **family name** der Familienname, der Nachname 1 **first name** der Vorname 1 **What's your name?** Wie heißt du? 1

Längere Ausdrücke findest du meist unter mehr als einem Stichwort, z. B. *first name* unter *first* und unter *name*.

Die Ziffern 1, 2 usw. zeigen, dass ein Wort mehrere Bedeutungen hat oder sogar als unterschiedliche Wortarten vorkommt. Lies also immer den ganzen Eintrag und entscheide dann, welche Bedeutung die richtige ist.

first [fɜːst]:
1. erste(r, s) 1
2. zuerst, als Erstes 1
at first zuerst, am Anfang 1
first name [ˈfɜːst neɪm] der Vorname

Du erfährst, wie das gesuchte Wort geschrieben und ausgesprochen wird. Schau dir für die Aussprache und Betonung die Lautschrift in den eckigen Klammern an.

▶ English sounds, p. 236

In Online-Wörterbüchern stellst du nur die Suchrichtung (E–D oder D–E) ein und tippst dann das Wort ein.
Durch einen Klick auf das Lautsprechersymbol kannst du dir ein Wort anhören.

Was muss ich bei einem deutsch-englischen Wörterbuch beachten?

Schlage bei Verben immer den Infinitiv (die Grundform) nach, also z. B. „singen" statt „gesungen".

Wenn ein Wort mehrere Übersetzungen hat, dann lies alle Einträge genau, um die passende Bedeutung zu finden.

Merkaufgabe 3

Was heißt *column* in diesen Sätzen?
a) One of the most famous columns in London is Nelson's Column.
b) Make a table with five columns.
(Die Lösung findest du auf Seite 138.)

SF 4

Im Internet recherchieren

▸ Unit 1 | p. 30 ▸ Unit 4 | p. 112

Im Internet kannst du dir schnell und einfach Informationen zu allen Themen besorgen. Mit ein paar Tricks behältst du trotz der Menge an Informationen den Überblick.

Benutze auch andere Quellen wie Bücher aus der Bücherei, Zeitungen und Magazine.

Suchen

- Überlege dir Suchbegriffe, die zu deinem Thema passen.
- Gib nicht nur einen Suchbegriff ein, sondern zwei oder mehrere. Du suchst z. B. Informationen zu Nessie. Wenn du nur *monster* eingibst, wirst du weniger Passendes finden, als wenn du *Scotland* + *Loch Ness* + *monster Nessie* eingibst.

Auswählen und prüfen

Beschäftige dich nur mit den Seiten und Links, die wirklich zu deiner Aufgabe passen und glaubwürdig sind. Nicht alle Informationen, die du findest, sind wichtig und richtig. Prüfe sie also sorgfältig:

- Passen die Informationen zu deinem Thema? Sind sie wichtig? Um dir einen Eindruck zu verschaffen, überfliege die Seite und achte auf Überschriften und Bilder.
- Sind die Informationen korrekt? Fakten sind gut, wenn sie wahr und überprüfbar sind. Es gibt aber auch gefälschte „Fakten“ und Statistiken. Prüfe daher:
  - Woher stammt die Information? Ist es z. B. ein Online-Lexikon oder ein Chat-Forum? Achte auf die Endung der Internetadresse oder URL (http://www...), sie kann dir wichtige Hinweise geben:
    .com bedeutet, es ist eine kommerzielle Webseite, die auch (versteckte) Werbung enthalten kann.
    .gov weist auf eine offizielle Webseite der amerikanischen Regierung hin.
    .uk bedeutet, dass es eine britische Seite ist.
- Verlasse dich nicht nur auf eine einzige Internetseite als Quelle, sondern ziehe zwei oder drei heran.
- Überprüfe, wer den Text verfasst hat. Verfolgt er oder sie ein bestimmtes Ziel? Ist die Person neutral und sachlich? Handelt es sich um Experten?

Unseriöse Quellen erkennst du z. B. an reißerischen oder unpassenden Überschriften, fehlenden Angaben zur Autorin oder zum Autor, fehlenden Belegen oder einem veralteten Datum.

Vorsicht bei Wikipedia. Das Online-Lexikon ist von freiwilligen Helfern geschrieben und kann Fehler enthalten.

Es ist natürlich in Ordnung, eine eigene Meinung zu äußern oder die Meinung anderer Leute wiederzugeben, solange sie auf Fakten basiert und respektvoll vorgetragen wird.

Sichern

- Setze *bookmarks*, also Lesezeichen oder Favoriten, in deinem Browser, um die ausgewählten Seiten später schnell wieder aufzurufen.
- Wenn du Inhalte einer Webseite verwendest, nenne immer die Autorin oder den Autor der Seite und die dazugehörige Internetadresse, die du direkt in dein digitales Dokument hineinkopieren kannst. Schreibe auch das Datum dazu, wann du die Webseite zuletzt aufgerufen hast.
- Mache dir Notizen oder drucke wichtige Seiten sofort aus und markiere wichtige Textstellen. Schreibe die Texte nicht wörtlich ab – gib die Inhalte in deinen eigenen Worten wieder. Ordne deine Ergebnisse in deinem Heft oder in einem Dokument auf dem Rechner mit Überschriften oder sortiere sie in einer Mindmap.
- Wenn du Inhalte wörtlich übernehmen möchtest, kennzeichne sie durch Anführungszeichen als Zitat und nenne die Quelle. Z. B. *„A lot of people think that the Loch Ness monster is real and have lovingly named it Nessie.“ (Loch Ness Times vom 11.11.2023)*

Bookmarks setzt du so: Du navigierst im Browser zu der Webseite, die du zu einem Favoriten machen möchtest, und klickst dann, je nach Browser, im Menü auf „Favoriten“ oder „Lesezeichen“, gibst den Namen des Lesezeichens in die Adressleiste ein und bestätigst mit ↵.

notes

- place: ... near ...
- tickets: £ ...
- open: ...
- fun facts: ...

Bilder verwenden

Wenn du ein Bild aus dem Internet verwendest, ist es wichtig, dass du die Quelle angibst, also den Ort, wo du das Bild gefunden hast. Dazu klickst du in deinen Suchergebnissen auf das Bild, das du nutzen möchtest, und gehst auf die eigentliche Seite, auf der es zu finden ist. Dann kopierst du die URL der Seite und setzt sie in deinem Dokument unter das Bild. Nenne auch die Fotografin oder den Fotografen, wenn du die Angabe findest. Am besten verwendest du eigene oder lizenzfreie Bilder *(creative commons)*, die gemeinfrei sind.

Denke daran, dass eine Suchmaschine keine Quelle ist, d. h. du musst immer die Adresse der Webseite angeben, auf der das Bild tatsächlich steht.

Wenn du Fotos mit anderen Personen machst und verwendest, musst du diese Personen um Erlaubnis bitten.

Merkaufgabe 4

Wenn dein Poster oder deine Folien z. B. auf der Webseite deiner Schule stehen, also an die Öffentlichkeit kommen, darfst du dann Fotos aus dem Internet verwenden, ja oder nein?

(Die Lösung findest du auf Seite 138.)

SF 5

Die eigene Meinung äußern

▶ Unit 2 | p. 60 ▶ Unit 4 | p. 116

Wie drücke ich aus, was ich denke?

Zu Beginn einer Diskussion sagst du, was du über ein Thema denkst. Dann begründest du deine Meinung.

In my opinion, ...
I think / believe that ...
I would say that ...
If you ask me ...

Wie frage ich nach der Meinung?

In Diskussionen geht es nicht nur um die eigene Meinung. Daher fragst du die anderen nach ihrer Meinung.

What do you think?

Wie reagiere ich angemessen?

Gehe auf die Beiträge anderer ein und respektiere andere Meinungen. Sei auch bei Meinungsverschiedenheiten sachlich und höflich. Wenn du etwas nicht richtig gehört oder verstanden hast, bitte dein Gegenüber, es zu wiederholen oder langsamer zu sprechen:
Can you say that again, please?
Don't speak so fast, please.

I (completely) agree.
Yes, you're so right.
That's a good point.

I'm not sure here.
I see it a bit differently.
I don't think that's true.
I don't agree with you (at all).

Was mache ich, wenn mir Wörter nicht einfallen?

Fehlt dir beim Sprechen ein Wort oder fällt es dir nicht ein, kannst du es umschreiben, z. B. durch einen Oberbegriff *(umbrella word)*, mit Wörtern, die eine ähnliche oder gleiche Bedeutung haben, oder mit gegensätzlichen Wörtern. Auch mit Relativsätzen kannst du Eigenschaften des gesuchten Begriffes erklären.

It's a place where ...
It's very similar to ...
It's the opposite of ...
It's somebody who ...

Füllwörter

Um ein Gespräch nicht stocken zu lassen, kannst du Füllwörter verwenden. Wenn du Zeit zum Nachdenken brauchst, kannst du diese mit *Let me see ...* oder *Well, ...* überbrücken.

Well, ...
Just a minute.
Let me think.

Merkaufgabe 5

Überlege dir passende Umschreibungen für „Zehen“ und „Küche“.
(Die Lösung findest du auf Seite 138.)

SF 6

Eine Geschichte planen

▸ Unit 3 | p. 88

Schritt 1: Ideen sammeln

Damit deine Geschichte verständlich und interessant wird, sammelst du zuerst wichtige Ideen und Wörter, z. B. in einer Liste oder einer Mindmap. Beantworte dafür die *wh*-Fragen: *Who? When? Where? What? Why? (+ How?)*

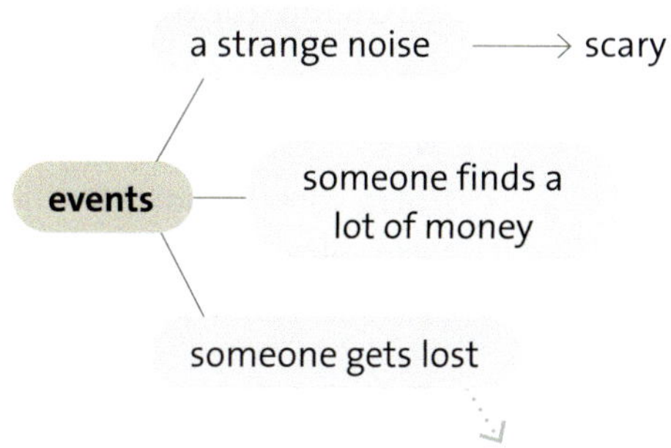

Schritt 2: Die Geschichte strukturieren

Deine Geschichte ist viel besser zu verstehen, wenn du sie sinnvoll gliederst. Unterteile sie deshalb in:

- **Anfang** *(beginning)*: In einem einleitenden Satz beschreibst du die Ausgangssituation: den Schauplatz und die Personen.
- **Mittelteil** *(middle)*: Im Mittelteil beschreibst du die Handlung deiner Geschichte.
- **Schluss** *(end)*: Schließe deine Geschichte mit einem Happy End, einer Auflösung oder einer neuen Situation ab.

Schritt 3: Einen Textentwurf erstellen

Möchtest du die Geschichte mündlich vortragen, mache dir nun Stichpunkte. Schreibe dafür wichtige Wörter auf Karteikarten und übe, sie frei sprechend vorzutragen.

Möchtest du die Geschichte aufschreiben, erstelle einen Textentwurf – auf einem Blatt Papier oder am Computer.

Überlege dir eine sinnvolle Reihenfolge und beginne bei neuen Punkten mit einer neuen Zeile, z. B. nach deiner Einleitung und vor deinem Schluss.

Joe and Salim wanted to go fishing. →
They packed and went out in the boat. →
It started to get dark and Joe was scared. →
A storm started.
Joe fell into the water. →
Salim pulled Joe into the boat. →
Salim called 999. →
A lifeguard rescued Joe and Salim.

Schritt 4: Deine Geschichte interessant klingen lassen

Deine Geschichte klingt interessanter, wenn du Adjektive verwendest, um Personen, Orte oder Dinge zu beschreiben. So kann sich dein Publikum deine Geschichte besser vorstellen. Verbinde deine Sätze mithilfe von Bindewörtern *(linking words)*, z. B. *eventually, first, finally, however, in the end, then, therefore.*

Gute Adjektive für die Geschichte von Joe und Salim könnten zum Beispiel sein: *black, careful, cold, dark, exciting, extreme, hard, happy, helpful, horrible, scared, wild, ...*

Merkaufgabe 6

Fallen dir noch fünf weitere *linking words* ein, die nicht auf dieser Seite stehen?

(Die Lösung findest du auf Seite 138.)

SF 7

Einen Kurzvortrag halten

▸ Unit 4 | p. 119

Um einen guten Kurzvortrag vor der Klasse halten zu können, musst du ihn gut vorbereiten und üben.

Meinen Kurzvortrag vorbereiten

- Nutze verschiedene Medien, um Informationen zu sammeln: Internet, Bücher, Zeitschriften, Zeitungen. Sammle und ordne deine Ideen.
- Ein Kurzvortrag sollte folgendermaßen aufgebaut sein:
  - **Einleitung:** Hier nennst du dein Thema.
  - **Hauptteil:** Nun nennst du deine Hauptpunkte. Dann erzählst du mehr zu jedem Punkt.
  - **Schluss:** Du fasst deine Hauptpunkte zusammen, bedankst dich fürs Zuhören und erkundigst dich, ob jemand Fragen hat.

I'd like to talk about …

To begin with, I'd like to tell you about …
To sum up …

Thank you for listening.
Do you have any questions?

- MK Veranschauliche deinen Vortrag mit einem Poster, Folien mit Bildern oder Gegenständen.
- Mache dir für die Präsentation kurze Notizen auf Karteikarten. Strukturiere deine Notizen genauso wie deine Präsentation. Hebe die wichtigsten Begriffe mit verschiedenen Farben hervor. Du kannst auch kleine Erinnerungen zum Ablauf deines Vortrags notieren.

▸ Skills file 12, p. 151

- Übe deinen Vortrag mehrmals vor dem Spiegel oder mit jemandem. Gebt euch gegenseitig Tipps, wie ihr euch verbessern könnt. Du kannst dich auch selbst mit dem Smartphone aufnehmen. Achte auf die Zeit.

Meinen Kurzvortrag halten

Überprüfe zu Beginn, ob alles vorbereitet ist. Dann schaue dein Publikum an und warte, bis es ruhig ist. Sprich langsam, laut und deutlich. Zeige während deines Vortrags auf Bilder oder dein Poster.

Merkaufgabe 7

Wenn dir etwas nicht einfällt und du Zeit zum Nachdenken benötigst, welche Satzanfänge kannst du dann verwenden, um Zeit zu gewinnen?

(Eine mögliche Lösung findest du auf Seite 138.)

Checkliste Computerpräsentation

- ✓ Wähle ein einfaches Folienlayout.
- ✓ Verwende eine Schriftgröße von mindestens 16 Punkt.
- ✓ Beschränke dich auf wenig Text.
- ✓ Wähle nur ein Bild pro Folie.
- ✓ Schreibe die Adresse der Internetseite dazu, von der du das Bild hast.

SF 8

Hörtexte verstehen

▸ Unit 1 | p. 17 ▸ Unit 2 | p. 46 ▸ Unit 3 | p. 78 ▸ Unit 4 | p. 105

Es kommt in der Begegnung mit dem Englischen sowohl im Alltag als auch im Unterricht darauf an zu verstehen, was gesagt wurde. Gesichtsausdruck und Körpersprache, die beim Verstehen helfen, fehlen meist bei Höraufgaben im Unterricht. Mit ein paar Tipps wird das Verstehen des Gehörten und das Lösen der Aufgaben dazu leichter.

Nutze die zahlreichen Möglichkeiten, um englische Texte zu hören. Wähle etwas aus, was dir gefällt, z. B. dein Lieblingslied oder dein Lieblingsbuch als Hörbuch auf Englisch. Schaue Filme und Serien auf Englisch. Blende englische Untertitel ein, falls du Probleme beim Verstehen hast. Blende sie aus, wenn du dich sicherer fühlst oder eine Episode schon mehrfach gesehen hast.

Vor dem Hören

Lies dir die Aufgabenstellung genau durch und überlege, was du tun sollst. Finde die Schlüsselwörter in der Aufgabenstellung. Geht es um ein allgemeines Thema oder um Details? Stelle dir die Situation bzw. das Thema vor – was erwartest du? Welche Leute sind beteiligt? Was weißt du schon über das Thema und welche Wörter wären wohl typisch?

Beim Hören

Versuche, zunächst grob zu verstehen, worum es in dem Text geht. Konzentriere dich auf die Schlüsselwörter aus der Aufgabenstellung und achte auch auf Hintergrundgeräusche. Wenn du ein wichtiges Wort nicht verstehst, dann denke an die Situation, um die es geht. Manchmal können dir andere Wörter im Satz oder ähnliche Wörter im Deutschen oder anderen Sprachen, die du sprichst, helfen.
Mache dir kurze Notizen. Bleib ruhig, wenn du beim ersten Mal nicht alles verstehst. Du hörst den Text meist zweimal.

Die Aufgaben stehen in der Regel in der gleichen Reihenfolge, in der die Stellen, die du für die Lösung brauchst, im Hörtext vorkommen.

Nach dem Hören

Vervollständige deine Notizen sofort und vergleiche sie. Lies noch einmal genau durch, was du geschrieben hast. Passen deine Antworten zu den Fragen?
Konzentriere dich beim zweiten Hören auf das, was du beim ersten Mal nicht verstanden hast, und beantworte die Fragen.

▸ Skills file 12, p. 151

Auch wenn du es nicht geschafft hast, alles aufzuschreiben, kannst du die Informationen noch aus deinem Gedächtnis abrufen.

Merkaufgabe 8

Welche dieser beiden Aufgaben fragt nach allgemeinen Dingen, welche nach Details?

a) *What topic do Ali and Pearl talk about?*
b) *What food and drinks do the kids order?*

(Die Lösung findest du auf Seite 138.)

SF 9

Lesetexte verstehen

▶ Unit 1 | p. 26 ▶ Unit 2 | p. 48 ▶ Unit 3 | p. 80 ▶ Unit 4 | p. 114 ▶ Unit 5 | p. 132

In diesem Buch findest du viele verschiedene Texte, z. B. Artikel, Dialoge, Geschichten. Die folgenden Tipps helfen dir beim Verstehen der Texte und Lösen der Aufgaben.

Je mehr englische Texte du liest, desto größer wird dein Wortschatz und desto schneller und besser verstehst du Texte.

Vor dem Lesen

Schaue dir die Aufgaben zum Text an und achte auf Schlüsselwörter. Überlege dir, was du tun sollst und welche Lesestrategie gefordert ist.

Lesestrategien: *Skimming* und *Scanning*

Skimming und *Scanning* sind Lesestrategien, die dich bei bestimmten Fragestellungen unterstützen können.

Skimming hilft dir, einen schnellen Überblick über den Inhalt eines Textes zu bekommen. Dafür siehst du dir diese Dinge an:

- Überschrift und Zwischenüberschriften sowie Bilder und Bildunterschriften,
- den ersten Satz jedes Absatzes, der oft die Hauptidee des Absatzes enthält,
- den letzten Absatz des Textes, der oft eine Zusammenfassung des Textes enthält.

Du musst nicht jedes Wort in einem Text verstehen, um den Inhalt zu verstehen. Um einen schnellen Überblick über den Inhalt zu bekommen, überfliegst du den Text.

Scanning hilft dir, nach bestimmten Informationen zu suchen.

- Überlege dir Stichwörter. Suchst du z. B. Öffnungszeiten, könnten das Ziffern oder Wörter sein wie *open, hours, days*.
- Überfliege den Text und suche nach den Stichwörtern. Du kannst dabei mit dem Finger in einer „S-Form“ über den Text gehen.
- Lies die Textstelle, die dein Stichwort enthält, um zu sehen, ob du dort die gesuchten Informationen findest. Wenn nicht, scanne weiter.

Wenn du mit Texten im Internet arbeitest, kann dein Browser dir viel Arbeit abnehmen: Mit Strg+F (Cmd+F am Mac) kannst du nach deinen Stichworten suchen und nur die Textstellen lesen, in denen ein Stichwort markiert ist. Auf deinem Handy findest du die Suche im Menü des Browsers.

Merkaufgabe 9

Schaue dir die Webseite auf S. 90 zu Edinburgh an. Scanne die Informationen nach den Eintrittspreisen der Burg und des Zoos.

(Die Lösung findest du auf S. 138.)

SF 10

Mediation

► Unit 1 | p. 20 ► Unit 2 | p. 49 ► Unit 3 | p. 75 ► Unit 4 | p. 109

In manchen Situationen musst du zwischen zwei Sprachen vermitteln, um Personen zu helfen, die wenig oder kein Englisch oder Deutsch können. Dies nennt man Sprachmittlung *(mediation)*. Du überträgst die wichtigsten Informationen von der einen Sprache in die andere, entweder mündlich oder schriftlich.

Gib nur die wichtigsten Informationen weiter

Lasse unwichtige Wörter und Satzteile weg und bilde kurze und einfache Sätze.

> Normalerweise gibst du nur den wesentlichen Inhalt wieder. Nur bei Gebrauchsanweisungen ist es wichtig, genau zu sein.

Keine Panik vor unbekannten Wörtern

Wenn du für jemandem z. B. während einer Stadtführung vermitteln oder einen englischen Artikel auf Deutsch erläutern möchtest, musst du nicht alle Details übersetzen. Deshalb ist es auch in Ordnung, wenn du nicht jedes Wort, sondern nur die zentrale Aussage verstehst. Wenn du ein Wort nicht kennst, versuche es mit anderen Wörtern zu umschreiben. Wenn dir zum Beispiel das englische Wort für „Onkel" nicht einfällt, kannst du auch sagen *my mum's / dad's brother*.

> **Checkliste Mediation**
> - ✓ nur die wichtigen Infos weitergeben
> - ✓ unbekannte Wörter umschreiben
> - ✓ auf Pronomen achten: An wen wendest du dich?
> - ✓ kulturelle Unterschiede bedenken

Achte in Gesprächen auf die Pronomen

Überlege immer, an wen du dich gerade wendest, und passe die Pronomen entsprechend an (siehe Foto).

Achte auf kulturelle Unterschiede

Überlege, was für dein Gegenüber wichtig ist, um die Situation und die Inhalte verstehen zu können.

Merkaufgabe 10

Du bist mit deiner Familie in Belfast und deine kleine Schwester möchte wissen, worum es auf dem Wandgemälde in Bild D auf S. 13 geht. Was sagst du ihr?

a) Hier wird Werbung für Traumreisen auf Kreuzfahrtschiffen gemacht.

b) Es geht um ein Schiffsunglück bei dem viele Menschen ihr Leben verloren haben.

(Die Lösung findest du auf Seite 138.)

SF 11

Bilder beschreiben

▶ Intro | p. 12 ▶ Unit 2 | p. 46 ▶ Unit 3 | p. 73

Wie gehe ich vor?

Wenn du ein Bild beschreiben möchtest, dann erwähne zuerst, was du beschreibst, z. B. ein Foto oder ein Poster, und die dargestellte Situation.Danach kümmerst du dich um die Details. Sage, wo sich was im Bild befindet. Wichtige Personen und Dinge befinden sich meist im Vordergrund.

I want to talk about this photo / poster / ...
It shows a group of people in the street.

In the foreground / On the right I can see a boy with bagpipes.
In the middle I can see happy people. On the left there is a man.

Beschreibe die Personen genauer, z. B. die Kleidung oder das Alter: *The piper is young. He is wearing a green top.*

Wer macht was?
The boy is playing the bagpipes. The people are dancing.
One man is clapping his hands.

Wenn du die Position von Dingen oder Menschen näher beschreiben willst, kannst du auch folgende Präpositionen verwenden:

behind • between • in front of • next to • over • under

The people are standing next to each other.

Am Ende deiner Beschreibung kannst du noch sagen, was du von der Abbildung hältst und warum:
I like / don't like this picture because ...

Denke daran: Benutze immer das *present progressive*, wenn du beschreibst, was jemand in einem Bild macht. Andere Dinge im Bild kannst du mit *"You can see ..."* oder *"There is / are ..."* beschreiben.

Merkaufgabe 11

Suche dir ein Bild in Unit 1 und beschreibe es.
Welcher Satz wäre z. B. richtig für Bild E auf S. 32?

a) *The person is playing the guitar.*
b) *The person plays the guitar.*

(Die Lösung findest du auf Seite 138.)

SF 12

Texte markieren und Notizen erstellen

▶ Unit 1 | p. 30 ▶ Unit 2 | p. 61
▶ Unit 3 | p. 83 ▶ Unit 4 | p. 119

Oft ist es hilfreich, wenn du Wesentliches in Texten hervorhebst und dir Notizen machst, z. B. wenn du einen Kurzvortrag vorbereitest oder wenn du den Inhalt eines Textes zusammenfassen oder nacherzählen möchtest.

Textstellen markieren

Auf Kopien von Texten kannst du Informationen markieren, um sie hervorzuheben und einfacher wiederzufinden. Konzentriere dich dabei auf die Informationen, die du laut Aufgabe aus dem Text heraussuchen sollst, wie z. B. die fünf *wh*-Fragen. Markiere nur die wichtigsten Informationen. Oft reichen ein oder zwei Wörter in einem Satz. Zusätzlich kannst du dir zu dem Text auch Notizen machen.

Checkliste Text markieren
Du kannst die wichtigen Stellen
- ✓ mit Textmarker markieren
- ✓ unterstreichen
- ✓ umkreisen
- ✓ mit Symbolen und Abkürzungen markieren (?, !, →, ☺, ☹)
- ✓ durch Notizen am Rand hervorheben

Wie erstelle ich Notizen?

- Verwende für deine Notizen kleine Zettel oder Karteikarten.
- Du kannst deine Notizen z. B. in einer Tabelle sammeln, in der du *wh*-Fragewörter *(what, where, when, who, why, how)* als Überschriften verwendest. Eine solche Tabelle ist gut, wenn du Fragen zu einem (Hör-)Text beantwortest, weil sie sehr strukturiert ist.

Who?	What?	When?	...
...	...	...	...

- Ein Notizzettel ist gut, wenn du möglichst frei sprechen möchtest, z. B. bei einem kleinen Vortrag. Schreibe deine Notizen gleich in der Reihenfolge auf, in der du deine Gedanken vortragen möchtest. Strukturiere deine Notizen optisch, z. B. durch Überschriften und Absätze.

My London sight
· what it is and where it is
· what to see and what to do
· history, stories and fun facts
· when it's open and how much it costs

- Schreibe keine ganzen Sätze, sondern das, was für dich wichtig ist, in Stichpunkten auf *(keywords)*.
  - Schreibe Ziffern anstelle von Zahlwörtern, z. B. „15“ statt „fifteen“, und verwende Abkürzungen, z. B. „Aug“ statt „August“, „+“ statt „and“, „/“ statt „or“.
  - Verwende Symbole und Zeichnungen anstelle von Stichwörtern, z. B. Smileys für Gefühle, Flaggen für Länder, Strichzeichnungen für Personen usw.

Es gibt auch Apps, mit denen du deine Notizen anfertigen kannst, wenn es deine Eltern erlauben. Das bietet sich vor allem dann an, wenn du über einen längeren Zeitraum Notizen machst, die du bearbeiten und ergänzen möchtest, wie z. B. bei einem kleinen Projekt. Du kannst deine Notizen zu Hause am Computer anfangen und später auf dem Handy ergänzen.

Merkaufgabe 12

Probiere es gleich aus. Suche dir ein Wunschurlaubsziel für den nächsten Sommer und mache dir Notizen dazu.

SF 13

Texte überprüfen und verbessern

▶ Unit 1 | p. 31 ▶ Unit 3 | p. 89
▶ Unit 4 | p. 113

Ein Text ist noch nicht fertig, wenn du ihn zu Ende geschrieben hast. Du solltest ihn noch mehrmals durchlesen bzw. in Partnerkorrektur durchlesen lassen und auf folgende Punkte achten:

Überprüfe und korrigiere deinen Text

Mache nach dem Schreiben eine kurze Pause. Dann fange an, den Text inhaltlich und sprachlich zu verbessern. Prüfe:

- Hast du irgendwo ein Wort vergessen?
- Sind die Sätze gut verständlich?
- Ist die Reihenfolge der Sätze sinnvoll?
- Hast du Absätze gemacht?
- Hast du *linking words* (Bindewörter) benutzt?
- Hast du Personen, Orte oder Dinge mithilfe von Adjektiven beschrieben?

Beim Korrekturlesen empfehlen sich mehrere Durchgänge, in denen du nacheinander auf folgende Dinge achtest:

- Sprache: Stimmen Rechtschreibung, Zeichensetzung, Grammatik?
- Aufbau und Lesbarkeit: Hat dein Text eine logische Struktur, ist er verständlich und liest sich flüssig?
- Ausdruck: Verwendest du eine abwechslungsreiche und lebendige Sprache und vermeidest Wiederholungen?
- Gestaltung: Benötigst du eine Überschrift? Hast du Abschnitte eingefügt? Hast du bei einem Brief oder einer E-Mail an Anrede und Schluss gedacht?
- typische Fehlerquellen wie ...
  - Groß- und Kleinschreibung, denn im Englischen schreibt man fast alles klein.
  - die richtige Zeitform: Schreibst du über die Gegenwart? Oder über Dinge, die du regelmäßig machst? Dann brauchst du das *simple present (I often go to the swimming pool.)*. Oder schreibst du über Sachen, die schon passiert sind? Dann brauchst du das *simple past (Yesterday I went to the swimming pool.)*.

Checkliste typische Fehlerquellen

- ✓ Groß- und Kleinschreibung
- ✓ unregelmäßige Pluralformen *(child – children, man – men)*
- ✓ gleicher Klang, aber unterschiedliche Schreibweisen und Bedeutungen *(to – too – two, their – there – they're)*
- ✓ Präpositionen *(by train, in the picture, on the bus)*
- ✓ unregelmäßige Verben (siehe die Liste auf S. 238–239)
- ✓ Wörter mit stummen Buchstaben *(climb, know)*

▶ Wichtige Schreibregeln im Englischen, p. 167

Merkaufgabe 13

Probiere es gleich aus. Nimm dir einen englischen Text, den du in letzter Zeit geschrieben hast. Lies ihn dir zweimal durch und überprüfe ihn anhand der obigen Schritte.

Inhalt

Erklär-film Dieses Symbol zeigt dir, dass du einen Erklärfilm zu diesem Thema in der App findest.

LF 1 Revision

Die Wortstellung *(Word order)*

a) Aussagesätze *(Statements)*

Subject	Verb	Object
We	love	summer evenings.

In einfachen Aussagesätzen ist die Wortstellung **S(ubject)** - **V(erb)** - **O(bject)**.

b) Orts- und Zeitangaben *(Phrases of place and time)*

Time		Place or time
	Put the books	on the table.
	I'm very busy	today.
Yesterday	I was bored.	
Last year	we got married.	

	Place	Time
Orla came	here	on Friday.
My dad moved	to Dresden	in 2020.

Ortsangaben (*on the table, at school* usw.) stehen meist am Ende des Satzes (häufig nach Verb und Objekt).
Zeitangaben (*today, yesterday, at 2 o'clock* usw.) stehen ganz am Anfang oder ganz am Ende des Satzes.

Beim Zusammentreffen von Orts- und Zeitangaben in einem Satz gilt im Englischen die Regel: **O**rt vor **Z**eit.

LF 1 Revision

c) Häufigkeitsadverbien *(Adverbs of frequency)*

	Frequency	
Pearl	always	goes out at weekends.
I	sometimes	feel unhappy.

Häufigkeitsadverbien (*always, often, sometimes, rarely, never* usw.) stehen im Englischen meist direkt vor dem Hauptverb (*go, feel* usw.).

LF 2 Revision

Erklärfilm

Die einfache Gegenwart *(The simple present)*

I always get up at 7 o'clock.
Ich stehe immer um 7 Uhr auf.
My sister doesn't usually go to parties.
Meine Schwester geht normalerweise nicht auf Partys.
We all love Indian food.
Wir alle lieben indisches Essen.
Where do you live?
Wo wohnen Sie?

Mit dem *simple present* sagst du, was oft, regelmäßig, jeden Tag oder auch selten oder nie geschieht oder was immer so ist (Dauerzustände).

Oft findest du diese Signalwörter in Sätzen im *simple present*: *always, never, often, rarely, sometimes, usually*.

a) Bejahte Aussagesätze *(Positive statements)*

I You We They	start.
He She It	starts.

He, she, it – ein -s muss mit!

Ebenso:

Your dad Lily The show	starts.

Bei *I, you, we* und *they* hat das Verb im *simple present* dieselbe Form wie der Infinitiv (die Grundform) des Verbs.

Aber bei der 3. Person Singular (*he, she, it* oder *your dad, Lily* usw.) musst du immer ein *-s* ans Verb anhängen.

! Manchmal gibt es Besonderheiten, z. B.:

do → does	*tidy → tidies*
go → goes	*wash → washes*
have → has	*watch → watches*

LF 2 Revision

Erklärfilm

b) Verneinte Aussagesätze *(Negative statements)*

I / You / We / They	don't start.
He / She / It	doesn't start.
We	don't do the shopping online.
Steve	doesn't do sports.

Aussagen im *simple present* musst du mit *don't* oder *doesn't* verneinen. Das Verb steht dann immer im Infinitiv (der Grundform): *He doesn't start.*

! Auch das Vollverb *do* („machen", „tun", „ausführen") verneint man im *simple present* mit *don't / doesn't*.

c) Entscheidungsfragen und Kurzantworten *(Yes/No-questions and short answers)*

Do	I you we they / your parents	like music?
Does	he / your dad she / Lily it	like music?

Bejahte Antwort	Verneinte Antwort
Yes, I do.	No, I don't.
Yes, you do.	No, you don't.
Yes, he / she / it does.	No, he / she / it doesn't.
Yes, we do.	No, we don't.
Yes, they do.	No, they don't.

Fragen, auf die man mit „Ja" oder „Nein" antworten kann, heißen Entscheidungsfragen. Sie beginnen mit *Do* oder *Does*.
Mit *I, you, we, they* verwendest du *Do*.
Mit *he, she, it* verwendest du *Does*.

Es ist unhöflich, auf Entscheidungsfragen nur mit *yes* oder *no* zu antworten. Besser ist eine Kurzantwort.

LF 2 Revision

Erklär-film

d) Fragen mit Fragewörtern *(Questions with question words)*

Where do the pets sleep?
Wo schlafen die Tiere?
Who does Luca love?
Wen liebt Luca?
What do you think?
Was meinst du?

Who loves Luca?
Wer liebt Luca?
What makes you sad?
Was macht dich traurig?

Auch Fragen mit Fragewörtern stellst du mit *do* oder *does*. Das Fragewort steht wie im Deutschen am Anfang.

! Wenn mit *Who* oder *What* nach dem Subjekt des Satzes gefragt wird, bildest du die Frage ohne *does / do*.

LF 3 Revision

Erklär-film

Die Verlaufsform der Gegenwart *(The present progressive)*

I'm reading a comic.
Ich lese gerade einen Comic.
Dad is cooking dinner.
Papa macht gerade das Abendessen.
What are you doing at the moment?
Was machst du jetzt gerade?
I'm working.
Ich bin gerade am Arbeiten. /
Ich arbeite gerade.

Mit dem *present progressive* sagst du, was jemand jetzt gerade tut. Damit beschreibst du auch, was auf Bildern passiert.

Folgende Zeitangaben findest du oft in Sätzen im *present progressive*:
now, at the moment, today.

Im Deutschen sagst du meist „Ich bin gerade am / beim ...“ oder „Ich ... gerade.“.

a) Bejahte und verneinte Aussagesätze *(Positive and negative statements)*

Bejahte Aussagesätze	
I'm You're He's / She's / It's We're They're	working.

Verneinte Aussagesätze	
I'm not You aren't He / She / It isn't We aren't They aren't	working.

Das *present progressive* besteht aus zwei Teilen: Form von *be* + *ing*-Form des Verbs.

am ('m) *are ('re)* *is ('s)* Verneinung: *am not ('m not)* *are not (aren't)* *is not (isn't)*	+ *ing*-Form des Verbs

! Bei Verben, die auf *-e* enden, fällt das *-e* bei der *ing*-Form weg:
have → *having*; *make* → *making*;
give → *giving*

! Bei einigen Verben wird der letzte Buchstabe verdoppelt, z. B.:
plan → *planning*; *stop* → *stopping*;
sit → *sitting*

b) Fragen und Antworten *(Questions and answers)*

Am I Are you	working?	No, you aren't. Yes, I am.
Where is he	going?	Home.
What are they	doing?	They're working.

In Fragen vertauscht man das Subjekt und *am / are / is*:
I am → *am I?*

LF 4 Revision

Erklär-film

Die einfache Vergangenheit *(The simple past)*

Yesterday Dad and I visited Grandma.
Gestern besuchten Papa und ich Oma.
Last week I didn't have any homework.
Letzte Woche hatte ich keine Hausaufgaben auf.
Did you watch the fireworks last night?
Hast du gestern Abend das Feuerwerk gesehen?

Mit dem *simple past* sprichst du über Dinge, die in der Vergangenheit geschehen sind.

Du verwendest es oft mit Zeitangaben wie *yesterday, last week / last year / last summer, two weeks ago, in 2022.*

a) Bejahte Aussagesätze *(Positive statements)*

I / You He / She / It We / They	helped.

Die Vergangenheitsform der Verben ist für alle Personen gleich:

- Bei regelmäßigen Verben hängst du *-ed* an das Verb: *walk* → *walked*.
- Bei Verben, die auf *-e* enden, wird nur *-d* angehängt: *arrive* → *arrived*.
- Einige Konsonanten werden verdoppelt: *plan* → *planned; stop* → *stopped*.

! Unregelmäßige Formen musst du lernen: *go* → *went; have* → *had; see* → *saw*.
Du kannst sie auf S. 238–239 nachschlagen.

b) Verneinte Aussagesätze *(Negative statements)*

I / You He / She / It We / They	didn't help.

Wenn du sagen willst, dass etwas nicht geschah, setzt du *didn't* vor das Verb. Das Verb steht dann immer im Infinitiv (der Grundform), z. B. *help*, nicht: *helped*.

c) Entscheidungsfragen und Kurzantworten *(Yes/No-questions and short answers)*

Did	I / you he / she / it we / they	help?	Yes, I did. Yes, she did. No, they didn't.

Entscheidungsfragen im *simple past* bildest du mit *Did* und dem Infinitiv (der Grundform) des Verbs, z. B. *help*, nicht *helped*.
Auch in Kurzantworten verwendest du *did* oder *didn't* (ohne folgenden Infinitiv).

LF 4 Revision

Erklär-film

d) Fragen mit Fragewörtern *(Questions with question words)*

What	did	she	watch?
When	did	it	finish?
Where	did	they	go?

Who said that?
Wer hat das gesagt?
What made you unhappy?
Was hat dich unglücklich gemacht?

Auch bei Fragen mit Fragewörtern verwendest du *did* und das Verb im Infinitiv, z. B. *watch*, *go* (nicht *watched*, *went*).

! Wenn mit *Who* oder *What* nach dem Subjekt des Satzes gefragt wird, bildest du die Frage ohne *did*.

LF 5 Revision

Erklär-film

Die Zukunft mit *will* *(The will-future)*

I think you'll have a great party.
Ich glaube, du wirst eine tolle Party haben.
Wait – I'll help you.
Warte – ich helfe dir.

Du verwendest das *will-future*
- für Dinge, die in der Zukunft vermutlich geschehen werden. Die Sätze beginnen oft mit *I think*, *maybe*, *I'm sure*.
- für spontane Entscheidungen.

a) Bejahte und verneinte Aussagesätze *(Positive and negative statements)*

Bejahte Aussagesätze		
It	will 'll	be sunny tomorrow.

Verneinte Aussagesätze		
It	will not won't	be sunny tomorrow.

Du bildest das *will-future* mit will und dem Infinitiv (der Grundform) des Verbs.
Nach Pronomen *(I, we, you, they, he, she, it)* kannst du die Kurzform verwenden:
Die Kurzform von *will* ist *'ll*.
Die Kurzform von *will not* ist won't.

I'll tidy my room later.

b) Fragen und Antworten *(Questions and answers)*

Will it be sunny?	Yes, it will. No, it won't.
What will the world be like in 100 years?	It will be a very different place.

In Fragen vertauscht man das Subjekt und *will*:
it will → *will it?*

LF 6

Erklärfilm

Bedingungssätze Typ I *(Conditional sentences type 1)*

▶ Unit 1 | p. 19

If you send me a message, I'll come.
Wenn du mir eine Nachricht schickst, komme ich.
If it rains tomorrow, we won't play football.
Wenn es morgen regnet, spielen wir nicht Fußball.

We won't play football if it rains tomorrow.
Wir spielen nicht Fußball, wenn es morgen regnet.

Mit Bedingungssätzen sagst du, was unter bestimmten Bedingungen geschehen wird.
Sie bestehen aus zwei Teilen:
- einem Nebensatz mit *if (if-clause)* im *simple present*, der die Voraussetzung nennt,
- einem Hauptsatz *(main clause)* mit *will*, *'ll* oder *won't*, der die Folge nennt.

Der *if*-Teil kann auch nach dem Hauptsatz stehen.

LF 7 Revision

Erklärfilm

Die Steigerung der Adjektive *(Comparison of adjectives)*

a) Steigerung mit *-er / -est (Comparison with -er / -est)*

Ella is taller than Pete.
Ella ist größer als Pete.
The airport is busier during the holidays.
Der Flughafen ist in den Ferien stärker ausgelastet.

Adjektive kann man steigern und in Vergleichen benutzen.
Bei einsilbigen Adjektiven und bei zweisilbigen Adjektiven, die auf *-y* enden, hängst du *-er / -est* an das Adjektiv:
- *tall* → *taller* (Komparativ = erste Steigerungsform)
- *tall* → *(the) tallest* (Superlativ = Höchstform)

The biggest tree in the park is 90 years old.
Der größte Baum im Park ist 90 Jahre alt.
The earliest train leaves at 7 a.m.
Der früheste Zug fährt um 7 Uhr morgens.

! Bei einigen Adjektiven musst du bei der Schreibung aufpassen (z. B. bei *big* → *bigger / biggest; hot* → *hotter / hottest* oder *busy* → *busier / busiest; early* → *earlier / earliest*).

The weather today is better than yesterday.
Das Wetter ist heute besser als gestern.
The worst part of the film was the ending.
Der schlimmste Teil des Films war das Ende.

! Beachte diese Ausnahmen:
good → *better* → *(the) best*
bad → *worse* → *(the) worst*

LF 7 Revision

b) Steigerung mit *more / most (Comparison with more / most)*

Thea's job is more interesting than Leo's.
Theas Job ist interessanter als der von Leo.
The most expensive house in the world is Buckingham Palace.
Das teuerste Haus der Welt ist der Buckingham Palace.

Bei längeren (vor allem dreisilbigen) Adjektiven setzt man *more / most* vor das Adjektiv:

- *expensive → more expensive* (Komparativ = erste Steigerungsform)
- *interesting → most interesting* (Superlativ = Höchstform)

LF 8

Erklär-film

Die Zukunft mit *going to* (*The* going to-*future*)

► Unit 2 | p. 49

We're going to have a picnic on Sunday.
Wir haben vor, am Sonntag zu picknicken.
Are you going to come to the party?
Wirst du zur Party kommen?

Mit *going to* ... sagst du, was du vorhast oder planst.

Going to hat hier nichts mit dem deutschen „gehen" zu tun, sondern bedeutet „werden" oder „wollen".

a) Bejahte und verneinte Aussagesätze *(Positive and negative statements)*

Bejahte Aussagesätze		
I'm		
You're		
He's / She's / It's	going to	ask.
We're		
They're		

Verneinte Aussagesätze		
I'm not		
You aren't		
He / She / It isn't	going to	ask.
We aren't		
They aren't		

Das *going to-future* besteht aus drei Teilen: Form von *be* + *going to* + Verb.

am ('m) *are ('re)* *is ('s)* Verneinung: *am not ('m not)* *are not (aren't)* *is not (isn't)*	+ *going to*	+ Verb

Das Verb bleibt immer im Infinitiv:
I'm going to watch a video.

! Nicht: *I'm going to ~~watching~~ a video.*

LF 8

b) Fragen und Antworten *(Questions and answers)*

Are you	going to	ask?	No, I'm not.
Where is he	going to	live?	In York.

In Fragen vertauscht man das Subjekt und *am / are / is*:
you are going to → are you going to?

LF 9

Reflexivpronomen *(Reflexive pronouns)*

▶ Unit 2 | p. 52

He has cut himself.
Er hat sich geschnitten.
We can look after ourselves.
Wir können uns um uns selbst kümmern.

I wash myself.	We wash ourselves.
You wash yourself.	You wash yourselves.
He washes himself.	They wash themselves.
She washes herself.	
It washes itself.	

Reflexivpronomen enden auf *-self* oder *-selves*. Du sagst damit, dass jemand etwas selbst tut. Vergleiche:

He washed the baby.	Er wusch das Baby.
He washed himself.	Er wusch sich selbst.

Merke dir diese Ausdrücke:

Help yourself.	Greif zu. / Bediene dich.
Enjoy yourself!	Viel Spaß!

LF 10

Erklär-film

Adverbien der Art und Weise *(Adverbs of manner)*

▶ Unit 3 | p. 76

Please speak slowly and clearly.
Bitte sprich langsam und deutlich.
Sarah ate her breakfast quickly.
Sarah aß ihr Frühstück schnell auf.

Adjektiv	Adverb	Adjektiv	Adverb
clear	clearly	angry	angrily
nervous	nervously	happy	happily
quick	quickly	full	fully

You speak English very well.
Du sprichst sehr gut Englisch.
Rhona worked hard.
Rhona hat hart gearbeitet.
Grace can run fast.
Grace kann schnell laufen.

Adverbien der Art und Weise beschreiben, wie man etwas tut oder wie etwas geschieht. Sie beschreiben also ein Verb. Vergleiche:

Adjektiv		Adverb
a careful driver	→	*she drives carefully*
a slow worker	→	*he works slowly*

Die meisten Adverbien bildet man, indem man die Endung *-ly* an das Adjektiv anhängt.

! Manchmal gibt es Unregelmäßigkeiten bei der Schreibung (z. B. *angrily* oder *fully*).

! Beachte diese Ausnahmen:
- Das Adverb zu *good* ist *well*.
- Bei *hard* und *fast* sind Adjektiv und Adverb gleich.

LF 11

Erklär-
film

Das *present perfect* (*The present perfect*)

▶ Unit 3 | p. 79

I have just finished my homework.
Ich habe gerade meine Hausaufgaben beendet.
I have never eaten sushi.
Ich habe noch nie Sushi gegessen.
Has Leo ever been to Rome?
Ist Leo schon mal in Rom gewesen? / War Leo schon mal in Rom?

Mit dem *present perfect* sagst du, dass jemand etwas – irgendwann – in der Zeit bis jetzt gemacht oder nicht gemacht hat. Der genaue Zeitpunkt ist unwichtig oder unbekannt und wird nicht genannt.

Oft hat die Handlung Folgen in der Gegenwart.

Signalwörter: *already, just, ever, never, not yet, once, twice, lots of times*

a) Bejahte und verneinte Aussagesätze (*Positive and negative statements*)

▶ Unit 3 | p. 79

Bejahte Aussagesätze	
I You We They	have started early. 've started early.
He / She / It	has started early. 's started early.

Verneinte Aussagesätze	
I You We They	haven't started early.
He / She / It	hasn't started early.

Das *present perfect* besteht aus zwei Teilen: *have / has* + dritte Form des Verbs (*past participle*).

have ('ve) *has ('s)* Verneinung: *have not (haven't)* *has not (hasn't)*	+ *past participle*

Wie bildest du das *past participle*?

- Bei regelmäßigen Verben hängst du *-ed* an das Verb: *walk* → *walked*.
- Bei Verben, die auf *-e* enden, wird nur *-d* angehängt: *arrive* → *arrived*.

! Unregelmäßige *past participle*-Formen musst du lernen, z. B.:

be → *been* *do* → *done* *eat* → *eaten*
go → *gone* *have* → *had* *see* → *seen*

Du kannst sie in der dritten Spalte der *List of irregular verbs* auf S. 238–239 nachschlagen.

LF 11

b) Fragen und Antworten *(Questions and answers)*

▶ Unit 3 | p. 81

Has it started yet?	Yes, it has. / No, it hasn't.
Where has he been?	At school.

In Fragen vertauscht man das Subjekt und *have / has*:
it has → has it?

LF 12

Possessivbegleiter und Possessivpronomen
(Possessive determiners and possessive pronouns)

▶ Unit 4 | p. 104

This is my phone. It's mine.
Das ist mein Handy. Es ist meins. / Es gehört mir.
I think it's her bike. It's hers.
Ich glaube, es ist ihr Fahrrad. Es ist ihrs.
I've found this book. Is it yours?
Ich habe dieses Buch gefunden. Ist es deins?

mit Nomen	ohne Nomen
my game	mine
your game	yours
his / her / its game	his / hers / its
our game	ours
your game	yours
their game	theirs

The dog has eaten its food.
But it's (= it is) still hungy.

Possessivbegleiter und Possessivpronomen zeigen an, wem etwas gehört.

Die Possessivbegleiter *my*, *your*, *his*, *her*, *its*, *our*, *their* werden vor einem Nomen (z. B. *game*) gebraucht.

Die Possessivpronomen *mine*, *yours*, *his*, *hers*, *its*, *ours*, *yours*, *theirs* stehen allein, ohne Nomen.

LF 13

Erklär-
film

Relativsätze *(Relative clauses)*

▸ Unit 4 | p. 112

Are you the boy who won the first prize?
Bist du der Junge, der den ersten Preis gewonnen hat?
This is the girl who we met yesterday.
Das ist das Mädchen, das wir gestern getroffen haben.
This is Polly, the parrot who can speak over 100 words.
Das ist Polly, der Papagei, der über 100 Wörter sprechen kann.

This is the girl that I told you about.
Das ist das Mädchen, von dem ich dir erzählt habe.
The phone that she uses is new.
Das Handy, das sie benutzt, ist neu.

I know a shop which sells really cool shoes.
Ich kenne einen Laden, der richtig coole Schuhe verkauft.
The game which you gave me is great.
Das Spiel, das du mir geschenkt hast, ist toll.

Mit Relativsätzen kannst du zusätzliche Informationen über eine Person oder eine Sache geben. Relativsätze werden in der Regel durch die Relativpronomen *who*, *that* oder *which* eingeleitet:

- Für Personen (und Haustiere mit Namen) verwendest du *who* oder *that*.
- Für Dinge (und Tiere ohne Namen) verwendest du *that* oder *which*.

Das Relativpronomen *that* kannst du also immer verwenden.

Die meisten englischen Relativsätze werden **nicht** durch **ein Komma** vor *who, which, that* abgetrennt, anders als im Deutschen. Man nennt sie ***defining relative clauses*** (bestimmende Relativsätze).

Grammatical terms *(Grammatische Fachbegriffe in diesem Buch)*

adjective	Adjektiv	*old, good, popular*
adverb of frequency	Häufigkeitsadverb	*often, always, sometimes, rarely, never*
adverb of manner	Adverb der Art und Weise	*well, carefully, quietly, angrily*
article	Artikel	***a / the** book, **an / the** apple*
comparative	Komparativ	*older, better, more popular*
comparison	Steigerung	*old – older – (the) oldest*
conditional sentence	Bedingungssatz	*If it's rainy, I'll stay at home.*
contact clause	Relativsatz ohne Relativpronomen	*a boy I know; things we eat*
going to-future	Futur mit *going to*	*I'm going to eat ...; We're going to watch ...*
if-clause	Nebensatz mit *if*	*If it rains, ...*
infinitive	Infinitiv (Grundform)	*(to) do, (to) go, (to) love*
irregular adjective / adverb / verb	unregelmäßiges Adjektiv / Adverb / Verb	adjective: *bad – **worse** – **worst**;* adverb: *good – **well**;* verb: *(to) do – **did** – **done***
long form	Langform	*I am, we do not, you are*
main clause	Hauptsatz	*If it rains, **I won't go out**.*
modal verb	modales Hilfsverb	*can, must, shouldn't*
negative	verneinte Form	***don't** go, **can't** go, **aren't** going, **hasn't** gone*
noun	Nomen / Substantiv	*friend, car, competition*
object	Objekt	*I like **cats**.*
past participle	Partizip Perfekt (3. Form)	*loved, eaten, seen, done, gone*
personal pronoun	Personalpronomen	*I, you, he, she, it, we, they*
plural	Plural, Mehrzahl	*book**s**, child**ren**, potato**es**, stor**ies***
possessive determiner	Possessivbegleiter	*my, your, his, her, its, our, their*
possessive pronoun	Possessivpronomen	*mine, yours, his, hers, its, ours, theirs*
preposition	Präposition	***in** the house, **on** the desk, **near** the river*
present perfect	Perfekt	*He has gone.; Have you seen?*
present progressive	Verlaufsform der Gegenwart	*I**'m** speak**ing**, she**'s** look**ing**, we**'re** talk**ing**, they **aren't** listen**ing***
reflexive pronoun	Reflexivpronomen	*myself, yourself, ourselves*
regular verb	regelmäßiges Verb	*(to) move – moved – moved*
relative clause	Relativsatz	*someone **who loves**, a shop **which sells***
relative pronoun	Relativpronomen	*who, which, that*
short answer	Kurzantwort	*Yes, I do. / No, I'm not. / Yes, she does.*
short form	Kurzform	*I**'m**, we **don't**, you**'re***
simple past	einfache Vergangenheit	*it was; I went; he talked*
simple present	einfache Gegenwart	*it is; I go; he talks*
singular	Singular, Einzahl	*book, child, potato, story*
state verb	Zustandsverb	*(to) be, (to) become, (to) feel, (to) look, (to) seem, (to) smell, (to) sound, (to) taste*
statement	Aussage(satz)	*I like oranges. I don't like bananas.*

subject	Subjekt	***They*** *eat dinner.;* ***The cat*** *is cute.*
substitute	Ersatzform	*He* ***was able to*** *run.* ***Will*** *you* ***be allowed to*** *…?*
superlative	Superlativ	*(the) oldest, (the) best, (the) most popular*
tense	Zeitform	*present progressive, simple past, future*
verb	Verb	*(to) go, (to) do, (to) have, (to) think, (to) love*
wh-question	Frage mit Fragewort	*What's this? Who are you?*
will-future	Futur mit *will*	*Noah* ***will*** *phone, you'****ll*** *see, he* ***won't*** *buy*
word order	Wortstellung	*subject – verb – object: We know them.*
yes/no-question	Entscheidungsfrage	*Are you OK?; Will she go?; Did it go well?*

Wichtige Schreibregeln im Englischen

Groß- und Kleinschreibung

Im Englischen wird fast alles kleingeschrieben. Merke dir nur diese Ausnahmen:

- das Wort *I* (ich)
- Monatsnamen *(January, February, …)*
- Wochentage *(Monday, Tuesday, …)*
- Eigennamen und geografische Namen *(Tom, Lisa, Brighton, …)*
- Länder, deren Bewohner und Bewohnerinnen, Sprachen und Nationalitäten *(Germany, the Germans, German)*
- das erste Wort am Satzanfang und in Überschriften

Stumme Buchstaben

Manche Wörter enthalten Buchstaben, die du zwar schreibst, aber nicht sprichst:

b *lamb*
c *science*
d *sandwich*
g *design*
h *technology*
i *fruit*
k *(to) know, knife*
l *(to) walk, (to) talk*
u *guitar, building*
t *(to) listen*
w *(to) answer, wrong*

Verdoppelung der Endkonsonanten

(to) stop – stopping, stopped
(to) win – winning, winner

-y wird zu *-ie*

- im Plural: *a pony – three ponies*
- in der 3. Person Singular: *(to) tidy – he tidies*
- bei der Steigerung von Adjektiven: *busy – busier – busiest, easy – easier – easiest*

Buchstabenverbindungen

Merke dir häufige Buchstabenverbindungen bei der Schreibung englischer Wörter:

-ee- *(to) see, deep, (to) meet, street*
-ea- *beach, meat, pea*
-igh- *sight, fight, right, night*
-oo- *book, good, look*
-ous- *dangerous, nervous, famously*
-tion *station, competition*

Kleine Unterschiede Deutsch–Englisch

Achte auf diese kleinen Unterschiede bei der Schreibung englischer Wörter

- k wird zu c: Musik – *music*
- f wird zu ph: Foto – *photo*
- isch wird zu ic: elektrisch – *electric*
- el wird zu le: Titel – *title*, Artikel – *article*
- sch wird zu sh: britisch – *British*
- deutsches -e am Wortende entfällt: Lampe – *lamp*, Ende – *end*

Wordbank 1: On the street

▶ Unit 1 | p. 21

Excuse me, how do I get to ...? /
Sorry, I'm lost. Could you tell me the way to ...?

Directions

Go straight on.

Turn left.

Turn right.

Take the first / second / third street on the left / right.

Go across the road.

Go along the river.

Go down the steps.

Go over the bridge.

Go past the cinema.

Go to the end of the street.

Go through the park.

Go up the hill.

Places

block of flats

car park

office building

petrol station

roundabout

skyscraper

traffic lights

zebra crossing

Wordbank 2: Giving opinions

▸ Unit 1 | p. 25

Words for 'good'

- amazing
- awesome
- brilliant
- cool
- excellent
- fantastic
- fine
- great
- perfect
- wonderful

Words for 'bad'

- awful
- horrible
- lousy
- nasty
- not my thing
- poor
- rubbish
- shocking
- terrible
- useless

Wordbank 3: Describing clothes and accessories

▸ Unit 2 | p. 46, 47

Materials *(Materialien)*

canvas *(Segeltuch)*

cotton *(Baumwolle)*

leather *(Leder)*

metal *(Metall)*

polyester *(Polyester)*

rubber *(Gummi)*

silk *(Seide)*

wool *(Wolle)*

Colours and patterns *(Farben und Muster)*

checked *(kariert)*

colourful *(farbenfroh)*

dark / light *(dunkel / hell)*

flowery *(geblümt)*

patterned *(gemustert)*

plain *(einfarbig)*

dotted *(gepunktet)*

striped *(gestreift)*

fit ***(Passform)***: baggy, tight

style: cool, casual, trendy, unusual, designer, sporty, vintage, smart

(to) buy clothes: shop, shopping centre, online

"green": second-hand, eco-friendly, recycled, flea-market

Wordbank 4: Feelings

▶ Unit 2 | p. 54

all right / OK	*in Ordnung*
amazing	*fantastisch, erstaunlich*
brave	*mutig*
calm	*ruhig, gelassen*
cheerful	*fröhlich*
confident	*selbstbewusst, sicher*
content	*zufrieden*
creative	*kreativ*
energetic	*energiegeladen, aktiv*
excellent	*hervorragend*
excited	*aufgeregt, gespannt*
fantastic	*fantastisch*
fine	*gut, prima*
great	*großartig*
happy	*froh, glücklich*
motivated	*motiviert*
proud	*stolz*
relaxed	*entspannt*
strong	*stark*
surprised	*überrascht*
wonderful	*wunderbar*

angry	*wütend, zornig*
awful	*schrecklich*
bored	*gelangweilt*
disappointed	*enttäuscht*
embarrassed	*peinlich berührt, verlegen*
fed up	*genervt, sauer*
frustrated	*frustriert*
horrible	*schrecklich*
jealous	*eifersüchtig*
lonely	*einsam*
nasty	*scheußlich*
nervous	*nervös*
puzzled	*verwirrt, ratlos*
sad	*traurig*
scared	*verängstigt*
shocked	*schockiert*
stressed	*gestresst*
terrible	*furchtbar*
tired	*müde*
upset	*verärgert, bestürzt*
useless	*nutzlos*
worried	*besorgt*

Wordbank 5: Scary creatures

▸ Unit 3 | p. 76, 77

I know a scary story about a / an …

dragon, ghost, mermaid, merman, monster, vampire

demon

gargoyle

goblin

mummy

ogre

werewolf

witch

wizard

zombie

Wordbank 6: Sports

▸ Unit 3 | p. 81

I play ...
badminton, basketball, cricket, football, hockey, table tennis, tennis

handball

rugby

volleyball

I go ...
bowling, climbing, cycling, dancing, hiking, horse riding, paddleboarding, running, skateboarding, skiing, surfing, swimming, walking

canoeing

ice skating

rowing

I do ...
fitness, judo, trampolining, yoga

archery

athletics

boxing

scuba diving

gymnastics

karate

Wordbank 7: Nature

▶ Unit 3 | p. 82, 83

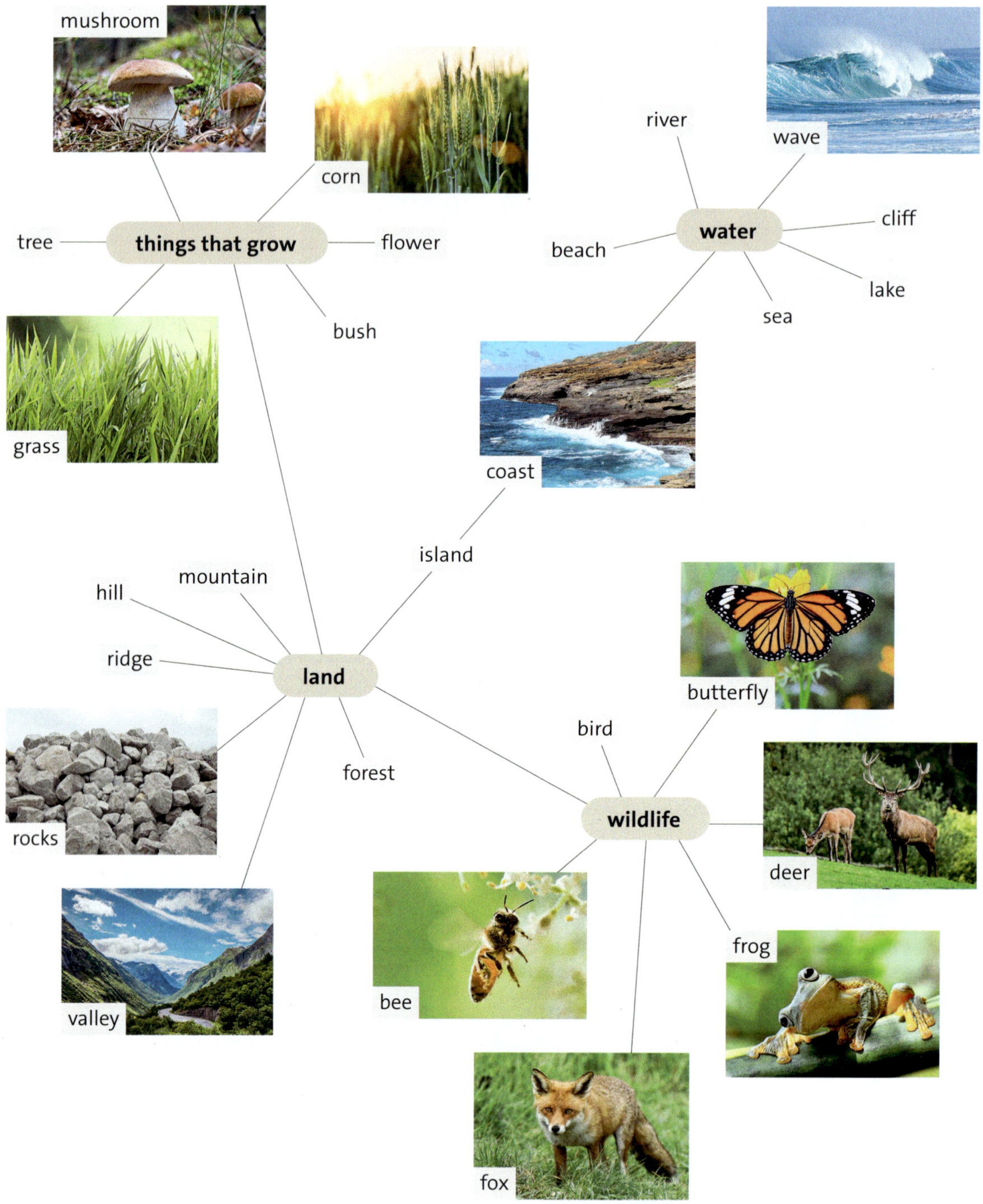

a beautiful / wild landscape	*eine schöne / wilde Landschaft*
a blue / cloudy sky	*ein blauer / bewölkter Himmel*
a narrow / wide river	*ein schmaler / breiter Fluss*
a high mountain	*ein hoher Berg*
a sandy / rocky beach	*ein Sandstrand / ein steiniger Strand*

Wordbank 8: Sights and places to visit

▸ Unit 4 | p. 103

In my area there is a/an …

art gallery, castle, escape room, library, museum, TV tower, theatre, zoo

harbour

national park

old town

palace

theme park

tower

town hall

town / village square

waterfall

Wordbank 9: Tech instructions

▶ Unit 4 | p. 108

Show the order of instructions
First ... / Second ... / Third ...
Then ... / Next ... / After that ...
Finally...

Get started
(to) switch on / off a device
(to) charge a device / a laptop / a tablet
(to) check the connection
(to) connect to Wi-Fi
(to) enter / put in a password
(to) log on

Prepare
(to) choose / download an app / software / a program
(to) install an app / software / a program
(to) pair with another device
(to) set up a device

Use a device
(to) click on a link (with a mouse)
(to) press a key (on a keyboard)
(to) scroll up / down a page
(to) swipe a screen
(to) tap an icon
(to) use a search engine

Files, texts and videos
(to) add captions / music / text effects
(to) copy / cut / paste text
(to) edit a text / video / vlog
(to) save data / a file
(to) upload a file / photos / a video

Hier findest du englische Sätze mit ihrer deutschen Übersetzung. Da jede Sprache anders funktioniert, ist eine wortwörtliche Übersetzung oft nicht möglich. Achte daher auf die kleinen Unterschiede.

1 Sich und andere vorstellen

Sich kennenlernen

	Hello, I'm ... / Hi! I'm ...	Hallo, ich bin ...
	Hi, my name is ... What's your name?	Hallo, ich heiße ... Wie heißt du?
	How old are you?	Wie alt bist du?
	I'm ... (years old). What about you?	Ich bin ... (Jahre alt). Und du?
	Nice to meet you. – Nice to meet you too.	Freut mich, dich / euch / Sie kennenzulernen. – Freut mich auch.
	I'm from (Manchester in England).	Ich komme aus (Manchester in England).
	I grew up in (Inverness in Scotland).	Ich bin in (Inverness in Schottland) aufgewachsen.

Über Interessen und Dinge sprechen, die einem wichtig sind

	What's your favourite book / film / ...?	Was ist dein Lieblingsbuch / -film / ...?
	What do you like to do in your free time?	Was machst du gerne in deiner Freizeit?
	What do(n't) you like / love?	Was magst / liebst du (nicht)?
	What kind of (music) do you like?	Welche Art von (Musik) magst du?
	I'm not really a fan of (history).	Ich bin nicht wirklich ein (Geschichts-)Fan.
	I think ... is the best (film) ever.	Ich finde, dass ... der beste (Film) überhaupt ist.
	I'm sorry, I think it's (boring).	Es tut mir leid, ich finde es / sie / ihn (langweilig).
Unit 2	My favourite sport / ... is ... because it's ...	Mein Lieblingsport / ... ist ..., weil es ...
	(My family) is really important to me because ...	(Meine Familie) ist mir sehr wichtig, weil ...
	What's important to you?	Was ist dir wichtig?
	Are / Is ... important to you?	Sind / Ist dir ... wichtig?
Unit 3	Do you like ... or do you like ... (better)?	Magst du ... oder magst du ... (lieber)?
	Which place / activity / ... looks the most interesting?	Welche(r) Ort / Aktivität / ... sieht am interessantesten aus?
	Have you ever (slept in a tent)?	Hast du schonmal (in einem Zelt geschlafen)?

Sich und andere beschreiben

	She has (brown) eyes and (blond) hair.	Sie hat (braune) Augen und (blondes) Haar.
	I have curly / straight hair.	Ich habe lockiges / glattes Haar.
	My mum is (tall) and my dad is (short).	Meine Mutter ist (groß) und mein Vater ist (klein).

2 Sich verabreden und etwas planen

	What are we doing this (weekend)?	Was machen wir am (Wochenende)?
	Are you doing anything (today)?	Machst du (heute) irgendetwas?
	What are you going to do on (Sunday) morning / afternoon / evening?	Was machst du am (Sonntag-)morgen / -nachmittag / -abend?
	(Saturday) would be best.	(Samstag) wäre am besten.
	Let's meet at (the station) / in (the park) at (7.30 p.m.).	Lass uns um (19.30 Uhr) am (Bahnhof) / im (Park) treffen.
	I'm sorry, I'm really busy.	Tut mir leid, ich bin sehr beschäftigt.
	Sorry, I can't. I'm going to ...	Tut mir leid, ich kann nicht. Ich werde ...
Unit 1	I can show you (the city) if you like.	Ich kann dir (die Stadt) zeigen, wenn du magst.
	What about (the London Eye)?	Wie wäre es mit (dem London Eye)?
	Let's go to ..	Lass uns zu ... gehen.
	Sure, what's there?	Klar, was gibt es dort (zu sehen)?
	See you on (Saturday).	Wir sehen uns am (Samstag).
Unit 4	Are you free later after dinner?	Hast du später nach dem Abendessen Zeit?

3 Leben in der Stadt

Öffentliche Verkehrsmittel nutzen

	How much does (a bus ticket) cost?	Wie viel kostet (eine Busfahrkarte)?
Unit 1	We have to / don't have to change lines.	Wir müssen / müssen nicht umsteigen.
	I have to buy a ticket.	Ich muss eine Fahrkarte kaufen.
	Let's take (the tube) to ...	Lass uns (die U-Bahn) nach / zu ... nehmen.
	We can take the bus / tram / ... from here.	Von hier können wir den Bus / die Straßenbahn / ... nehmen.
	How long does it take by taxi / bike / ...?	Wie lange dauert es mit dem Taxi / Fahrrad / ...?

Nach dem Weg fragen und Wege beschreiben

Unit 1	Go straight on / across / along / past / ...	Gehe geradeaus / über / entlang / an ... vorbei / ...
	Turn left / right.	Biege links / rechts ab.
	If you turn ..., you'll see a ...	Wenn du ... abbiegst, siehst du eine/n ...
	Take the first / second / ... road on the right / left.	Nimm die erste / zweite / ... Straße auf der rechten / linken Seite.
	Just follow (the river) that way until you come to ...	Folge (dem Fluss) in diese Richtung bis du bei / an ... ankommst.
	South / North / East / West from ...	Südlich / Nördlich / Östlich / Westlich von ...

Essen gehen und in einem Restaurant bestellen

	Are you hungry?	Hast du Hunger?
	I'm really hungry. / No, I'm not hungry.	Ich bin echt hungrig. / Nein, ich habe keinen Hunger.
	My favourite dish is (pizza).	Mein Lieblingsgericht ist (Pizza).
	Would you like some more (water)?	Möchtest du / Möchten Sie noch etwas mehr (Wasser)?
	Enjoy your meal!	Guten Appetit!
Unit 1	Everything looks wonderful.	Das sieht alles sehr lecker aus.
	Hi, are you ready to order?	Hi, mögt ihr / mögen Sie bestellen?
	What would you like to drink / eat?	Was möchtest du / mögen Sie essen / trinken?
	Could I have (some tea), please?	Könnte ich bitte (einen Tee) bekommen?
	I'd like (a cola), please.	Ich hätte gerne (eine Cola).
	I'll have (the falafel), please.	Ich bekomme (die Falafel), bitte.
	Can you tell me what ... is?	Können Sie mir sagen, was ... ist?
	Could we have some bread too, please?	Könnten wir bitte noch etwas Brot bekommen?

4 Über Umwelt, Natur(schutz) und Nachhaltigkeit sprechen

Unit 1	We live in a green city.	Wir leben in einer nachhaltigen Stadt.
	I think ... is very / not very green.	Ich finde ... sehr / nicht besonders nachhaltig.
	There's (not) a lot of ...	Es gibt (nicht) viele ...
Unit 2	Fast fashion is a big problem.	Fast Fashion ist ein großes Problem.
Unit 3	Is nature important to you?	Ist dir die Natur / die Umwelt wichtig?
	Nature is important because it gives us food / clean air / ...	Die Natur ist wichtig, weil sie uns Nahrung / frische Luft / ... gibt.
	I like to be in nature / go camping / watch birds / ...	Ich mag es, in der Natur zu sein / zu Campen / Vögel zu beobachten / ...
	I don't like to go outside because (there are lots of insects).	Ich gehe nicht gerne nach draußen / in die Natur, weil (es da viele Insekten gibt).

5 Miteinander reden

Über Probleme sprechen und Ratschläge erteilen

Unit 2	What can I do?	Was kann / soll ich machen?
	Should I ...?	Sollte ich ...?
	I understand that you're (feeling) unhappy / sad / disappointed / ...	Ich verstehe, dass du unglücklich / traurig / enttäuscht / ... bist.
	Do you have any advice for me?	Kannst du / Können Sie mir einen Rat geben?

	What (else) should I do?	Was könnte / sollte ich (noch) tun?
	I need some advice.	Ich brauche einen Rat.
	I'm sorry that you feel bad.	Es tut mir leid, dass du dich schlecht fühlst.
	I really like that idea.	Das ist eine gute Idee.
	I think you have to talk to someone.	Ich denke, du solltest mit jemandem (darüber) sprechen.
Unit 4	Could you help me, please?	Könntest du mir bitte helfen?

Komplimente machen

Unit 2	I think you're funny / brave / ...	Ich finde dich witzig / mutig / ...
	You're amazing at ...	Du kannst hervorragend ...
	I want to tell you that you're very kind / great at football / ...	Ich möchte dir sagen, dass du sehr nett bist / sehr gut Fußball spielst / ...
	Thank you, that's nice of you.	Danke, das ist lieb / nett von dir.
	You're welcome!	Gern geschehen!

Einen Konflikt lösen und sich entschuldigen

Unit 3	I'm sorry, it was a bad idea to (take a different path).	Es tut mir leid, es war eine schlechte Idee (einen anderen Weg zu nehmen).
	I don't know why I thought that was (a good idea).	Ich weiß nicht, warum ich dachte, dass das (eine gute Idee) wäre.
	Thank you for saying sorry.	Danke für deine Entschuldigung.
	I feel better now.	Jetzt fühle ich mich besser.
	Next time, you should ...	Beim nächsten Mal solltest du ...

Hilfe anbieten, erbitten und annehmen

Unit 4	I'd like to (use social media). But I don't know where to start.	Ich möchte gerne (soziale Medien nutzen). Aber ich weiß gar nicht, wo ich anfangen soll.
	I can help you if you like.	Ich kann dir helfen, wenn du magst.
	Could you / Can you please help me (to make an account)?	Könntest / Kannst du mir bitte helfen (einen Account einzurichten)?
	No problem.	Kein Problem.
	Would you like me to ...?	Möchtest du, dass ich ...?
	No, thanks, I'm OK.	Alles gut, danke. / Nein, danke.
	Shall I help you with ...?	Soll ich dir mit ... helfen?

6 Technologie im Alltag

Über Technologie und soziale Medien im Alltag sprechen

Unit 4	I often / sometimes / never / ... use social media.	Ich nutze soziale Medien oft / manchmal / nie / ...
	I'm (not) allowed to use social media.	Ich darf soziale Medien (nicht) nutzen.
	I believe that social media is a good / bad thing for teens because ...	Ich denke, dass soziale Medien gut / schlecht für Jugendliche sind, weil ...
	I think one of the problems with social media is that ...	Ich denke, ein Problem der sozialen Medien ist, dass ...
	Social media (also) helps people ...	Soziale Medien helfen (auch) ...
	I use social media / my phone / my smartwatch / ... to ...	Ich nutze soziale Medien / mein Smartphone / meine Smartwatch / ..., um ...
	Do you use social media? Why (not)?	Nutzt du soziale Medien? Warum (nicht)?
	I think it is(n't) a good idea to edit photos because ...	Ich finde, es ist (k)eine gute Idee, Fotos zu bearbeiten, weil ...

Ein Telefongespräch führen

Unit 4	Hi, (Dylan). How are things?	Hi, (Dylan). Wie geht's?
	Are you free later / after dinner?	Hast / Hättest du später / nach dem Abendessen Zeit?
	Can you say that again, please?	Kannst du das bitte nochmal wiederholen?
	Can you hear me now?	Kannst du mich jetzt hören?
	I can't hear you.	Ich kann dich nicht hören.
	Oh, one more thing.	Oh, eine Sache noch.
	Sorry, I have to go now.	Entschuldige, ich muss jetzt los.
	Bye. See you later / tomorrow.	Tschüss. Bis später / morgen.

7 Seine Meinung äußern und diskutieren

	I think that's true / false.	Ich glaube, das ist richtig / falsch.
	I'm sorry, I don't understand.	Es tut mir leid, das verstehe ich nicht.
	That's not a good idea.	Das ist keine gute Idee.
	I'm not really a fan of ...	Ich bin nicht wirklich Fan von ...
	For me that isn't true.	Für mich ist das nicht so.
	That's a great idea!	Das ist eine sehr gute Idee!
Unit 2	In my opinion ...	Meiner Meinung nach ...
	If you ask me ...	Wenn du mich fragst ...
	I don't agree with you (at all).	Ich stimme dir (ganz und gar) nicht zu.

	I (completely) agree.	Ich stimme (voll und ganz) zu.
	Maybe, you're right.	Vielleicht hast du recht.
	That's a good point.	Das ist ein gutes Argument.
	I see it a little differently.	Ich sehe das etwas anders.
	I would say that ...	Ich würde sagen, dass ...
Unit 4	Just a minute.	Moment.

8 Feedback geben

	You can use more words or pictures.	Du kannst mehr Wörter oder Bilder verwenden.
	Your presentation was quite long / short.	Deine Präsentation war ziemlich lang / kurz.
	Please speak more loudly / clearly.	Sprich bitte ein bisschen lauter / deutlicher.
	Don't speak so fast, please.	Sprich bitte nicht so schnell.
	That was useful information.	Das waren nützliche Informationen.
	Your notes are really helpful.	Deine Notizen sind wirklich nützlich.
	Next time, check your spelling.	Prüfe deine Rechtschreibung beim nächsten Mal.
	Your presentation needs a better structure.	Deine Präsentation sollte besser strukturiert werden.
	You've done a great job!	Das hast du toll gemacht!
	The text on your slides was a bit small.	Der Text auf deinen Folien war etwas zu klein.
	You spoke loudly and clearly.	Du hast laut und deutlich gesprochen.
	I understood most of / some of what you said.	Ich habe das meiste / einiges von dem, was du gesagt hast, verstanden.
	You looked at your cards.	Du hast auf deine Karten geschaut.
	Please look at me / us more.	Schau mich / uns bitte öfter an.
	You smiled / didn't smile.	Du hast gelächelt / nicht gelächelt.
Unit 1	You gave interesting reasons. Good job!	Du hast interessante Gründe genannt. Gut gemacht!
Unit 3	You used lots of (adjectives).	Du hast viele (Adjektive) verwendet.
Unit 4	Those are great reasons.	Das ist eine großartige Begründung.

Classroom English

You and your teacher	Du und deine Lehrerin / dein Lehrer
Good morning, Mr / Mrs / Ms ... *(bis 12 Uhr)*	Guten Morgen, Herr / Frau ...
Good afternoon, Mr / Mrs / Ms ... *(bis 12 Uhr)*	Guten Tag, Herr / Frau ...
Sorry, I'm late.	Entschuldigung, dass ich zu spät komme.
Can I open / close the window, please?	Kann ich bitte das Fenster öffnen / zumachen?
Can I go to the toilet, please?	Kann ich bitte zur Toilette gehen?

Homework and exercises	Hausaufgaben und Übungen
Sorry, I don't have my exercise book.	Es tut mir leid, ich habe mein Heft nicht dabei.
I don't understand this exercise.	Ich verstehe die Übung nicht.
I can't do number 3.	Ich kann Nummer 3 nicht lösen.
Sorry, I haven't finished.	Entschuldigung, ich bin noch nicht fertig.
I have ... Is that right too?	Ich habe ... Ist das auch richtig?
Sorry, I don't know.	Es tut mir leid, das weiß ich nicht.
What's for homework?	Was haben wir (als Hausaufgabe) auf?

You need help	Du brauchst Hilfe
Can you help me, please?	Können Sie / Kannst du mir bitte helfen?
What page is it, please?	Auf welcher Seite sind wir / steht das?
What's ... in English / German?	Was heißt ... auf Englisch / Deutsch?
Can you write it on the board, please?	Können Sie das bitte an die Tafel schreiben?
Can I say it in German?	Kann ich das auf Deutsch sagen?
Can you speak more loudly, please?	Können Sie / Kannst du bitte lauter sprechen?
Can you say / play that again, please?	Können Sie das bitte noch einmal sagen / abspielen?

Work with a partner	Partnerarbeit
Can I work with Julian?	Kann ich mit Julian arbeiten?
Can I use your (pen), please?	Kann ich bitte deinen (Stift) benutzen?
Yes, here you are.	Hier, bitte.
It's my / your turn.	Ich bin dran. / Du bist dran.
Let's make / draw a / an ...	Lass uns ein / eine / einen ... machen / zeichnen.
Let's act out the story / the dialogue.	Lass uns die Geschichte / den Dialog spielen.

What your teacher says	Was deine Lehrerin / dein Lehrer sagt
Let's start.	Lasst uns anfangen. / Los geht's.
Listen, please. / Quiet, please.	Hört bitte zu. / Ruhe bitte.
Open your books at page 24, please.	Schlagt bitte Seite 24 auf.
Do exercise 5 for homework, please.	Macht bitte Übung 5 als Hausaufgabe.
Write the correct words.	Schreibt die richtigen Wörter (auf).
Correct the false sentences.	Korrigiert die falschen Sätze.
Where's your book, Dana?	Wo ist dein Buch, Dana?
Try again!	Versuche es noch einmal.
That's all for today. You can go now.	Das ist alles für heute. Ihr könnt jetzt gehen.

Im *Vocabulary* findest du alle neuen Wörter und Wendungen, die du lernen musst.
Sie stehen in der Reihenfolge, in der sie im Buch zum ersten Mal vorkommen.
Höre dir in der App jedes Wort beim Lernen genau an und sprich es nach.

Inhalt

Symbole und Abkürzungen

► p. 10 ► pp. 12/13	Die Seitenzahl in der linken Spalte zeigt dir, wo das Wort zum ersten Mal in diesem Buch vorkommt. *(p. = page, Seite; pp. = pages, Seiten)*
►► **cycle lane**	Die doppelten Pfeile weisen auf ein Wort mit gleicher Bedeutung hin, das du bereits kennst.
cheap ◄► **expensive**	Das „Gegenteil"-Zeichen bedeutet: *cheap* ist das Gegenteil von *expensive.*
! **the sea** – das Meer, die See **the lake** – der See	Das ! bedeutet: Vorsicht, hier keinen Fehler machen!
German **"Frau":** • She's a nice **woman**. (eine nette Frau) • That's **Mrs/Ms** Smith. (Frau Smith) • This is Anne, my **wife**. (meine Frau)	In den Merkboxen findest du wichtige Hinweise zu den neuen Wörtern und Wendungen.
sb. = somebody / sth. = something	*adj = adjective* (Adjektiv)
infml = informal (informell, umgangssprachlich)	*adv = adverb* (Adverb)
pl = plural (Plural, Mehrzahlform)	*conj = conjunction* (Konjunktion)
AE = American English / BE = British English	*prep = preposition* (Präposition)

Hinweise

Tipps zum Vokabellernen findest du im **Skills file** auf S. 139–141.
Die **Wordbanks** (S. 168–176) bieten dir nach wichtigen Themen gesammelte Stichwörter.
Let's talk (S. 177–183) enthält Wendungen für wichtige Situationen, z. B. „Feedback geben".
Eine **Liste mit unregelmäßigen Verben** findest du auf den Seiten 238–239.
Englische Wörter, die Wörtern im Deutschen ähnlich sind, findest du auf S. 240.
Im **Dictionary** (S. 215–235) kannst du englische und deutsche Wörter nachschlagen.

Hello!

pp. 10/11	**north** [nɔːθ]	der Norden; nördlich; Nord-	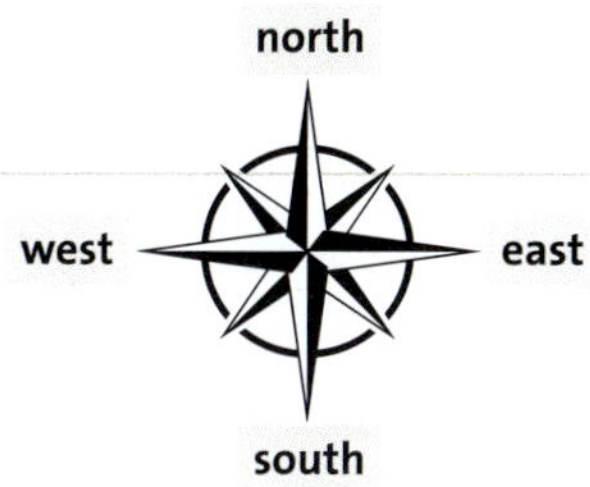
	south [saʊθ]	der Süden; südlich; Süd-	
	east [iːst]	der Osten; östlich; Ost-	
	west [west]	der Westen; westlich; West-	
	northern [ˈnɔːðən]	nördliche(r, s), Nord-	nouns: **north, east, south, west** adj: **northern, eastern, southern, western** ! Aussprache: **south** [saʊθ] **– southern** [ˈsʌðən]
	republic [rɪˈpʌblɪk]	die Republik	! Betonung auf der 2. Silbe: **republic** [rɪˈpʌblɪk]
	island [ˈaɪlənd]	die Insel	• **isle** [aɪl] (*kurz für* **island**) = die Insel, das Eiland • **the British Isles** *(pl)* = die Britischen Inseln
pp. 12/13	**life** [laɪf], *pl* **lives** [laɪvz]	das Leben	! one **life** – nine **lives**
	bagpipes *(pl)* [ˈbægpaɪps]	der Dudelsack	! *German:* **Dudelsack spielen** *English:* (to) **play the bagpipes**  bagpipes
	lake [leɪk]	der See	! **the sea** – das Meer, die See **the lake** – der See The word for **lake** in Scotland is **loch** [lɒx], [lɒk].
	skyscraper [ˈskaɪskreɪpə]	der Wolkenkratzer	 skyscrapers
	mural [ˈmjʊərəl]	das Wandgemälde	a big picture on a wall or a building
	canal [kəˈnæl]	der Kanal	 a **canal**

foreground [ˈfɔːgraʊnd]	der Vordergrund	There is a woman in the **foreground**. In the **background**, you can see some mountains. 
background [ˈbækgraʊnd]	der Hintergrund	

Unit 1 London: City life

► pp. 14/15

tower [ˈtaʊə]	der Turm	 a **tower**

The royal family

royal [ˈrɔɪəl]	königlich	**prince** [prɪns]	der Prinz
king [kɪŋ]	der König	**princess** [prɪnˈses]	die Prinzessin
queen [kwiːn]	die Königin		

wheel [wiːl]	das Rad	**big wheel** = das Riesenrad
palace [ˈpæləs]	der Palast, das Schloss	 a **palace** ! Betonung auf der 1. Silbe: **palace** [ˈpæləs]

Topic 1

► p. 16

public [ˈpʌblɪk]	öffentlich	Are there any **public** toilets near here? **public transport** *(no pl)* = die öffentlichen Verkehrsmittel
underground [ˈʌndəgraʊnd]	die U-Bahn	• Travelling on the **underground** is fast, but you don't see anything of the city. • The **underground** in London is also called "the tube".
way [weɪ]	die Art und Weise	The underground is a great **way** to travel in London.

way

1. die Strecke, der Weg	We still have a long **way** to go.	eine weite Strecke
	You're **in the way**.	im Weg
2. die Richtung	The station is **this way** /	hier entlang, in diese(r) Richtung /
	The station is **that way**!	da entlang, in jene(r) Richtung
	Look **both ways**.	in beide Richtungen
	You're walking **the wrong way!**	in die falsche Richtung
3. die Art und Weise	Do it **(in) this way**!	auf diese Art/Weise
	You can do it **in different ways**.	auf unterschiedliche Art/Weise

line [laɪn]	die (U-Bahn-)Linie, die (Zug-)Strecke	! **line** = **1.** die Zeile; die Reihe; **2.** die (U-Bahn-)Linie, die (Zug-)Strecke

	(to) **hire** ['haɪə]	mieten, leihen; *(Person:)* einstellen	verb: (to) **hire** – Let's **hire** a boat and have fun on the lake! noun: **hire** – There's a boat **hire** over there. (der Verleih, die Vermietung)
	bike lane ['baɪk leɪn]	der Radweg	►► **cycle lane** **lane** = die Gasse
	traffic ['træfɪk]	der (Straßen-)Verkehr	There was a lot of **traffic**, so it took us an hour to drive home.
	(to) **forget** [fə'get], *simple past:* **forgot** [fə'gɒt]	vergessen	It's dad's birthday tomorrow. Don't **forget** it. (to) **forget** ◄► (to) **remember**
	(to) **drive** [draɪv], *simple past:* **drove** [drəʊv]	*(mit dem Auto)* fahren	I usually take the bus. I don't like to **drive**. (= I don't like to take the car.) verb: (to) **drive** – noun: **driver** (der Fahrer, die Fahrerin)
	(to) **cross** [krɒs]	kreuzen, überqueren	verb: (to) **cross** – Don't **cross** the road here. It's too dangerous. noun: **cross** (das Kreuz) – Put a **cross** (x) next to your favourite kind of music.
► p. 17	**stall** [stɔːl]	der (Markt-)Stand, die Bude	 a **stall**
	cheap [tʃiːp]	billig, preiswert	**cheap** ◄► **expensive**

Topic 2

► p. 18	**ghost** [gəʊst]	der Geist, das Gespenst	 a **scary ghost** **ghost tour** = die Geistertour *(Stadtführung mit gruseligen Themen/Elementen)*
	classic ['klæsɪk]	klassisch	adj: **classic** – noun: **classic** (der Klassiker)
	(to) **join** sb./sth. [dʒɔɪn]	sich jm. anschließen; bei etwas mitmachen	• (to) **join a club** = in einen Klub eintreten • (to) **join a group** = sich einer Gruppe anschließen
	enough [ɪ'nʌf]	genug	Is one sandwich **enough**? Or are you still hungry?
	prime minister [praɪm 'mɪnɪstə]	der Premierminister, die Premierministerin	The British **prime minister** lives at 10 Downing Street. ! Betonung: **prime minister** ['mɪnɪstə]
	except (for) [ɪk'sept]	außer, bis auf	In my family everyone is tall **except (for)** me.
► p. 19	**type (of)** [taɪp]	die Art (von), die Sorte (von)	►► **kind (of), sort (of)**

	(to) **smell** [smel]	riechen; schlecht riechen	verb: (to) **smell** – noun: **smell** (der Geruch; der Gestank)
	(to) **miss** [mɪs]	verpassen; versäumen, auslassen	! (to) **miss** = **1.** vermissen – I enjoyed my trip to France, but I **missed** my friends. **2.** verpassen – I'm late! I'll **miss** the bus. **3.** versäumen, auslassen – I was so late that I **missed** the first lesson.
► p. 20	**umbrella** [ʌm'brelə]	der (Regen-)Schirm	
	per cent (%) [pə 'sent]	das Prozent	There are eight kids: four are girls. That's 50 **per cent**.
	central ['sentrəl]	zentral	**in central London** = in der Londoner Innenstadt / Stadtmitte adj: **central** – noun: **centre**
► p. 21	**virtual** ['vɜːtʃuəl]	virtuell	! Betonung auf der 1. Silbe: **virtual** ['vɜːtʃuəl]
	square [skweə]	der Platz *(in der Stadt)*	• noun: stalls in the market **square** • adj: a **square** table/room (rechteckig)
	roundabout ['raʊndəbaʊt]	der Kreisverkehr	
	column ['kɒləm]	die Säule; die Spalte *(in Texten)*	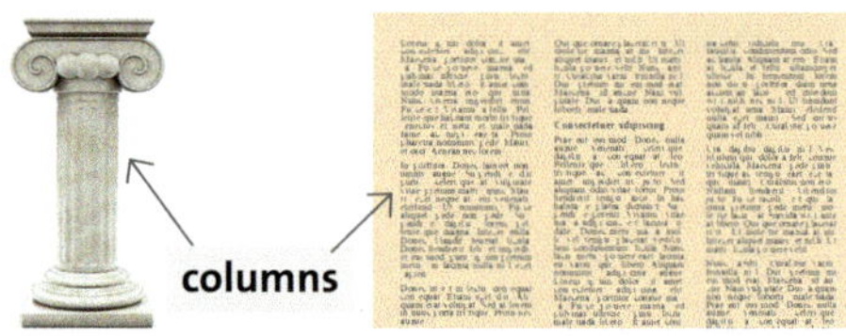
	guard [gɑːd]	der Wärter, die Wärterin; die Wache; der/die Sicherheits-bedienstete	noun: **guard** – The people in uniform are the king's **guards**. verb: (to) **guard sth.** – They **guard** the king's palace. (etwas schützen, bewachen) **Changing of the Guards** = die Wachablösung
	capsule ['kæpsjuːl]	die Kapsel; die Raumkapsel; die Kabine *(auf einem Riesenrad)*	

Topic 3

► p. 22	**menu** ['menju:]	die Speisekarte	What can we eat at this restaurant? Let's look at the **menu.** ! Betonung auf der 1. Silbe: **menu** ['menju:]
	chickpea ['tʃɪkpi:]	die Kichererbse	
	cucumber ['kju:kʌmbə]	die Gurke *(Salatgurke)*	
	sesame ['sesəmi]	der Sesam	! Aussprache: ['sesəmi] – mit scharfem **s** und [i] am Ende
	juice [dʒu:s]	der Saft	**orange juice** 
	bottomless ['bɒtəmləs]	bodenlos, unerschöpflich; mit kostenlosem Nachschank *(bei Getränken z. B. in Cafés)*	with no bottom; a **bottomless** drink means you can get as much of it as you want *(in a cafe, restaurant)*
	I'll have ...	Ich nehme ... *(beim Essen, z. B. im Restaurant)*	**I'll have** the chicken and some water, please.
► p. 23	**careless** ['keələs]	unvorsichtig, leichtsinnig	**careless ◄ ► careful**

-ful / -less

-ful	**careful**	['keəfl]	vorsichtig	**beautiful**	['bju:tɪfl]	(wunder)schön
	colourful	['kʌləfl]	farbig, bunt	**successful**	[sək'sesfl]	erfolgreich
	helpful	['helpfl]	hilfsbereit, hilfreich	**wonderful**	['wʌndəfl]	wunderbar
	useful	['ju:sfl]	nützlich			
-less	**careless**	['keələs]	unvorsichtig, leichtsinnig	**bottomless**	['bɒtəmləs]	bodenlos, unerschöpflich
	colourless	['kʌləlǝs]	farblos	**endless**	['endləs]	endlos, unendlich
	helpless	['helpləs]	hilflos	**homeless**	['həʊmləs]	obdachlos
	useless	['ju:sləs]	nutzlos, unnütz			

	(to) **order** ['ɔ:də]	bestellen	verb: (to) **order** – Are you ready to **order**? noun: **order** – Can I take your **orders**? (... Ihre Bestellungen aufnehmen?)
	waiter ['weɪtə], **waitress** ['weɪtrəs]	der Kellner, die Kellnerin	a **waiter** and two customers 
	(to) speak: you **spoke** [spəʊk]	sprechen: du sprachst; du hast gesprochen	In her talk Dr. Grey **spoke** about robots that can help us with chores at home.
► p. 25	**global** ['gləʊbl]	global, weltweit	! Betonung auf der 1. Silbe: **global** ['gləʊbl] adj: **global** – noun: **globe** (der Globus; die Kugel) **across the globe** = **all (a)round the globe** = all over the world

goal [gəʊl]	das Ziel *(Absicht; Lebensziel)*; das Tor *(im Sport)*	What are your **goals** in life? What do you want to do when you finish school? Our team scored a **goal** in the last minute!
(to) **make** sb. sth.	jn. zu etwas machen	• We **made Joe the new coach** of our team. (... machten Joe zum neuen Trainer ...) • My grandparents came from Turkey and **made Germany their new home**. (... machten Deutschland zu ihrer neuen Heimat.)
reason [ˈriːzn]	der Grund, die Begründung	What could be **the reason why** Jill did this? (der Grund dafür, dass ...) ! *German:* **aus diesem Grund** *English:* **for this reason**
(to) **disagree** [dɪsəˈgriː]	nicht zustimmen, widersprechen	Sorry, but I **disagree** with you. (= I don't agree with you. I think you're wrong.) (to) **agree** ◄► (to) **disagree**

Story

► p. 26	(to) **answer the phone**	ans Telefon gehen	That's your phone ... don't you want to **answer it**? ! *German:* **ans Telefon gehen** *English:* (to) **answer the phone** *German:* **(die Haustür) aufmachen, zur / an die Tür gehen** *English:* (to) **answer the door**
	(to) send: she **sent** [sent]	senden, schicken: sie schickte; sie hat geschickt	Yesterday Jill **sent** me this funny photo.
	right after school	gleich / direkt nach der Schule	• **right by the sea** = direkt am Meer • **right from the start** = gleich / direkt von Anfang an • **right now / then** = genau jetzt / dann ! **right** = **1.** richtig; **2.** (nach) rechts; **3.** (das) Recht; **4.** gleich, direkt
	department store [dɪˈpɑːtmənt stɔː]	das Kaufhaus	►► a big shop
	(to) **be lost** [lɒst]	sich verlaufen/verirrt haben	Can I help you? **Are** you **lost**? – Yes, I'm looking for the library ...
	we **should ...** [ʃʊd]	wir sollten ...	What **should** I do? – I think you **should** talk to your parents.
► p. 27	**doorkeeper** [ˈdɔːkiːpə]	der Pförtner, die Pförtnerin	A **doorkeeper** guards the doors of a building, like a big shop.
	directions *(pl)* [dəˈrekʃnz]	die Wegbeschreibung(en)	! (to) **give directions** = den Weg beschreiben (to) **ask for directions** = nach dem Weg fragen
	suddenly [ˈsʌdənli]	plötzlich, auf einmal	**Suddenly** the music stopped and it was very quiet.

	grass [grɑːs]	das Gras; der Rasen	
	memorial (to sb./sth.**)** [məˈmɔːriəl]	das Denkmal (für jn./etwas), die Gedenkstätte	This is a **memorial** to people who died when they tried to save others.
	fountain [ˈfaʊntən]	der (Spring-/Trink-)Brunnen	**memorial fountain** = der Gedenkbrunnen
	wife [waɪf], *pl* **wives** [waɪvz]	die (Ehe-)Frau	Zoe married Carl, so she is now Carl's **wife**. Carl is Zoe's **husband**. *German* **Frau**: • She's a nice **woman**. (eine nette Frau) • That's **Mrs/Ms** Smith. (Frau Smith) • This is Anne, my **wife**. (meine Frau)
	(to) **follow** [ˈfɒləʊ]	(be)folgen; verfolgen	• Someone was **following** me on my way home. (folgen, verfolgen) • Always **follow** the rules, please. (befolgen)
	(to) **hurry** [ˈhʌri]	sich beeilen; eilen	verb: (to) **hurry** – It's late. We have to **hurry**. **Hurry up**! (Beeil dich!) noun: **hurry** (Eile) – We're **in a hurry**! (Wir sind in Eile. / Wir haben es eilig!)
	(to) **catch** [kætʃ], *simple past:* **caught** [kɔːt]	einholen; fangen; erwischen; nehmen *(z. B. einen Zug, einen Bus)*	• If we hurry, we'll **catch** Joe. He has only just left! (einholen) • Our cat sometimes **catches** mice. (fangen) • I want to **catch** the train at 12:55. (nehmen)
	statue [ˈstætʃuː]	die Statue	This is a famous **statue**. 
▶ p. 28	**clue** [kluː]	der (Lösungs-)Hinweis; der Anhaltspunkt	• They don't know who killed the man and are still looking for **clues** in his flat. • I don't have a **clue**. / I have no **clue**. *(infml)* = Ich habe keine Ahnung. / Keine Ahnung.
	once [wʌns]	einmal; einst	• I've only been to York **once**. (einmal) • This city was **once** a small town. (einst) • **at once** = auf einmal – You shouldn't all speak **at once**.
	(to) **discuss** [dɪˈskʌs]	diskutieren (über); besprechen	Mum and I **discussed** my problems with these maths exercises. She helped a lot! verb: (to) **discuss** – noun: **discussion** (die Diskussion)
	event [ɪˈvent]	das Ereignis	The first day at school is a big **event** for most kids.

Viewing

▶ p. 29	**community** [kəˈmjuːnəti]	die Gemeinschaft, die Gemeinde	My favourite football club has a big **community** of fans all over Europe.

	(to) **volunteer** [vɒlən'tɪə]	freiwillig / ehrenamtlich arbeiten *(unbezahlt)*	verb: (to) **volunteer** – I **volunteer** in a charity shop two afternoons a week. noun: **volunteer** (der/die Freiwillige; der/die ehrenamtliche Mitarbeiter/in) – I'm a **volunteer** and work in a charity shop (= I get no money for my work).
	(to) **get involved (in)** [ɪn'vɒlvd]	sich engagieren (für, bei); sich beteiligen (an)	I often **get involved in** clean-ups on our beaches. Try **not to get involved**. (Versuche, dich da rauszuhalten.)
	(to) **make a difference**	etwas bewirken, etwas ausmachen	Do clean-ups and recycling things **make a difference**? What do you think?
	two years **ago** [ə'gəʊ]	vor zwei Jahren	! *German:* **vor zwei Jahren / fünf Minuten** *English:* **two years / five minutes ago**

Study skills

► p. 30	**research** [rɪ'sɜːtʃ]	die Forschung(en), die Recherche(n)	noun: **research** – I'd like to do some **research**. verb: (to) **research** – I'd like to **research** this topic. (erforschen, untersuchen, recherchieren)
	keyword ['kiːwɜːd]	das Stichwort, das Schlagwort	What do you think about when you hear the **keyword** "game"?
	fact [fækt]	die Tatsache	This isn't a new building. The **fact** is, it's very old. **In fact**, it's over 500 years old. **in fact** = tatsächlich, in Wirklichkeit, genau genommen

Unit task

► p. 31	**audio** ['ɔːdiəʊ]	Audio-, Ton-	Do we need a video? Or is an **audio** recording enough? (= a recording only of sound/music)

Irregular verbs

Infinitive	Simple past		Infinitive	Simple past	
(to) **catch**	**caught**	fangen; einholen; nehmen *(Zug, Bus, ...)*	(to) **forget**	**forgot**	vergessen
			(to) **send**	**sent**	senden, schicken
(to) **drive**	**drove**	(Auto) fahren	(to) **speak**	**spoke**	sprechen

Unit 2 Manchester: Who we are

► pp. 44/45	**secondary school** ['sekəndri skuːl]	die weiterführende Schule	I'm 11. I go to **secondary school** now.
	(to) **support** [sə'pɔːt]	unterstützen	(to) give help to sb.; (to) be a fan of a sports team verb: (to) **support** – My parents always **support** my dreams and plans. nouns: • **support** (die Unterstützung) – My parents are a great **support**. • *(person)* **supporter** – I'm a Manchester United **supporter**.

	disability [dɪsəˈbɪləti]	die Behinderung	Ms Adu has a **disability**. She's in a wheelchair. noun: **disability** – adj: **disabled** [dɪsˈeɪbld] ((körper)behindert)
	annoying [əˈnɔɪɪŋ]	ärgerlich *(unangenehm)*	adj: **annoy<u>ing</u>** – I find it very **annoying** that the trains are always late. **annoy<u>ed</u>** – I'm often **annoyed** about the trains. (verärgert) verb: (to) **annoy** sb. – It **annoys** me that the trains are always late. (jn. ärgern)

Topic 1

► p. 46	**ripped** [rɪpt]	zerrissen, (ein)gerissen	(to) **rip** = zerreißen, (ein)reißen  **ripped** jeans
	comfortable [ˈkʌmftəbl]	bequem, gemütlich	Please wear **comfortable** clothes for your yoga class. **comfortable** ◄► **uncomfortable** (unbequem, ungemütlich)
	skirt [skɜːt]	der Rock	 a **skirt**
	sock [sɒk]	die Socke	**socks** 
	brand [brænd]	die (Produkt-)Marke	This shop doesn't sell expensive **brands**, but their bikes are very good. What **brand** is your new bike?
	at a good price	zu einem guten Preis	I got my bike **at a very good price**. *German:* **zu einem guten Preis** *English:* **at a good price**
	(to) **borrow** [ˈbɒrəʊ]	(aus)leihen, sich borgen	Can I **borrow** your glue stick, please?
	normal [ˈnɔːml]	normal	! Betonung auf der 1. Silbe: <u>nor</u>mal

Topic 2

► p. 48	**friendship** [ˈfrendʃɪp]	die Freundschaft	Sue is my best friend. My **friendship** with Sue is very important to me. nouns: **friendship**; *(person)* **friend** – adj: **friendly**

	advice *(no pl)* [əd'vaɪs]	der Rat, der Ratschlag, die Ratschläge	**!** **advice** ist unzählbar: *German:* **Er gab mir einen Rat.** *English:* **He gave me some advice. /** **He gave me a piece of advice.** (*never:* He gave me ~~an advice~~.) Take my **advice**: Go and see a doctor. (Hör auf meinen Rat: ...)
	(to) **be in love (with** sb.**)**	verliebt sein (in jn.)	(to) **fall in love (with** sb.**)** = sich verlieben (in jn.)
	(to) **do well**	gut abschneiden, erfolgreich sein	Joe **did well** in his maths test. My sister started a new business, and it's **doing very well**. (to) **do well** ◄► (to) **do badly** (schlecht abschneiden, keinen Erfolg haben)
	frustrating [frʌ'streɪtɪŋ]	frustrierend	adj: **frustrating** (frustrierend); **frustrated** (frustriert) verb: (to) **frustrate** sb. (jn. frustrieren)
	(to) **be allowed to do** sth. [ə'laʊd]	etwas tun dürfen	• We**'re not allowed to** eat in class. • **Are** you **allowed to** use dictionaries in your English tests? – No, dictionaries **are not allowed**. (... sind nicht erlaubt.)
	(to) **have a crush (on** sb.**)** [krʌʃ]	in jn. verliebt sein	►► (to) **be in love with** sb. **crush** = die Schwärmerei, das Verliebtsein; der Schwarm *(jd., in den/die man verliebt ist)*
	shy [ʃaɪ]	scheu, schüchtern	**shy ◄► confident**
► p. 49	**serious** ['sɪəriəs]	ernst(haft)	Jen is a very **serious** person. (ernst) Are you **serious**? (Meinst du das ernst?)
► p. 50	**they**	er/sie *(geschlechtsneutral)*	

they = he or she

A nice teacher will always help you if **they** can. = if he or she can

Not every student can talk to **their** parents about **their** problems. = his or her parents / problems

Our friend Chris doesn't feel that **they** are a man or a woman.
We use the pronouns "**they / them / their**" for **them**.

(to) **tell** sb. **(not) to do** sth.	jn. auffordern, etwas (nicht) zu tun; jm. sagen, dass er/sie etwas (nicht) tun soll	The teacher **told** the students **to be** quiet. She **told** them **not to chat** during lessons.
myself [maɪ'self]	(ich) mich/mir	

Reflexive pronouns

I	► **myself** [maɪ'self]	mir, mich	I'm trying to teach **myself** the guitar.
you	► **yourself** [jɔː'self]	dir, dich	Don't climb that tree. **You** could fall and hurt **yourself**.
he	► **himself** [hɪm'self]	sich	I didn't know if **he** was talking to me or to **himself**.
she	► **herself** [hɜː'self]	sich	**My sister** ordered tea for me and coffee for **herself**.
it	► **itself** [ɪt'self]	sich	**The cat** fell off a tree and hurt **itself**.
we	► **ourselves** [aʊə'selvz]	uns	Our team is great – **we** can be proud of **ourselves**!
you	► **yourselves** [jɔː'selvz]	euch	**You** must believe in **yourselves**, kids!
they	► **themselves** [ðəm'selvz]	sich	**Small children** can't look after **themselves**.

! Merk dir auch die Wendung **Enjoy yourselves.** = Viel Spaß! / Amüsiert euch gut!

tonight [tə'naɪt]	heute Nacht, heute Abend	It's so hot today, but we can sit in the garden **tonight** when it gets cooler.
tomorrow [tə'mɒrəʊ]	morgen	Today is Friday, so **tomorrow** is Saturday.
(to) **write** sth. **down** [raɪt 'daʊn], *simple past:* **wrote** [rəʊt]	etwas aufschreiben	I can remember new words better if I **write** them **down**. 
so far [səʊ 'fɑː]	bis jetzt, bis hierher	 **So far** my holiday has been great. ►► till/until now
option ['ɒpʃn]	die Wahl(möglichkeit), die Option	No idea what to do tonight? These are your **options**: ... (= things that you can choose from)
truth [truːθ]	die Wahrheit	• (to) **tell the truth** = (to) say (only) things that are true Are you telling the **truth**? = Is it true what you're saying? • **To tell the truth**, I hate parties. (Ehrlich gesagt, ...) noun: **truth** – adj: **true**
safe [seɪf]	sicher *(gefahrlos)*	adj: **safe** – noun: **safety** (die Sicherheit) 
chance [tʃɑːns]	die Chance, die Gelegenheit; das Risiko	I'll try parkour if I get the **chance**. Don't **take any chances**! (Geh auf Nummer sicher! / Geh keine Risiken ein!)
► p. 51 (to) **compare (to/with)** [kəm'peə]	vergleichen (mit)	Work with a partner and **compare** your texts. = **Compare** your text **to/with** your partner's.
(to) **rest** [rest]	ruhen; sich ausruhen	verb: (to) **rest** – noun: **rest** (Ruhe, Pause, Erholung) (to) **take a rest** = eine Pause machen
healthy ['helθi]	gesund	Stay fit and **healthy** – join our jogging club. adjective: **healthy** – noun: **health** (Gesundheit)

(to) **clap (your hands)** [klæp]	(in die Hände) klatschen	It was a great concert. At the end everyone **clapped** and **cheered**.	
(to) **cheer** [tʃɪə]	jubeln, *(Sportler/innen)* anfeuern		

Topic 3

▶ p. 52	**confidence** [ˈkɒnfɪdəns]	das (Selbst-)Vertrauen, die Zuversicht	noun: **confidence** – adj: **confident**
	young [jʌŋ]	jung	The youth centre is a place for **young** people. adj: **young** – noun: **youth** **young ◄► old**
▶ p. 53	(to) **make** sb. **do** sth. [meɪk]	jn. dazu bringen, etwas zu tun	You can give people good tips, but you can't **make them do** what you want. Listening to music always **makes me feel** good.
	that's why	deshalb, darum	Sam was alone. **That's why** she felt sad.
	(to) **take care of** sb./sth. [keə]	sich um jn./etwas kümmern	

care – (to) care – careful

- nouns:

care	Choose your words **with care.** **Take care.** Can you **take care of** our dog next week?	mit Sorgfalt, sorgfältig Pass auf dich auf. sich kümmern um	**care** *(n)* = **1.** die Sorgfalt, die Vorsicht; **2.** die Versorgung, die Betreuung; die Pflege
carer	I think we will need a **carer** for Grandpa soon.	die Pflegekraft; der Betreuer, die Betreuerin	

- verbs:

(to) **care for** sb. (betreuen, pflegen; sich kümmern um; aufpassen auf)	Who is going to **care for** our dog when we're on holiday?	Wer kümmert sich um unseren Hund ...?
(to) **care about** sth. (wichtig nehmen)	I really **care about** animals. I don't **care about** money.	Tiere liegen mir sehr am Herzen. Geld ist mir nicht wichtig. / Geld ist mir egal.

- adjective:

careful (vorsichtig)	Be **careful** when you cross the road.	Sei vorsichtig, wenn du die Straße überquerst.

role model [ˈrəʊl mɒdl]	das Vorbild	a person that you like very much, and you try to be like them
poor [pɔː], [pʊə]	arm	**Poor George!** = Der arme George! / Armer George! **poor ◄► rich** adj: **poor** – noun: **poverty** [ˈpɒvəti] (die Armut)
(to) write: **he has written** [ˈrɪtn]	schreiben: er hat geschrieben	I have no ideas for my homework – so far I **haven't written** anything!

	penalty [ˈpenəlti]	der Strafstoß; der Elfmeter *(Fußball)*	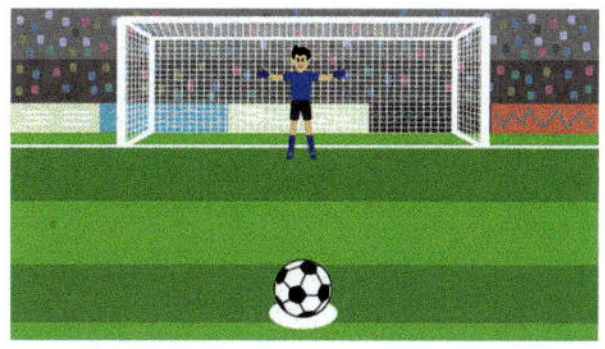 (to) **miss a penalty** = einen Elfmeter verschießen *(nicht treffen)*
	racist [ˈreɪsɪst]	der Rassist, die Rassistin; rassistisch	nouns: **racism** (der Rassismus); *(person)* **racist** adj: **racist** ! Betonung auf der 1. Silbe: **racist** [ˈreɪsɪst], **racism** [ˈreɪsɪzəm]
	whenever [wenˈevə]	wann (auch) immer	You can come and visit us **whenever** you like.
	interested (in) [ˈɪntrəstɪd]	interessiert (an)	Are you **interested in** science? Then join the Science Club. ! (to) **be interested in** sth. = an etwas interessiert sein, sich für etwas interessieren (to) **be interesting** = interessant sein
▸ p. 54	(to) **appear** [əˈpɪə]	erscheinen; auftauchen	• A funny picture **appeared** on the screen. (erscheinen) • Suddenly a cat **appeared** behind the car. (auftauchen) • He **appeared** to be very sad. (zu sein scheinen)
	(to) **interrupt** [ɪntəˈrʌpt]	unterbrechen	It's not OK to **interrupt** people when they're talking.
	actually [ˈæktʃuəli]	eigentlich; tatsächlich	Let's take a rest. **Actually**, I'm really hungry!
▸ p. 55	**compliment** [ˈkɒmplɪmənt]	das Kompliment	! Betonung auf der 1. Silbe: **compliment** [ˈkɒmplɪmənt] (to) **pay** sb. **a compliment** = jm. ein Kompliment machen
	classmate [ˈklɑːsmeɪt]	der Mitschüler, die Mitschülerin	The other students in your class are your **classmates**.

Story

▸ p. 56	**pitch** [pɪtʃ]	der Platz *(Sport)*, das Spielfeld	a **football pitch** 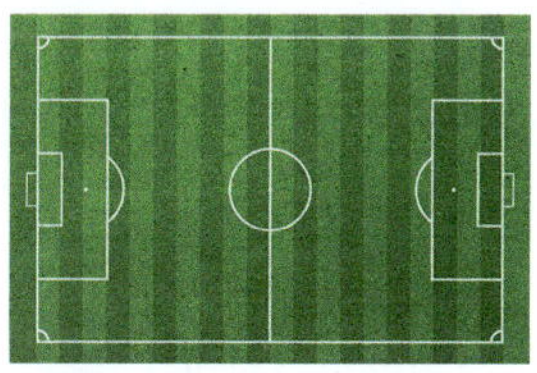
▸ p. 57	**half-time** [hɑːf ˈtaɪm]	die Halbzeit(pause)	! *German:* **in der Halbzeit** *English:* **at half-time** • noun: **half,** *pl* **halves** = die Hälfte – **the first half** *(Sport)* = die erste Halbzeit • adv: **half** – **half full, half empty** = halb voll, halb leer • **half the time, half the money** = die Hälfte der Zeit, die Hälfte des Geldes **half an hour** = eine halbe Stunde

goalkeeper [ˈɡəʊlkiːpə]	der Torwart, die Torhüterin	
far [fɑː]	weit (entfernt)	**far** ◀ ▶ **near**
additional [əˈdɪʃənl]	zusätzliche(r, s)	I could move to York, but first I'd like some **additional** information about the city. **additional time** = die Nachspielzeit *(Fußball)*
finger [ˈfɪŋɡə]	der Finger	You have ten **fingers** – five on each hand. (to) **cross your fingers** = die Daumen drücken / halten *(jm. Glück / gutes Gelingen wünschen)*
(to) **call** sb. **names**	jn. beschimpfen	What? Mike really **called you names** in front of all your friends? How mean!
(to) **keep doing** sth. [kiːp], *simple past:* **kept** [kept]	etwas dauernd/immer wieder tun	(to) **keep going** = (immer) weiter gehen

(to) keep, kept

1. (to) **keep**	Here's some tea to **keep** you warm. / Don't tell them. Let's **keep** it secret.	**halten**
	Can I **keep** your pencil? / **Keep** the change.	**behalten**
	Where do you **keep** vegetables? / We **keep** our biscuits in this box.	**aufbewahren**
2. (to) **keep doing** sth.	I told him to stop, but he **kept calling** me names. / **Keep walking** till you get to the bridge.	**etwas dauernd / immer wieder / immer weiter tun**
3. (to) **keep** sb. **busy.**	Here's a list of activities to **keep** the children **busy**.	**jn. beschäftigen, auf Trab halten**

	ahead [əˈhed]	voran, voraus	There's an accident on the road **ahead**! Let's take a different route. Just walk **ahead**, don't wait for me.
▶ p. 58	**beginning** [bɪˈɡɪnɪŋ]	der Anfang	**beginning** ◀ ▶ **end** **!** *German:* **am Anfang** *English:* **in the beginning** noun: **beginning** – verb: (to) **begin,** *simple past:* **began** (anfangen, beginnen)
	(to) **freeze** [friːz], *simple past:* **froze** [frəʊz]	(ge)frieren; erstarren	Rivers and lakes sometimes **freeze** in winter. Suddenly the lights went out, and I **froze**.
	ending [ˈendɪŋ]	die Endung; das Ende *(Text, Geschichte)*	**!** *German:* **Happy End** *English:* **happy ending**
	(to) **say sorry to** sb.	sich bei jm. entschuldigen	I don't know why I did that. I really want to **say sorry to** all of you.
	conflict [ˈkɒnflɪkt]	der Konflikt, die Auseinandersetzung, der Streit	**!** Betonung auf der 1. Silbe: **conflict** [ˈkɒnflɪkt]

Viewing

► p. 59	**coach** [kəʊtʃ]	der (Reise-)Bus	 buses  a coach
	police *(pl)*	die Polizei	**!** **police** ist ein Pluralwort: Where **are** the **police**? Did you call **them**? (Wo **ist** die **Polizei**? Hast du **sie** gerufen?)
	service station [ˈsɜːvɪs steɪʃn]	die Tankstelle; die (Autobahn-)Raststätte	a **service station** 

Study skills

► p. 60	**stupid** [ˈstjuːpɪd]	dumm, blöd; albern	That's a **stupid** idea. (= not a clever idea)
	completely [kəmˈpliːtli]	völlig, absolut	verb: (to) **complete** – Please **complete** the list. (vervollständigen) adj: **complete** – Is the list **complete** now? (vollständig, komplett) adv: **completely** – My clothes don't need to be **completely** new. I'm happy with second-hand clothes too.
	point	das Argument, der Standpunkt	

point

(to) **make your point**	ein Argument vorbringen	(to) **take a point**	einen Standpunkt verstehen
Make your point.	Leg deinen Standpunkt dar. / Sag, wie du darüber denkst.	**I take your point.**	Ich verstehe, was du sagen willst. / Einverstanden.
That's a good point.	Das ist ein gutes Argument.		

	quick [kwɪk]	schnell	►► **fast** **quick / fast** ◄► **slow**

Unit task

► p. 61	**argument** [ˈɑːgjumənt]	das Argument; der Streit	noun: **argument** [ˈɑːgjumənt] – verb: (to) **argue** [ˈɑːgjuː] (argumentieren) • (to) **argue for/against** sth. = sich für/gegen etwas aussprechen • (to) **argue an opinion** = eine Meinung vertreten • (to) **argue (about)** – (sich) streiten (über / wegen)
	topic [ˈtɒpɪk]	das Thema	The **topic** of my presentation is "animals in zoos".

personality [pɜːsəˈnæləti]	die Persönlichkeit; der Charakter	Ann has the perfect **personality** to be a good student. nouns: **person**; **personality** – adj: **personal** *(persönlich)*
difficult [ˈdɪfɪkəlt]	schwierig, schwer	This exercise is really **difficult**. (= really hard)
result [rɪˈzʌlt]	das Ergebnis	**as a result** = folglich, demzufolge

Irregular verbs

Infinitive	Simple past		Infinitive	Simple past	
(to) **begin**	**began**	anfangen, beginnen	(to) **keep**	**kept**	(be)halten; aufbewahren
(to) **freeze**	**froze**	(ge)frieren; erstarren	(to) **write**	**wrote**	schreiben

Unit 3 Scotland: Adventure

▸ pp. 72/73	**capital (city)** [ˈkæpɪtl]	die Hauptstadt	! **capital** = **1.** (= capital city) die Hauptstadt **2.** (= capital letter) der Großbuchstabe
	the Highlands *(pl)* [ˈhaɪləndz]	das schottische Hochland	an area with high mountains in Scotland
	kayak [ˈkaɪæk]	der/das Kajak	 **kayaking** = das Kajakfahren **kayaker** = der/die Kajakfahrer/in
	coast [kəʊst]	die Küste	! *German:* an **der Küste** *English:* on **the coast**
	(to) **hike** [haɪk]	wandern	**Hiking** in the mountains is fun. verb: (to) **hike** – nouns: **hike** (die Wanderung); *(person)* **hiker**
	high [haɪ]	hoch	In our holidays we climb **high** mountains.

Topic 1

▸ p. 74	**legend** [ˈledʒənd]	die Legende, die Sage	! Betonung auf der 1. Silbe: **legend** [ˈledʒənd]
	mile [maɪl]	die Meile *(ca. 1,6 km)*	! *German:* mit 30 **Meilen pro Stunde** *English:* at 30 **miles per hour** **per** = pro
	deep [diːp]	tief	a **deep** lake / **deep** snow
	neck [nek]	der Hals, der Nacken	It was horrible – he fell down the stairs and broke his **neck**.
	since then [sɪns ˈðen]	seit damals, seitdem	The first week was sunny, but the weather has been very bad **since then**.

	scientist [ˈsaɪəntɪst]	der (Natur-)Wissenschaftler, die (Natur-)Wissenschaftlerin	I love science. I want to become a **scientist**.
	fake [feɪk]	falsch, gefälscht	This isn't real gold, it's only **fake**. Is this true? Or is it just **fake** news? adj: **fake** – noun: **fake** (der/das Fake, die Fälschung) – verb: (to) **fake sth.** (etwas faken, fälschen, vortäuschen)
	even [ˈiːvn]	sogar, selbst	• **even** (sogar) – Everybody helped, **even** the children. • **even if** (selbst wenn) – **Even if** I'm tired, I must do my homework. • **not even** (nicht einmal) – He doesn't like sweets, **not even** ice cream.
	eel [iːl]	der Aal	 an **eel**
▶ p. 75	**a one-day tour**	eine eintägige Tour	! *German:* eine **eintägige** Tour • eine **einstündige** Bootsfahrt • ein **dreiwöchiger** Urlaub *English:* a **one-day** tour • a **one-hour** boat trip • a **three-week** holiday
	(to) **explore** [ɪkˈsplɔː]	erforschen, erkunden	Let's walk around and **explore** the village.
	adult [ˈædʌlt]	der/die Erwachsene	someone 18 years old or older
▶ p. 76	**soldier** [ˈsəʊldʒə]	der Soldat, die Soldatin	**soldiers** 
	(to) **carry** [ˈkæri]	tragen; bei sich haben; befördern	• Let me help you **carry** those bags! (tragen) • You're not allowed to **carry** knives on a plane. (bei sich haben) • This car can **carry** five people. (befördern)
▶ p. 77	**tunnel** [ˈtʌnl]	der Tunnel	! Aussprache: **tunnel** [ˈtʌnl]
	(to) **get lost** [lɒst]	sich verlaufen, sich verirren	• (to) **get lost** – Be careful that you don't **get lost** when you go hiking. • (to) **be lost** – But if you**'re lost**, phone for help.
	(to) **lose** [luːz], **lost, lost** [lɒst]	verlieren	! (to) **win** ◀▶ (to) **lose**: We **lost** the match. (to) **find** ◀▶ (to) **lose**: I've **lost** my ticket!
	(to) **decide** [dɪˈsaɪd]	beschließen, sich entscheiden	• (to) **decide to do** sth. – We **decided to do** a project about clothes. • (to) **decide on** sth. – We can't **decide on** a name for our baby.

piper [ˈpaɪpə]	der Dudelsackspieler, die Dudelsackspielerin	a bagpipe player
sudden [ˈsʌdn]	plötzliche(r, s)	His **sudden** arrival surprised us all. (Seine plötzlicher Ankunft ...) = We were surprised when he **suddenly** arrived. (..., als er plötzlich ankam)
nobody [ˈnəʊbədi] **/** **no one** [ˈnəʊ wʌn]	niemand	**No one / Nobody** is at home. The house is very quiet.

Topic 2

► p. 78 **outdoor** activity [ˈaʊtdɔː]	die Outdoor-Aktivität; die Aktivität für draußen / im Freien	I like **outdoor activities** like hiking and cycling. adv: **outdoors** [aʊtˈdɔːz] – I like to be **outdoors**. (im Freien, draußen)
off [ɒf]	weg von; hinunter von	You could break your neck if you jump **off** a tree.

off

(to) fall off	My friend **fell off** his bike / a wall.	herunterfallen
(to) get off	He hurt his leg when he **got off** his horse / his bike.	absteigen
	Be careful when you **get off** the train / the bus.	aussteigen

cliff [klɪf]	die Klippe	**cliff jumping** = das Klippenspringen
tent [tent]	das Zelt	 **tents** on a campsite
(to) sleep: I **slept,** I **have slept** [slept]	schlafen: ich schlief; ich habe geschlafen	I hate to get up early. Last Sunday I **slept** till 10:30. I**'ve** never **slept** in a tent. And you?
before [bɪˈfɔː]	zuvor; vorher; schon einmal	Have you ever been to Scotland **before**?

before

1. *(prep)* **vor**	**before** school / **before** lunch / ...	**vor** der Schule / **vor** dem Mittagessen / ...
2. *(conj)* **bevor**	**before** you read the text / **before** we eat / ...	**bevor** du den Text liest / bevor wir essen / ...
3. *(adv)* **vorher; schon einmal**	I've never been to Scotland **before**. I've seen this film **before**.	Ich war **vorher** noch nie in Schottland. Ich habe diesen Film **schon mal** gesehen.

(to) ride: I **have ridden** [ˈrɪdn]	reiten / (Rad) fahren: ich bin geritten / (Rad) gefahren	I**'ve ridden** a horse only once. Horses scare me.
(to) drive: I **have driven** [ˈdrɪvn]	*(mit dem Auto)* fahren: ich bin gefahren	It's a long way to Israel. We always fly, we**'ve** never **driven** there.
► p. 79 (to) read [riːd]: I **read** [red], I **have read** [red]	lesen: ich las; ich habe gelesen	You **haven't read** this book? I **read** it last week. It's great, you should read it!

	present ['preznt]	die Gegenwart	nouns: the **past** (die Vergangenheit) / the **present** / the **future** adj: **present** (gegenwärtige(r, s)) / **past** (vergangene(r, s)) / **future** – Here's a list of all the **present** and **past** members of the club.
	(to) **pack** [pæk]	packen, einpacken	(to) **pack** ◄ ► (to) **unpack** [ʌn'pæk] (auspacken)
	(to) forget: I **have forgotten** [fə'gɒtn]	vergessen: ich habe vergessen	Oh no, where's my phone? I think **I've forgotten** it at home.
► p. 80	**instructor** [ɪn'strʌktə]	der Lehrer, die Lehrerin; der Ausbilder, die Ausbilderin	She's an **instructor** at the outdoor centre and teaches all kinds of outdoor activities.

Topic 3

► p. 81	**example** [ɪg'zɑːmpl]	das Beispiel	! *German:* **zum Beispiel** *English:* **for example**
	(to) **take notes** [teɪk 'nəʊts]	(sich) Notizen machen *(beim Lesen oder Zuhören)*	! **(to) take notes** benutzt du, wenn du dir beim Lesen o. Zuhören Notizen machst. **(to) make notes** verwendest du, wenn du eigene Ideen aufschreibst, z. B. als Vorbereitung für einen Vortrag.
► p. 82	**nature** ['neɪtʃə]	die Natur	noun: **nature** – adj: **natural** ['nætʃrəl] (natürlich, Natur-) **natural history** = die Naturkunde
	(to) **protect (from / against)** [prə'tekt]	(be)schützen (vor)	An umbrella **protects** you **from** the rain.
	path [pɑːθ]	der Weg, der Pfad	 a **path**
	gate [geɪt]	das Tor	Who left the garden **gate** open? 
	flower ['flaʊə]	die Blume; die Blüte	 colourful **flowers**
	plant [plɑːnt]	die Pflanze	noun: **plant** – Which **plants** do you have in your garden? verb: (to) **plant** – What else would you like to **plant** in your garden? (pflanzen)

► p. 83	(to) **recycle** [riːˈsaɪkl]	recyceln, wiederverwerten	verb: (to) **recycle** – noun: **recycling** (das Recycling)
	less [les]	weniger	This winter we had **less** snow than last winter. (= not as much snow as last winter) **less** ◄ ► **more**
	wild [waɪld]	wild	On our safari we saw many **wild** animals. ! Aussprache: **wild** [waɪld]
	air [eə]	die Luft	We all need **air** to breathe.
	climate [ˈklaɪmət]	das Klima	Is this weird weather still normal or is **climate change** the reason? **climate change** = der Klimawandel
	protest [ˈprəʊtest]	der Protest, die Protestdemonstration	nouns: **protest** [ˈprəʊtest]; *(person)* **protester** [prəˈtestə] (der/die Demonstrant/in) verb: (to) **protest** [prəˈtest]

Story

► p. 84	**trainer** [ˈtreɪnə]	der Sportschuh	**trainer** = **1.** der/die Trainer/in; **2.** der Sportschuh 
	view (of) [vjuː]	der (An-)Blick; die (Aus-)Sicht (auf)	From our hotel room we had a great **view of** the sea. noun: **view** – verb: (to) **view sth.** (sich etwas anschauen)
► p. 85	**valley** [ˈvæli]	das Tal	There's a river in the **valley**. 
	(to) **cry** [kraɪ]	weinen; rufen, schreien	! Schreibung: (to) **cry,** *simple past:* **cried** – The baby **cried** a lot. *but:* **crying** – He's **crying**. verb: (to) **cry** – noun: **cry** (der Schrei, der Ruf)
	rescue [ˈreskjuː]	die Rettung	verb: (to) **rescue** (retten) – There was a fire at the old house. Firefighters **rescued** a man from the top floor. nouns: **rescue**; *(person)* **rescuer** – For the **rescuers**, it was a very difficult and dangerous **rescue**.

(to) hear: they **heard** [hɜːd], they **have heard** [hɜːd]	hören: sie hörten, sie haben gehört	This sounds like my favourite band, but **I've** never **heard** this song before! But I **heard** they have a new album out.
helicopter [ˈhelɪkɒptə]	der Hubschrauber	 a **helicopter**
while [waɪl]	während	We met Simon **while** we were in Cornwall.

German "während"
- vor Nebensatz: **while** – I slept **while** my friends watched the film.
- vor Nomen: **during** – I slept **during** the film.

both [bəʊθ]	beide	Do you want to buy **both** T-shirts? = Do you want to buy **both** the red **and** the green T-shirt? (... sowohl das rote als auch das grüne T-Shirt ...) **both ... and ...** = sowohl ... als auch ...
embarrassed [ɪmˈbærəst]	verlegen, peinlich berührt	adj: • **embarrassed** – Aren't you **embarrassed**? / Don't you feel **embarrassed**? • **embarrassing** (peinlich) – Sometimes I do **embarrassing** things. verb: (to) **embarrass sb.** (jn. in Verlegenheit bringen, jm. peinlich sein) – Her questions **embarrassed** me.
▶ p. 86 **choice** [tʃɔɪs]	die (Aus-)Wahl; die Entscheidung	noun: **choice** – • Stay at school or find a job? You have the **choice**! / It's your **choice**! • I don't have a **choice** – I'll have to take a taxi. (Ich habe keine Wahl ...) verb: (to) **choose, chose, chosen**; (to) **choose to do** sth. (sich entscheiden / beschließen, etwas zu tun) – I asked him some questions, but he **chose** not to answer them.
(to) **blame** sb. **(for** sth.**)** [bleɪm]	jm. die Schuld geben (an etwas), es jm. übelnehmen	Don't **blame** me **for** all the bad things in your life! The teacher didn't explain this very well, so you can't **blame** the students if they don't know the answers!
mistake [mɪˈsteɪk]	der Fehler	There are some **mistakes** in your text. Please correct them. Is this your pen? I'm sorry, I took it **by mistake**. (aus Versehen; versehentlich)

Viewing

▸ p. 87	**cave** [keɪv]	die Höhle	 a **cave**

Study skills

▸ p. 88	(to) **shout** [ʃaʊt]	rufen, schreien	verbs: (to) **shout** – "Leave me alone!" he **shouted**. (to) **shout at** sb. – Don't **shout at me**. (jn. anschreien) noun: **shout** – We heard angry **shouts** in the street. (der Ruf, der Schrei)

Unit task

▸ p. 89	**middle** [ˈmɪdl]	die Mitte	**in the middle (of)** = in der Mitte (von)
	correct [kəˈrekt]	korrekt	adj: **correct** – verb: (to) **correct** (korrigieren)

Irregular verbs

Infinitive	Simple past	Past participle	
(to) **choose**	**chose**	**chosen**	(aus)wählen
(to) **drive**	**drove**	**driven**	*(Auto)* fahren
(to) **forget**	**forgot**	**forgotten**	vergessen
(to) **go**	**went**	**gone**	gehen; fahren
(to) **hear**	**heard**	**heard**	hören
(to) **hurt**	**hurt**	**hurt**	verletzen; wehtun

Infinitive	Simple past	Past participle	
(to) **keep**	**kept**	**kept**	(be)halten
(to) **lose**	**lost**	**lost**	verlieren
(to) **read** [iː]	**read** [e]	**read** [e]	lesen
(to) **ride**	**rode**	**ridden**	reiten; *(Rad)* fahren
(to) **sleep**	**slept**	**slept**	schlafen
(to) **write**	**wrote**	**written**	schreiben

Unit 4 Wales: Digital life

▸ pp. 102/103	**digital** [ˈdɪdʒɪtl]	digital	adj: **digital** – I have a **digital** camera. adv: **digitally** – I take all my photos **digitally**. ! Betonung auf der 1. Silbe: **digital(ly)** [ˈdɪdʒɪtl], [ˈdɪdʒɪtəli]
	donkey [ˈdɒŋki]	der Esel	 a **donkey**
	national [ˈnæʃnəl]	national	adj: **national, international** [ɪntəˈnæʃnəl] (international) – noun: **nation** [ˈneɪʃn] (die Nation)

sheep [ʃiːp], *pl* **sheep**	das Schaf	 ! one **sheep** two **sheep**
official [əˈfɪʃl]	offiziell	Is it true? What does the actor's **official** website say? **official language** = die Amtssprache
dragon [ˈdræɡən]	der Drache	**dragons** 
million [ˈmɪljən]	die Million	►► **1,000,000** ! **three million people** – *but:* **millions of people**
choir [ˈkwaɪə]	der Chor	 a **choir**
social media [səʊʃl ˈmiːdiə]	die sozialen Medien	• **social** = sozial • **media** = die Medien ! *German:* **in den sozialen Medien** *English:* **on social media**

Topic 1

► p. 104 **mine** [maɪn]	meine, meiner, meins	

Possessive pronouns

I	► **mine** [maɪn]	meine, meiner, meins	This isn't your bike. It's **mine**. (= It's my bike.)
you	► **yours** [jɔːz]	deine, deiner, deins; Ihrer, Ihre, Ihres	These aren't my shorts. Are they **yours**?
he	► **his** [hɪz]	seiner, seine, seins	Nick has a phone like that. So maybe it's **his**?
she	► **hers** [hɜːz]	ihrer, ihre, ihres	Lucie has two rulers. You can use one of **hers**.
it	► **its** [ɪts]	seiner, seine, seins; ihrer, ihre, ihres	*(Das Possessivpronomen zu „it" heißt „its", aber es wird kaum verwendet.)*
we	► **ours** [ɑːz], [ˈaʊəz]	unserer, unsere, unseres	Your house is really nice. **Ours** is smaller and older.
you	► **yours** [jɔːz]	eurer, eure, eures; Ihrer, Ihre, Ihres	Our bikes are over there. Where are **yours**?
they	► **theirs** [ðeəz]	ihrer, ihre, ihrs	This isn't the Millers' car. **Theirs** is blue.

! *Am Briefschluss:* **Yours, Jill** = Deine / Ihre / Eure Jill

(to) **edit** [ˈedɪt]	bearbeiten, editieren	(to) change a text / video to make it better
because of [bɪˈkɒz əv]	wegen	We went home **because of** the rain. (= ... **because** it was raining.)
► p. 105 **voice** [vɔɪs]	die Stimme	You can sing very well. You have a great **voice**! **voice message** = die Sprachnachricht ! *German:* **mit tiefer / hoher Stimme** *English:* **in a deep / high voice**

Topic 2

► p. 106	**without** [wɪˈðaʊt]	ohne	**Without** clouds, there can't be rain. **with ◄ ► without**
► p. 107	**letter** [ˈletə]	der Brief	! **letter** = **1.** der Brief; **2.** der Buchstabe
	several [ˈsevrəl]	mehrere, einige	The shop has **several** bikes for under £400. ►► some, but not a lot
	medicine [ˈmedsn], [ˈmedɪsn]	die Medizin, die Arznei, das Medikament	! Betonung auf der 1. Silbe: **medicine** [ˈmedsn], [ˈmedɪsn]
► p. 108	**link** [lɪŋk]	die Verbindung; der Link	noun: **link** – Is there a **link** between stress and headaches? (die Verbindung) I'll send you the **link** to the website. (der Link) verb: (to) **link (to/with)** (verbinden (mit)) – **Link** your sentences with *but*, *or* or *and*.
	watch [wɒtʃ]	die Armbanduhr	 a **watch** **smartwatch** = die Smartwatch
	How are things?	Wie geht's (so)?	I haven't seen you for a long time! **How are things** with you? (= How are you?)
	(to) **charge** [tʃɑːdʒ]	aufladen *(Smartphone, Batterie, ...)*	Do you have to **charge** your phone every day? verb: (to) **charge** – noun: **charger** (das Ladegerät)
	(to) **swipe** [swaɪp]	wischen *(auf Touchscreen)*; durchziehen, einlesen *(z. B. Kreditkarte)*	• To view the next picture, **swipe** left. • We had to **swipe** a card at the door to get into our hotel room. 
	(to) **tap** sth. [tæp]	tippen an / auf etwas; (leise) klopfen	verb: (to) **tap** – **Tap** an icon on the screen. noun: **tap** – Give that icon on the screen a little **tap**. (das (leise) Klopfen) (to) **tap your fingers** = mit den Fingern klopfen
	(to) **switch** sth. **on / off** [swɪtʃ ˈɒn], [swɪtʃ ˈɒf]	etwas einschalten / ausschalten	verb: (to) **switch** sth. **on / off** – Please **switch off** the lights when you leave the house. noun: **switch** – I couldn't find the light **switch** in the dark. (der Schalter)  a **light switch**
► p. 109	**instruction** [ɪnˈstrʌkʃn]	die Anweisung	Do you always read the **instructions** when you get a new phone?

(to) **pair** sth. **(with** sth.**)** [peə]	etwas (mit etwas) koppeln *(z. B. Geräte)*	You can use Bluetooth to **pair** your phone with your smartwatch. verb: (to) **pair** – noun: **pair**
command [kə'mɑːnd]	der Befehl, das Kommando	My dog knows some simple **commands**: When I say "sit", he sits down.

Topic 3

▸ p. 110	(to) **debate** (sth.) [dɪ'beɪt]	debattieren; diskutieren (über etwas)	verb: (to) **debate** (sth.) – Let's **debate** this. noun: **debate** (die Debatte) – Let's **hold / have a debate** about this. (eine Debatte führen)
	versus (**v** *or* **vs**) ['vɜːsəs]	gegen *(bei Wettkämpfen)*; gegenüber	What an exciting match: Manchester City **versus / vs / v** Manchester United!
	(to) **subscribe to** sth. [səb'skraɪb]	etwas abonnieren	We **subscribe to** a daily newspaper. (= We pay money to get a paper every day.)
	channel ['tʃænl]	der Sender, der (TV-)Kanal	I watched an old film, but when the football match started, I changed **channels**. (= I switched to a different **channel**.) **the (English) Channel** = der Ärmelkanal
	(to) **delete** [dɪ'liːt]	löschen	I **deleted** the message from my phone.
	whole [həʊl]	ganze(r, s)	I can't eat a **whole** pizza. Let's eat half a pizza each.
	thought [θɔːt]	der Gedanke	We could do it this way. – Oh, that's true! Good **thought**! (= good idea) verb: (to) **think, thought, thought** – noun: **thought**
	(to) **hit** [hɪt], **hit, hit**	treffen auf, schlagen, prallen, stoßen gegen/auf	**(to) hit** **treffen** – The ball **hit** a window. **schlagen** – Don't **hit** your little sister. **prallen/ stoßen** – They almost **hit** a tree with their car. **!** *German:* Ich **habe mir den Kopf gestoßen**. *English:* I **hit my head**.
▸ p. 111	**Shall** I ...? [ʃæl], [ʃəl]	Soll ich ...?	It's hot in here. **Shall I** open the window?
	There you go.	Hier, bitte schön.; *(auch:)* Da hast du's! / Na siehst du!	• **There you go**, two veggie burgers. That's £5.60, please. (Hier, bitte schön.) • **There you go!** I told you it would look great. (Na siehst du!)
	private ['praɪvət]	privat; persönlich	**!** Betonung auf der 1. Silbe: **private** ['praɪvət] **private** ◂ ▸ **public**

	Would you like me to ...?	Möchtest du, dass ich ...?	**Would you like me to do** the shopping?

„Möchtest du, dass ich ...?" – „Ich möchte, dass du ..."

Im Deutschen benutzt du „**dass**"-Sätze, wenn du möchtest, dass **jemand etwas tut**:

- Ich **möchte, dass du** den Geschirrspüler ausräumst.
- **Möchtest du, dass ich** einkaufen gehe?

Im Englischen darf auf **would like** und **want** nicht ein **"that"**-Satz folgen. Vergleiche:

- I **want you to** empty the dishwasher. / I **would like you to** empty the dishwasher.
- **Would you like me to** do the shopping?

Nie: ~~I want that you ...~~ / ~~Would you like that I ...?~~

	biography [baɪ'ɒgrəfi], (*kurz auch:* **bio** ['baɪəʊ])	die Biografie	! Betonung auf der 2. Silbe: **biography** [baɪ'ɒgrəfi]
► p. 112	**cyberbullying** ['saɪbəbʊliɪŋ]	das Cybermobbing	using social media or messages to bully somebody
	statistic [stə'tɪstɪk]	die statistische Tatsache, die statistische Größe	! Meist wird der Plural **statistics** verwendet: **Statistics** show that ... = die Statistik zeigt ... / die Statistiken zeigen, dass ...
	one in five	jede/r fünfte, eine/r von fünf(en)	**One in three** children in the UK have never climbed a tree. ! Auf **One in xxx kids / teens / cars / ...** kann ein Verb im Plural oder im Singular folgen: **One in three kids have never climbed ...** oder **One in three kids has never climbed ...**
	however [haʊ'evə]	allerdings, jedoch	She was born in France. She isn't French, **however**. (= But she isn't French.)
	positive ['pɒzətɪv]	positiv	**positive** ◄► **negative**
	a teenager **who** ... / teenagers **who** ...	ein Teenager, der ... / Teenager, die ...	! Das Relativpronomen **who** benutzt du für Personen: I know a girl **who** has four sisters.
	victim ['vɪktɪm]	das Opfer	No one should become a **victim** of bullying.
	it says that ...	es heißt (im Text), dass ...	**It says here that** the artist lives in Spain now. (Hier steht, **dass** ...)
	emotional [ɪ'məʊʃənl]	emotional	adj: **emotional** – noun: **emotion** (die Emotion, das Gefühl) ! Betonung auf der 2. Silbe: **emotion** [ɪ'məʊʃn], **emotional** [ɪ'məʊʃənl]
	side [saɪd]	die Seite *(z. B. Straßenseite)*	How can I get to the other **side** of the river? ! *German* "Seite": **1.** *(Buchseite u.Ä.)* **page** **2.** *(Straßenseite u.Ä.)* **side**
► p. 113	**organization** [ɔ:gənaɪ'zeɪʃn]	die Organisation	verb: (to) **organize** (organisieren) – nouns: **organization**; *(person)* **organizer** (der/die Organisator/in)

Story

► p. 114	(to) **skim a text** [skɪm]	einen Text überfliegen *(um den Inhalt grob zu erfassen)*	(to) read a text quickly to find the main idea(s)
	(to) **lie (to** sb.**)** [laɪ]	(jn. an)lügen	verb: (to) **lie** – Jo didn't tell the truth. She **lied to** us. noun: **lie** (die Lüge) – Jo didn't tell the truth. She told us **lies**. ! (to) **lie, lied, lied** *but:* **lying** – I don't believe him. I think he**'s lying.**
	(to) **reply (to)** [rɪˈplaɪ]	antworten (auf)	►► (to) answer verb: (to) **reply** – noun: **reply** (die Antwort)
	exchange [ɪksˈtʃeɪndʒ]	der Schüleraustausch; der Austausch, der Wechsel	• **exchange class** = *die Schulklasse, die am Schüleraustausch teilnimmt* • **exchange student / exchange partner** = der/die Austauschschüler/in, -partner/in noun: **exchange** – verb: (to) **exchange** (tauschen, austauschen)
	confused [kənˈfjuːzd]	verwirrt	Now I'm **confused**. Is Jim your uncle or your cousin?
► p. 115	**comment (about / on** sth.**)** [ˈkɒment]	der Kommentar (über / zu etwas)	noun: **comment (about / on)** – Can you **make a comment on** these events? (einen Kommentar abgeben) verb: (to) **comment (about / on** sth.**)** – Can you **comment on** these events? ((etwas) kommentieren)
	breath [breθ]	der Atem(zug)	(to) **take a deep breath** = tief durchatmen noun: **breath** – verb: (to) **breathe**
	(to) sit (down): he **sat (down)** [sæt], he **has sat down**	sitzen: er saß, er hat gesessen / sich setzen: er setzte sich (hin), er hat sich (hin)gesetzt	**Have** you ever **sat** right at the front of a plane? I **sat** there when I flew to London last week.
	jealous (of) [ˈdʒeləs]	neidisch (auf); eifersüchtig	You get so much pocket money! I'm really **jealous**. She was **jealous of** her baby brother. She thought her parents loved him more.
	right [raɪt]	das Recht	Nobody has the **right** to read my emails. (das Recht, ... zu lesen)
► p. 116	(to) **recognize** [ˈrekəgnaɪz]	(wieder)erkennen	He has changed so much that I didn't **recognize** him.
	lighting [ˈlaɪtɪŋ]	die Beleuchtung	Good **lighting** in public spaces is important so that people feel safe at night.
	pose [pəʊz]	die Pose, die Haltung	This yoga **pose** is sometimes called "the snake". **power pose** = die Machtpose noun: **pose** – verb: (to) **pose** (posieren)
	pretty [ˈprɪti]	hübsch	Plockton is a **pretty** village on the Scottish coast.

Viewing

► p. 117	**costume** [ˈkɒstjuːm]	das Kostüm, die Verkleidung	! Betonung auf der 1. Silbe: <u>cos</u>tume
	(to) **sew** [səʊ], **sewed** [səʊd], **sewn** [səʊn]	nähen	! Aussprache: **sew** [səʊ], **sewed** [səʊd], **sewn** [səʊn] I'd like to learn to **sew** and design and make my own fashion.  a **sewing machine**
	paint [peɪnt]	die Farbe, der Lack	noun: **paint** – Let's go and buy some blue **paint**. verb: (to) **paint** (malen; (an)streichen) – Then we can **paint** this chair blue.
	skin [skɪn]	die Haut; die Schale *(z. B. Banane)*	• No one should experience bullying because of their **skin** colour. • There's a banana **skin** on the floor.
	headpiece [ˈhedpiːs]	der Kopfschmuck	 a **headpiece**
	interest (in) [ˈɪntrəst]	das Interesse (an)	noun: **interest (in)** – Do you have an **interest in** hiking? (= Are you interested ...?) verb: (to) **interest** sb. (**in** sth.) – Can I **interest** you **in** our school magazine? (jn. (für etwas) interessieren) adj: **interesting** (interessant); **interested (in)** (interessiert (an))

Study skills

► p. 118	(to) **flow** [fləʊ]	fließen; strömen	verb: (to) **flow** – The water **flows** very fast here. noun: **flow** (der Fluss; der Strom) – • Don't try to swim against the **flow** of the water. • The village isn't happy about the endless **flow** of tourists.
	(to) **order** [ˈɔːdə]	ordnen, anordnen	verb: (to) **order** – Please **order** your ideas and give your text a better structure. noun: **order** (die Reihenfolge, die Ordnung) – Please put these pictures **in order** (in eine Reihenfolge) / **in the correct order** (in die richtige Reihenfolge).
	habit [ˈhæbɪt]	die (An-)Gewohnheit	something that you do regularly Eating too many sweets is a bad **habit**.

Irregular verbs

Infinitive	Simple past	Past participle		Infinitive	Simple past	Past participle	
(to) **do**	**did**	**done**	machen, tun	(to) **send**	**sent**	**sent**	senden, schicken
(to) **feel**	**felt**	**felt**	(sich) fühlen	(to) **sew** [əʊ]	**sewed** [əʊ]	**sewn** [əʊ]	nähen
(to) **give**	**gave**	**given**	geben	(to) **sit**	**sat**	**sat**	sitzen; sich (hin)setzen
(to) **hit**	**hit**	**hit**	treffen, schlagen, stoßen	(to) **stand**	**stood**	**stood**	stehen
(to) **meet**	**met**	**met**	(sich) treffen	(to) **take**	**took**	**taken**	(mit)nehmen
(to) **put**	**put**	**put**	stellen, legen	(to) **tell**	**told**	**told**	erzählen, sagen
(to) **say** [eɪ]	**said** [e]	**said** [e]	sagen	(to) **think**	**thought**	**thought**	denken
(to) **see**	**saw**	**seen**	sehen	(to) **win**	**won**	**won**	gewinnen

°Unit 5 Two Irelands: Together

Die Unit 5 ist keine Pflicht-Unit, daher sind die neuen Wörter alle mit einem Kringel (°) markiert. Wenn ihr die Unit bearbeitet, kannst du die neuen Wörter lernen, aber sie werden nicht in Band 4 vorausgesetzt.

pp. 130/131	**°peace** [piːs]	der Friede(n)	Will there ever be **peace** in the world? (to) **keep (the) peace** = (den) Frieden erhalten, sichern
	°the Troubles *(pl)* [ˈtrʌblz]	der Nordirlandkonflikt (*wörtlich:* die Unruhen)	Der Nordirlandkonflikt war eine jahrzehntelange Phase bewaffneter Konflikte zwischen Katholiken und Protestanten zur Frage, ob Nordirland Teil des Vereinigten Königreichs bleiben sollte. Sie endete 1998 mit dem „Karfreitagsabkommen".
	°violence [ˈvaɪələns]	die Gewalt; die Gewalttätigkeit	Try to talk to each other. You never solve problems with **violence**!

Topic 1

▸ p. 132	**°... as well as ...** [əz ˈwel əz]	sowohl ... als auch ...	I have a bike **as well as** a car.
	°(to) **take a break**	(eine) Pause machen	I can't work any more. Let's **take a break** and get something to eat.
	°local [ˈləʊkl]	einheimisch, am/vom Ort	Do all your friends go to the **local** school? (= Gehen ... hier im Ort zur Schule?)
	°ship [ʃɪp]	das Schiff	 a ship
	°sadly [ˈsædli]	traurigerweise	We still miss our cat. **Sadly** he died last year.
	°(to) **build** [bɪld], **built, built** [bɪlt]	bauen	They **built** a new bridge across the river. The bridge **was built** in 2017. = Die Brücke wurde ... gebaut.

	°(to) **scan** (a text **for** sth.) [skæn]	(einen Text) überfliegen, (einen Text) absuchen (nach etwas)	(to) read a text quickly, looking only for important information
	°**specific** [spəˈsɪfɪk]	bestimmte(r, s), spezielle(r, s); genau, präzise	• Any **specific** time when you need the car back? (bestimmte(r, s)) • She gave us very **specific** instructions. (genau, präzise)
► p. 133	°**bed and breakfast (B&B)** [bed ən ˈbrekfəst]	das Zimmer mit Frühstück; die Frühstückspension	We stayed at a nice **B&B** in York last year. **Bed and breakfast** can be quite expensive.
	°**kettle** [ˈketl]	der Wasserkocher *(elektrisch)*	a **kettle** 
	°**guest** [gest]	der Gast	someone who visits someone else
	°**muesli** [ˈmjuːzli]	das Müsli	 **muesli**
	°**cold meat** [kəʊld ˈmiːt]	der (Braten-/Wurst-)Aufschnitt	! **meat** = **1.** *unzählbar:* I don't eat **meat**. (Fleisch) **2.** *zählbar:* **meats** = die Fleischsorten **cold meats** = die Aufschnittsorten

Viewing

► p. 134	°**times** [taɪmz]	mal	Six **times** three is eighteen.
	°**wish** [wɪʃ]	der Wunsch	noun: **wish** – verb: (to) **wish (for** sth.**)** If you had three **wishes**, what would you **wish for**?
	°(to) **wish (for** sth.**)** [wɪʃ]	(sich etwas) wünschen	
	°**absolutely** [ˈæbsəluːtli]	total, absolut, vollkommen	The show was **absolutely** amazing. Is that true? Are you **absolutely** sure? ! Betonung auf der 1. Silbe: **absolutely** [ˈæbsəluːtli]
	°**spectacular** [spekˈtækjələ]	spektakulär, aufsehenerregend	! Betonung auf der 2. Silbe: **spectacular** [spekˈtækjələ]
	°(to) **lock** [lɒk]	abschließen *(z. B. Tür)*	• (to) **lock** sb. **in** = jn. einsperren • (to) **lock** sb. **in a room / a wardrobe** = jn. in ein Zimmer / einen Kleiderschrank sperren

Im *English-German Dictionary* kannst du nachschlagen, was ein Wort bedeutet oder wie es ausgesprochen wird.

Es werden folgende **Abkürzungen und Symbole** verwendet:

infml = informal (umgangssprachlich) *pl = plural* (Mehrzahl)
sb. = somebody (jemand) *sth. = something* (etwas)
jd. = jemand jm. = jemandem jn. = jemanden

° Mit diesem Kringel sind Wörter markiert, die nicht zum Lernwortschatz gehören.

Die **Fundstellenangaben** zeigen, wo ein Wort zum ersten Mal vorkommt.
Die Ziffern in Klammern bezeichnen Seitenzahlen.

1 = Lighthouse 1 2 = Lighthouse 2 3: 1 (16) = Lighthouse 3, Unit 1, Seite 16

A

a [ə] ein, eine 1 **one hour a day** eine Stunde pro Tag 2

about [ə'baʊt]:
1. ungefähr 2
2. **about me/you/...** über mich/dich/... 1
What about ... ? Wie wäre es mit ... ? 1 **What about you?** Und du? / Was ist mit dir? 1

above [ə'bʌv] über, oberhalb (von); oben 2

°absolutely ['æbsəluːtli] total, absolut, vollkommen

accident ['æksɪdənt]:
1. der Unfall 2
2. der Zufall 2
by accident zufällig 2

account [ə'kaʊnt] das (Bank-)Konto; der Account 2

acoustic [ə'kuːstɪk] akustisch 2

across [ə'krɒs] über *(quer über)* 2

act [ækt]: Theater spielen, schauspielern; aufführen 2 **act out** aufführen, vorspielen 2

action ['ækʃn] die Aktion, die (spannende) Handlung 1

activist ['æktɪvɪst] der/die Aktivist/in 2

activity [æk'tɪvəti] die Aktivität, die Tätigkeit 1

actor ['æktə] der/die Schauspieler/in 2

actually ['æktʃuəli] eigentlich; tatsächlich 3: 2 (54)

ad [æd] *(infml) siehe* **advert**

add [æd] hinzufügen; addieren 1

additional [ə'dɪʃənl] zusätzliche(r, s) 3: 2 (57)

additional time [ə'dɪʃənl taɪm] die Nachspielzeit *(Fußball)* 3: 2 (57)

address [ə'dres] die Adresse 1

adult ['ædʌlt] der/die Erwachsene 3: 3 (75)

adventure [əd'ventʃə] das Abenteuer 2

advert ['ædvɜːt] *infml auch* **ad** die Anzeige, das Inserat; der Werbespot 2

advice *(no pl)* [əd'vaɪs] der Rat(schlag), Ratschläge 3: 2 (48) **give sb. advice** jm. Rat geben 3: 2 (48) **take sb.'s advice** auf js. Rat hören 3: 2 (48)

after ['ɑːftə]:
1. **after (school)** nach (der Schule) 1
2. **after (you read)** nachdem (du liest) 1

afternoon [ɑːftə'nuːn] der Nachmittag 1 **in the afternoon** nachmittags, am Nachmittag 1

again [ə'gen] wieder, noch einmal 1

against [ə'genst] gegen 2

°age [eɪdʒ] das Alter

agent ['eɪdʒənt] der/die Agent/in 2

ago [ə'gəʊ]: **two years ago** vor zwei Jahren 3: 1 (29)

agree [ə'griː]: **agree (with sb./sth.)** jm. zustimmen; mit etwas einverstanden sein 2 **agree on** sich einigen auf 2

ahead [ə'hed] voran, voraus 3: 2 (57)

air [eə] die Luft 3: 3 (83)

album ['ælbəm] das Album 2

°alien ['eɪliən]:
1. außerirdisch
2. der/die Außerirdische

all [ɔːl] alle(s) 1 **all day** der ganze Tag, den ganzen Tag (lang) 2 **all over** total, ganz und gar 2 **all over the world** überall auf der Welt, auf der ganzen Welt, weltweit 2 **all the family** die ganze Familie 2 **all the time** die ganze Zeit, ständig 2 **not ... at all** überhaupt nicht(s), gar nicht(s); überhaupt kein/e, gar kein/e 2

allergic (to) [ə'lɜːdʒɪk] allergisch (gegen) 1

allowed [ə'laʊd] erlaubt 3: 2 (48) **be allowed to do sth.** etwas tun dürfen 3: 2 (48)

almost ['ɔːlməʊst] fast, beinahe 2

alone [ə'ləʊn] allein 1

along the river [ə'lɒŋ] den Fluss entlang, am Fluss entlang 2

alphabet ['ælfəbet] das Alphabet 1

already [ɔːl'redi] schon 1

also ['ɔːlsəʊ] auch 1

°altogether [ɔːltə'geðə] insgesamt

always ['ɔːlweɪz] immer 1

am [æm]: **I'm (= I am)** ich bin 1

a.m. [eɪ'em]: **4 a.m.** 4 Uhr (früh-)morgens 1 **9 a.m.** 9 Uhr vormittags 1

amazing [ə'meɪzɪŋ] erstaunlich; großartig 1

ambulance ['æmbjələns] der Krankenwagen 2

an [ən] ein/e *(vor Vokalen)* 1

and [ænd], [ənd] und 1

angry ['æŋgri] wütend 1

animal ['ænɪml] das Tier 1

animal charity ['ænɪml tʃærəti] die wohltätige Organisation, die Tiere unterstützt 2

ankle ['æŋkl] der Knöchel, das Fußgelenk 2

annoy sb. [ə'nɔɪ] jn. ärgern 3: 2 (44/45)

annoyed [ə'nɔɪd] verärgert, ärgerlich 3: 2 (44/45)

annoying [ə'nɔɪɪŋ] ärgerlich *(unangenehm)* 3: 2 (44/45)

°anonymous [ə'nɒnɪməs] anonym

°another [ə'nʌðə] ein/e andere/r/s; noch ein/e

answer ['ɑːnsə]:
1. die Antwort 1
2. (be)antworten 1
answer the door aufmachen, zur/an die Tür gehen 3: 1 (26) **answer the phone** ans Telefon gehen 3: 1 (26)

any ['eni] jede(r/s) (beliebige), jegliche(r/s) 2 **(at) any time** zu jeder Zeit, jederzeit 2 **Do you have any questions?** Habt ihr / Hast du (irgendwelche) Fragen? 1 **not (...) any more** nicht mehr 2 **there aren't any ...** es gibt keine ... 1

anybody ['enibɒdi] irgendjemand; jede/r (beliebige) 2 **not (...) anybody** niemand 2

anyone ['eniwʌn] irgendjemand; jede/r (beliebige) 2 **not (...) anyone** niemand 2

anything ['eniθɪŋ] (irgend)etwas; alles; egal, was 2 **not ... anything** nichts 2

apartment [ə'pɑːtmənt] die Wohnung 2

app [æp] die App 1

appear [ə'pɪə] auftauchen, erscheinen 3: 2 (54) **appear to be/do** zu sein/zu tun scheinen 3: 2 (54)

apple ['æpl] der Apfel 1

April ['eɪprəl] der April 1

°aqueduct ['ækwɪdʌkt] der/das Aquädukt *(Brücke für eine Wasserleitung / einen Kanal)*

architect ['ɑːkɪtekt] der/die Architekt/in 2

are [ɑː]: **The books are £2.** Die Bücher kosten 2 Pfund. 2 **they are** sie sind 1 **they aren't** sie sind nicht 1 **you are** du bist / ihr seid 1
area ['eəriə] der Bereich, die Gegend, die Fläche 1
argue ['ɑːgjuː]:
1. argumentieren 3: 2 (61)
argue an opinion eine Meinung vertreten 3: 2 (61) **argue for/against sth.** sich für/gegen etwas aussprechen 3: 2 (61)
2. **argue (about)** (sich) streiten (über/wegen) 3: 2 (61)
argument ['ɑːgjumənt]:
1. das Argument 3: 2 (61)
2. der Streit 3: 2 (61)
arm [ɑːm] der Arm 2
around ... [ə'raʊnd] um (... herum), in ... umher 2 **all around the globe** auf der ganzen Welt 3: 1 (25)
arrival [ə'raɪvl] die Ankunft 2
arrive [ə'raɪv] ankommen 2
art [ɑːt] die Kunst 1
°article ['ɑːtɪkl] der Artikel
artist ['ɑːtɪst] der/die Künstler/in 2
as [æz], [əz]:
1. als, während *(Konjunktion)* 2
as they walk während sie gehen 2
2. als *(Präposition)* 2
as a teacher als Lehrer/in 2
3. wie *(Präposition)* 2
(not) as bad as (nicht) so schlecht/ schlimm wie 2 **°... as well as ...** sowohl ... als auch ...
ask [ɑːsk]:
1. fragen 1
ask a question eine Frage stellen 1
2. **ask sb. for sth.** jn. um etwas bitten 1
ask sb. to do sth. jn. bitten, etwas zu tun 1
asleep [ə'sliːp]: **be asleep** schlafen 2 **fall asleep** einschlafen 2
assembly [ə'sembli] die Schulversammlung 1
assistant [ə'sɪstənt]
1. der/die Assistent/in 2
2. *(= shop assistant)* der/die Verkäufer/in 2
at [æt], [ət] an; in; bei; auf 1 **at 8 o'clock** um 8 Uhr 1 **at a good price** zu einem guten Preis 3: 2 (46) **at least** wenigstens, zumindest 2 **at night** nachts, in der Nacht 2 **at the cinema** im Kino 1 **at the top (of)** oben, am oberen Ende (von); an der Spitze (von) 1 **at work** bei der Arbeit, am Arbeitsplatz 1 **be good at sth. / at doing sth.** etwas gut können; gut in etwas sein 1 **Open your books at page 10.** Schlagt eure Bücher auf Seite 10 auf. 1
ate [eɪt], [et] *siehe* **eat**
°attack [ə'tæk] angreifen
audio ['ɔːdiəʊ] Audio-, Ton- 3: 1 (31)
August ['ɔːgəst] der August 1
aunt [ɑːnt] die Tante 1
away [ə'weɪ] weg, fort 1

B

baby ['beɪbi] das Baby 2
babysat ['beɪbisæt] *siehe* **babysit**
babysit ['beɪbisɪt], **babysat, babysat** babysitten 2
babysitter ['beɪbisɪtə] der/die Babysitter/in 2
babysitting ['beɪbisɪtɪŋ] das Babysitten 2
back [bæk]:
1. zurück 2
back at home wieder zu Hause 2 **like/love sb. back** js. Liebe erwidern, jn. auch mögen/lieben 3: 2 (48)
2. **at the back (of the bus/cinema)** hinten (im Bus/im Kino) 2 **at the back of the book** hinten im Buch 2 **on the back of the card** auf der Rückseite der Karte 2
background ['bækgraʊnd] der Hintergrund 3: (12/13)
bad [bæd] schlecht; schlimm 1
badly ['bædli]: **do badly** schlecht abschneiden, keinen Erfolg haben 3: 2 (48)
bag [bæg] die Tasche 1
bagpipes *(pl)* ['bægpaɪps] der Dudelsack 3: (12/13)
bake [beɪk] backen 2
baker ['beɪkə] der/die Bäcker/in 2
bakery ['beɪkəri] die Bäckerei 2
ball [bɔːl] der Ball 1
balloon [bə'luːn] der Ballon 1
banana [bə'nɑːnə] die Banane 1
band [bænd] die Band, die Musikgruppe 1
bank [bæŋk] die Bank *(Geldinstitut)* 2
bank account ['bæŋk əkaʊnt] das Bankkonto 2
barbecue ['bɑːbɪkjuː] das Grillfest, das Grillen 2
bark (at sb.) [bɑːk] (jn. an)bellen 1
basketball ['bɑːskɪtbɔːl] der Basketball 1
°bass [beɪs] der Bass *(Instrument; Stimmlage)*
bathroom ['bɑːθruːm] das Bad(ezimmer) 1
be [biː], **was/were, been** sein 1 **I want to be a firefighter.** Ich möchte Feuerwehrmann/-frau werden. 2
beach [biːtʃ] der Strand 1 **on the beach** am Strand 1 **to the beach** zum Strand, an den Strand 1
°beaten ['biːtn]: **it cannot be beaten** es ist unschlagbar *(wörtlich: es kann nicht geschlagen / besiegt werden)*
beautiful ['bjuːtɪfl] wunderschön 2
beauty ['bjuːti] die Schönheit 2
became [bɪ'keɪm] *siehe* **become**
because [bɪ'kɒz] weil 1
because of [bɪ'kɒz əv] wegen 3: 4 (104)
become [bɪ'kʌm], **became, become** werden 2
bed [bed] das Bett 1 **go to bed** ins Bett gehen 1
°bed and breakfast (B&B) [bed ən 'brekfəst] das Zimmer mit Frühstück; die Frühstückspension
bedroom ['bedruːm] das Schlafzimmer 1
been [biːn] *siehe* **be**
before [bɪ'fɔː]:
1. **before (school / the lesson)** vor (der Schule / der Unterrichtsstunde) 1
2. **before (you read)** bevor (du liest) 1
3. vorher; zuvor; schon einmal 3: 3 (78)
began [bɪ'gæn] *siehe* **begin**
begin [bɪ'gɪn], **began, begun** anfangen, beginnen 3: 2 (58)
beginning [bɪ'gɪnɪŋ] der Anfang 3: 2 (58)
°begun [bɪ'gʌn] *siehe* **begin**
behind [bɪ'haɪnd] hinter 1
believe (in) [bɪ'liːv] glauben (an) 2
°bell [bel] die Klingel, die Glocke
below [bɪ'ləʊ] unter(halb von); unten 2
best [best] beste(r, s); am besten 1 **like sth. best** etwas am liebsten mögen 2
better ['betə] besser 2 **like sth. better** etwas lieber mögen 2
between [bɪ'twiːn] zwischen 2
big [bɪg]:
1. groß 1
2. schwer, dick *(Person)* 2
big wheel [bɪg 'wiːl] das Riesenrad 3: 1 (14/15)
bike [baɪk] das Fahrrad 1
bike lane ['baɪk leɪn] der Radweg 3: 1 (16)
bio ['baɪəʊ] *siehe* **biography**
biography [baɪ'ɒgrəfi] *kurz auch* **bio** die Biografie 3: 4 (111)
bird [bɜːd] der Vogel 2
birthday ['bɜːθdeɪ] der Geburtstag 1 **Happy birthday!** Herzlichen Glückwunsch zum Geburtstag! 1 **My birthday is in April.** Ich habe im April Geburtstag. 1 **on my birthday** an meinem Geburtstag 1 **When's your birthday?** Wann hast du Geburtstag? 1
biscuit ['bɪskɪt] der Keks, das Plätzchen 2
bit [bɪt]: **a bit** ein bisschen, ein wenig 2
black [blæk] schwarz 1
blame sb. (for sth.) [bleɪm] jm. die Schuld geben (an etwas), es jm. übelnehmen 3: 3 (86)
blanket ['blæŋkɪt] die Decke *(zum Zudecken u. Ä.)* 2
blog [blɒg]:
1. bloggen 3: 1 (25)
2. der/das Blog *(Internet-Tagebuch)* 3: 1 (25)
blond [blɒnd] blond 2
blue [bluː] blau 1
board [bɔːd] die Tafel 1
boat [bəʊt] das Boot; das Schiff 1
body ['bɒdi] der Körper 2

book [bʊk] das Buch 1
°bookmark [ˈbʊkmɑːk] das Lesezeichen
boot [buːt] der Stiefel 2
bored [bɔːd] gelangweilt 2 **be bored / get bored** sich langweilen 2 **I'm bored** mir ist langweilig 2
boring [ˈbɔːrɪŋ] langweilig 2
born [bɔːn]: **he was born** er wurde geboren 2
borrow [ˈbɒrəʊ] (aus)leihen, sich borgen 3: 2 (46)
boss [bɒs] der Boss, der/die Chef/in 2
both [bəʊθ] beide 3: 3 (85) **both ... and ...** sowohl ... als auch ... 3: 3 (85)
bottle [ˈbɒtl] die Flasche 2
bottom [ˈbɒtəm] das untere Ende 2
bottomless [ˈbɒtəmləs] bodenlos, unerschöpflich; mit kostenlosem Nachschank *(bei Getränken z. B. in Cafés)* 3: 1 (22)
bought [bɔːt] *siehe* **buy**
bowling [ˈbəʊlɪŋ] das Bowling, das Kegeln 1
box [bɒks] die Box, der Kasten 2
boy [bɔɪ] der Junge 1
boyfriend [ˈbɔɪfrend] der (feste) Freund 2
braces *(pl)* [ˈbreɪsɪz] die Zahnspange, die Zahnklammer 2
°bracket [ˈbrækɪt] die *(runde)* Klammer *(in Texten)*
°brainstorm [ˈbreɪnstɔːm] Ideen (ungeordnet) sammeln
brand [brænd] die (Produkt-) Marke 3: 2 (46)
brave [breɪv] mutig 2
bread [bred] das Brot 1
break [breɪk] die Pause 1 **°take a break** (eine) Pause machen
break [breɪk], **broke, broken** (zer-) brechen 2 **break the fast** das Fasten brechen 2
breakfast [ˈbrekfəst] das Frühstück 1
breath [breθ] der Atem(zug) 3: 4 (115) **take a deep breath** tief durchatmen 3: 4 (115)
breathe (in/out) [briːð] (ein-/aus-) atmen 2
bridge [brɪdʒ] die Brücke 2
bring [brɪŋ] bringen, mitbringen 1
Britain [ˈbrɪtn] Großbritannien 1
British [ˈbrɪtɪʃ] britisch 1
British Isles *(pl)* [brɪtɪʃ ˈaɪlz] die Britischen Inseln 3: (10/11)
broke [brəʊk] *siehe* **break**
broken [ˈbrəʊkən]: **be broken** zerbrochen, kaputt, sein 2
brother [ˈbrʌðə] der Bruder 1
brown [braʊn] braun 1
brunch [brʌntʃ] das Brunch 2
brush [brʌʃ]:
1. die Bürste 1
2. bürsten 1
brush your teeth (sich) die Zähne putzen 1
°build [bɪld], **built, built** bauen
building [ˈbɪldɪŋ] das Gebäude 1
°built [bɪlt] *siehe* **build** **it was built** es wurde gebaut
bully [ˈbʊli]:
1. der/die Mobber/in; der/die Tyrann/in 1
2. tyrannisieren, mobben 1
burger [ˈbɜːgə] der Hamburger *(Frikadelle)* 3: 1 (20)
bus [bʌs] der Bus 1 **by bus** mit dem Bus 1 **on the bus** im Bus 1
business [ˈbɪznəs] das Geschäft, der Betrieb 2 **start a business** ein Geschäft aufmachen, einen Betrieb gründen/eröffnen 2
business card [ˈbɪznəs kɑːd] die Visitenkarte, die Geschäftskarte 2
business owner [ˈbɪznəs əʊnə] der/die Geschäftsinhaber/in 2
busy [ˈbɪzi] (viel)beschäftigt 1 **be busy** beschäftigt sein, (viel) zu tun haben 1
but [bʌt], [bət] aber 1
butter [ˈbʌtə] die Butter 1
buy [baɪ], **bought, bought** kaufen 1
by [baɪ]: **by bus** mit dem Bus 1 **by the sea** am Meer, an der See 1 **pay by card** mit Karte (be)zahlen *(z. B. Bankkarte)* 2
Bye. [baɪ] Tschüs. 1

C

°caber [ˈkeɪbə] der Baumstamm
cafe [ˈkæfeɪ] das Café 1
cake [keɪk] der Kuchen, die Torte 1
calendar [ˈkælɪndə] der Kalender 2
call [kɔːl]:
1. nennen; rufen; anrufen 2
call sb. names jn. beschimpfen 3: 2 (57)
2. der Ruf 2
3. *(kurz für:* **phone call***)* der (Telefon-) Anruf 2
called [kɔːld]: **be called** heißen 1
calm [kɑːm] ruhig, besonnen 2
came [keɪm] *siehe* **come**
camera [ˈkæmərə] die Kamera 2
camping [ˈkæmpɪŋ] das Camping 3: 3 (80)
campsite [ˈkæmpsaɪt] der Campingplatz 2
can [kæn], [kən] können 1
canal [kəˈnæl] der Kanal 3: (12/13)
candle [ˈkændl] die Kerze 2
can't [kɑːnt]: **I can't (= cannot)** ich kann nicht 1
canteen [kænˈtiːn] die Kantine, die (Schul-)Mensa 1
cap [kæp] die (Schirm-)Mütze, die Kappe 1
cape [keɪp] das Cape *(Umhang)* 2
capital [ˈkæpɪtl]:
1. **capital (city)** die Hauptstadt 3: 3 (72/73)
2. **capital (letter)** der Großbuchstabe 3: 3 (72/73)
capsule [ˈkæpsjuːl] die Kapsel; die Raumkapsel; die Kabine *(auf einem Riesenrad)* 3: 1 (21)
°caption [ˈkæpʃn] die Bildunterschrift
car [kɑː] das Auto 1
card [kɑːd] die Karte 1 **business card** die Visitenkarte, die Geschäftskarte 2 **pay by card** mit Karte (be)zahlen *(z. B. Bankkarte)* 2 **playing card** die Spielkarte 1
care [ˈkeə]:
1. die Sorgfalt, die Vorsicht 2
take care vorsichtig sein, aufpassen 2
2. die Versorgung, die Betreuung; die Pflege 3: 2 (53)
take care of sb./sth. sich um jn./etwas kümmern 3: 2 (53)
3. **care about sth.** etwas wichtig nehmen 3: 2 (53)
care for betreuen, pflegen; sich kümmern um; aufpassen auf 3: 2 (53)
I care about animals. Tiere liegen mir am Herzen. 3: 2 (53)
careful [ˈkeəfl] vorsichtig 1
careless [ˈkeələs] unvorsichtig, leichtsinnig 3: 1 (23)
carer [ˈkeərə] die Pflegekraft; der/die Betreuer/in 3: 2 (53)
carnival [ˈkɑːnɪvl] der Karneval 2
carrot [ˈkærət] die Möhre, die Karotte 1
carry [ˈkæri] tragen; bei sich haben; befördern 3: 3 (76)
cartoon [kɑːˈtuːn] der Zeichentrickfilm; der Comic, der Cartoon 2
case [keɪs] das Etui, der Behälter, der Kasten 1
cash [kæʃ] das Cash, das Bargeld 2 **pay (in) cash** bar bezahlen 2
cash machine [ˈkæʃ məʃiːn] der Geldautomat 2
castle [ˈkɑːsl] die Burg 2
cat [kæt] die Katze 1
catch [kætʃ], **caught, caught** fangen; erwischen; nehmen *(z. B. Zug, Bus)* 3: 1 (27)
caught [kɔːt] *siehe* **catch**
cave [keɪv] die Höhle 3: 3 (87)
celebrate [ˈselɪbreɪt] feiern 2
celebration [selɪˈbreɪʃn] die Feier, das Fest 2
°Celtic [ˈkeltɪk] keltisch
cent [sent] der Cent 2
central [ˈsentrəl] zentral 3: 1 (20)
centre [ˈsentə] das Zentrum; die Mitte 1
chair [tʃeə] der Stuhl 1
champion [ˈtʃæmpiən] der/die Meister/in *(in einer Sportart)*, der Champion 3: 2 (53)
chance [tʃɑːns]:
1. die Chance, die Gelegenheit 3: 2 (50)
2. das Risiko 3: 2 (50)
Don't take any chances! Geh auf Nummer sicher! / Geh keine Risiken ein! 3: 2 (50)
change [tʃeɪndʒ]:
1. **change (into)** (sich) (ver)ändern (zu/in); wechseln; (sich) verwandeln (in), werden (zu) 2
change (clothes) sich umziehen *(frische Kleidung anziehen)* 2

change (trains) umsteigen 2
2. die Veränderung, der Wechsel, die Verwandlung 2
a change of clothes die (frische) Kleidung zum Wechseln 2 Changing of the Guards die Wachablösung 3: 1 (21)
3. das Wechselgeld 2

channel ['tʃænl] der Sender, der (TV-) Kanal 3: 4 (110) the (English) Channel der Ärmelkanal 3: 4 (110)

character ['kærəktə] der Charakter; die Figur *(aus einer Geschichte)* 2

charge [tʃɑːdʒ] aufladen *(Smartphone, Batterie, ...)* 3: 4 (108)

charger ['tʃɑːdʒə] das Ladegerät 3: 4 (108)

charity ['tʃærəti] die wohltätige Organisation 2 animal charity die wohltätige Organisation, die Tiere unterstützt 2

charity shop ['tʃærəti ʃɒp] *das Geschäft, das gespendete Waren für wohltätige Zwecke verkauft* 2

chat [tʃæt]:
1. chat (with) chatten (mit); sich unterhalten (mit) 2
2. die Unterhaltung; der Chat 2
have a chat eine Unterhaltung führen, sich unterhalten 2

cheap [tʃiːp] billig, preiswert 3: 1 (17)

check [tʃek]:
1. die (Über-)Prüfung, die Kontrolle 1
2. (über)prüfen, kontrollieren 1
check sb./sth. out *(infml)* sich jn./etwas anschauen, anhören; etwas ausprobieren 2

checklist ['tʃeklɪst] die Checkliste 2

°checkpoint ['tʃekpɔɪnt] der Kontrollpunkt

cheer [tʃɪə] jubeln, *(Sportler/innen)* anfeuern 3: 2 (51)

cheese [tʃiːz] der Käse 1

chemical ['kemɪkl]:
1. Chemikalie 2
2. chemisch 2

chicken ['tʃɪkɪn] das Huhn; das (Brat-)Hähnchen 1

chickpea ['tʃɪkpiː] die Kichererbse 3: 1 (22)

child [tʃaɪld], *pl* children das Kind 2

children ['tʃɪldrən] *Plural von child*

chips *(pl)* [tʃɪps] die Pommes frites 1 fish and chips der Fisch mit Pommes Frites 1

chocolate ['tʃɒklət] die Schokolade 1 hot chocolate der Kakao, die heiße (Trink-)Schokolade 1

choice [tʃɔɪs] die (Aus-)Wahl; die Entscheidung 3: 3 (86)

choir ['kwaɪə] der Chor 3: 4 (102/103)

choose [tʃuːz], chose, chosen (aus) wählen 2 choose to do sth. sich entscheiden, beschließen etwas zu tun 3: 3 (86)

chore [tʃɔː] die (Haus-)Arbeit, die *(lästige)* Pflicht 2 do chores (Haus-)Arbeiten erledigen 2

chose [tʃəuz] *siehe choose*

chosen ['tʃəuzn] *siehe choose*

Christmas ['krɪsməs] (das) Weihnachten 2

Christmas Day [krɪsməs 'deɪ] der 1. Weihnachtstag (25. 12.) 2

church [tʃɜːtʃ] die Kirche 2

cinema ['sɪnəmə] das Kino 1 at the cinema im Kino 1

circle ['sɜːkl] der Kreis 1

circus ['sɜːkəs] der Zirkus 1

city ['sɪti] die (Groß-)Stadt 1

clap (your hands) [klæp] (in die Hände) klatschen 3: 2 (51)

class [klɑːs] die Klasse; der Unterricht; der Kurs 1 in class im Unterricht 1

class teacher ['klɑːs tiːtʃə] der/die Klassenlehrer/in 1

classic ['klæsɪk]:
1. der Klassiker 3: 1 (18)
2. klassisch 3: 1 (18)

classical ['klæsɪkl] klassisch 2

classical music [klæsɪkl 'mjuːzɪk] klassische Musik 2

classmate ['klɑːsmeɪt] der/die Mitschüler/in 3: 2 (55)

classroom ['klɑːsruːm] das Klassenzimmer 1

clean [kliːn]:
1. sauber 1
2. sauber machen, putzen 1
clean sth. up etwas aufräumen, sauber machen 1

clean-up ['kliːn ʌp] das Säubern, das Saubermachen 1

clean-up day ['kliːn ʌp deɪ] der Dreck-weg-Tag *(Aktionstag zum Müllsammeln)* 1

cleaner ['kliːnə] die Reinigungskraft 1

clear [klɪə] klar, deutlich 2

clever ['klevə] schlau, klug 1

click [klɪk]:
1. der Klick, das Klicken 2
2. click (on) klicken (auf), anklicken 2

cliff [klɪf] die Klippe 3: 3 (78)

cliff jumping ['klɪf dʒʌmpɪŋ] das Klippenspringen 3: 3 (78)

climate ['klaɪmət] das Klima 3: 3 (83)

climate change ['klaɪmət tʃeɪndʒ] der Klimawandel 3: 3 (83)

climb [klaɪm]:
1. der Aufstieg, die Klettertour; der Anstieg 2
2. klettern (auf) 2

climber ['klaɪmə] der Kletterer, die Kletterin 2

clock [klɒk] die (Wand-, Stand-, Turm-)Uhr 1

close [kləuz] schließen, zumachen 1

closed [kləuzd] geschlossen 1

clothes *(pl)* [kləuðz] die Kleidung, die Kleidungsstücke 1 a change of clothes (frische) Kleidung zum Wechseln 2

clothes swap ['kləuðz swɒp] der Kleidertausch, die Kleidertauschparty 1

cloud [klaud] die Wolke 1

cloudy ['klaudi] wolkig, bewölkt 1

clown [klaun] der Clown 1

club [klʌb] der Klub, der Verein 1 school club die AG *(in der Schule)* 1

clue [kluː] der (Lösungs-)Hinweis; der Anhaltspunkt 3: 1 (28) I don't have a clue. / I have no clue. *(infml)* Ich habe keine Ahnung. / Keine Ahnung. 3: 1 (28)

coach [kəutʃ] der (Reise-)Bus 3: 2 (59)

°coal [kəul] die Kohle

coast [kəust] die Küste 3: 3 (72/73)

cocoa ['kəukəu] der Kakao 1

code [kəud] programmieren *(Computer)*; kodieren 1

coding ['kəudɪŋ] das Programmieren *(Computer)* 1

coffee ['kɒfi] der Kaffee 1

coin [kɔɪn] die Münze 2

cola ['kəulə] die Cola 1

cold [kəuld]:
1. kalt 1
be cold frieren 1
2. die Kälte 1
3. die Erkältung 1
have a cold erkältet sein 1

°cold meat [kəuld 'miːt] der (Braten-/Wurst-)Aufschnitt cold meats *(pl)* die Aufschnittsorten

collect [kə'lekt] (ein)sammeln 1

°Cologne [kə'ləun] Köln

colour ['kʌlə] die Farbe 1 What colour is ...? Welche Farbe hat ...? 1

colourful ['kʌləfl] farbig, bunt 3: 1 (23)

colourless ['kʌlələs] farblos 3: 1 (23)

column ['kɒləm] die Säule; die Spalte *(in Texten)* 3: 1 (21)

come [kʌm], came, come (mit)kommen 1 come after sb. hinter jm. herkommen 3: 1 (27) come off (sth.) abgehen (von etwas), (herunter-) fallen (von etwas), sich lösen (von etwas) 3: 3 (78)

comfortable ['kʌmftəbl] bequem, gemütlich 3: 2 (46)

comic ['kɒmɪk] der Comic 1

command [kə'mɑːnd] der Befehl, das Kommando 3: 4 (109)

comment (about/on sth.) ['kɒment]:
1. (etwas) kommentieren 3: 4 (115)
2. der Kommentar (über/zu etwas) 3: 4 (115)

°common ['kɒmən]: have sth. in common etwas gemeinsam haben

community [kə'mjuːnəti] die Gemeinschaft, die Gemeinde 3: 1 (29)

compare (to/with) [kəm'peə] vergleichen (mit) 3: 2 (51)

competition [kɒmpə'tɪʃn] der Wettbewerb 1

complete [kəm'pliːt]:
1. vervollständigen 3: 2 (60)
2. vollständig, komplett 3: 2 (60)

completely [kəm'pliːtli] völlig, absolut *(Adv.)* 3: 2 (60)

compliment ['kɒmplɪmənt] das Kompliment 3: 2 (55) pay sb. a compliment jm. ein Kompliment machen 3: 2 (55)

computer [kəm'pjuːtə] der Computer 1

computing [kəmˈpjuːtɪŋ] die Informatik 1
concert [ˈkɒnsət] das Konzert 2
confidence [ˈkɒnfɪdəns] das (Selbst-) Vertrauen, die Zuversicht 3:2 (52)
confident [ˈkɒnfɪdənt] (selbst)sicher; zuversichtlich 2
conflict [ˈkɒnflɪkt] der Konflikt, die Auseinandersetzung, der Streit 3:2 (58)
confused [kənˈfjuːzd] verwirrt 3:4 (114)
console [kənˈsəʊl] die Konsole 1
contact [ˈkɒntækt]:
1. der Kontakt 2
2. **contact sb.** Kontakt aufnehmen mit jm., sich in Verbindung setzen mit jm. 2
°**conversation** [kɒnvəˈseɪʃn] das Gespräch
cook [kʊk]:
1. der Koch, die Köchin 1
2. kochen 1
cooking [ˈkʊkɪŋ] das Kochen 1
cool [kuːl] cool 1
°**copy** [ˈkɒpi]:
1. kopieren, abschreiben
2. die Kopie; das Exemplar
correct [kəˈrekt]:
1. korrekt 3:3 (89)
2. korrigieren 3:3 (89)
cosplay [ˈkɒspleɪ] das Cosplay *(Sich-verkleiden als eine Figur z. B. aus einem Manga)* 3:4 (117)
cost [kɒst]:
1. die Kosten; der Preis 1
2. **cost, cost, cost** kosten 1
costume [ˈkɒstjuːm] das Kostüm, die Verkleidung 3:4 (117)
cough [kɒf]:
1. husten 2
2. der Husten 2
could [kʊd]:
1. **I could** ich konnte 2
2. **he could** er könnte 2
°**count** [kaʊnt] zählen
country [ˈkʌntri] das Land, *(auch:)* die ländliche Gegend 1
course [kɔːs]:
1. der Kurs 2
2. **main course** das Hauptgericht 1
cousin [ˈkʌzn] der Cousin, die Cousine 1
crafts *(pl)* [krɑːfts] das Kunsthandwerk, das Basteln 1
crazy [ˈkreɪzi] verrückt 2 **be crazy about sth.** wild auf etwas sein, versessen auf etwas sein 2
cream [kriːm] die Sahne 1
create [kriˈeɪt] (er)schaffen, erstellen 2
creative [kriˈeɪtɪv] kreativ 2
°**creative commons** [krieɪtɪv ˈkɒmənz] „das schöpferische Gemeingut" *(gemeinnützige Organisation, die das einfache Verbreiten von Nutzungsrechten zum Ziel hat)*
cricket [ˈkrɪkɪt] das Kricket *(Mannschaftssportart)* 1
cross [krɒs]:
1. das Kreuz 3:1 (16)
2. kreuzen, überqueren 3:1 (16)
cross your fingers die Daumen drücken/halten *(jm. Glück / gutes Gelingen wünschen)* 3:2 (57)
°**crowd** [kraʊd] die (Menschen-) Menge
°**crown** [kraʊn] die Krone
crush [krʌʃ]:
1. die Schwärmerei, das Verliebtsein 3:2 (48)
have a crush (on sb.) in jn. verliebt sein 3:2 (48)
2. der Schwarm *(jd., in den/die man verliebt ist)* 3:2 (48)
cry [kraɪ]:
1. der Schrei, der Ruf 3:3 (85)
2. weinen; rufen, schreien 3:3 (85)
cucumber [ˈkjuːkʌmbə] die Gurke *(Salatgurke)* 3:1 (22)
cupcake [ˈkʌpkeɪk] der Cupcake *(kleiner Muffin-ähnlicher Kuchen)* 2
curl [kɜːl] die Locke 2
curly [ˈkɜːli] lockig 2
curry [ˈkʌri] das Curry *(Gewürz und auch Gericht)* 2
cushion [ˈkʊʃn] das Kissen 1
custard [ˈkʌstəd] der Custard *(Vanillesoße)* 1
customer [ˈkʌstəmə] der Kunde, die Kundin 2
cut [kʌt]:
1. der Schnitt 1
2. schneiden 1
cute [kjuːt] niedlich, süß 1
cyberbullying [ˈsaɪbəbʊliɪŋ] das Cybermobbing 3:4 (112)
cycle [ˈsaɪkl] Rad fahren 1
cycle lane [ˈsaɪkl leɪn] der Radweg 3:1 (16)
cycling [ˈsaɪklɪŋ] das Radfahren 1
°**Cymru** [ˈkʌmri] *Name für Wales auf Welsh*

D

dad [dæd] der Papa, der Vati 1
dance [dɑːns]:
1. tanzen 1
2. der Tanz 1
dancer [ˈdɑːnsə] der/die Tänzer/in 1
dancing [ˈdɑːnsɪŋ] das Tanzen 1
danger [ˈdeɪndʒə] die Gefahr 2
dangerous [ˈdeɪndʒərəs] gefährlich 2
dark [dɑːk]:
1. dunkel 2
2. das Dunkel, die Dunkelheit 3:1 (18)
date [deɪt] das Datum 1 **birthday date** das Datum des Geburtstags 1
daughter [ˈdɔːtə] die Tochter 2
day [deɪ] der Tag 1 **the days of the week** *(pl)* die Wochentage 1 **work long days** lange arbeiten, lange Arbeitstage haben 1
dead [ded] tot 1 **My phone is dead.** Mein Telefon-Akku ist leer. 3:1 (26)
°**deal with** [ˈdiːl wɪð], **dealt, dealt** klarkommen mit, fertigwerden mit, umgehen mit
°**dealt** [delt] *siehe* **deal with**
°**dear** [dɪə]: **be dear to sb.** jm. lieb (und teuer) sein *(jm. sehr wichtig sein)*
Dear ... [dɪə] Liebe/r ... 2
debate [dɪˈbeɪt]:
1. debattieren 3:4 (110)
2. die Debatte 3:4 (110)
hold/have a debate eine Debatte führen 3:4 (110)
December [dɪˈsembə] der Dezember 1
decide [dɪˈsaɪd] beschließen, sich entscheiden 3:3 (77) **decide on sth.** etwas beschließen, sich für etwas entscheiden 3:3 (77) **decide to do sth.** beschließen, sich entscheiden etwas zu tun 3:3 (77)
decorate [ˈdekəreɪt] dekorieren, schmücken 2
decoration [dekəˈreɪʃn] der Dekoration, der Schmuck, die Verzierung 2
deep [diːp] tief 3:3 (74)
°**definition** [defɪˈnɪʃn] die Definition
delete [dɪˈliːt] löschen 3:4 (110)
delicious [dɪˈlɪʃəs] köstlich, lecker 2
department store [dɪˈpɑːtmənt stɔː] das Kaufhaus 3:1 (26)
describe [dɪˈskraɪb] beschreiben 2
description [dɪˈskrɪpʃn] die Beschreibung 2
design [dɪˈzaɪn]:
1. die Gestaltung, das Design 1
2. entwerfen, gestalten 2
design and technology [dɪzaɪn ən tekˈnɒlədʒi] das Werken, der Werkunterricht 1
designer [dɪˈzaɪnə] der/die Designer/in 2
desk [desk]:
1. der Schreibtisch 1
2. der Schalter *(z. B. Verkaufs-, Postschalter)* 3:1 (27)
dessert [dɪˈzɜːt] die Nachspeise, das Dessert 1 **for dessert** zum/als Nachtisch 1
°**Dia Duit!** [dʒɪə ˈxʊɪtʃ] Hallo! *(irisches Gälisch; wörtlich: Gott sei mit dir/euch/Ihnen!)*
dictionary [ˈdɪkʃənri] das Wörterbuch, das *(alphabetische)* Wörterverzeichnis 2
did [dɪd] *siehe* **do** **I didn't buy ... (= did not)** ich kaufte nicht; ich habe nicht gekauft 2
die (of) [daɪ] sterben (an) 2
difference [ˈdɪfrəns] der Unterschied 1 **make a difference** etwas bewirken, etwas ausmachen 3:1 (29)
different (to) [ˈdɪfrənt] verschieden; anders (als) 1
difficult [ˈdɪfɪkəlt] schwierig, schwer 3:2 (61)
dig [dɪg] graben 1
digital [ˈdɪdʒɪtl] digital 3:4 (102/103)
dining area [ˈdaɪnɪŋ eəriə] der Essbereich, die Essecke 1

dining room [ˈdaɪnɪŋ ruːm] das Esszimmer 1
dinner [ˈdɪnə] das Abendessen 1 **for dinner** zum Abendessen 1
dip [dɪp] der Dip 3: 1 (22)
directions *(pl)* [dəˈrekʃnz] die Wegbeschreibung(en) 3: 1 (27) **ask for directions** nach dem Weg fragen 3: 1 (27) **give directions** den Weg beschreiben 3: 1 (27)
dirty [ˈdɜːti] schmutzig 1
disability [dɪsəˈbɪləti] die Behinderung 3: 2 (44/45)
disabled [dɪsˈeɪbld] (körper)behindert 3: 2 (44/45)
disagree [dɪsəˈgriː] nicht zustimmen, widersprechen 3: 1 (25)
°disaster [dɪˈzɑːstə] die Katastrophe, das Unglück
disco [ˈdɪskəʊ] die Disco 2
discover [dɪˈskʌvə] entdecken 2
discuss [dɪˈskʌs] diskutieren 3: 1 (28)
discussion [dɪˈskʌʃn] die Diskussion 3: 1 (28)
dish [dɪʃ]:
1. die Schüssel, die Schale 1
2. das Gericht *(Mahlzeit)* 1
main dish das Hauptgericht 1
dishwasher [ˈdɪʃwɒʃə] die Geschirrspülmaschine 2
°ditch sth. [dɪtʃ] *(infml)* etwas über Bord werfen
do [duː], **did, done** machen, tun 1 **do badly** schlecht abschneiden, keinen Erfolg haben 3: 2 (48) **do well** gut abschneiden, erfolgreich sein 3: 2 (48) **do your homework** Hausaufgaben machen 1
doctor (Dr) [ˈdɒktə] der Arzt, die Ärztin; der/die Doktor/in (Dr.) 2
dog [dɒg] der Hund 1
dolphin [ˈdɒlfɪn] der Delfin 2
done [dʌn] *siehe* **do** **Well done.** Gut gemacht! 1
donkey [ˈdɒŋki] der Esel 3: 4 (102/103)
donut [ˈdəʊnʌt] der Donut *(ringförmiges Gebäck aus Hefeteig)* 2
door [dɔː] die Tür 1 **answer the door** aufmachen, zur/an die Tür gehen 3: 1 (26)
doorkeeper [ˈdɔːkiːpə] der/die Pförtner/in 3: 1 (27)
°double [ˈdʌbl] doppelt, Doppel-
down [daʊn] hinunter, herunter 2
download [ˈdaʊnləʊd]:
1. der/das Download 3: 4 (108)
2. herunterladen 3: 4 (108)
dragon [ˈdrægən] der Drache 3: 4 (102/103)
draw [drɔː] zeichnen 1
drawing [ˈdrɔːɪŋ]:
1. die Zeichnung 1
2. das Zeichnen 1
dream [driːm]:
1. der Traum 1
2. **dream (of/about sth.)** träumen (von etwas) 1
dress [dres]:
1. das Kleid 2
2. sich kleiden, sich anziehen 2
dressed [drest]: **get dressed** sich anziehen 1
drink [drɪŋk]:
1. das Getränk 1
2. trinken 1
drive [draɪv], **drove, driven** *(mit dem Auto)* fahren 3: 1 (16)
driven [ˈdrɪvn] *siehe* **drive**
drone [drəʊn] die Drohne 1
°drop the beat [drɒp ðə ˈbiːt] den/einen Beat unter die Musik legen
drove [drəʊv] *siehe* **drive**
°dungeon [ˈdʌndʒən] der Kerker, das Verlies *(in einer Burg)*
during [ˈdjʊərɪŋ] während 2

E

each [iːtʃ] jede(r, s) (einzelne), jeweils 2
each other [iːtʃ ˈʌðə] einander, sich (gegenseitig) 2
°ear [ɪə] das Ohr
earlier [ˈɜːliə] vorhin; vorher, früher 3: 1 (27)
early [ˈɜːli] früh 2
earn [ɜːn] verdienen *(Geld)* 2
earth [ɜːθ] die Erde 2
east [iːst] der Osten; östlich; Ost- 3: (10/11)
Easter [ˈiːstə] (das) Ostern 2
eastern [ˈiːstən] östlich(r,s), Ost- 3: (10/11)
easy [ˈiːzi] einfach, leicht 1
eat [iːt], **ate, eaten** essen; fressen 1
eaten [ˈiːtn] *siehe* **eat**
edit [ˈedɪt] bearbeiten, editieren 3: 4 (104)
eel [iːl] der Aal 3: 3 (74)
egg [eg] das Ei 1
eight [eɪt] acht 1
eighteen [eɪˈtiːn] achtzehn 1
eighty [ˈeɪti] achtzig 1
°electric [ɪˈlektrɪk] elektrisch, Elektro-
electro [ɪˈlektrəʊ] der Electro, die Elektromusik 2
electronic [ɪlekˈtrɒnɪk] elektronisch 2
electronics *(pl)* [ɪlekˈtrɒnɪks] die Elektronik; die elektronischen Geräte 2
elephant [ˈelɪfənt] der Elefant 1
eleven [ɪˈlevən] elf 1
else [els]: **What else?** Was sonst noch? 2 **Would you like anything else?** Möchten Sie sonst noch etwas? 2
email [ˈiːmeɪl]:
1. die E-Mail 2
2. **email sb.** jm. mailen, eine E-Mail schicken 2
embarrass sb. [ɪmˈbærəs] jn. in Verlegenheit bringen, jm. peinlich sein 3: 3 (85)
embarrassed [ɪmˈbærəst] verlegen, peinlich berührt 3: 3 (85) **be/feel embarrassed** peinlich berührt sein 3: 3 (85)
embarrassing [ɪmˈbærəsɪŋ] peinlich 3: 3 (85)
emoji [ɪˈməʊdʒi] das Emoji 3: 4 (111)
emotion [ɪˈməʊʃn] die Emotion, das Gefühl 3: 4 (112)
emotional [ɪˈməʊʃənl] emotional 3: 4 (112)
empty [ˈempti]:
1. leer 2
2. leeren 2
end [end]:
1. enden; beenden 1
2. das Ende, der Schluss 1
at the end (of) am Ende (von) 1 **in the end** schließlich; zum Schluss 1
ending [ˈendɪŋ] die Endung; das Ende *(Text, Geschichte)* 3: 2 (58)
endless [ˈendləs] endlos 3: 1 (23)
energetic [enəˈdʒetɪk] aktiv, tatkräftig, energiegeladen 2
energy [ˈenədʒi] Energie 2
England [ˈɪŋglənd] England 1
English [ˈɪŋglɪʃ] Englisch; englisch 1
enjoy [ɪnˈdʒɔɪ] genießen 1 **enjoy doing sth.** es genießen, etwas zu tun 1 **Enjoy your meal.** Guten Appetit! 2 **Enjoy yourselves.** Viel Spaß! Amüsiert euch gut! 3: 2 (50) **Enjoy!** Viel Vergnügen! / Guten Appetit! 1
enough [ɪˈnʌf] genug 3: 1 (18)
especially [ɪˈspeʃəli] insbesondere 2
estate [ɪˈsteɪt] die Wohnsiedlung; das Gewerbegebiet 1
°EU (= European Union) [iː ˈjuː] die EU (Europäische Union)
euro [ˈjʊərəʊ], *pl* **euros** Euro 1
°European Union [jʊərəpiːən ˈjuːniən] die Europäische Union
even [ˈiːvn] sogar, selbst 3: 3 (74) **even if** selbst wenn, sogar wenn 3: 3 (74) **not even** nicht einmal 3: 3 (74)
evening [ˈiːvnɪŋ] der Abend 1 **in the evening** abends, am Abend 1
event [ɪˈvent] das Ereignis 3: 1 (28)
ever [ˈevə] jemals, schon einmal 2 **the best party ever** die beste Party überhaupt / die beste Party, die man sich wünschen kann 1 **°for ever** für immer, ewig (lange)
every [ˈevri] jede(r, s) 2 **every 30 minutes** alle 30 Minuten 2
everybody [ˈevribɒdi] jeder; alle 1 **Hello everybody!** Hallo allerseits! 1
everyone [ˈevriwʌn] jeder, alle 1
everything [ˈevriθɪŋ] alles 2
everywhere [ˈevriweə] überall 1
example [ɪgˈzɑːmpl] das Beispiel 3: 3 (81) **for example** zum Beispiel 3: 3 (81)
except (for) [ɪkˈsept] außer, bis auf 3: 1 (18)
exchange [ɪksˈtʃeɪndʒ]:
1. der Schüleraustausch; der Austausch, der Wechsel 3: 4 (114)
2. **exchange sth. for sth.** austauschen, etwas in/gegen etwas umtauschen 3: 4 (114)

exchange class [ɪksˈtʃeɪndʒ klɑːs] *die Schulklasse, die am Schüleraustausch teilnimmt* 3: 4 (114)
exchange partner [ɪksˈtʃeɪndʒ pɑːtnə] der/die Austauschpartner/in 3: 4 (114)
exchange student [ɪksˈtʃeɪndʒ stjuːdnt] der/die Austauschschüler/in 3: 4 (114)
excited [ɪkˈsaɪtɪd] aufgeregt, gespannt 2
exciting [ɪkˈsaɪtɪŋ] aufregend 2
Excuse me, ... [ɪksˈkjuːz miː] Entschuldigung, ... / Entschuldigen Sie, ... 1
exercise [ˈeksəsaɪz] die Übung, die Aufgabe 1
exercise book [ˈeksəsaɪz bʊk] das Schulheft, das Übungsheft 1
expensive [ɪkˈspensɪv] teuer 1
experience [ɪkˈspɪəriəns]:
1. die Erfahrung; das Erlebnis 2
2. **experience sth.** etwas erfahren; erleben 2
explain sth. to sb. [ɪkˈspleɪn] jm. etwas erklären 1
explanation [ekspləˈneɪʃn] die Erklärung 1
explore [ɪkˈsplɔː] erforschen, erkunden 3: 3 (75)
extra [ˈekstrə] Extra-, zusätzliche(r, s) 2
eye [aɪ] das Auge 2

F

face [feɪs] das Gesicht 2
fact [fækt] die Tatsache 3: 1 (30)
in fact tatsächlich, in Wirklichkeit, genau genommen 3: 1 (30)
fair [feə] fair 2
fake [feɪk]:
1. falsch, gefälscht 3: 3 (74)
2. der/das Fake, die Fälschung 3: 3 (74)
3. **fake sth.** etwas faken, fälschen, vortäuschen 3: 3 (74)
falafel [fəˈlæfl] die/das Falafel 3: 1 (22)
fall [fɔːl], **fell, fallen** fallen; hinfallen 2
°fallen [ˈfɔːlən] *siehe* **fall**
false [fɔːls] falsch, unrichtig 2
false friend [fɔːls ˈfrend] der „falsche Freund" *(Übersetzungsfalle)* 2
fame [feɪm] Ruhm 2
family [ˈfæməli] die Familie 1
famous (for) [ˈfeɪməs] berühmt (für, wegen) 2
fan [fæn] der Fan 1
far [fɑː] weit (entfernt) 3: 2 (57)
so far bis jetzt, bis hierher 3: 2 (50)
farm [fɑːm] der Bauernhof, die Farm 2
fashion [ˈfæʃn] die Mode, die Fashion 3: 1 (25)
fast [fɑːst] schnell 1
fast [fɑːst]:
1. fasten 2
2. das Fasten, die Fastenzeit 2
break the fast das Fasten brechen 2
father [ˈfɑːðə] der Vater 2
favourite [ˈfeɪvərɪt]:
1. der Liebling, der/die Favorit/in 1
2. Lieblings- 1

February [ˈfebruəri] der Februar 1
°feedback (on sth.) *(no pl)* [ˈfiːdbæk] das Feedback (zu etwas) *(Rückmeldung)*
feel [fiːl], **felt, felt** sich fühlen; fühlen 1 **feel sorry for sb.** Mitleid haben mit jm. 1
feeling [ˈfiːlɪŋ] das Gefühl 1
feet [fiːt] *Plural von* **foot**
fell [fel] *siehe* **fall**
felt [felt] *siehe* **feel**
festival [ˈfestɪvl] das Fest(ival) 2
few [fjuː]: **a few** ein paar, einige 2
°field [fiːld] das Feld; die Weide
fifteen [fɪfˈtiːn] fünfzehn 1
fifty [ˈfɪfti] fünfzig 1
fight [faɪt]:
1. der Kampf 2
2. **fight, fought, fought** kämpfen, bekämpfen 2
fight (with sb. about/over sth.) sich (mit jm. um etwas) streiten 2
fighter [ˈfaɪtə] der Kämpfer die Kämpferin 2
file [faɪl] die Datei; der Ordner, die Liste 1
film [fɪlm]:
1. der Film 1
2. **film sth.** etwas filmen 3: 1 (21)
filter [ˈfɪltə]:
1. der Filter 3: 4 (116)
2. filtern 3: 4 (116)
finally [ˈfaɪnəli] schließlich, endlich 1
find [faɪnd], **found, found** finden 1
find out (about) herausfinden; sich informieren (über) 1
fine [faɪn] gut, in Ordnung; schön 2
He feels fine. Er fühlt sich gut. / Es geht ihm gut. 2
finger [ˈfɪŋgə] der Finger 3: 2 (57)
tap your fingers mit den Fingern klopfen 3: 4 (108)
finish [ˈfɪnɪʃ]:
1. das Ende, das Ziel *(z. B. beim Sport)* 2
2. enden; beenden, zu Ende machen 2
be finished fertig(gestellt) sein 3: 4 (104)
fire [ˈfaɪə] das Feuer 2
stop a fire ein Feuer löschen 2
firefighter [ˈfaɪəfaɪtə] der Feuerwehrmann, die Feuerwehrfrau 2
fireworks *(pl)* [ˈfaɪəwɜːks] das Feuerwerk 2
first [fɜːst]:
1. erste(r, s) 1
2. zuerst, als Erstes 1
at first zuerst, am Anfang 1
fish [fɪʃ] der Fisch 1
fish and chips [fɪʃ ən ˈtʃɪps] der Fisch mit Pommes Frites 1
°fit [fɪt] passen (zu)
five [faɪv] fünf 1
fix sth. [fɪks] *(infml)* etwas in Ordnung bringen; etwas reparieren 2
flag [flæg] die Fahne, die Flagge 2
flat [flæt] die Wohnung 1
flew [fluː] *siehe* **fly**

floor [flɔː]:
1. der Fußboden 1
2. die Etage, der Stock, das Stockwerk 1
top floor die oberste Etage, der oberste Stock, das oberste Stockwerk 1
flour [ˈflaʊə] das Mehl 1
flow [fləʊ]:
1. der Fluss; der Strom 3: 4 (118)
2. fließen; strömen 3: 4 (118)
flower [ˈflaʊə] die Blume; die Blüte 3: 3 (82)
°flown [fləʊn] *siehe* **fly**
fly [flaɪ], **flew, flown** fliegen 2
fold [fəʊld] falten 2
follow [ˈfɒləʊ] (be)folgen; verfolgen 3: 1 (27)
follower [ˈfɒləʊə] der Follower 3: 4 (113)
food [fuːd] das Essen, das Lebensmittel; das Futter 1
foot [fʊt], *pl* **feet**:
1. der Fuß *(Körperteil)* 2
2. der Fuß *(Längenmaß; ca. 30 cm)* 2
football [ˈfʊtbɔːl] der Fußball 1
footballer [ˈfʊtbɔːlə] der/die Fußballspieler/in 2
for [fɔː] für 1 **for light** als Licht(quelle) 3: 4 (106) **change for the better** sich verbessern, zum Bessern verändern 3: 1 (29) **to change sth. for the better** etwas verbessern, zum Bessern verändern 3: 1 (29) **What's for homework?** Was haben wir als Hausaufgabe(n) auf? 1 **°for 30 seconds** für 30 Sekunden, 30 Sekunden lang
foreground [ˈfɔːgraʊnd] der Vordergrund 3: (12/13)
forest [ˈfɒrɪst] der Wald 2
°forever, for ever [fərˈevə] für immer, ewig (lange)
forget [fəˈget], **forgot, forgotten** vergessen 3: 1 (16)
forgot [fəˈgɒt] *siehe* **forget**
forgotten [fəˈgɒtn] *siehe* **forget**
forty [ˈfɔːti] vierzig 1
forward [ˈfɔːwəd]: **look forward to doing sth.** sich darauf freuen, etwas zu tun 2 **look forward to sth.** sich auf etwas freuen 2
fought [fɔːt] *siehe* **fight**
found [faʊnd] *siehe* **find**
fountain [ˈfaʊntən] der (Spring-/Trink-)Brunnen 3: 1 (27) **memorial fountain** der Gedenkbrunnen 3: 1 (27)
four [fɔː] vier 1
fourteen [fɔːˈtiːn] vierzehn 1
free [friː]:
1. frei 1
free time die Freizeit, die freie Zeit 1 **Are you free after school?** Hast du nach der Schule Zeit? 1
for free kostenlos, umsonst 2
2. kostenlos 1
freeze [friːz], **froze, frozen** erstarren; (ge)frieren 3: 2 (58)

°freeze-frame [ˈfriːz freɪm] das Standbild *(Film)*
Friday [ˈfraɪdeɪ], [ˈfraɪdi] der Freitag 1
fried [fraɪd] frittiert, gebraten 1
friend [frend] der/die Freund/in 1
friendly [ˈfrendli] freundlich, nett 1
friendship [ˈfrendʃɪp] die Freundschaft 3: 2 (48)
°frightening [ˈfraɪtnɪŋ] beängstigend, erschreckend
from [frɒm] von, aus 1
front [frʌnt]: **a house with trees in front** ein Haus mit Bäumen davor 1 **in front of** vor 1
front door [frʌnt ˈdɔː] die Haustür, die Eingangstür 2
froze [frəʊz] *siehe* **freeze**
°frozen [ˈfrəʊzn] *siehe* **freeze**
fruit [fruːt] das Obst 1
frustrate sb. [frʌˈstreɪt] jn. frustrieren 3: 2 (48)
frustrated [frʌˈstreɪtɪd] frustriert 3: 2 (48)
frustrating [frʌˈstreɪtɪŋ] frustrierend 3: 2 (48)
fry [fraɪ] braten; frittieren 1
frying pan [ˈfraɪɪŋ pæn] die Bratpfanne 1
full [fʊl]:
1. voll 2
full of … voller … 2
2. satt 2
fun [fʌn]: **be fun** Spaß machen; lustig sein 1 **have fun** Spaß haben 1
funny [ˈfʌni] witzig, komisch 1
future [ˈfjuːtʃə]:
1. die Zukunft 2
2. zukünftige(r, s) 2

G

°Gaelic [ˈgeɪlɪk] Gälisch *(Sprache)*
°gallery [ˈgæləri] die Galerie
game [geɪm]:
1. das Spiel 1
2. Computerspiele spielen 2
gamer [ˈgeɪmə] der/die Gamer/in *(Computerspieler/in)* 2
gaming [ˈgeɪmɪŋ] das Gaming *(Spielen am Computer)* 2
°gap [gæp] die Lücke, der Abstand
garden [ˈgɑːdn] der Garten 1
gate [geɪt] das Tor 3: 3 (82)
gave [geɪv] *siehe* **give**
geography [dʒiˈɒgrəfi] die Geografie, die Erdkunde 1
German [ˈdʒɜːmən] deutsch; Deutsch; der/die Deutsche 1
Germany [ˈdʒɜːməni] Deutschland 1
get [get], **got, got**:
1. bekommen 1
get sth. sich etwas holen/besorgen 1
2. werden 1
get ready (for) sich fertig machen (für), sich vorbereiten (auf) 2
get wet nass werden 1
3. **get (to)** gelangen, (hin)kommen (nach) 2
Get down! Komm (da) runter! 2
get off your bike/your horse vom Fahrrad / vom Pferd absteigen 3: 3 (78) **get up** aufstehen 1
get on a train/bus in einen Zug/Bus einsteigen 2 **get off a train/bus** aus einem Zug/Bus aussteigen 2
°4. **get sth.** etwas verstehen, mitbekommen
°Don't get me wrong. Versteh(t) mich nicht falsch.
ghost [gəʊst] der Geist, das Gespenst 3: 1 (18)
ghost tour [ˈgəʊst tʊə] die Geistertour *(Stadtführung mit gruseligen Themen/Elementen)* 3: 1 (18)
gift [gɪft] das Geschenk, die Gabe; das Talent 2
gift shop [ˈgɪft ʃɒp] der Geschenk(artikel)laden, der Souvenirladen 2
girl [gɜːl] das Mädchen 1 **a girls' group** eine Mädchengruppe, eine Gruppe für Mädchen 1
girlfriend [ˈgɜːlfrend] die (feste) Freundin 2
give [gɪv], **gave, given** geben 1
give up aufgeben 3: 4 (117)
°give in (to sb./sth.) (jm./einer Sache) nachgeben
given [ˈgɪvn] *siehe* **give**
glasses *(pl)* [ˈglɑːsɪz] die Brille 2
global [ˈgləʊbl] global, weltweit 3: 1 (25)
globe [gləʊb] der Globus; die Kugel 3: 1 (25) **across the globe** auf der ganzen Welt 3: 1 (25) **all (a)round the globe** auf der ganzen Welt 3: 1 (25)
glove [glʌv] der Handschuh 2
glue [gluː] der Kleber, der Klebstoff 1
glue stick [ˈgluː stɪk] der Klebestift 1
go [gəʊ], **went, gone**:
1. gehen, fahren 1
go out rausgehen, weggehen; ausgehen 2 **How's it going?** *(infml)* Wie geht's? / Wie läuft's? 2 **There you go.** Hier, bitte schön.; *(auch:)* Da hast du's! / Na siehst du! 3: 4 (111)
°it goes *bong* es macht *bong*
2. werden 1
go green grün/umweltbewusst werden 1 **go red** erröten, rot werden 1
3. **I'm going to …** ich werde … *(Plan, Vorhaben)* 2
go-kart [ˈgəʊ kɑːt] der/das Gokart 3: 3 (78)
goal [gəʊl] das Ziel *(Absicht, Lebensziel)*; das Tor *(im Sport)* 3: 1 (25)
goalkeeper [ˈgəʊlkiːpə] der Torwart, die Torhüterin 3: 2 (57)
goat [gəʊt] die Ziege 2
god [gɒd] der Gott 2
gold [gəʊld]:
1. das Gold 1
2. goldfarben 1
°golden [ˈgəʊldn] golden, aus Gold
gone [gɒn] *siehe* **go**
good [gʊd]:
1. gut 1
be good at sth. etwas gut können; gut in etwas sein 1 **be good with …** gut umgehen können mit … 1
2. brav 2
Goodbye. [gʊdˈbaɪ] Auf Wiedersehen! 1
got [gɒt] *siehe* **get**
grandma [ˈgrænmɑː] die Oma 1
grandpa [ˈgrænpɑː] der Opa 1
grandparents *(pl)* [ˈgrænpeərənts] die Großeltern 2
grass [grɑːs] das Gras; der Rasen 3: 1 (27)
great [greɪt]:
1. großartig, toll 1
2. groß *(bedeutend, angesehen)* 2
Great Britain [greɪt ˈbrɪtn] Großbritannien 1
green [griːn]:
1. grün 1
2. umweltbewusst 1
go green grün/umweltbewusst werden 1
°greeting [ˈgriːtɪŋ] die Begrüßung
grey [greɪ] grau 1
ground [graʊnd] der (Erd-)Boden 1
ground floor [graʊnd ˈflɔː] das Erdgeschoss 1
group [gruːp] die Gruppe 1
guard [gɑːd]:
1. schützen, bewachen 3: 1 (21)
2. der/die Wärter/in; die Wache; der/die Sicherheitsbedienstete 3: 1 (21)
Changing of the Guards die Wachablösung 3: 1 (21)
guess [ges]:
1. die Vermutung 1
2. (er)raten 1
guessing game das Ratespiel 1
3. glauben, annehmen 1
I guess ich glaube, ich nehme an 1
°guest [gest] der Gast
guide [gaɪd]:
1. führen, leiten 1
2. *(= tour guide)* der/die Reiseleiter/in; der/die Fremdenführer/in 1
guide dog [ˈgaɪd dɒg] der Blindenhund 1
guitar [gɪˈtɑː] die Gitarre 1
°guy [gaɪ] *(infml)* der Typ, der Kerl

H

habit [ˈhæbɪt] die (An-)Gewohnheit 3: 4 (118)
had [hæd] *siehe* **have**
hair [heə] das Haar, die Haare 2
haircut [ˈheəkʌt] der Haarschnitt 3: 1 (29) **give sb. a haircut** jm. die Haare schneiden 3: 1 (29)
hairdresser [ˈheədresə] der/die Friseur/in 2
hairdresser's [ˈheədresəz] der Friseursalon 2
half [hɑːf]:
1. halbe(r, s) 3: 2 (57)
half an hour eine halbe Stunde 3: 2 (57) **half full** halb voll 3: 2 (57) **half past 6** halb 7 2 **half the time / half the money** die Hälfte der Zeit / des Geldes 3: 2 (57)

2. *pl* **halves** die Hälfte; *(Fußball)* die Halbzeit 3: 2 (57)
half-time [hɑːf ˈtaɪm] die Halbzeit(pause) 3: 2 (57)
hall [hɔːl]:
1. der Flur, die Diele 1
2. die Halle, der Saal 1
sports hall die Sporthalle 1
halloumi [həˈluːmi] der Halloumi *(Käse)* 3: 1 (22)
Halloween [hæləʊˈiːn] das Halloween *(Abend des 31. Oktober)* 2
°Halò! [ˈhʌləʊ] Hallo! *(schottisches Gälisch)*
halves [hɑːvz] *Plural von* **half**
ham [hæm] der Schinken 1
hamster [ˈhæmstə] der Hamster 1
hand [hænd] die Hand 1 **put your hand up** sich melden, aufzeigen 1
handball [ˈhændbɔːl] der Handball 2
handy [ˈhændi] praktisch, nützlich; handlich; griffbereit, zur Hand 2
°hang [hæŋ], **hung, hung: hang out** rumhängen, abhängen **hang sth. (up)** etwas aufhängen
happen (to sb.) [ˈhæpən] (jm.) geschehen, passieren 2
happy [ˈhæpi] glücklich, froh 1 **Happy birthday!** Herzlichen Glückwunsch zum Geburtstag! 1
hard [hɑːd] schwer, schwierig; hart 1
hard-working [hɑːd ˈwɜːkɪŋ] fleißig 2
has [hæz], [həz]: **he/she/it has** er/sie/es hat 1
hashtag [ˈhæʃtæg] das/der Hashtag *(Rautezeichen in einem elektronischen Text)* 3: 4 (114)
hat [hæt] der Hut, die Mütze 1
hate [heɪt]:
1. hassen 2
2. der Hass 2
have [hæv], **had, had** haben 1
have to do sth. etwas tun müssen 2
I have to go. Ich muss Schluss machen. *(am Telefon/Briefschluss)* 2
I'll have ... Ich nehme ... *(beim Essen, z. B. im Restaurant)* 3: 1 (22)
he [hiː] er 1 **he's (= he is)** er ist 1
head [hed] der Kopf 1
headache [ˈhedeɪk] Kopfschmerzen 2
have a headache Kopfschmerzen haben 2
headphones *(pl)* [ˈhedfəʊnz] der Kopfhörer 1
headpiece [ˈhedpiːs] der Kopfschmuck 3: 4 (117)
health [helθ] die Gesundheit 3: 2 (51)
healthy [ˈhelθi] gesund 3: 2 (51)
hear [hɪə], **heard, heard** hören 1
heard [hɜːd] *siehe* **hear**
°heavy [ˈhevi] schwer *(Gewicht)*
°held [held] *siehe* **hold**
helicopter [ˈhelɪkɒptə] der Hubschrauber 3: 3 (85)
Hello. [həˈləʊ] Hallo. 1 **Hello everybody!** Hallo allerseits! 1
helmet [ˈhelmɪt] der Helm 2
help [help]:
1. helfen 1
2. die Hilfe 1
helpful [ˈhelpfl] hilfsbereit; hilfreich, nützlich 1
helpless [ˈhelpləs] hilflos 3: 1 (23)
her [hɜː], [hə]:
1. sie; ihr 1
2. **her friends** ihre Freunde/Freundinnen 1
here [hɪə] hier; hierher 1 **Here you are.** Bitte schön. / Hier, bitte. 1
hero [ˈhɪərəʊ], *pl* **heroes** der/die Held/in 2
hers [hɜːz] ihrer, ihre, ihres *(zu „she")* 3: 4 (104)
herself [hɜːˈself] sich (selbst) *(zu „she")* 3: 2 (50)
Hi. [haɪ] Hallo. 1
high [haɪ] hoch 3: 3 (72/73)
°Highland Games *(pl)* [haɪlənd ˈgeɪmz] *die traditionelle schottische Veranstaltung mit sportlichen Wettkämpfen*
Highlands [ˈhaɪləndz]: **the Highlands** *(pl)* das schottische Hochland 3: 3 (72/73)
highlight [ˈhaɪlaɪt]:
1. der Höhepunkt, das Schlaglicht 1
2. hervorheben, markieren, unterstreichen 1
hike [haɪk]:
1. die Wanderung 3: 3 (72/73)
2. wandern 3: 3 (72/73)
hiker [ˈhaɪkə] der Wanderer, die Wanderin 3: 3 (72/73)
hiking [ˈhaɪkɪŋ] das Wandern 3: 3 (72/73)
°hill [hɪl] der Hügel
him [hɪm] ihm, ihn 1
himself [hɪmˈself] sich (selbst) *(zu „he")* 3: 2 (50)
hire [ˈhaɪə]:
1. der Verleih, die Vermietung 3: 1 (16)
2. mieten, leihen; *(Person:)* einstellen 3: 1 (16)
his [hɪz]:
1. seiner, seine, seins *(zu „he")* 3: 4 (104)
2. **his room** sein Zimmer 1
history [ˈhɪstri] die Geschichte *(vergangene Zeiten)* 1
hit [hɪt], **hit, hit:**
1. schlagen 3: 4 (110)
2. stoßen gegen, zusammenstoßen mit; treffen auf 3: 4 (110)
hobby [ˈhɒbi] das Hobby 1
hockey [ˈhɒki] das Hockey 1
°hold [həʊld], **held, held** halten
holiday [ˈhɒlədeɪ] der Urlaub 1
holidays die Ferien 1 **on holiday** im/in den Urlaub 1
home [həʊm]:
1. das Heim, das Zuhause 1
at home zu Hause 1
2. nach Hause 1
go home nach Hause gehen 1
homeless [ˈhəʊmləs] obdachlos 3: 1 (23)
°hometown [həʊmˈtaʊn] die Heimatstadt
homework [ˈhəʊmwɜːk] die Hausaufgabe(n) 1 **do your homework** Hausaufgaben machen 1 **What's for homework?** Was haben wir als Hausaufgabe(n) auf? 1
honest [ˈɒnɪst] ehrlich 2
hope [həʊp]:
1. hoffen 2
2. die Hoffnung 2
°hopeless [ˈhəʊpləs] hoffnungslos
°horn [hɔːn] die Hupe *(Auto)*; das Horn
horoscope [ˈhɒrəskəʊp] das Horoskop 2
horrible [ˈhɒrəbl] schrecklich 1
horse [hɔːs] das Pferd 1
hospital [ˈhɒspɪtl] das Krankenhaus 1
hot [hɒt] heiß, warm 1
hot chocolate [hɒt ˈtʃɒklət] der Kakao, die heiße (Trink-)Schokolade 1
hot dog [ˈhɒt dɒg] das Hot Dog *(heißes Würstchen in einem Brötchen)* 2
hot meal [hɒt ˈmiːl] die warme Mahlzeit 1
hotel [həʊˈtel] das Hotel 2
hour [ˈaʊə] die Stunde 1
per hour pro Stunde 3: 3 (74)
work long hours lange arbeiten, Überstunden machen 2
house [haʊs] das Haus 1
how [haʊ] wie 1 **How are you?** Wie geht's? / Wie geht es dir/euch/Ihnen? 2 **How much is/are ...?** Was (Wie viel) kostet/kosten ...? 2
how to do sth. wie man etwas tut / tun kann / tun soll 1
however [haʊˈevə] allerdings, jedoch 3: 4 (112)
hug [hʌg]:
1. die Umarmung 2
2. **hug (sb.)** (jn.) umarmen; einander umarmen 2
hummus [ˈhʊməs] der/das Hummus 3: 1 (22)
hundred [ˈhʌndrəd]: **a/one hundred** (ein)hundert 1
°hung [hʌŋ] *siehe* **hang**
hungry [ˈhʌŋgri] hungrig 1
I'm hungry. Ich habe Hunger. 1
hurry [ˈhʌri]:
1. sich beeilen; eilen 3: 1 (27)
Hurry up! Beeil dich! / Beeilt euch! 3: 1 (27)
2. die Eile 3: 1 (27)
in a hurry in Eile 3: 1 (27)
hurt [hɜːt], **hurt, hurt** verletzen; wehtun 2 **be hurt** verletzt sein 2
get hurt sich verletzen 2
husband [ˈhʌzbənd] der Ehemann 1

I

I [aɪ] ich 1 **I'm (= I am)** ich bin 1
°ice [aɪs] das Eis *(gefrorenes Wasser)*
ice cream [aɪs ˈkriːm] das (Speise-)Eis 1
ice rink [ˈaɪs rɪŋk] die Schlittschuhbahn 1
icing [ˈaɪsɪŋ] die Glasur, der Zuckerguss 1

icing sugar ['aɪsɪŋ ʃʊgə] der Puderzucker 1
idea [aɪ'dɪə] die Idee 1
if [ɪf]:
1. wenn, falls 1
even if selbst wenn, sogar wenn 3: 3 (74) **What if ...?** Was wäre, wenn ...? 1
2. ob 1
ill [ɪl] krank 2
illness ['ɪlnəs] die Krankheit 2
°**imagine sth.** [ɪ'mædʒɪn] sich etwas vorstellen
important (for/to sb.) [ɪm'pɔːtnt] wichtig (für jn.) 2
in [ɪn] in; auf 1 **in English** auf Englisch 1 **in the afternoon** nachmittags, am Nachmittag 1 **in the country** auf dem Land 1 **in the evening** abends, am Abend 1 **in the morning** morgens, am Morgen 1 **in the photo** auf dem Foto 1 **in the picture** auf dem Bild 1 **in town** in der Stadt 1 **one in five** jede/r fünfte, eine/r von fünf(en) 3: 4 (112) °**in the field** auf der Weide
°**indoor** ['ɪndɔː] im Haus/Gebäude, drinnen stattfindend
°**industry** ['ɪndəstri] die Industrie
influencer ['ɪnfluənsə] der/die Influencer/in 2
information [ɪnfə'meɪʃn] die Information(en) 1 **visitor information centre** die Touristeninformation, das Fremdenverkehrsbüro 1
insect ['ɪnsekt] Insekt 2
inside [ɪn'saɪd] innerhalb (von) 1 **inside the house** im Haus 1
instruction [ɪn'strʌkʃn] die Anweisung 3: 4 (109)
instructor [ɪn'strʌktə] der/die Lehrer/in, der/die Ausbilder/in 3: 3 (80)
interest ['ɪntrəst]:
1. **interest (in)** das Interesse (an) 3: 4 (117)
2. **interest sb. (in sth.)** jn. (für etwas) interessieren 3: 4 (117)
interested (in) ['ɪntrəstɪd] interessiert (an) 3: 2 (53)
interesting ['ɪntrəstɪŋ] interessant 1
international [ɪntə'næʃnəl] international 3: 4 (102/103)
internet ['ɪntənet] das Internet 1
interrupt [ɪntə'rʌpt] unterbrechen 3: 2 (54)
interview ['ɪntəvjuː] das Interview 2
into ['ɪntu], ['ɪntə] in (... hinein) 2 **cut sth. into pieces** etwas in Stücke schneiden 2
intro ['ɪntrəʊ] (*kurz für* **introduction**) die Einführung, die Einleitung 3: 4 (118)
°**introduction** [ɪntrə'dʌkʃn] die Einführung, die Einleitung
invitation (to) [ɪnvɪ'teɪʃn] die Einladung (zu, nach) 1
invite (to) [ɪn'vaɪt] einladen (zu, nach) 1
involved [ɪn'vɒlvd]: **get involved (in)** sich engagieren (für, bei); sich beteiligen (an) 3: 1 (29) **Try not to get involved.** Versuche, dich da rauszuhalten 3: 1 (29)
Ireland ['aɪələnd] Irland 3: (10/11)
is [ɪz] *(er/sie/es)* ist 1 **he isn't (= is not)** er ist nicht 1 **The football is £3.** Der Fußball kostet 3 Pfund. 2
island ['aɪlənd] die Insel 3: (10/11)
isle [aɪl] die Insel, das Eiland *(kurz für „island")* 3: (10/11) **British Isles** *(pl)* die Britischen Inseln 3: (10/11)
it [ɪt] es *(bei Sachen und Tieren auch:* er; sie*)* 1
°**item** ['aɪtəm] der Gegenstand, der Artikel
its [ɪts]:
1. sein/seine, ihr/ihre *(besitzanzeigend: Dinge und Tiere)* 1
2. seiner, seine, seins; ihrer, ihre, ihres *(zu „it")* 3: 4 (104)
itself [ɪt'self] sich (selbst) (zu *„it"*) 3: 2 (50)

J

jacket ['dʒækɪt] die Jacke, das Jackett 2 **rain jacket** die Regenjacke 2
January ['dʒænjuəri] der Januar 1
jazz [dʒæz] der Jazz 2
jealous (of) ['dʒeləs] neidisch (auf); eifersüchtig 3: 4 (115)
jeans *(pl)* [dʒiːnz] die Jeans(hose) 2
°**jewellery** ['dʒuːəlri] der Schmuck
°**jewels** *(pl)* ['dʒuːəlz] die Juwelen
jigsaw (puzzle) ['dʒɪgsɔː] das Puzzle 1
job [dʒɒb] der Job, die (Arbeits-)Stelle; die Aufgabe 2
join sb./sth. [dʒɔɪn] sich jm. anschließen; bei etwas mitmachen 3: 1 (18) **join a club** in einen Klub eintreten 3: 1 (18) **join a group** sich einer Gruppe anschließen 3: 1 (18)
joke [dʒəʊk] der Witz, der Scherz 2
journey ['dʒɜːni] die Reise, die Fahrt; der Weg 1
judo ['dʒuːdəʊ] das Judo 2 **do judo** Judo machen 2
juggle ['dʒʌgl] jonglieren 1
juice [dʒuːs] der Saft 3: 1 (22)
July [dʒu'laɪ] der Juli 1
jump [dʒʌmp] springen; *(vor Schreck)* zusammenzucken 2
June [dʒuːn] der Juni 1
just [dʒʌst]:
1. nur, bloß; einfach 1
It's just us. Es sind nur wir. 1
2. gerade (eben) 2
3. **just then / just there** genau dann / genau dort 2

K

karaoke [kæri'əʊki] das Karaoke 2
karate [kə'rɑːti] Karate 2
kayak ['kaɪæk] das Kajak 3: 3 (72/73)
kayaker ['kaɪækə] der/die Kajakfahrer/in 3: 3 (72/73)
kayaking ['kaɪækɪŋ] das Kajakfahren 3: 3 (72/73)
kebab [kɪ'bæb] der Kebab 2
keep [kiːp], **kept, kept:**
1. halten; behalten; aufbewahren 3: 2 (57)
2. **keep doing sth.** etwas dauernd/immer wieder tun 3: 2 (57)
keep going (immer) weiter gehen 3: 2 (57)
kept [kept] *siehe* **keep**
ketchup ['ketʃəp] Ketchup 3: 2 (60)
°**kettle** ['ketl] der Wasserkocher *(elektrisch)*
key [kiː] der Schlüssel; Schlüssel- 2
keyword ['kiːwɜːd] das Stichwort, das Schlagwort 3: 1 (30)
kid [kɪd] das Kind, der/die Jugendliche 1
kill [kɪl] töten 2
killer ['kɪlə] der Mörder, die Mörderin 2
kilometre (km) ['kɪləmiːtə] der Kilometer 2
kind [kaɪnd] nett, freundlich 1
kind (of) [kaɪnd] die Art (von), die Sorte (von) 1
king [kɪŋ] der König 3: 1 (14/15)
Kingdom ['kɪŋdəm]: **the United Kingdom (= the UK)** das Vereinigte Königreich 2
kitchen ['kɪtʃɪn] die Küche 1
knew [njuː] *siehe* **know**
knit [nɪt] stricken 2
knock [nɒk] stoßen, klopfen 2 **knock at (sth.)** (an)klopfen an (etwas, z. B. Tür) 2 **knock sth. over** etwas umstoßen 2
know [nəʊ], **knew, known** wissen; kennen 1 **you know** nämlich, weißt du 3: 1 (27)
°**known** [nəʊn] *siehe* **know**

L

°**label** ['leɪbl] das Etikett *(auch: wenn man abgestempelt wird)*
lake [leɪk] der (Binnen-)See 3: (12/13)
lamb [læm] das Lamm(fleisch) 2
lamp [læmp] die Lampe 1
land [lænd]:
1. das Land *(Grund und Boden)* 2
2. landen 2
lane [leɪn] die Gasse 3: 1 (16) **bike lane** der Radweg 3: 1 (16) **cycle lane** der Radweg 3: 1 (16)
language ['læŋgwɪdʒ] die Sprache 2
large [lɑːdʒ] groß 2
last [lɑːst] letzte(r, s); als letztes 2 **last week/month/year** die letzte/vorige Woche, der letzte/vorige Monat, das letzte/vorige Jahr 2
late [leɪt] (zu) spät 1 **I'm late.** Ich habe mich verspätet. 1
later ['leɪtə] später 1 **Speak later.** Tschüs. / Bis später. 1
laugh [lɑːf]:
1. das Lachen 2

2. **laugh (at)** lachen (über) 2
laugh out loud laut auf-/loslachen 2
°**lazy** ['leɪzi] faul
learn [lɜːn] lernen 1
least [liːst] am wenigsten 2 **at least** wenigstens, zumindest 2 **the least favourite chores** die Arbeiten (im Haus), die man am wenigsten gerne macht 2
leave [liːv], **left, left** lassen; verlassen; zurücklassen 2 **leave sb. alone** jn. allein lassen; jn. in Ruhe lassen 2
left [left] *siehe* **leave**
left [left] links; nach links 2
on the left links, auf der linken Seite 2 **to the left of ...** links von ... 2
leg [leg] das Bein 2
legend ['ledʒənd] die Legende, die Sage 3: 3 (74)
lemon ['lemən] die Zitrone 1
lemonade [leməˈneɪd] die Limonade 1
less [les] weniger 3: 3 (83)
lesson ['lesn] die (Unterrichts-) Stunde 1
let's (= let us) [lets] lass(t) uns 1
letter ['letə]:
1. der Brief 3: 4 (107)
2. der Buchstabe 3: 4 (107)
level ['levl] der Grad, die Stufe; das Niveau, die Ebene 2
library ['laɪbrəri] die Bücherei, die Bibliothek 1
lie [laɪ]:
1. die Lüge 3: 4 (114)
tell a lie / lies lügen 3: 4 (114)
2. **lie (to sb.)** (jn. an)lügen 3: 4 (114)
life [laɪf], *pl* **lives** das Leben 3: (12/13)
°**life skills** *(pl)* ['laɪf skɪlz] die Alltagskompetenzen, die lebenswichtigen Fertigkeiten
light [laɪt] das Licht; die Lampe 1
lighting ['laɪtɪŋ] die Beleuchtung 3: 4 (116)
like [laɪk]:
1. mögen 1
I like singing. Ich singe gerne. 1
I'd (= I would) like ... Ich hätte gern ... / Ich möchte ... 1 **I'd (= I would) like to meet ....** Ich würde mich gerne mit ... treffen. 1 **Would you like me to ...?** Möchtest du, dass ich ...? 3: 4 (111)
2. liken *(in sozialen Netzwerken: positiv bewerten)* 3: 4 (114)
3. der Like *(positive Rückmeldung / „Gefällt mir" in sozialen Netzwerken)* 3: 4 (110)
like [laɪk] wie; wie zum Beispiel 2
like a vampire wie ein Vampir 2 **like this** so, auf diese Art 1 **a story like this** so/solch eine Geschichte 1
What's ... like? Wie ist ...? / Wie sieht ... aus? 1
line [laɪn]:
1. die Reihe 1
2. die Linie 3: 1 (16)
3. die Zeile 1
4. die (U-Bahn-)Linie, die (Zug-) Strecke 3: 1 (16)

link [lɪŋk]:
1. die Verbindung; der Link 3: 4 (108)
2. **link (to/with)** verbinden (mit) 3: 4 (108)
lion ['laɪən] der Löwe 1
list [lɪst]:
1. die Liste 1
2. (auf)listen 1
listen (to) ['lɪsn] (sich etwas) anhören; zuhören 1 **listening to music** Musik (an)hören 1
listener ['lɪsənə] der/die Zuhörer/in 3: 2 (52)
little ['lɪtl]:
1. klein 2
2. **a little** ein wenig, ein bisschen 2
live [lɪv] leben, wohnen 1
lives [laɪvz] *Plural von* **life**
living room ['lɪvɪŋ ruːm] das Wohnzimmer 1
lizard ['lɪzəd] die Eidechse 1
°**local** ['ləʊkl] einheimisch, am/vom Ort
loch [lɒx] *schottisches Wort für „lake"* 3: (12/13)
°**lock** [lɒk] abschließen *(z. B. Tür)* **(to) lock sb. in** jn. einsperren **(to) lock sb. in a room / a wardrobe** jn. in ein Zimmer / einen Kleiderschrank sperren
lonely ['ləʊnli] einsam 2
long [lɒŋ] lang 1 **work long days** lange arbeiten, lange Arbeitstage haben 1 **work long hours** lange arbeiten, Überstunden machen 2
look [lʊk]:
1. aussehen 1
2. sehen, schauen 1
look after sb./sth. sich um jn./etwas kümmern; auf jn./etwas aufpassen 2 **look at sth.** sich etwas anschauen 1 **look for** suchen; Ausschau halten nach 2 **look forward to doing sth.** sich darauf freuen , etwas zu tun 2 **look forward to sth.** sich auf etwas freuen 2 **look sth. up** etwas nachschlagen 1
lose [luːz], **lost, lost** verlieren 3: 3 (77)
°**loss** [lɒs] der Verlust **loss of life** Verluste an Menschenleben
lost [lɒst] *siehe* **lose** **be lost** sich verlaufen/verirrt haben 3: 1 (26) **get lost** sich verlaufen, sich verirren 3: 3 (77)
lot [lɒt]: **a lot (of) / lots (of)** viel/e 1
a lot sehr 1
loud [laʊd] laut 1 **laugh out loud** laut auf-/loslachen 2
love [lʌv]:
1. die Liebe 1
be in love (with sb.) verliebt sein (in jn.) 3: 2 (48) **fall in love (with sb.)** sich verlieben (in jn.) 3: 2 (48)
2. lieben, sehr mögen 1
I'd (= I would) love ... Ich hätte liebend gern ... / Ich möchte liebend gern ... 1 **I'd (= I would) love to meet ...** Ich würde mich liebend gerne mit ... treffen. 1
lucky ['lʌki]: **be lucky** Glück haben 1

lunch [lʌntʃ] das Mittagessen 1
What's for lunch? Was gibt es zum Mittagessen? 1
lunchtime ['lʌntʃtaɪm] die Mittagszeit 2 **at lunchtime** zur Mittagszeit 2

M

machine [məˈʃiːn] der Automat, die Maschine 2 **ticket machine** der Fahrkartenautomat 2
made [meɪd] *siehe* **make**
mag [mæg] *siehe* **magazine**
magazine [mægəˈziːn], *infml auch* **mag** die Zeitschrift 2
magic ['mædʒɪk]:
1. magisch 2
2. die Zauberei 2
do magic zaubern 2
magic show [mædʒɪk ˈʃəʊ] die Zaubershow 2
magic trick [mædʒɪk ˈtrɪk] der Zaubertrick 2
main [meɪn] Haupt-, wichtigste(r, s) 1
main course [meɪn ˈkɔːs] das Hauptgericht 1
main dish [meɪn ˈdɪʃ] das Hauptgericht 1
make [meɪk], **made, made** machen, herstellen 1 **make (money)** (Geld) verdienen 2 **make sb. do sth.** jn. dazu bringen, etwas zu tun 3: 2 (53)
make sb. sth. jn. zu etwas machen 3: 1 (25) °**make sth. up** etwas bilden, ausmachen
make-up ['meɪk ʌp] das Make-up 2
man [mæn], *pl* **men** der Mann 2
mango ['mæŋgəʊ], *pl* **mangoes** die Mango 2
many ['mæni] viele 1 **how many?** wie viele? 1
map [mæp] die Landkarte, der Stadtplan 1
March [mɑːtʃ] der März 1
marina [məˈriːnə] der Jachthafen 1
market ['mɑːkɪt] der Markt 1
married (to) ['mærid] verheiratet (mit) 1 **get married (to sb.)** jn. heiraten 2
marry ['mæri] heiraten 2
mask [mɑːsk] die Maske 2
°**match** (passend) zusammenfügen
match to zuordnen
match [mætʃ] das Spiel, der Wettkampf 1
maths [mæθs] die Mathe(matik) 1
May [meɪ] der Mai 1
may [meɪ] dürfen 2 **May I ...?** Darf ich ...? 2 °**May the best team win!** Möge das beste Team gewinnen!
maybe ['meɪbi] vielleicht 1
me [miː]:
1. mich; mir 1
2. *(in bestimmten Wendungen)* ich 1
It's me. Ich bin's. 1 **Not me!** Ich nicht! *(= Ich bin/war/habe/... es/das nicht!)* 1
meal [miːl] die Mahlzeit, das Essen 1
Enjoy your meal. Guten Appetit! 2
hot meal die warme Mahlzeit 1

mean [miːn]:
1. bedeuten 1
2. meinen *(sagen wollen)* 1
°**mean to do sth.** etwas mit Absicht tun, etwas tun wollen

mean [miːn] gemein, fies 1

meaning [ˈmiːnɪŋ] die Bedeutung 1

meat [miːt] das Fleisch 1 °**meats** *(pl)* die Fleischsorten °**cold meat** der (Braten-/Wurst-)Aufschnitt

mechanic [mɪˈkænɪk] der/die Mechaniker/in 2

media [ˈmiːdiə] die Medien 3: 4 (102/103)

°**mediation** [miːdiˈeɪʃn] die Vermittlung, die Sprachmittlung

medicine [ˈmedsn], [ˈmedɪsn] die Medizin, die Arznei, das Medikament 3: 4 (107)

medium [ˈmiːdiəm] medium *(Kleidergröße: mittelgroß/M)* 2

meet [miːt], **met, met** kennenlernen; (sich) treffen 1 **Nice to meet you.** Freut mich, dich/euch/Sie kennenzulernen. 1

meeting [ˈmiːtɪŋ] das Meeting *(Treffen, Zusammenkunft)* 2

melon [ˈmelən] die Melone 1

member [ˈmembə] das Mitglied 2

memorial (to sb./sth.) [məˈmɔːriəl] das Denkmal (für jn./etwas), die Gedenkstätte 3: 1 (27)

memorial fountain [məˈmɔːriə faʊntənl] der Gedenkbrunnen 3: 1 (27)

men [men] *Plural von* **man**

menu [ˈmenjuː] die Speisekarte 3: 1 (22)

°**merman** [ˈmɜːmən], *pl* **mermen** der Nix, der Wassermann, der Meermann

mess [mes] das Chaos, die Unordnung 1

message [ˈmesɪdʒ] die Nachricht, die Mitteilung 1

messy [ˈmesi] unordentlich 1

met [met] *siehe* **meet**

metre [ˈmiːtə] der Meter 2

mice [maɪs] *Plural von* **mouse**

middle [ˈmɪdl] die Mitte 3: 3 (89) **in the middle (of)** in der Mitte (von) 3: 3 (89)

mile [maɪl] die Meile *(ca. 1,6 km)* 3: 3 (74)

miles per hour (mph) [maɪlz pər ˈaʊə] Meilen pro Stunde 3: 3 (74) **at 30 miles per hour** mit 30 Meilen pro Stunde 3: 3 (74)

milk [mɪlk] die Milch 1

°**millennium** [mɪˈleniəm] das Jahrtausend

million [ˈmɪljən] die Million 3: 4 (102/103)

mind [maɪnd] der Geist, der Verstand; die Gedanken; der Kopf *(im übertragenen Sinn)* 2 **make up your mind / make your mind up** sich entscheiden, sich entschließen 2

mind map [ˈmaɪnd mæp] Gedankenkarte, Wörternetz, Mindmap 1

°**mind sth.** [maɪnd] auf etwas achten, auf etwas aufpassen **Mind the gap.** Achten Sie auf den Abstand zwischen Zug und Bahnsteigkante.

mine [maɪn] meine, meiner, meins 3: 4 (104)

°**mine** [maɪn] das Bergwerk

mini [ˈmɪni] Mini- 1

mini-drone [ˈmɪnɪ drəʊn] die Minidrohne 1

minigolf [ˈmɪnigɒlf] das Minigolf 2

minute [ˈmɪnɪt] die Minute 1

mirror [ˈmɪrə] der Spiegel 2

miss [mɪs]:
1. vermissen 2
2. verpassen 3: 1 (19)
miss a penalty einen Elfmeter verschießen *(= nicht treffen)* 3: 2 (53)
3. versäumen, auslassen 3: 1 (19)

mistake [mɪˈsteɪk] der Fehler 3: 3 (86) **by mistake** aus Versehen; versehentlich 3: 3 (86)

mix [mɪks] (ver)mischen 1

mixture [ˈmɪkstʃə] die Mischung 1

°**model** [ˈmɒdl] das Modell; das Fotomodell

modern [ˈmɒdn] modern 2

moment [ˈməʊmənt] der Moment 1 **at the moment** im Moment, zurzeit 1

Monday [ˈmʌndeɪ], [ˈmʌndi] der Montag 1

money [ˈmʌni] das Geld 1 **pocket money** das Taschengeld 2

monkey [ˈmʌŋki] der Affe 1

monster [ˈmɒnstə] das Monster 3: 3 (74)

month [mʌnθ] der Monat 1

more [mɔː] mehr, weitere 1 **three more** noch drei, drei weitere 1

morning [ˈmɔːnɪŋ] der Morgen 1 **in the morning** morgens, am Morgen 1

mosque [mɒsk] die Moschee 2

most schools [məʊst] die meisten Schulen 1

mother [ˈmʌðə] die Mutter 2

motto [ˈmɒtəʊ] das Motto 3: 3 (80)

mountain [ˈmaʊntən] der Berg 2

mountain biking [ˈmaʊntən baɪkɪŋ] das Mountainbiking 2

mouse [maʊs], *pl* **mice** die Maus 1

move [muːv]:
1. (sich) bewegen 2
2. **move (to)** (um)ziehen (nach) 2

Mr Lee [ˈmɪstə] Herr Lee 1

Mrs Lee [ˈmɪsɪz] Frau Lee *(Anrede für verheiratete Frauen)* 1

Ms Lee [mɪz] Frau Lee *(allgemeine Anrede f. Frauen)* 1

much [mʌtʃ] viel; sehr 1 **How much is/are ...?** Was (Wie viel) kostet/kosten ...? 2 **Thank you very much.** Vielen Dank. / Danke vielmals. 1

°**muesli** [ˈmjuːzli] das Müsli

multicultural [mʌltiˈkʌltʃərəl] multikulturell 2

mum [mʌm] die Mama, die Mutti 1

mural [ˈmjʊərəl] das Wandgemälde 3: (12/13)

museum [mjuˈziːəm] das Museum 1

music [ˈmjuːzɪk] die Musik 1 **classical music** klassische Musik 2

musical [ˈmjuːzɪkl] das Musical 2

musician [mjuˈzɪʃn] der/die Musiker/in 2

must [mʌst] müssen 1

mustn't do [ˈmʌsnt] nicht tun dürfen 2

my [maɪ] mein/e 1

myself [maɪˈself] mich/mir (selbst) 3: 2 (50)

N

name [neɪm] der Name 1 **call sb. names** jn. beschimpfen 3: 2 (57) **What's your name?** Wie heißt du? 1

nation [ˈneɪʃn] die Nation 3: 4 (102/103)

national [ˈnæʃnəl]:
1. national 3: 4 (102/103)
2. national, National- 3: 4 (102/103)

°**national park** [næʃnəl ˈpɑːk] der Nationalpark *(staatliches Naturschutzgebiet)*

natural [ˈnætʃrəl] natürlich, Natur- 3: 3 (82)

natural history [nætʃrəl ˈhɪstri] die Naturkunde 3: 3 (82)

nature [ˈneɪtʃə] die Natur 3: 3 (82)

near [nɪə] nahe (bei), in der Nähe von 1

neck [nek] der Hals, der Nacken 3: 3 (74)

need [niːd] brauchen 1 **need to do sth.** etwas tun müssen 1

negative [ˈnegətɪv] negativ 3: 4 (112)

neighbour [ˈneɪbə] der/die Nachbar/in 1

neighbourhood [ˈneɪbəhʊd] die Nachbarschaft, die Gegend, das Viertel 1

nervous [ˈnɜːvəs] nervös, aufgeregt 2

nest [nest] das Nest 2

never [ˈnevə] nie, niemals 1

new [njuː] neu 1

news [njuːz] die Nachrichten 1

newsagent [ˈnjuːzeɪdʒənt] der/die Zeitungshändler/in 2

newsagent's [ˈnjuːzeɪdʒənts] der Zeitschriftenladen, der Zeitungskiosk 2

newspaper [ˈnjuːspeɪpə] die (Tages-) Zeitung 1

next [nekst]:
1. nächste(r, s) 1
the next day am nächsten Tag 1
2. **Next ...** Als Nächstes ... 1

next to [ˈnekst tə] neben 1

nice [naɪs] nett, schön 1

night [naɪt] die Nacht 2 **at night** nachts, in der Nacht 2

nine [naɪn] neun 1

nineteen [naɪnˈtiːn] neunzehn 1

ninety [ˈnaɪnti] neunzig 1

no [nəʊ]:
1. nein 1
2. kein/e; verboten 1
No dogs! Hunde verboten! 1

no one [ˈnəʊ wʌn] niemand 3: 3 (77)

nobody [ˈnəʊbədi] niemand 3: 3 (77)

noise [nɔɪz] das Geräusch; der Lärm 1
noisy ['nɔɪzi] laut, voller Lärm; lärmend 1
normal ['nɔːml] normal 3: 2 (46)
north [nɔːθ] der Norden; nördlich; Nord- 3: (10/11)
north-east [nɔːθ'iːst] der Nordosten, nordöstlich; Nordost- 3: (10/11)
north-west [nɔːθ'west] der Nordwesten, nordwestlich; Nordwest- 3: (10/11)
northern ['nɔːðən] nördliche(r,s), Nord- 3: (10/11)
nose [nəʊz] die Nase 2
not [nɒt] nicht 1 **I'm not a boy.** Ich bin kein Junge. 1
note [nəʊt] die Notiz; der kurze Brief 1 **make notes** (sich) Notizen machen *(zur Vorbereitung)* 1 **take notes** (sich) Notizen machen *(beim Lesen oder Zuhören)* 3: 3 (81) °**sticky note** die Haftnotiz, der Klebezettel
°**nothing** ['nʌθɪŋ] nichts
notice ['nəʊtɪs]:
1. (be)merken 2
2. der Anschlag, die Bekanntmachung *(an einem Schwarzen Brett)* 2
November [nəʊ'vembə] der November 1
now [naʊ] nun, jetzt 1
°**nowhere** ['nəʊweə] nirgendwo(hin)
number ['nʌmbə] die Zahl, die Ziffer, die Nummer 1
nurse [nɜːs] der Krankenpfleger, die Krankenpflegerin 2

O

o'clock [ə'klɒk]: **at 8 o'clock** um 8 Uhr 1
October [ɒk'təʊbə] der Oktober 1
of [ɒv], [əv] von 1 **bags of rubbish** Tüten/Säcke mit/voller Müll 1 **the days of the week** *(pl)* die Wochentage 1 **the first of April (1st April)** der erste April 1
of course [əv 'kɔːs] natürlich, selbstverständlich 1
off [ɒf]:
1. weg von; hinunter von 3: 3 (78) **get off (a train/bus)** aussteigen (aus einem Zug/Bus) 2 **get off your bike/your horse** vom Fahrrad / vom Pferd absteigen 3: 3 (78) °**off the coast** vor der Küste
2. **be off** aus sein *(ausgeschaltet sein)* 2
°**offer** ['ɒfə] (an)bieten
office ['ɒfɪs] das Büro 1
official [ə'fɪʃl] offiziell 3: 4 (102/103)
official language [əfɪʃl 'læŋgwɪdʒ] die Amtssprache 3: 4 (102/103)
often ['ɒfn], ['ɒftən] oft 1
°**ogre** ['əʊgə] das Ungeheuer, das Monster
oh [əʊ] Null *(im gesprochenen Englisch)* 1

OK [əʊ'keɪ] okay, in Ordnung 1 **Are you OK?** Geht es dir gut? / Bist du okay? 1 **I'm OK.** Es geht mir gut. 1
old [əʊld] alt 1
on [ɒn]:
1. auf 1 **on holiday** im/in den Urlaub 1 **on Monday** am Montag 1 **on Mondays** an jedem Montag, montags 1 **on my birthday** an meinem Geburtstag 1 **on the beach** am Strand 1 **on the bus** im Bus 1 **get on (a train/bus)** einsteigen (in einen Zug/Bus) 2
2. **be on** gezeigt werden *(Kino, Fernsehen)*, stattfinden, „laufen"; an sein *(eingeschaltet sein)* 2
once [wʌns]:
1. einst 3: 1 (28)
2. einmal 3: 1 (28)
at once auf einmal 3: 1 (28)
one [wʌn]:
1. eins 1 **one way** eine Strecke *(= ohne Rückfahrt/Rückflug)* 2 **one-way ticket** die einfache Fahrkarte *(= ohne Rückfahrt)* 2 **a one-day tour** eine eintägige Tour 3: 3 (75) **a one-hour boat trip** eine einstündige Bootsfahrt 3: 3 (75)
2. **the round one** der/die/das Runde 2
onion ['ʌnjən] die Zwiebel 2
online [ɒn'laɪn] online, Online- 1
only ['əʊnli] nur, bloß; erst 1
onto the table ['ɒntu], ['ɒntə] auf den Tisch 2
open ['əʊpən]:
1. öffnen; aufschlagen *(Buch)* 1
2. offen, geöffnet 1
3. sich öffnen, aufgehen 3: 1 (30)
opinion [ə'pɪnjən] die Meinung 2 **in my opinion** meiner Meinung nach 2
opposite ['ɒpəzɪt] das Gegenteil 1
option ['ɒpʃn] die Wahl(möglichkeit), die Option 3: 2 (50)
or [ɔː] oder; sonst 1
orange ['ɒrɪndʒ]:
1. orange(farben) 1
2. die Orange, die Apfelsine 1
order ['ɔːdə]:
1. ordnen, anordnen 3: 4 (118)
2. die Reihenfolge; die Ordnung 3: 4 (118)
in order in eine(r) Reihenfolge 3: 4 (118) **in the correct order** in der richtigen Reihenfolge, in die richtige Reihenfolge 3: 4 (118)
order ['ɔːdə]:
1. die Bestellung 3: 1 (23)
2. **order sth.** etwas bestellen 3: 1 (23)
organization [ɔːgənaɪ'zeɪʃn] die Organisation 3: 4 (113)
organize ['ɔːgənaɪz] organisieren 3: 4 (113)
organizer ['ɔːgənaɪzə] der/die Organisator/in 3: 4 (113)
other ['ʌðə] andere(r, s) 1 **each other** einander, sich (gegenseitig) 2 **the others** die anderen 1
our ['aʊə] unser/e 1

ours [ɑːz], ['aʊəz] unserer, unsere, unseres 3: 4 (104)
ourselves [aʊə'selvz] uns (selbst) 3: 2 (50)
out (of ...) [aʊt]:
1. **out** heraus, hinaus, nach draußen 2 **go out** rausgehen, weggehen; ausgehen 2
2. **out of ...** aus ... (heraus/hinaus) 2
outdoor ['aʊtdɔː] Outdoor- 3: 3 (78)
outdoor activity ['aʊtdɔː] die Outdoor-Aktivität; die Aktivität für draußen / im Freien 3: 3 (78)
outdoors [aʊt'dɔːz] im Freien, draußen 3: 3 (78)
outfit ['aʊtfɪt] das Outfit 3: 2 (46)
outside [aʊt'saɪd] außerhalb (von) *(Präp.)* 1 **outside the house** außerhalb des Hauses 1
oven ['ʌvn] der Backofen 1
over ['əʊvə]:
1. **over 50** über / mehr als 50 1 **over here** hier herüber; hier drüben 1 **over there** da drüben, dort drüben 1 **all over the world** überall auf der Welt, auf der ganzen Welt, weltweit 2
2. hinüber, herüber 2 **come / walk over** hinüberkommen/-gehen, rüberkommen/-gehen 2
own [əʊn]:
1. **my/your own room** mein/dein/ein eigenes Zimmer 1
2. **own sth.** etwas besitzen 2
owner ['əʊnə] der/die Besitzer/in 2

P

pack [pæk] packen, einpacken 3: 3 (79)
packet ['pækɪt] die Packung, das Päckchen 1
°**paddleboarding** ['pædlbɔːdɪŋ] das Stehpaddeln, Paddleboardfahren
page (= p.) [peɪdʒ] die (Buch-/Heft-) Seite 1 **Open your books at page 10.** Schlagt eure Bücher auf Seite 10 auf. 1
paint [peɪnt]:
1. die Farbe, der Lack 3: 4 (117)
2. (an)malen; lackieren, (an)streichen 3: 4 (117)
pair [peə]:
1. das Paar 2
2. **pair sth. (with sth.)** etwas (mit etwas) koppeln *(z. B. Geräte)* 3: 4 (109)
palace ['pæləs] der Palast, das Schloss 3: 1 (14/15)
pan [pæn] die Pfanne 1
paper ['peɪpə]:
1. die (Tages-)Zeitung 1
2. das Papier 1
parade [pə'reɪd] die Parade, der Umzug 2
°**paragraph** ['pærəgrɑːf] der (Text-) Abschnitt
°**parallel** ['pærəlel] parallel, Parallel-
parents *(pl)* ['peərənts] die Eltern 1
park [pɑːk] der Park 1

parkour [pɑːˈkʊə] der Parkour *(akrobatischer Hindernislauf in der Stadt)* 1
°parliament [ˈpɑːləmənt] das Parlament **the Houses of Parliament** *(pl)* das Parlamentsgebäude in London
parrot [ˈpærət] der Papagei 1
part (of) [pɑːt] der Teil (von) 1
partner [ˈpɑːtnə] der/die Partner/in 1
party [ˈpɑːti] die Party 1
past [pɑːst]:
1. die Vergangenheit 3: 3 (79)
2. vergangene(r, s) 3: 3 (79)
past [pɑːst]:
1. nach *(bei Uhrzeitangaben)* 2 **half past 6** halb 7 2 **quarter past 7** viertel nach 7 2
2. vorbei an, vorüber an 2
pasta [ˈpæstə] die Pasta *(italienische Bezeichnung für Teigwaren)* 1
path [pɑːθ] der Weg, der Pfad 3: 3 (82)
pay (for sth.) [peɪ] zahlen; (etwas) bezahlen 1 **pay by card** mit Karte (be)zahlen *(z. B. Bankkarte)* 2
PE (= physical education) [piː ˈiː] der (Schul-)Sport 1
pea [piː] die Erbse 1
°peace [piːs] der Friede(n) **keep (the) peace** (den) Frieden erhalten, sichern
°peer pressure [pɪə ˈpreʃə] der Gruppendruck
pen [pen] der Kugelschreiber, der Stift; der Füller 1
penalty [ˈpenəlti] der Strafstoß; der Elfmeter *(Fußball)* 3: 2 (53)
pence [pens] *Plural von penny*
pencil [ˈpensl] der Bleistift 1
pencil case [ˈpensl keɪs] das Federmäppchen 1
pencil sharpener [ˈpensl ʃɑːpnə] der Bleistift(an)spitzer 1
penny (= p) [ˈpeni] Penny *(kleinste britische Münze)* 2
people *(pl)* [ˈpiːpl] die Leute, die Menschen 1
per [pɜː], [pə] pro 3: 3 (74) **miles per hour (mph)** Meilen pro Stunde 3: 3 (74)
per cent (%) [pə ˈsent] das Prozent 3: 1 (20)
perfect [ˈpɜːfɪkt] perfekt 1
perfectly (still) [ˈpɜːfɪktli] ganz/völlig (still) 1
perhaps [pəˈhæps] vielleicht 2
person [ˈpɜːsn] die Person 1
personal [ˈpɜːsənl] persönlich 3: 2 (61)
personality [pɜːsəˈnæləti] die Persönlichkeit; der Charakter 3: 2 (61)
pet [pet] das (Haus-)Tier 1
phone [fəʊn]:
1. anrufen; telefonieren 1
2. das Telefon 1
answer the phone ans Telefon gehen 3: 1 (26) **on the phone** am Telefon 1
phone call [ˈfəʊn kɔːl] der (Telefon-)Anruf 2
phone number [ˈfəʊn nʌmbə] die Telefonnummer 1
photo [ˈfəʊtəʊ] das Foto 1 **in the photo** auf dem Foto 1 **take photos** Fotos machen 1 **taking photos** das Fotografieren *(Hobby)* 1
photography [fəˈtɒɡrəfi] die Fotografie *(Hobby)*, das Fotografieren 2
°phrase [freɪz] der Ausdruck, die (Rede-)Wendung
physical education (PE) [fɪzɪkl edʒuˈkeɪʃn] der (Schul-)Sport 1
pick [pɪk] (aus)wählen, aussuchen 2 **pick sb./sth. up** jn./etwas abholen 2 **pick sth. up** etwas aufheben *(vom Boden)*, etwas hochheben 2
picnic [ˈpɪknɪk] das Picknick 1 **have a picnic** ein Picknick machen 1
picture [ˈpɪktʃə] das Bild 1
pier [pɪə] der Pier, die Seebrücke 1
pig [pɪɡ] das Schwein 1
piggy bank [ˈpɪɡi bæŋk] das Sparschwein 2
pink [pɪŋk] rosa 1
piper [ˈpaɪpə] der/die Dudelsackspieler/in 3: 3 (77)
°piping [ˈpaɪpɪŋ] das Dudelsackspielen
°pit [pɪt] die Grube
pitch [pɪtʃ] der Platz *(Sport)*, das Spielfeld 3: 2 (56)
pizza [ˈpiːtsə] die Pizza 2
place [pleɪs] der Ort, der Platz 1 **take place** stattfinden 2
plan [plæn]:
1. der Plan 2
2. planen 2
plan to do sth. planen, etwas zu tun 2
plane [pleɪn] das Flugzeug 2
planet [ˈplænɪt] der Planet 2
plant [plɑːnt]:
1. die Pflanze 3: 3 (82)
2. pflanzen 3: 3 (82)
plastic [ˈplæstɪk] das Plastik, der Kunststoff 2
platform [ˈplætfɔːm] der Bahnsteig 2 **at platform 4** auf Gleis 4 2
play [pleɪ] spielen 1
player [ˈpleɪə] der/die Spieler/in 1
playing card [ˈpleɪɪŋ kɑːd] die Spielkarte 1
playlist [ˈpleɪlɪst] die Playlist 1
please [pliːz] bitte 1
plumber [ˈplʌmə] der/die (Sanitär-)Installateur/in 2
p.m. [piːˈem]: **4 p.m.** 4 Uhr nachmittags, 16 Uhr 1 **9 p.m.** 9 Uhr abends, 21 Uhr 1
pocket [ˈpɒkɪt] die Tasche *(an Kleidungsstücken)* 2
pocket money [ˈpɒkɪt mʌni] das Taschengeld 2
podcast [ˈpɒdkɑːst] der Podcast *(Audiodatei zum Herunterladen aus dem Internet)* 3: 2 (52)
poem [ˈpəʊɪm] das Gedicht 2
point [pɔɪnt]:
1. der Punkt 1
2. das Argument, der Standpunkt 3: 2 (60)
I take your point. Ich verstehe, was du sagen willst. 3: 2 (60) **make a/your point** ein Argument vortragen/vorbringen 3: 2 (60) **Make your point.** Leg deinen Standpunkt dar. / Sag, wie du darüber denkst. 3: 2 (60) **take a point** einen Standpunkt verstehen 3: 2 (60) **That's a good point.** Das ist ein gutes Argument. 3: 2 (60)
°point (at/to) [pɔɪnt] zeigen, deuten (auf)
police *(pl)* [pəˈliːs] die Polizei 3: 2 (59)
polite [pəˈlaɪt] höflich 1
°pony [ˈpəʊni] das Pony
pool [puːl] *(kurz für swimming pool)* das Schwimmbad 1
poor [pɔː], [pʊə] arm 3: 2 (53) **Poor George!** Der arme George! / Armer George! 3: 2 (53)
pop (music) [ˈpɒp mjuːzɪk] der Pop, die Popmusik 2
popular (with) [ˈpɒpjələ] beliebt, populär (bei) 1
pork [pɔːk] das Schweinefleisch 1
pose [pəʊz]:
1. posieren 3: 4 (116)
2. die Pose, die Haltung 3: 4 (116)
power pose die Machtpose 3: 4 (116)
positive [ˈpɒzətɪv] positiv 3: 4 (112)
post [pəʊst]:
1. der Post *(Teil eines Blogs)* 1
2. posten *(im Internet veröffentlichen)* 1
poster [ˈpəʊstə] das Poster 1
potato [pəˈteɪtəʊ], *pl* **potatoes** die Kartoffel 1
pound (£) [paʊnd] das Pfund *(britische Währung)* 1
poverty [ˈpɒvəti] die Armut 3: 2 (53)
powder [ˈpaʊdə] das Pulver 1
power [ˈpaʊə] die Kraft, die Macht, die Energie; der (elektrische) Strom 2
power pose [ˈpaʊə pəʊz] die Machtpose 3: 4 (116)
°powerful [ˈpaʊəfl] kräftig, stark, mächtig
practice [ˈpræktɪs] die Übung(en) 2
practise [ˈpræktɪs] üben 2
pray [preɪ] beten 2
prayer [preə] das Gebet 2
prediction [prɪˈdɪkʃn] die Vorhersage, die Voraussage 2
preparation [prepəˈreɪʃn] die Vorbereitung; die Zubereitung 2
prepare (for) [prɪˈpeə] vorbereiten, zubereiten; sich vorbereiten (auf) 2
present [ˈpreznt] das Geschenk 1
present [ˈpreznt]:
1. die Gegenwart 3: 3 (79)
2. gegenwärtig 3: 3 (79)
present sth. (to sb.) [prɪˈzent] (jm.) etwas präsentieren, vorstellen 1
presentation [preznˈteɪʃn] das Referat, die Präsentation 1
°pressure [ˈpreʃə]:
1. **pressure sb. (into sth.)** jn. (zu etwas) drängen
2. der Druck
peer pressure der Gruppendruck
pretty [ˈprɪti]:
1. hübsch 3: 4 (116)

°2. **pretty busy/old/cool/...** ziemlich hektisch/alt/cool/...
price [praɪs] der (Kauf-)Preis 2
pride [praɪd] der Stolz 2
prime minister [praɪm ˈmɪnɪstə] der/die Premierminister/in 3:1 (18)
prince [prɪns] der Prinz 3:1 (14/15)
princess [prɪnˈses] die Prinzessin 3:1 (14/15)
°**print (out)** [prɪnt] (aus)drucken
private [ˈpraɪvət] privat; persönlich 3:4 (111)
prize [praɪz] der Preis, der Gewinn 1
prize show [ˈpraɪz ʃəʊ] die Preisverleihung *(Zeremonie)* 1
problem [ˈprɒbləm] das Problem 1
profile [ˈprəʊfaɪl] das Profil; die Beschreibung, das Portrait 2
program [ˈprəʊɡræm]:
1. das (Computer-)Programm 2
2. programmieren 2
programme [ˈprəʊɡræm] das (Fernseh-)Programm, die Sendung 2
programmer [ˈprəʊɡræmə] der/die Programmierer/in 2
project [ˈprɒdʒekt] das Projekt 1
protect (from/against) [prəˈtekt] (be)schützen (vor) 3:3 (82)
protest [ˈprəʊtest] der Protest, die Protestdemonstration 3:3 (83)
protest [prəˈtest] protestieren 3:3 (83)
protester [prəˈtestə] der/die Demonstrant/in 3:3 (83)
proud (of) [praʊd] stolz (auf) 2
public [ˈpʌblɪk] öffentlich 3:1 (16)
public transport *(no pl)* [pʌblɪk ˈtrænspɔːt] die öffentlichen Verkehrsmittel 3:1 (16)
punk [pʌŋk] der Punk 2
purple [ˈpɜːpl] violett, lila 1
put [pʊt], **put, put** *(etwas wohin)* tun, legen, stellen, stecken 1 **put sth. on** etwas anziehen *(Kleidung)*, aufsetzen *(z. B. Hut, Brille)* 2 **put your hand up** sich melden, aufzeigen 1
puzzle [ˈpʌzl] das Rätsel 1

Q

quarter [ˈkwɔːtə]: **quarter past 7** viertel nach 7 2 **quarter to 7** viertel vor 7 2
queen [kwiːn] die Königin 3:1 (14/15)
question [ˈkwestʃən] die Frage 1 **ask a question** eine Frage stellen 1
quick [kwɪk] schnell 3:2 (60)
quiet [ˈkwaɪət] ruhig, still, leise 1
quiz [kwɪz], *pl* **quizzes** das Quiz, das Ratespiel; der Test 1 **do a quiz** ein Quiz / ein Ratespiel / einen Test machen 1
quizzes [ˈkwɪzɪz] *Plural von quiz*

R

rabbit [ˈræbɪt] das Kaninchen 1
racism [ˈreɪsɪzəm] der Rassismus 3:2 (53)
racist [ˈreɪsɪst]:
1. der/die Rassist/in 3:2 (53)
2. rassistisch 3:2 (53)
radio [ˈreɪdiəʊ] das Radio 3:2 (52)
°**rafting** [ˈrɑːftɪŋ] das Rafting *(Schlauchbootfahren auf Flüssen)*
rain [reɪn]:
1. der Regen 1
2. regnen 1
rain jacket [ˈreɪn dʒækɪt] die Regenjacke 2
rainbow [ˈreɪnbəʊ] der Regenbogen 2
rainy [ˈreɪni] regnerisch 1
rap [ræp]:
1. der Rap 2
2. rappen 2
read [red] *siehe* **read**
read [riːd], **read, read** lesen 1
reader [ˈriːdə] der/die Leser/in 1
ready [ˈredi] fertig, bereit 1 **get ready (for)** sich fertig machen (für), sich vorbereiten (auf) 2
real [rɪəl] echt, wirklich 2
realistic [riːəˈlɪstɪk] realistisch 2
really [ˈriːəli], [ˈrɪəli] wirklich 1
reason [ˈriːzn] der Grund, die Begründung 3:1 (25) **for this reason** aus diesem Grund 3:1 (25) **the reason why ...** der Grund dafür, dass ... 3:1 (25)
recipe [ˈresəpi] das (Koch-)Rezept 1
recipe book [ˈresəpi bʊk] das Kochbuch 1
recognize [ˈrekəɡnaɪz] (wieder)erkennen 3:4 (116)
°**recommend sth. (to sb.)** [rekəˈmend] (jm.) etwas empfehlen
record [rɪˈkɔːd] aufnehmen, aufzeichnen 1
recording [rɪˈkɔːdɪŋ] die Aufnahme 1
recycle [riːˈsaɪkl] recyceln, wiederverwerten 3:3 (83)
recycling [rɪˈsaɪklɪŋ] das Recycling 3:1 (25)
red [red] rot 1 **go red** erröten, rot werden 1
relax [rɪˈlæks] sich entspannen 2
relaxed [rɪˈlækst] entspannt 2
relaxing [rɪˈlæksɪŋ] entspannend 2
remember [rɪˈmembə]:
1. daran denken, nicht vergessen 1
remember to do sth. daran denken, etwas zu tun 1
2. sich erinnern an 1
remember doing sth. sich daran erinnern, etwas getan zu haben 1
repeat [rɪˈpiːt] wiederholen 2
reply (to) [rɪˈplaɪ]:
1. antworten (auf) 3:4 (114)
2. die Antwort (auf) 3:4 (114)
republic [rɪˈpʌblɪk] die Republik 3: (10/11)
rescue [ˈreskjuː]:
1. retten 3:3 (85)
2. die Rettung 3:3 (85)
rescuer [ˈreskjuːə] der/die Retter/in 3:3 (85)
research [rɪˈsɜːtʃ]:
1. erforschen, untersuchen, recherchieren 3:1 (30)
2. die Forschung(en), die Recherche(n) 3:1 (30)
do research recherchieren 3:1 (30)
respect [rɪˈspekt]:
1. respektieren, achten 2
2. **respect (for)** der Respekt (vor) 2
rest [rest]:
1. ruhen; sich ausruhen 3:2 (51)
2. die Ruhe, die Pause, die Erholung 3:2 (51)
take a rest Pause machen 3:2 (51)
restaurant [ˈrestrɒnt] das Restaurant 2
result [rɪˈzʌlt] das Ergebnis 3:2 (61)
as a result folglich, demzufolge 3:2 (61)
return [rɪˈtɜːn]:
1. zurückkehren, zurückkommen 2
2. *(kurz für: **return ticket**)* (Hin- und) Rückfahrkarte 2
return ticket [rɪˈtɜːn tɪkɪt] (Hin- und) Rückfahrkarte 2
rhyme [raɪm]:
1. (sich) reimen 2
2. der Reim 2
rice [raɪs] der Reis 1
rich [rɪtʃ] reich 2
ridden [ˈrɪdn] *siehe* **ride**
ride [raɪd], **rode, ridden: ride a bike** mit dem Fahrrad fahren 2 **ride a horse** reiten 2
right [raɪt]:
1. richtig *(Adj.)* 1
be right Recht haben 1
2. das Recht 3:4 (115)
You had no right to do this. Du hattest kein Recht, das zu tun. 3:4 (115)
3. *(adv.)* genau, gerade, direkt 3:1 (26)
right after school gleich/direkt nach der Schule 3:1 (26) **right by the sea** direkt am Meer 3:1 (26) **right from the start** gleich/direkt von Anfang an 3:1 (26) **right now** gerade jetzt, genau jetzt 3:1 (26) **right then** genau dann 3:1 (26)
right [raɪt] rechts; nach rechts 2 **on the right** rechts, auf der rechten Seite 2 **to the right of ...** rechts von ... 2
ring [rɪŋ] der Ring 1 **wedding ring** der Ehering 2
rip [rɪpt] zerreißen, (ein)reißen 3:2 (46)
ripped [rɪpt] zerrissen, (ein)gerissen 3:2 (46)
river [ˈrɪvə] der Fluss 2
road [rəʊd] die Straße *(in oder zwischen Orten)* 1
road trip [ˈrəʊd trɪp] die Autoreise 3:3 (87)
robot [ˈrəʊbɒt] der Roboter 1
rock [rɒk] der Rock *(Rockmusik)* 2
rode [rəʊd] *siehe* **ride**
role [rəʊl] die Rolle *(Film, Theater)* 2
role model [ˈrəʊl mɒdl] das Vorbild 3:2 (53)

role-play ['rəʊlpleɪ]:
1. das Rollenspiel 2
2. **role-play sth.** etwas in einem Rollenspiel darstellen 2
room [ruːm] der Raum, das Zimmer 1
round [raʊnd]:
1. rund *(Adj.)* 2
2. **round ...** um (... herum), in ... umher 2
all round the globe auf der ganzen Welt 3: 1 (25) **all round the stadium** überall im Stadion, im ganzen Stadion 3: 2 (57)
roundabout ['raʊndəbaʊt] der Kreisverkehr 3: 1 (21)
route [ruːt] die Route, der Weg 3: 1 (28)
royal ['rɔɪəl] königlich 3: 1 (14/15)
rubber ['rʌbə] das Radiergummi 1
rubbish ['rʌbɪʃ] der (Haus-)Müll, der Abfall 1
rucksack ['rʌksæk] der Rucksack 1
rugby ['rʌgbi] das Rugby *(Ballsportart)* 3: 4 (102/103)
rule [ruːl] die Regel 2
ruler ['ruːlə] das Lineal 1
run [rʌn] rennen, laufen 1
running ['rʌnɪŋ] das Laufen *(Sport)* 1

S

sad [sæd] traurig 1
°**sadly** ['sædli] traurigerweise
safe [seɪf] sicher *(gefahrlos)* 3: 2 (50)
safety ['seɪfti] die Sicherheit 3: 2 (50)
said [sed] *siehe* **say**
°**sailor** ['seɪlə] der Seemann, die Seemännin; der Matrose, die Matrosin
°**Saint (= St)** [seɪnt] Sankt (St)
salad ['sæləd] der Salat *(als Gericht oder Beilage)* 1
same [seɪm]: **the same** gleich; derselbe/dieselbe/dasselbe; dieselben 1
sandwich ['sænwɪtʃ], ['sænwɪdʒ] das Sandwich 1
sang [sæŋ] *siehe* **sing**
°**sank** [sæŋk] *siehe* **sink**
sari ['sɑːri] der Sari *(Kleid/Gewand indischer Frauen)* 2
sat [sæt] *siehe* **sit**
Saturday ['sætədeɪ], ['sætədi] der Samstag 1
sauce [sɔːs] die Soße 1
sausage ['sɒsɪdʒ] das (Brat-, Bock-)Würstchen, die Wurst 1
save [seɪv]:
1. retten 2
2. sparen 2
savings *(pl)* ['seɪvɪŋz] die Ersparnisse 2
savings account ['seɪvɪŋz əkaʊnt] das Sparkonto 2
saw [sɔː] *siehe* **see**
say [seɪ], **said, said** sagen 1 **say sorry to sb.** sich bei jm. entschuldigen 3: 2 (58) **it says that ...** es heißt (im Text), dass ... 3: 4 (112)
°**scan (a text for sth.)** [skæn] (einen Text) überfliegen, (einen Text) absuchen (nach etwas)
scare sb. [skeə] jn. erschrecken, jm. Angst machen 2
scared [skeəd]: **be scared (of)** Angst haben (vor) 1
scarf [skɑːf], *pl* **scarves** Schal 2
scarves [skɑːvz] *Plural von* **scarf**
scary ['skeəri] unheimlich, beängstigend, gruselig 2
scene [siːn] die Szene 1
school [skuːl] die Schule 1 **at school** in der Schule 1
school club ['skuːl klʌb] die AG *(in der Schule)* 1
school uniform [skuːl 'juːnɪfɔːm] die Schuluniform 1
sci-fi ['saɪ faɪ] *siehe* **science fiction**
science ['saɪəns] die Naturwissenschaft 1
science fiction [saɪəns 'fɪkʃn] *infml auch* **sci-fi** die Sciencefiction 2
scientist ['saɪəntɪst] der/die (Natur-)Wissenschaftler/in 3: 3 (74)
score [skɔː]:
1. der Score *(Spielstand, Spielergebnis)* 2
2. scoren *(einen Punkt / ein Tor / einen Treffer erzielen)* 2
Scotland ['skɒtlənd] Schottland 3: (10/11)
screen [skriːn] der Bildschirm; die Leinwand *(Kino)* 2
sea [siː] das Meer, die See 1 **by the sea** am Meer, an der See 1
sea level ['siː levl] der Meeresspiegel 2
seagull ['siːgʌl] die Möwe 1
°**season** ['siːzn] die Jahreszeit; die Saison
°**seat** [siːt] der (Sitz-)Platz
°**second** ['sekənd] die Sekunde
second (2nd) ['sekənd] zweite(r, s) 1
second-hand [sekənd 'hænd] secondhand *(gebraucht, aus zweiter Hand)* 3: 2 (61)
second-hand shop [sekənd hænd 'ʃɒp] der Secondhandladen 3: 2 (61)
secondary school ['sekəndri skuːl] die weiterführende Schule 3: 2 (44/45)
secret ['siːkrət]:
1. geheim 1
2. das Geheimnis 1
see [siː], **saw, seen** sehen 1
See you soon. Bis bald! 1
See you. Bis dann. / Tschüs. 1
seen [siːn] *siehe* **see**
sell [sel], **sold, sold** verkaufen 1
send [send], **sent, sent** senden, schicken 1
sent [sent] *siehe* **send**
°**sentence** ['sentəns] der Satz
°**separate** ['sepəreɪt] trennen
September [sep'tembə] der September 1
°**series** ['sɪəriːz], *pl* **series** die Serie, die Sendereihe
serious ['sɪəriəs] ernst(haft) 3: 2 (49) **Are you serious?** Meinst du das ernst? 3: 2 (49)
service station ['sɜːvɪs steɪʃn] die Tankstelle; die (Autobahn-)Raststätte 3: 2 (59)
sesame ['sesəmi] der Sesam 3: 1 (22)
set [set], **set, set** stellen, legen, setzen 2 **set the table** den Tisch decken 2
setting ['setɪŋ] das Setting *(die Einstellung, z. B. bei Geräten)* 3: 4 (109)
seven ['sevn] sieben 1
seventeen [sevn'tiːn] siebzehn 1
seventy ['sevnti] siebzig 1
several ['sevrəl] mehrere, einige 3: 4 (107)
sew [səʊ], **sewed, sewn** nähen 3: 4 (117)
sewing machine ['səʊɪŋ məʃiːn] die Nähmaschine 3: 4 (117)
sewn [səʊn] *siehe* **sew**
Shall I ...? [ʃæl], [ʃəl] Soll ich ...? 3: 4 (111)
shame [ʃeɪm]: **a shame** schade; eine Schande 1 **That's / It's a shame!** Das/Es ist schade! 1 **What a shame!** Wie schade! 1
°**shard** [ʃɑːd] die Scherbe
share [ʃeə] teilen 1
sharpener ['ʃɑːpnə] der Anspitzer 1
she [ʃiː] sie *(weibliche Person)* 1
she's (= she is) sie ist 1
sheep [ʃiːp], *pl* **sheep** das Schaf 3: 4 (102/103)
shelf [ʃelf], *pl* **shelves** das Regal(brett) 1
shelves [ʃelvz] *Plural von* **shelf**
°**ship** [ʃɪp] das Schiff
shirt [ʃɜːt] das Shirt, das Hemd 2
shoe [ʃuː] der Schuh 1
shop [ʃɒp]:
1. das Geschäft, der Laden 1
be at the shops Einkäufe erledigen 1
2. (ein)kaufen, „shoppen" 2
shop for sth. etwas kaufen (gehen) 2
shop assistant ['ʃɒp əsɪstənt] der/die Verkäufer/in 2
shopper ['ʃɒpə] der Kunde, die Kundin; der/die Einkäufer/in 2
shopping ['ʃɒpɪŋ] das Einkaufen; die Einkäufe 1 **do the shopping** die Einkäufe erledigen, einkaufen gehen 1
go shopping einkaufen gehen 1
shopping list ['ʃɒpɪŋ lɪst] die Einkaufsliste 1
short [ʃɔːt]:
1. kurz 1
2. klein *(Person; Körpergröße)* 1
shorts *(pl)* [ʃɔːts] die kurze Hose, die Shorts 2
should [ʃʊd]: **we should ...** wir sollten ... 3: 1 (26)
shout [ʃaʊt]:
1. der Ruf, der Schrei 3: 3 (88)
2. rufen, schreien 3: 3 (88)
shout at sb. jn. anschreien 3: 3 (88)
show [ʃəʊ]:
1. zeigen 2
2. die Show, die Aufführung; die Ausstellung 1
prize show die Preisverleihung *(Zeremonie)* 1

shower ['ʃaʊə] die Dusche 1
have a shower (sich) duschen 1
shy [ʃaɪ] scheu, schüchtern 3: 2 (48)
sick [sɪk] krank 2
sickness ['sɪknəs] die Krankheit 2
side [saɪd] die Seite *(z. B. Straßenseite)* 3: 4 (112)
sight [saɪt]:
1. die Sehenswürdigkeit 2
2. der Anblick, das Bild 2
sightseeing ['saɪtsiːɪŋ] das Sightseeing *(Besichtigung von Sehenswürdigkeiten)* 3: 3 (87)
sign [saɪn] das Zeichen; das Schild 2
°**silent** ['saɪlənt] still, lautlos **fall/go silent** still werden, verstummen
silver ['sɪlvə]:
1. Silber 2
2. silberfarben 2
°**similar** ['sɪmələ] ähnlich
simple ['sɪmpl] einfach 1
sing [sɪŋ], **sang, sung** singen 1
singer ['sɪŋə] der/die Sänger/in 1
singing ['sɪŋɪŋ] das Singen 1
single ['sɪŋgl] Einzel-, einzelne(r, s) 2
single ticket [sɪŋgl 'tɪkɪt] die einfache Fahrkarte *(= ohne Rückfahrt)* 2
°**sink** [sɪŋk], **sank, sunk** sinken
sister ['sɪstə] die Schwester 1
sit [sɪt], **sat, sat** sitzen; sich setzen 1
sit down sich hinsetzen 1
°**situation** [sɪtʃu'eɪʃn] die Situation
six [sɪks] sechs 1
sixteen [sɪks'tiːn] sechzehn 1
sixty ['sɪksti] sechzig 1
size [saɪz] die Größe 2 **What size do you take?** Welche Größe hast du? 2
skateboard ['skeɪtbɔːd]:
1. das Skateboard 1
2. Skateboard fahren 1
skateboarding ['skeɪtbɔːdɪŋ] das Skateboardfahren 1
skatepark ['skeɪt pɑːk] der Skatepark 1
ski [skiː]:
1. der Ski 1
2. Ski laufen, Ski fahren 1
go skiing (zum) Skilaufen gehen 1
skill [skɪl] die Fähigkeit, die Fertigkeit 2 °**life skills** die Alltagskompetenzen, die lebenswichtigen Fertigkeiten °**study skills** die Lerntechniken
skim a text [skɪm] einen Text überfliegen *(um den Inhalt grob zu erfassen)* 3: 4 (114)
skin [skɪn] die Haut; die Schale *(z. B. Banane)* 3: 4 (117)
°**skinny** [skɪni] mager, dünn *(sehr schlank)*
skirt [skɜːt] der Rock 3: 2 (46)
skyscraper ['skaɪskreɪpə] der Wolkenkratzer 3: (12/13)
sleep [sliːp]:
1. der Schlaf 1
2. **sleep, slept, slept** schlafen 1
°**sleepy** ['sliːpi] müde, schläfrig, verschlafen
slept [slept] *siehe* **sleep**
slide [slaɪd] das Dia; die Folie *(Präsentationssoftware)* 1
slippers *(pl)* [slɪpə] die Hausschuhe 2
slow [sləʊ] langsam 1
small [smɔːl] klein 1
smart [smɑːt]:
1. schick 1
2. intelligent, clever 1
smartwatch ['smɑːtwɒtʃ] die Smartwatch 3: 4 (108)
smell [smel]:
1. der Geruch; der Gestank 3: 1 (19)
2. riechen; schlecht riechen 3: 1 (19)
smile [smaɪl]:
1. das Lächeln 2
2. lächeln 2
smile at sb. jn. anlächeln 2
smiley ['smaɪli] das Smiley 2
snake [sneɪk] die Schlange 1
snow [snəʊ]:
1. der Schnee 1
2. schneien 1
snowboarding ['snəʊbɔːdɪŋ] das Snowboarding 2
snowy ['snəʊi] schneebedeckt; verschneit 1
so [səʊ]:
1. so 1
so weird so seltsam, so komisch 1
2. also, daher 1
3. **so (that)** sodass 2
so far [səʊ 'fɑː] bis jetzt, bis hierher 3: 2 (50)
social ['səʊʃl] sozial 3: 4 (102/103)
social media [səʊʃl 'miːdiə] die sozialen Medien 3: 4 (102/103)
on social media in den sozialen Medien 3: 4 (102/103)
sock [sɒk] die Socke 3: 2 (46)
sofa ['səʊfə] das Sofa 1
software ['sɒftweə] die Software 3: 4 (116)
sold [səʊld] *siehe* **sell**
soldier ['səʊldʒə] der/die Soldat/in 3: 3 (76)
solve [sɒlv] lösen *(Rätsel, Problem)*, lüften *(Geheimnis)* 2
some [sʌm], [səm] einige, ein paar; etwas, ein wenig 1
somebody ['sʌmbədi] jemand 1
someone ['sʌmwʌn] jemand 1
something ['sʌmθɪŋ] etwas 1
sometimes ['sʌmtaɪmz] manchmal 1
son [sʌn] der Sohn 1
song [sɒŋ] das Lied 1
soon [suːn] bald 2
sorry ['sɒri]: **Sorry. / I'm sorry.** Tut mir leid. / Entschuldigung. 1 **be/feel sorry for sb.** Mitleid haben mit jm. 1 **I'm / I feel sorry for him.** Ich habe Mitleid mit ihm. / Er tut mir leid. 1 **say sorry to sb.** sich bei jm. entschuldigen 3: 2 (58)
sound [saʊnd]:
1. der Laut; das Geräusch; der Klang 2
2. klingen *(sich … anhören)* 2
south [saʊθ] der Süden; südlich; Süd- 3: (10/11)
south-east [saʊθ'iːst] der Südosten, südöstlich; Südost- 3: (10/11)
south-west [saʊθ'west] der Südwesten; südwestlich; Südwest- 3: (10/11)
southern ['sʌðən] südlich(r,s), Süd- 3: (10/11)
souvenir [suːvə'nɪə] das Souvenir 3: 4 (105)
space [speɪs] der Weltraum; der Raum, die Fläche; der Platz 2
spaghetti [spə'geti] die Spaghetti 2
speak (to) [spiːk], **spoke, spoken** sprechen (mit) 1 **Speak later.** Tschüs. / Bis später. 1
speaking ['spiːkɪŋ] das Sprechen 1
special ['speʃl] besondere(r, s) 1 **… is special** … ist etwas Besonderes 1 **What's special about this place?** Was ist das Besondere an diesem Ort? 1
special effects *(pl)* [speʃl ɪ'fekts] die Special Effects *(in Filmen)* 2
°**specific** [spə'sɪfɪk] bestimmte(r, s), spezielle(r, s); genau, präzise
°**spectacular** [spek'tækjələ] spektakulär, aufsehenerregend
°**speech bubble** ['spiːtʃ bʌbl] die Sprechblase
spell [spel] buchstabieren 1
spelling ['spelɪŋ] die Schreibweise, die Rechtschreibung 1
spend [spend], **spent, spent: spend money (on …)** Geld ausgeben (für …) 2 **spend time** Zeit verbringen 2
spent [spent] *siehe* **spend**
spice [spaɪs] das Gewürz 1
spicy ['spaɪsi] würzig 1
spoke [spəʊk] *siehe* **speak**
°**spoken** ['spəʊkən] *siehe* **speak**
sport [spɔːt] der Sport; die Sportart 1
sports hall ['spɔːts hɔːl] die Sporthalle 1
°**spot sth.** [spɒt] etwas entdecken
square [skweə]:
1. der Platz *(in der Stadt)* 3: 1 (21)
2. rechteckig 3: 1 (21)
°**St = Saint** [seɪnt] St = Sankt
stadium ['steɪdiəm] das Stadion 1
stairs *(pl)* [steəz] die Treppe; die (Treppen-)Stufen 2
stall [stɔːl] der (Markt-)Stand, die Bude 3: 1 (17)
stand [stænd], **stood, stood** stehen; sich (hin)stellen 2 **stand up** (auf-) stehen 1
star [stɑː]:
1. der Stern 2
2. der (Film-/Pop-)Star 2
star sign ['stɑː saɪn] das Sternzeichen 2
start [stɑːt]:
1. der Anfang, der Start 1
2. beginnen, anfangen (mit) 1
start a business ein Geschäft aufmachen, einen Betrieb gründen/ eröffnen 2
°**statement** ['steɪtmənt] die Aussage, der Aussagesatz
station ['steɪʃn] der Bahnhof 1

statistic [stəˈtɪstɪk] die statistische Tatsache, die statistische Größe 3: 4 (112) **statistics** *(pl)* die Statistik(en) 3: 4 (112)
statue [ˈstætʃuː] die Statue 3: 1 (27)
stay [steɪ]:
1. der Aufenthalt 1
2. bleiben; übernachten 1
stay up aufbleiben *(nicht ins Bett gehen)* 2
step [step] die Stufe; der Schritt 1
stepbrother [ˈstepbrʌðə] der Stiefbruder 2
stepdad [ˈstepdæd] der Stiefvater 2
stepdaughter [ˈstepdɔːtə] die Stieftochter 2
stepfather [ˈstepfɑːθə] der Stiefvater 2
stepmother [ˈstepmʌθə] die Stiefmutter 2
stepmum [ˈstepmʌm] die Stiefmutter 2
stepsister [ˈstepsɪstə] die Stiefschwester 2
stepson [ˈstepsʌn] der Stiefsohn 2
°**stick** [stɪk], **stuck, stuck** kleben; stecken; (haften) bleiben
°**sticky note** [stɪki ˈnəʊt] die Haftnotiz, der Klebezettel
still [stɪl]:
1. (immer) noch 1
2. trotzdem 2
stood [stʊd] *siehe* **stand**
stop [stɒp]:
1. der Halt, der Haltepunkt; die Unterbrechung 1
2. (an)halten; stoppen; aufhören (mit) 1
stop a fire ein Feuer löschen 2
story [ˈstɔːri] die Geschichte *(Erzählung)* 1
straight [streɪt]:
1. gerade; *(Haare)* glatt 2
2. **straight on** geradeaus (weiter) 2
strawberry [ˈstrɔːbəri] die Erdbeere 1
stream [striːm] streamen 3: 4 (110)
streamer [ˈstriːmə] der/die Streamer/in *(Personen, die etwas streamen)* 3: 4 (110)
street [striːt] die Straße *(in Ortschaften)* 2
street musician [ˈstriːt mjuzɪʃn] der/die Straßenmusiker/in 2
strength [streŋθ] die Stärke, die Kraft 2
°**strict** [strɪkt] streng
strong [strɒŋ] stark 2
structure [ˈstrʌktʃə]:
1. die Struktur 1
2. strukturieren, aufbauen 1
°**stuck** [stʌk] *siehe* **stick**
student [ˈstjuːdnt] der/die Schüler/in; der/die Student/in 1
study [ˈstʌdi] studieren; lernen *(z. B. für Prüfungen)* 2
°**study skills** *(pl)* [ˈstʌdi skɪlz] die Lerntechniken
stuff [stʌf] *(infml)* das Zeug, der Kram 2
stupid [ˈstjuːpɪd] dumm, blöd; albern 3: 2 (60)
subject [ˈsʌbdʒɪkt] das (Schul-)Fach 1
subscribe to sth. [səbˈskraɪb] etwas abonnieren 3: 4 (110)
success [səkˈses] der Erfolg 2
successful [səkˈsesfl] erfolgreich 2
sudden [ˈsʌdn] plötzliche(r, s) 3: 3 (77)
suddenly [ˈsʌdənli] plötzlich, auf einmal 3: 1 (27)
sugar [ˈʃʊgə] der Zucker 1
suit [suːt] der (Herren-)Anzug; das (Damen-)Kostüm 2
summer [ˈsʌmə] der Sommer 1
sun [sʌn] die Sonne 1
Sunday [ˈsʌndeɪ], [ˈsʌndi] der Sonntag 1
°**sung** [sʌŋ] *siehe* **sing**
sunglasses *(pl)* [ˈsʌnglɑːsɪz] die Sonnenbrille 1
°**sunk** [sʌŋk] *siehe* **sink**
sunny [ˈsʌni] sonnig 1 **It's sunny.** Die Sonne scheint. 1
super [ˈsuːpə] super 2
superhero [ˈsuːpəhɪərəʊ], *pl* **superheroes** der/die Superheld/in 2
supermarket [ˈsuːpəmɑːkɪt] der Supermarkt 1
superpower [ˈsuːpəpaʊə] die Superkraft 2
support [səˈpɔːt]:
1. unterstützen 3: 2 (44/45)
2. die Unterstützung 3: 2 (44/45)
supporter [səˈpɔːtə] der/die Anhänger/in, der Fan 3: 2 (44/45)
sure [ʃʊə], [ʃɔː] sicher 1
surf [sɜːf] surfen 2
surfing [ˈsɜːfɪŋ] das Surfing 1
surprise [səˈpraɪz]:
1. überraschen 2
2. die Überraschung 2
surprised [səˈpraɪzd] überrascht 1
°**Sutmae?** [səˈmaɪ] Hallo, wie geht es dir/euch/Ihnen? *(walisisches Gälisch)*
swam [swæm] *siehe* **swim**
swap [swɒp]:
1. tauschen 1
2. der Tausch 1
clothes swap der Kleidertausch, die Kleidertauschparty 1
sweater [ˈswetə] der Sweater 3: 2 (46)
sweatshirt [ˈswetʃɜːt] das Sweatshirt 1
sweet [swiːt]:
1. süß 1
2. das Bonbon 1
sweets *(pl)* [swiːts] die Süßigkeiten 1
swim [swɪm], **swam, swum** schwimmen 1
swimmer [ˈswɪmə] der/die Schwimmer/in 1
swimming [ˈswɪmɪŋ] das Schwimmen 1
swimming pool [ˈswɪmɪŋ puːl] das Schwimmbad 1
swimsuit [ˈswɪmsuːt] der Badeanzug 2
swipe [swaɪp] wischen *(auf Touchscreen)*; (z. B. Kreditkarte) durchziehen, einlesen 3: 4 (108)
switch [swɪtʃ]:
1. der Schalter 3: 4 (108)
2. **switch sth. on/off** etwas einschalten / ausschalten 3: 4 (108)
swum [swʌm] *siehe* **swim**
°**symbol** [ˈsɪmbl] das Symbol

T

T-shirt [ˈtiː ʃɜːt] das T-Shirt 1
table [ˈteɪbl]:
1. der Tisch 1
set the table den Tisch decken 2
°2. die Tabelle
table tennis [ˈteɪbl tenɪs] das Tischtennis 1
take [teɪk], **took, taken**:
1. dauern, *(Zeit)* brauchen, in Anspruch nehmen 1
2. (mit)nehmen; bringen 1
take notes sich Notizen machen 3: 3 (81) **take out the rubbish** den Müll rausbringen 2 **take photos** Fotos machen 1 **take place** stattfinden 2 **take sb.'s advice** auf js. Rat hören 3: 2 (48) **take sth. off** etwas ausziehen *(Kleidung)*, ablegen *(z. B. Hut, Brille)* 2 **taking photos** das Fotografieren *(Hobby)* 1
taken [ˈteɪkn] *siehe* **take**
talk [tɔːk]:
1. das Gespräch; die Rede, der Vortrag 1
give a talk einen Vortrag halten 1
2. **talk (to)** sprechen, reden (mit) 1
talk about sprechen, reden über 1
tall [tɔːl] groß *(Person)*; hoch *(Gebäude)* 2
tap [tæp]:
1. das (leise) Klopfen 3: 4 (108)
2. **tap sth.** tippen an/auf etwas; (leise) klopfen 3: 4 (108)
tap your fingers mit den Fingern klopfen 3: 4 (108)
°**task** [tɑːsk] die Aufgabe **do a task** eine Aufgabe machen
°**taste** [teɪst] schmecken; kosten, probieren
taught [tɔːt] *siehe* **teach**
taxi [ˈtæksi] das Taxi 3: 1 (16)
tea [tiː] der Tee 1
teach [tiːtʃ], **taught, taught** lehren, unterrichten 2
teacher [ˈtiːtʃə] der/die Lehrer/in 1
team [tiːm] das Team, die Mannschaft 1
teamwork [ˈtiːmwɜːk] das Teamwork, die Zusammenarbeit 2
tech [tek] *(infml)* *siehe* **technology**
technology [tekˈnɒlədʒi], *infml auch:* **tech** die Technik, der Technikunterricht; die Technologie 1
teen [tiːn] der Teenager 3: 2 (52)
teenager [ˈtiːneɪdʒə] der Teenager 3: 2 (48)

teeth [ti:θ] *Plural von* **tooth brush your teeth** (sich) die Zähne putzen 1
tell [tel], **told, told** erzählen, sagen 1 **tell sb. (not) to do sth.** jn. auffordern, etwas (nicht) zu tun; jm. sagen, dass er/sie etwas (nicht) tun soll 3: 2 (50)
ten [ten] zehn 1
ten thousand [ten 'θaʊznd] zehntausend (10000) 2
tennis ['tenɪs] das Tennis 1
tent [tent] das Zelt 3: 3 (78)
terrarium [te'reəriəm] das Terrarium 1
terrible ['terəbl] schrecklich, fürchterlich 2
test [test]:
1. testen 1
2. der Test; die Klassenarbeit 1
text [tekst]:
1. der Text 1
2. die SMS 1
3. **text sb.** jm. eine SMS schicken 1
than [ðən]: **louder than ...** lauter als ... 2
thank sb. [θæŋk] jm. danken, sich bei jm. bedanken 2
thank you ['θæŋk ju:] danke (schön) 1 **Thank you very much.** Vielen Dank. / Danke vielmals. 1
thanks [θæŋks] danke (schön) 1
that [ðæt]:
1. das (dort) 1
that's (= that is) das (da) ist 1
2. dass *(leitet einen Nebensatz ein)* 3: 4 (112)
so that sodass 2
3. der, die, das *(Relativpronomen)* 1
things that people can use Dinge, die Menschen gebrauchen/benutzen können 1
the [ðə] der, die, das 1
theatre ['θɪətə] das Theater 2
their [ðeə] ihr/e *(Plural)* 1
theirs [ðeəz] ihrer, ihre, ihrs *(zu „they")* 3: 4 (104)
them [ðem], [ðəm] sie, ihnen 1
themselves [ðəm'selvz] sich (selbst) (zu *„they"*) 3: 2 (50)
then [ðen] dann, danach 1
there [ðeə] da, dort; dahin, dorthin 1 **there are** es sind ... / es gibt ... 1 **there's (= there is)** es ist ... / es gibt ... 1
these [ði:z] diese (hier) 1 **These are my friends.** Das hier sind meine Freunde/Freundinnen. 1
they [ðeɪ]:
1. sie *(Plural)* 1
they're (= they are) sie sind 1
2. er/sie *(geschlechtsneutral)* 3: 2 (50)
thing [θɪŋ] das Ding, die Sache 1 **How are things?** Wie geht's (so)? 3: 4 (108)
think [θɪŋk], **thought, thought** denken, meinen, glauben 1 **think about** nachdenken über 2 **think of sb./sth.** an jn./etwas denken 2 **think of sth.** sich etwas überlegen, ausdenken 2 **I think ...** Ich denke/meine/glaube/finde, ... 1 **°What do you think of ...?** Was denkst du über ...? / Was hältst du von ...?
third (3rd) [θɜ:d] dritte(r, s) 1
thirteen [θɜ:'ti:n] dreizehn 1
thirty ['θɜ:ti] dreißig 1
this [ðɪs] dies; diese(r, s) 1
those [ðəʊz] die dort, jene (dort) 2
thought [θɔ:t]:
1. *siehe* **think**
2. der Gedanke 3: 4 (110)
thousand ['θaʊznd] tausend 2
three [θri:] drei 1
threw [θru:] *siehe* **throw**
through [θru:] durch 2
throw [θrəʊ], **threw, thrown** werfen 2 **throw away** wegwerfen 2
°thrown [θrəʊn] *siehe* **throw**
thunderstorm ['θʌndəstɔ:m] das Gewitter 2
Thursday ['θɜ:zdeɪ], ['θɜ:zdi] der Donnerstag 1
°tick [tɪk] ankreuzen, abhaken
ticket ['tɪkɪt] die Eintrittskarte, die Fahrkarte, das Ticket 1 **one-way ticket** die einfache Fahrkarte *(= ohne Rückfahrt)* 2 **single ticket** die einfache Fahrkarte *(= ohne Rückfahrt)* 2
ticket machine ['tɪkɪt məʃi:n] der Fahrkartenautomat 2
tidy ['taɪdi]:
1. ordentlich 1
2. aufräumen 1
tie [taɪ] die Krawatte 1
till [tɪl] bis 2 **not ... till** erst, wenn ... 2
time [taɪm]:
1. die Zeit; die Uhrzeit 1
have a great/good time (viel) Spaß haben, sich vergnügen 2 **on time** pünktlich 2 **What's the time?** Wie spät ist es? 1
2. das Mal 2
for the first time zum ersten Mal 2 **this time** dieses Mal 2
°timeline ['taɪmlaɪn] der Zeitstrahl, die Zeitachse, die Chronik
°times [taɪmz] mal
timetable ['taɪmteɪbl] der Stundenplan 1
tip [tɪp] der Tipp 2
tired ['taɪəd] müde 1
title ['taɪtl] der Titel, die Überschrift 1
to [tu], [tə]:
1. zu, nach 1
to sb. an jn. *(z. B. schreiben an jn., eine E-Mail an jn.)* 1 **Have you ever been to London?** Bist du schon mal in London gewesen? 2 **the answer to the question** die Antwort auf die Frage 1
2. bis 1
(from) 2 o'clock to 5 o'clock (von) 2 Uhr / 14 Uhr bis 5 Uhr / 17 Uhr 1
3. (um) zu 1
how to do sth. wie man etwas tut / tun kann / tun soll 1 **things to eat** Dinge zum Essen 1
4. vor *(bei Uhrzeitangaben)* 2
quarter to 7 viertel vor 7 2
today [tə'deɪ] heute 1
together [tə'geðə] zusammen 1
toilet ['tɔɪlət] die Toilette 1
told [təʊld] *siehe* **tell**
tomato [tə'mɑ:təʊ], *pl* **tomatoes** die Tomate 1
tomato sauce [tə'mɑ:təʊ sɔ:s] die Tomatensoße 1
tomorrow [tə'mɒrəʊ] morgen 3: 2 (50)
tonight [tə'naɪt] heute Nacht, heute Abend 3: 2 (50)
too [tu:]:
1. auch 1
from York too auch aus York 1
2. **too slow** zu langsam 1
took [tʊk] *siehe* **take**
°tool [tu:l] das Werkzeug; das (Hilfs-)Mittel
tooth [tu:θ], *pl* **teeth** Zahn 1
top [tɒp] die Spitze, das obere Ende 1 **top floor** die oberste Etage, der oberste Stock, das oberste Stockwerk 1 **at the top (of)** oben, am oberen Ende (von); an der Spitze (von) 1 **the top five hobbies** die fünf besten/beliebtesten Hobbys 1
topic ['tɒpɪk] das Thema 3: 2 (61)
tour (of) [tʊə] Tour, Reise, Rundgang/Rundfahrt 1
tour guide ['tʊə gaɪd] der/die Reiseleiter/in; der/die Fremdenführer/in 1
tourist ['tʊərɪst] der/die Tourist/in 1
tower ['taʊə] der Turm 3: 1 (14/15)
town [taʊn] die Stadt 1
town centre [taʊn 'sentə] das Stadtzentrum 1
toy [tɔɪ] das Spielzeug 1
tradition [trə'dɪʃn] die Tradition 2
traditional [trə'dɪʃənl] traditionell 2
traffic ['træfɪk] der (Straßen-)Verkehr 3: 1 (16)
trailer ['treɪlə] der Trailer *(Filmvorschau)* 2
train [treɪn] der Zug, die Eisenbahn 1
train station ['treɪn steɪʃn] der Bahnhof 1
trainer ['treɪnə]:
1. der/die Trainer/in 1
2. der Sportschuh 3: 3 (84)
trampoline ['træmpəli:n] das Trampolin 1
trampolining ['træmpəli:nɪŋ] das Trampolinspringen/-turnen 1
transport *(no pl)* ['trænspɔ:t] das Fortbewegungsmittel; die Beförderung 2 **public transport** die öffentlichen Verkehrsmittel 3: 1 (16)
travel ['trævl]:
1. das Reisen 1
2. reisen, fahren 1
treat ['tri:t] der Hochgenuss, das besondere Vergnügen; die (besondere) Leckerei 2
tree [tri:] der Baum 1
trick [trɪk] der Trick, das Kunststück 1
trip [trɪp] der Ausflug; die Reise 2 **boat trip** der Bootsausflug, die Bootsfahrt 2 **go on a trip** eine Reise machen 2 **take a trip** eine Reise machen 2

troll [trəʊl] der Troll *(Provokateur/in in Online-Medien)* 3: 4 (118)
trophy [ˈtrəʊfi] die Trophäe; der Pokal 2
trouble [ˈtrʌbl] der Ärger, Schwierigkeiten 1 **be in trouble** Ärger haben, in Schwierigkeiten sein 1 °**the Troubles** *(pl)* der Nordirlandkonflikt (*wörtlich:* die Unruhen)
trousers *(pl)* [ˈtraʊzəz] die Hose 2
true [truː] wahr, richtig 2
truth [truːθ] die Wahrheit 3: 2 (50) **tell the truth** die Wahrheit sagen 3: 2 (50) **To tell the truth, ...** Ehrlich gesagt, ... 3: 2 (50)
try [traɪ]:
1. versuchen, (aus)probieren 2 **try sth. on** anprobieren *(Kleidung)* 2 **try to do sth.** versuchen, etwas zu tun 2
2. der Versuch 2 **Have a try! / Give it a try!** Versuch's/Probier's doch mal! 2
°**tube** [tjuːb] *(infml)* die Londoner U-Bahn
Tuesday [ˈtjuːzdeɪ], [ˈtjuːzdi] der Dienstag 1
tunnel [ˈtʌnl] der Tunnel 3: 3 (77)
turn [tɜːn]:
1. (sich) (um)drehen 1 **Turn it upside down.** Dreh/Stell es auf den Kopf. 1 **turn right/left** (nach) rechts/links abbiegen 2 **turn sth. (over)** etwas umdrehen 1 °**turn sth. up** etwas laut(er) stellen
2. **it is sb.'s turn (to do sth.)** jd. ist dran / an der Reihe (etwas zu tun) 1 **take turns (to do sth.)** sich abwechseln; sich dabei abwechseln, etwas zu tun 1
TV [tiːˈviː] der Fernseher; das Fernsehen 1
twelfth (12th) [twelfθ] zwölfte(r, s) 1
twelve [twelv] zwölf 1
twenty [ˈtwenti] zwanzig 1
two [tuː] zwei 1
type (of) [taɪp] die Art (von), die Sorte (von) 3: 1 (19)

U

°**Ugh!** [ɜː] Bah!
UK [juː ˈkeɪ] das Vereinigte Königreich 2
umbrella [ʌmˈbrelə] der (Regen-)Schirm 3: 1 (20)
uncle [ˈʌŋkl] der Onkel 1
uncomfortable [ʌnˈkʌmftəbl] unbequem, ungemütlich 3: 2 (46)
uncool [ʌnˈkuːl] uncool 2
under [ˈʌndə] unter 1
underground [ˈʌndəgraʊnd] die U-Bahn 3: 1 (16)
°**underground** [ʌndəˈgraʊnd] unterirdisch, unter der Erde
understand [ʌndəˈstænd], **understood, understood** verstehen 2
understood [ʌndəˈstʊd] *siehe* **understand**
unfair [ʌnˈfeə] unfair 2
unfriendly [ʌnˈfrendli] unfreundlich 1
unhappy [ʌnˈhæpi] unglücklich, unzufrieden 2
unhelpful [ʌnˈhelpfl] nicht hilfreich; nicht hilfsbereit 2
uniform [ˈjuːnɪfɔːm] die Uniform 1
unit [ˈjuːnɪt] die Unit *(Lerneinheit)* 1
United Kingdom (= the UK) [junaɪtɪd ˈkɪŋdəm] das Vereinigte Königreich 2
unkind [ʌnˈkaɪnd] unfreundlich, herzlos 2
unlucky [ʌnˈlʌki] unglücklich 2 **be unlucky** Pech haben 3: 2 (57)
unpack [ʌnˈpæk] auspacken 3: 3 (79)
untidy [ʌnˈtaɪdi] unordentlich, unaufgeräumt 2
until [ənˈtɪl] bis *(zeitlich)* 2 **not ... until** erst, wenn ... 2
up [ʌp] hinauf, hoch 2
upload [ʌpˈləʊd]:
1. der/das Upload 3: 4 (111)
2. uploaden, hochladen 3: 4 (111)
upside down [ʌpsaɪd ˈdaʊn] verkehrt herum, auf dem Kopf 1
us [ʌs], [əs] uns 1 **It's just us.** Es sind nur wir. 1
use [juːz] benutzen, verwenden 1
useful [ˈjuːsfl] nützlich, hilfreich 2
useless [ˈjuːsləs] nutzlos, unnütz 3: 1 (23)
user [ˈjuːzə] der/die (Be-)Nutzer/in 1
usually [ˈjuːʒuəli] normalerweise, meistens 2

V

vacuum [ˈvækjuəm] Staub saugen 2
vacuum cleaner [ˈvækjuəm kliːnə] der Staubsauger 2
valley [ˈvæli] das Tal 3: 3 (85)
vampire [ˈvæmpaɪə] der Vampir 2
vanilla [vəˈnɪlə] die Vanille 1
vegetables *(pl)* [ˈvedʒtəblz] das/die Gemüse 1
vegetarian [vedʒəˈteəriən], *infml auch* **veggie**:
1. der/die Vegetarier/in 1
2. vegetarisch 1
veggie [ˈvedʒi] *siehe* **vegetarian**
versus (v; vs) [ˈvɜːsəs] gegen *(bei Wettkämpfen)*; gegenüber 3: 4 (110)
very [ˈveri] sehr 1
vet [vet] der Tierarzt, die Tierärztin 1
victim [ˈvɪktɪm] das Opfer 3: 4 (112)
video [ˈvɪdiəʊ] das Video; Video- 1
video game [ˈvɪdiəʊ geɪm] das Videospiel 1
view [vjuː]:
1. **view (of)** der (An-)Blick; die (Aus-)Sicht (auf) 3: 3 (84)
2. **view sth.** sich etwas anschauen 3: 3 (84)
°**viewing** [ˈvjuːɪŋ] das Fernsehen, das Betrachten *(von DVDs, Filmen usw.)*
village [ˈvɪlɪdʒ] das Dorf 1
°**violence** [ˈvaɪələns] die Gewalt; die Gewalttätigkeit
virtual [ˈvɜːtʃuəl] virtuell 3: 1 (21)
visit [ˈvɪzɪt]:
1. der Besuch 1
2. besuchen 1
visitor [ˈvɪzɪtə] der/die Besucher/in; der Gast 1
visitor information centre [vɪzɪtə ɪnfəˈmeɪʃn sentə] die Touristeninformation, das Fremdenverkehrsbüro 1
vlog [ˈvlɒg] der/das Vlog *(Video-Blog)* 3: 3 (87)
vlogger [ˈvlɒgə] der/die Vlogger/in *(Video-Blogger/in)* 3: 3 (87)
vocab [ˈvəʊkæb] *siehe* **vocabulary**
vocabulary [vəˈkæbjələri], *infml auch* **vocab** der Wortschatz, das Vokabular; das Vokabelverzeichnis 1
voice [vɔɪs] die Stimme 3: 4 (105)
voice message [ˈvɔɪs mesɪdʒ] die Sprachnachricht 3: 4 (105)
volunteer [vɒlənˈtɪə]:
1. der/die Freiwillige; der/die ehrenamtliche Mitarbeiter/in 3: 1 (29)
2. freiwillig/ehrenamtlich arbeiten *(unbezahlt)* 3: 1 (29)

W

°**wagon** [ˈwægən] die (Kohle-)Lore (Güterwagen in Bergwerken *(auf Schienen)*)
wait (for) [weɪt] warten (auf) 2 **Wait a minute.** Warte mal. / Einen Moment. 2 **I can't wait!** Ich kann es kaum erwarten! 2
waiter [ˈweɪtə] der Kellner 3: 1 (23)
waitress [ˈweɪtrəs] die Kellnerin 3: 1 (23)
Wales [weɪlz] Wales 3: (10/11)
walk [wɔːk]:
1. der Spaziergang 1 **go for a walk** spazieren gehen, einen Spaziergang machen 3: 4 (110)
2. (zu Fuß) gehen, wandern 1 **walk over** hinübergehen, rübergehen 2
walking [ˈwɔːkɪŋ] das Wandern 1
walking boot [ˈwɔːkɪŋ buːt] der Wanderstiefel 2
wall [wɔːl] die Wand, die Mauer 2 **on the wall** an die Wand; an der Wand 2
want [wɒnt] wollen 1 **want sb. to do sth.** wollen, dass jd. etwas tut 3: 4 (111) **want to do sth.** etwas tun wollen 1
wardrobe [ˈwɔːdrəʊb] der Kleiderschrank 1
warm [wɔːm] warm 1
was [wɒz], [wəz] *siehe* **be**
wash [wɒʃ] (sich) waschen 2
washing [ˈwɒʃɪŋ] die Wäsche 2 **do the washing** die Wäsche erledigen, Wäsche waschen 2
watch [wɒtʃ] die Armbanduhr 3: 4 (108)
watch (sth.) [wɒtʃ] (sich etwas) anschauen; (etwas) beobachten 1
water [ˈwɔːtə] das Wasser 1
wave (to sb.) [weɪv] (jm. zu)winken 1

way [weɪ]:
1. die Strecke, der Weg 2
one way eine Strecke *(= ohne Rückfahrt)* 2 **one-way ticket** die einfache Fahrkarte *(= ohne Rückfahrt)* 2
2. die Art und Weise 3: 1 (16)
(in) this way auf diese Art/Weise 3: 1 (16) **in different ways** unterschiedlich *(Adv.)*, auf unterschiedliche Art/Weise 3: 1 (16)
3. die Richtung 3: 1 (16)
both ways in beide(n) Richtungen 3: 1 (16) **that way** da entlang, in jene(r) Richtung 3: 1 (16) **the wrong way** (in) die falsche Richtung 3: 1 (16) **this way** hier entlang, in diese(r) Richtung 3: 1 (16)

we [wiː] wir 1 **we're (= we are)** wir sind 1
wear [weə], **wore, worn** tragen, anhaben *(Kleidung)* 1
weather [ˈweðə] das Wetter, die Witterung 1
website [ˈwebsaɪt] die Website 2
wedding [ˈwedɪŋ] die Hochzeit 2
wedding ring [ˈwedɪŋ rɪŋ] der Ehering 2
Wednesday [ˈwenzdeɪ], [ˈwenzdi] der Mittwoch 1
week [wiːk] die Woche 1 **the days of the week** *(pl)* die Wochentage 1
weekday [ˈwiːkdeɪ] der Werktag, der Wochentag 1
weekend [wiːkˈend] das Wochenende 1 **at the weekend** am Wochenende 1
weird [wɪəd] seltsam, komisch 1
welcome [ˈwelkəm]: **Welcome (to ...)!** Willkommen (in/an ...)! 1 **You're welcome.** Bitte, gern geschehen. / Nichts zu danken. 1
well [wel] gut *(Adv.)* 1 **Well done.** Gut gemacht! 1 **do well** gut abschneiden, erfolgreich sein 3: 2 (48) °**... as well as ...** sowohl ... als auch ...
went [went] *siehe* **go**
were [wɜː], [wə] *siehe* **be**
west [west] der Westen; westlich; West- 3: (10/11)
western [ˈwestən] westlich(r,s), West- 3: (10/11)
what [wɒt]:
1. was 1
2. welche(r, s) 1
What about a ... ? Wie wäre es mit einer/einem ... ? 1 **What about you?** Und du? / Was ist mit dir? 1 **What's your name?** Wie heißt du? 1
wheel [wiːl] das Rad 3: 1 (14/15) **big wheel** das Riesenrad 3: 1 (14/15)
wheelchair [ˈwiːltʃeə] der Rollstuhl 1
when [wen]:
1. wann 1
2. wenn *(zeitlich)* 1
3. als *(zeitlich)* 2
whenever [wenˈevə] wann (auch) immer 3: 2 (53)
where [weə] wo; wohin 1
which [wɪtʃ] welche(r, s) 1 **Which part ...?** Welcher Teil ...? 1
while [waɪl] während 3: 3 (85)
white [waɪt] weiß 1
who [huː]:
1. wer 1
°2. wen; wem
3. **a teenager who / teenagers who** ein Teenager, der ... / Teenager, die ... 3: 4 (112)
whole [həʊl] ganze(r, s) 3: 4 (110)
why [waɪ] warum 1 **that's why** deshalb, darum 3: 2 (53) **the reason why ...** der Grund dafür, dass ... 3: 1 (25)
wife [waɪf], *pl* **wives** die (Ehe-)Frau 3: 1 (27)
wild [waɪld] wild 3: 3 (83)
will [wɪl]: **I'll (= I will) be ....** Ich werde ... sein. 2
win [wɪn], **won, won** gewinnen 1
wind [wɪnd] der Wind 1
window [ˈwɪndəʊ] das Fenster 1
windsurfing [wɪndsɜːfɪŋ] das Windsurfing 1
windy [ˈwɪndi] windig 1
winner [ˈwɪnə] der/die Gewinner/in; der/die Sieger/in 1
winter [ˈwɪntə] der Winter 1
°**wish** [wɪʃ]:
1. **wish (for sth.)** (sich etwas) wünschen
2. der Wunsch
make a wish sich etwas wünschen
with [wɪð] mit; bei 1 **popular with** beliebt bei 2
without [wɪˈðaʊt] ohne 3: 4 (106)
wives [waɪvz] *Plural von* **wife**
woman [ˈwʊmən], *pl* **women** die Frau 2
women [ˈwɪmɪn] *Plural von* **woman**
won [wʌn] *siehe* **win**
wonderful [ˈwʌndəfl] wunderbar 2
won't [wəʊnt]: **I won't (= I will not) be ...** Ich werde nicht ... sein. 2
word [wɜːd] das Wort 1 **words (of a song)** *(pl)* der (Song-)Text 2
°**wordbank** [ˈwɜːdbæŋk] die Wortbank *(Sammlung von Wörtern zu einem Thema)*
wore [wɔː] *siehe* **wear**
work [wɜːk]:
1. arbeiten; funktionieren 1
work sth. out etwas herausfinden, etwas erarbeiten, etwas verstehen 2
2. die Arbeit 1
at work bei der Arbeit, am Arbeitsplatz 1
work experience [ˈwɜːk ɪkspɪəriəns] die Arbeitserfahrung(en), die Praxiserfahrung(en); das Praktikum 2
world [wɜːld] die Welt 2 **the best place in the world** der beste Ort der Welt / auf der Welt 2
worn [wɔːn] *siehe* **wear**
worried (about) [ˈwʌrid] beunruhigt, besorgt (wegen) 2
worry [ˈwʌri]:
1. die Sorge 2
2. **worry (about)** sich Sorgen machen (wegen, um) 2
Don't worry. Mach dir keine Sorgen. 2
worse [wɜːs] schlechter, schlimmer 2
worst [wɜːst] der/die/das schlechteste, schlimmste; am schlechtesten, am schlimmsten 2
°**worth** [wɜːθ] wert **It is/was worth it.** Das ist/war es wert.
would [wʊd]: **I'd (= I would) like/ love ...** Ich hätte (liebend) gern ... / Ich möchte (liebend gern)... 1 **I'd love/ like to meet ....** Ich würde mich (liebend) gerne mit ... treffen. 1
write [raɪt], **wrote, written** schreiben 1 **write sth. down** etwas aufschreiben 3: 2 (50)
writer [ˈraɪtə] der/die Autor/in 2
written [ˈrɪtn] *siehe* **write**
wrong [rɒŋ] falsch 1 **be wrong** Unrecht haben 1 **Something is wrong.** Irgendetwas ist nicht in Ordnung. / Irgendetwas stimmt nicht. 2 **What's wrong?** Was ist los? / Was/Wo ist das Problem? 2
wrote [rəʊt] *siehe* **write**

Y

year [jɪə] das Jahr; der Jahrgang 1
yellow [ˈjeləʊ] gelb 1
yes [jes] ja 1
yesterday [ˈjestədeɪ] gestern 2
yet [jet]: **... yet?** ... schon ...? 2 **not ... yet** noch nicht ... 2
yoga [ˈjəʊgə] das Yoga 1
yoghurt [ˈjɒgət] der/die/das Joghurt 2
you [juː] du; dich; dir; ihr; euch; Sie; Ihnen 1
young [jʌŋ] jung 3: 2 (52)
your [jɔː], [jə] dein/e; euer/eure; Ihr/e 1
yours [jɔːz] deine, deiner, deins; eurer, eure, eures; Ihrer, Ihre, Ihres *(zu „you")* 3: 4 (104) **Yours, Jill** Deine/Ihre/Eure Jill *(am Briefschluss)* 3: 4 (104)
yourself [jəˈself] dir/dich (selbst) 3: 2 (50)
yourselves [jɔːˈselvz] ihr/euch (selbst) 3: 2 (50) **Enjoy yourselves.** Viel Spaß! Amüsiert euch gut! 3: 2 (50)
youth [juːθ] die Jugend; der Jugendliche 1
youth centre [ˈjuːθ sentə] das Jugendzentrum 1

The English alphabet

a	[eɪ]	h	[eɪtʃ]	o	[əʊ]	v	[viː]
b	[biː]	i	[aɪ]	p	[piː]	w	[ˈdʌbljuː]
c	[siː]	j	[dʒeɪ]	q	[kjuː]	x	[eks]
d	[diː]	k	[keɪ]	r	[ɑː]	y	[waɪ]
e	[iː]	l	[el]	s	[es]	z	[zed]
f	[ef]	m	[em]	t	[tiː]		
g	[dʒiː]	n	[en]	u	[juː]		

English sounds

Die Lautschrift zeigt dir die Aussprache von Wörtern und Lauten *(sounds)*.

Einige dieser Laute kommen im Deutschen nicht vor oder werden anders geschrieben. Sie sind hier mit einem Ausrufezeichen gekennzeichnet: **!**. Übe sie mit Hilfe der App.

	[iː]	green, he, sea
	[ɑː]	ask, class, car, park
!	[ɔː]	or, ball, door, four, morning
	[uː]	ruler, blue, too, two, you
	[ɜː]	early, her, girl, work, T-shirt
	[ɪ]	in, big, expensive
	[e]	yes, bed, again, breakfast
	[æ]	animal, apple, black, cat
	[ʌ]	mum, bus, colour
	[ɒ]	song, on, dog, what
	[ʊ]	book, good, put, bully
	[ə]	again, today, a sister
	[i]	happy, monkey
	[eɪ]	name, eight, play, great
	[aɪ]	I, time, right, my
	[ɔɪ]	boy, toilet, noise
	[əʊ]	old, no, road, yellow
	[aʊ]	now, house
	[ɪə]	here, material, really, year
	[eə]	where, pair, share, their
	[ʊə]	tour
	[b]	bike, table, verb
	[p]	pen, paper, shop

	[d]	day, window, good
	[t]	ten, letter, at
	[g]	go, again, bag
	[k]	kitchen, car, back
	[m]	man, remember, mum
	[n]	no, one, ten
!	[ŋ]	wrong, young, uncle, thanks
	[l]	like, old, small
	[r]	ruler, friend, sorry
!	[w]	we, where, one
	[j]	yes, you, uniform
	[f]	family, after, laugh
!	[v]	very, seven, have
	[s]	six, poster, yes
!	[z]	zoo, quiz, his, music, please
	[ʃ]	she, station, English
!	[ʒ]	usually, revision, garage
	[tʃ]	chain, teacher, watch
!	[dʒ]	job, German, project, orange
!	[θ]	thing, three, bathroom, north
!	[ð]	the, weather, with
	[h]	house, who, behind
	[x]	loch

0 oh, zero, nil [əʊ, ˈzɪərəʊ, nɪl]
1 one [wʌn]
2 two [tʊ:]
3 three [θri:]
4 four [fɔ:]
5 five [faɪv]
6 six [sɪks]
7 seven [ˈsevn]
8 eight [eɪt]
9 nine [naɪn]
10 ten [ten]

11 eleven [ɪˈlevn]
12 twelve [twelv]
13 thirteen [θɜ:ˈti:n]
14 fourteen [fɔ:ˈti:n]
15 fifteen [fɪfˈti:n]
16 sixteen [sɪksˈti:n]
17 seventeen [sevnˈti:n]
18 eighteen [eɪˈti:n]
19 nineteen [naɪnˈti:n]
20 twenty [ˈtwenti]

21 twenty-one [twentiˈwʌn]
22 twenty-two [twentiˈtu:]
23 twenty-three [twentiˈθri:]
...

30 thirty [ˈθɜ:ti]
40 forty [ˈfɔ:ti]
50 fifty [ˈfɪfti]
60 sixty [ˈsɪksti]
70 seventy [ˈsevnti]
80 eighty [ˈeɪti]
90 ninety [ˈnaɪntɪ]
100 a / one hundred [ə / wʌn ˈhʌndrəd]

101 one hundred and one
102 one hundred and two
...

1st first [fɜ:st]
2nd second [ˈsekənd]
3rd third [θɜ:d]
4th fourth [fɔ:θ]
5th fifth [fɪfθ]
6th sixth [sɪksθ]
7th seventh [ˈsevnθ]
8th eighth [eɪtθ]
9th ninth [naɪnθ]
10th tenth [tenθ]

11th eleventh [ɪˈlevnθ]
12th twelfth [twelfθ]
13th thirteenth [θɜ:ˈti:nθ]
14th fourteenth [fɔ:ˈti:nθ]
15th fifteenth [fɪfˈti:nθ]
16th sixteenth [sɪksˈti:nθ]
17th seventeenth [sevnˈti:nθ]
18th eighteenth [eɪˈti:nθ]
19th nineteenth [naɪnˈti:nθ]
20th twentieth [ˈtwentiəθ]

21st twenty-first [twentiˈfɜ:st]
22nd twenty-second [twentiˈsekənd]
23rd twenty-third [twentiˈθɜ:d]
...

30th thirtieth [ˈθɜ:tiəθ]
40th fortieth [ˈfɔ:tiəθ]
50th fiftieth [ˈfɪftiəθ]
60th sixtieth [ˈsɪkstiəθ]
70th seventieth [ˈsevntiəθ]
80th eightieth [ˈeɪtiəθ]
90th ninetieth [ˈnaɪntiəθ]
100th hundredth [ˈhʌndrədθ]

101st one hundred and first
102nd one hundred and second
...

infinitive	simple past	past participle	
(to) **babysit**	**babysat**	**babysat**	babysitten
(to) **be**	I/he/she/it **was**; you/we/they **were**	**been**	sein
(to) **beat**	**beat**	**beaten**	schlagen, besiegen
(to) **become**	**became**	**become**	werden
(to) **begin**	**began**	**begun**	anfangen, beginnen
(to) **blow**	**blew** [uː]	**blown**	pusten, blasen; wehen
(to) **break**	**broke**	**broken**	zerbrechen
(to) **bring**	**brought**	**brought**	(mit)bringen
(to) **build** [ɪ]	**built** [ɪ]	**built** [ɪ]	bauen
(to) **buy**	**bought**	**bought**	kaufen
(to) **catch**	**caught** [ɔː]	**caught** [ɔː]	(ein)fangen; erwischen
(to) **choose**	**chose**	**chosen**	(aus)wählen
(to) **come**	**came**	**come**	(mit)kommen
(to) **cost**	**cost**	**cost**	kosten
(to) **cut**	**cut**	**cut**	(aus)schneiden
(to) **deal with** [iː]	**dealt** [e]	**dealt** [e]	klarkommen (mit), fertigwerden (mit)
(to) **do**	**did**	**done** [ʌ]	tun, machen
(to) **draw**	**drew**	**drawn**	zeichnen
(to) **drink**	**drank**	**drunk**	trinken
(to) **drive** [aɪ]	**drove** [əʊ]	**driven** [ɪ]	fahren
(to) **eat** [iː]	**ate** [et, eɪt]	**eaten** [iː]	essen; fressen
(to) **fall**	**fell**	**fallen**	(hin)fallen
(to) **feed**	**fed**	**fed**	füttern; ernähren
(to) **feel**	**felt**	**felt**	fühlen, sich fühlen
(to) **fight**	**fought**	**fought**	(be)kämpfen
(to) **find**	**found**	**found**	finden
(to) **fly**	**flew**	**flown**	fliegen
(to) **forget**	**forgot**	**forgotten**	vergessen
(to) **get**	**got**	**got**	bekommen; (sich etw.) holen; werden
(to) **give** [ɪ]	**gave**	**given** [ɪ]	geben
(to) **go**	**went**	**gone**	gehen, fahren
(to) **grow (up)**	**grew (up)**	**grown (up)**	(auf)wachsen
(to) **hang out**	**hung out** [ʌ]	**hung out**	rumhängen, abhängen
(to) **have**	**had**	**had**	haben; etw. essen
(to) **hear** [ɪə]	**heard** [ɜː]	**heard**	hören
(to) **hit**	**hit**	**hit**	treffen auf, schlagen, stoßen gegen
(to) **hurt**	**hurt**	**hurt**	verletzen; wehtun
(to) **keep**	**kept**	**kept**	(be)halten; aufbewahren
(to) **know** [nəʊ]	**knew** [njuː]	**known** [nəʊn]	wissen; kennen
(to) **lead** [iː]	**led** [e]	**led** [e]	führen, leiten
(to) **leave**	**left**	**left**	lassen, zurücklassen, verlassen
(to) **let**	**let**	**let**	lassen
(to) **lie**	**lay**	**lain**	liegen
(to) **lose** [uː]	**lost**	**lost**	verlieren
(to) **make**	**made**	**made**	machen, herstellen
(to) **mean**	**meant**	**meant**	bedeuten, meinen

infinitive	simple past	past participle	
(to) **meet**	**met**	**met**	treffen; (sich) treffen
(to) **pay**	**paid**	**paid**	(be)zahlen
(to) **put**	**put**	**put**	legen, stellen, stecken
(to) **read** [iː]	**read** [e]	**read** [e]	lesen
(to) **rewrite**	**rewrote**	**rewritten**	neu schreiben, umschreiben
(to) **ride** [aɪ]	**rode**	**ridden** [ɪ]	reiten; *(Rad)* fahren
(to) **run**	**ran**	**run**	rennen, laufen
(to) **say**	**said** [sed]	**said** [sed]	sagen
(to) **see**	**saw**	**seen**	sehen
(to) **sell**	**sold**	**sold**	verkaufen
(to) **send**	**sent**	**sent**	senden, schicken
(to) **set**	**set**	**set**	stellen, legen, setzen
(to) **sew** [əʊ]	**sewed** [əʊ]	**sewn** [əʊ]	nähen
(to) **shake**	**shook**	**shaken**	schütteln; zittern
(to) **show**	**showed**	**shown**	zeigen
(to) **sing**	**sang**	**sung**	singen
(to) **sink**	**sank**	**sunk**	sinken
(to) **sit**	**sat**	**sat**	sitzen; sich setzen
(to) **sleep**	**slept**	**slept**	schlafen
(to) **slide**	**slid**	**slid**	rutschen; schieben; gleiten (lassen)
(to) **speak** [iː]	**spoke**	**spoken**	sprechen
(to) **spend**	**spent**	**spent**	*(Geld)* ausgeben, *(Zeit)* verbringen
(to) **split**	**split**	**split**	(sich) (auf)teilen, sich (auf)spalten
(to) **stand**	**stood**	**stood**	stehen; sich (hin)stellen
(to) **steal**	**stole**	**stolen**	stehlen, rauben
(to) **stick**	**stuck**	**stuck**	kleben; stecken
(to) **swim**	**swam**	**swum**	schwimmen
(to) **take**	**took**	**taken**	(mit)nehmen; bringen; dauern
(to) **teach**	**taught**	**taught**	lehren, unterrichten
(to) **tell**	**told**	**told**	sagen; erzählen, berichten
(to) **think**	**thought**	**thought**	denken, glauben, meinen
(to) **throw**	**threw** [uː]	**thrown**	werfen
(to) **understand**	**understood**	**understood**	verstehen
(to) **upset**	**upset**	**upset**	jn. erschüttern; jn. aufregen, ärgern
(to) **wear** [eə]	**wore** [ɔː]	**worn** [ɔː]	tragen, anhaben *(Kleidung)*
(to) **win**	**won** [ʌ]	**won** [ʌ]	gewinnen
(to) **write** [aɪ]	**wrote**	**written** [ɪ]	schreiben

Du kannst die unregelmäßigen Verben in Gruppen einteilen, damit das Lernen leichter wird:

- Alle drei Formen sind gleich *(chicken verbs)*: *put, put, put* – das klingt wie gackernde Hühner.
- Zwei Formen sind gleich:
  – (echo verbs): z. B. *bring, brought, brought* – (sandwich verbs): *become, became, become*
- Alle drei Formen sind verschieden: Da gibt es z. B. die *cat verbs*, bei denen der Klang der drei Formen an das Miau einer Katze erinnert: *sing, sang, sung*
  Wenn du diese Formen in ähnlichen Zweiergruppen lernst, kannst du sie besser behalten: *be, was, been – see, saw, seen* oder *break, broke, broken – speak, spoke, spoken*

Finde zu jeder Gruppe weitere Beispiele in der Übersicht auf diesen beiden Seiten.

Viele englische Wörter ähneln deutschen Wörtern: *a cowboy* = ein Cowboy
Beachte aber die Unterschiede 1–3!

(1) Nomen werden im Deutschen großgeschrieben, aber im Englischen klein.
(2) Manche Wörter haben im Deutschen andere Endungen, aber einen ähnlichen Stamm, z. B. planen – *(to) plan*.
(3) Oft unterscheidet sich die Aussprache. Höre dir die blau markierten Wörter in der App an und sprich sie nach.

active / activity
address
allergic (to)
alphabet
alternative
anonymous
April
article
August
balcony
ball
banana
barbecue
bass
biology
blues
bowling
Brexit
(to) bring
British
browser
bus
butter
cafe
camera
card
character
chocolate
circus
class
classroom
clever
club
coffee
comic
computer
console
cool
corridor
cost / (to) cost
cousin
creative
crown
culture
curry
dance / (to) dance
December
decoration
definition
detail
dialogue
drama
drink / (to) drink
electric
elephant
end / (to) end
England / English
experiment
family
February
film
(to) find
fish
football
friend / friendly
gallery
garage
garden
gold
group
guest
hamster
happy
hello
highlight
horn
house
hungry
idea
information
insect
January
jewels
July
June
karaoke
kebab
kilometre (km)
kiosk
lamp
market
maths
melon
milk
millilitre
minute
modern
moment
museum
music
name
negative
November
number
object
October
online
open
orange
parallel
partner
pasta
pause
perfect
person
photo
picnic
plan / (to) plan
pool
post
poster
problem
project
pronoun
rafting
respect
restaurant
ring
robot
room
rucksack
salad
sandwich
sauce
scene
school
(to) send
September
shopping centre
silver
(to) sink
skateboard
smart
sofa
software
song
sport
star
stop
story
student
summer
supermarket
surfing
sweatshirt
(to) swim
synagogue
test / (to) test
text / (to) text
title
toilet
tomato
top
tourist
tradition
trainer
trick
uniform
vanilla
vegan
vegetarian / veggie
video
warm
website
wind
winner
winter
word
yoghurt
zoo

Typical tasks	Häufige Arbeitsanweisungen
Act out the conversation / song / story.	Führt das Gespräch / das Lied / die Geschichte vor.
Add more ideas / points / ...	Füge weitere Ideen / Punkte / ... hinzu.
Answer the questions / partner B's questions.	Beantworte die Fragen / Partner Bs Fragen.
Brainstorm ideas.	Sammle spontane Einfälle / Gedanken.
Check the spelling / your answers / ideas (with a partner).	Überprüfe deine Rechtschreibung / Antworten / Ideen (mit einem/r Partner/-in).
Choose the correct answer / word.	Wähle die richtige Antwort / das richtige Wort aus.
Collect ideas / words / phrases / information.	Sammle Ideen / Wörter / Ausdrücke / Informationen.
Compare the pictures / your answers / ideas / ...	Vergleiche die Bilder / deine Antworten / Ideen / ...
Complete the table / list / sentences / conversation / ...	Vervollständige die Tabelle / Liste / Sätze / Unterhaltung / ...
Copy the table / list / notes.	Schreibe die Tabelle / die Liste / Notizen ab.
Correct the false / wrong sentences / answers.	Berichtige die falschen Sätze / Antworten.
Describe the picture / your room / ...	Beschreibe das Bild / dein Zimmer / ...
Discuss with a partner.	Diskutiere mit einem/r Partner/-in.
Explain what ... means.	Erkläre was ... bedeutet.
Find the answers / the correct / right / wrong words / information / images / ...	Finde die Antworten / die richtigen / falschen Wörter / Informationen / Bilder / ...
Find reasons for and against ...	Finde Gründe, die für und gegen ... sprechen.
Finish the sentences.	Vervollständige die Sätze.
Give advice / feedback.	Gib Ratschläge / Rückmeldung.
Give reasons.	Begründe (deine Antwort).
Give your opinion.	Sag / Äußere deine Meinung.
Have a conversation with (two partners).	Unterhalte dich mit (zwei Partner/-innen).
Listen and check / practise / repeat / guess / take notes.	Höre zu und überprüfe / übe / wiederhole / rate / mache Notizen.
Look at the photos / pictures / map / title.	Sieh dir die Fotos / Bilder / Karte / die Überschrift an.
Make groups (of six / ... students).	Bildet Gruppen (zu je sechs / ... Schüler/-innen).
Make sentences / notes / lists / a mind map.	Fertige Sätze / Notizen / Listen / eine Mindmap an.
Match the sentence parts / the words to ...	Verbinde die Satzhälften / die Wörter mit ...
Put the sentences / dialogue in the correct order.	Bringe die Sätze / den Dialog in die richtige Reihenfolge.
Read the conversation / text / story / article.	Lies den Dialog / Text / die Geschichte / den Artikel.
Swap cards / roles.	Tauscht die Karten / die Rollen.
Take notes (about ...).	Mache dir Notizen (zu ...).
Take turns.	Wechselt euch ab.
Talk to a partner / in groups.	Sprich mit einem/r Partner/-in / deiner Gruppe.
Tell your partner / the class.	Erzähle / Sage es deinem/r Partner/-in / der Klasse.
Think of (reasons for) ...	Überlege dir (Gründe für) ...
True, false or not in the text?	Richtig, falsch oder nicht im Text?
Use your notes / the words in a) / keywords / the information (in the table).	Benutze deine Notizen / die Wörter aus Aufgabe a) / Stichworte / die Informationen (aus der Tabelle).
Watch part 1 / scene 1 / all the film / the video.	Sieh dir Teil 1 / Szene 1 / den ganzen Film / das Video an.
Work alone / in pairs / in groups.	Arbeite allein / in Partnerarbeit / in Gruppen.
Work out the meaning of (the words).	Finde die Bedeutung (der Wörter) heraus.
Write the correct answers / sentences / questions.	Schreibe die richtigen Antworten / Sätze / Fragen (auf).
Write a short description / a blog post / an ending to the story ...	Schreibe eine kurze Beschreibung / einen Blogeintrag / ein Ende für die Geschichte ...

Titelbild
Cornelsen / li.: Shutterstock.com / Ron Ellis / courtesy of Transport for London; Personen: Chocolate Films; Hintergrund re.: stock.adobe.com / anatoliycherkas

Illustrationen
Cornelsen / Harald Ardeias: S. 21; S. 22 oben; S. 23 oben; S. 32; S. 52 unten; S. 55 unten; S. 56 unten li.; S. 57 oben, unten re.; S. 62 A–F; S. 68; S. 70; S. 71 oben; S. 77 1–6; S. 82 1–6; S. 84; S 85; S. 86 unten; S. 90 A, B; S. 98; S. 101; S. 126; S. 150; S. 168; **Cornelsen / Carlos Borrell Eiköter:** S. 1 Mitte; S. 26 oben; **Cornelsen / Inhouse / Josephine Bienert-Köhler:** S. 95; S. 148; S. 172; **Cornelsen / Jeongsook Lee:** S. 207 oben; **Cornelsen / Inhouse / Melina Frick:** S. 36 Mitte li.; **Cornelsen / Irina Zinner:** S. 155; S. 156; S. 157; S. 158; S. 159; S. 160; S. 163; S. 164; S. 165

Abbildungen
Umschlagseite vorne (U2): oben: Siehe S. 14, S. 16, S. 26; **S. 1** oben: Siehe S. 30, S. 31, S. 32; **S. 4:** Shutterstock.com / S–F; **S. 5** stock.adobe.com / Kaspars; **S. 6** Shutterstock.com / Fotimageon; **S. 7** stock.adobe.com / Tomas Marek; **S. 8** Shutterstock.com / John McGreevy; **S. 10** oben li.: Shutterstock.com / Aldiki Gustiyan; Flaggen: Shutterstock.com / SLdesign; Karte: stock.adobe.com / lesniewski; **S. 11** Pearl: Cornelsen / Chocolate Films; Orla: Cornelsen / Chocolate Films; Jack: Cornelsen / Chocolate Films; Dylan: Cornelsen / Chocolate Films; Grace: Cornelsen / Chocolate Films; Omar: Cornelsen / Chocolate Films; **S. 12** C: stock.adobe.com / zgphotography; A: mauritius images / Alexander Pöschel; B: Shutterstock.com / Dieter Hawlan; **S. 13** F: stock.adobe.com / coward_lion; E: stock.adobe.com / Tomas Marek; D: mauritius images / Prisma; **S. 14** A: mauritius images / Novarc Images; Lilly: Cornelsen / Anja Poehlmann; B: stock.adobe.com / sborisov; Ali: Cornelsen / Chocolate Films; **S. 15** D: stock.adobe.com / Mistervlad; C: Imago Stock & People GmbH / Westend61; E: stock.adobe.com / Photocreo Bednarek; **S. 16** b) unten: Shutterstock.com / Sampajano_Anizza; b) oben: mauritius images / age fotostock; b) Mitte: Shutterstock.com / Tupungato; unten: mauritius images / Simon Belcher; **S. 17** stock.adobe.com / I-Wei Huang; **S. 18** A: Imago Stock&People GmbH / Jeff Greenberg; C: stock.adobe.com / Юлия Клюева; B: mauritius images / alamy stock photo / Scott Sim; **S. 19** Cornelsen / Chocolate Films; **S. 20** stock.adobe.com / Nicola; **S. 22** Halloumi: Shutterstock.com / MariaKovaleva; Falafel: Shutterstock.com / Veliavik; Chicken and potatoes: Shutterstock.com / OlgaBombologna; Spicy sausages: Shutterstock.com / diplomedia; Blatt Symbol: Shutterstock.com / John_Dakapu; Spicy potatoes: Shutterstock.com / diplomedia; Hummus: Shutterstock.com / Pixel-Shot; Bread: stock.adobe.com / anaumenko; **S. 23** unten: Shutterstock.com / fizkes; **S. 24** oben: Shutterstock.com / Tyler Olson; unten: stock.adobe.com / FotoStuss; **S. 25** SDG wheel: courtesy of the UNITED NATIONS / Department of Global Communications (https://www.un.org/sustainabledevelopment) The content of this publication has not been approved by the United Nations and does not reflect the views of the United Nations or its officials or Member States.); **S. 26** Mitte: stock.adobe.com / Richie Chan; unten: mauritius images / Steve Vidler; **S. 27** Mitte: Cornelsen / Personen: Chocolate Films, Hintergrund: mauritius images / alamy stock photo / Fotomaton; oben: mauritius images / Loop Images; unten: mauritius images / Steve Vidler; **S. 28** Cornelsen / Chocolate Films; **S. 29** Digital Learning Ass. Ltd.; **S. 30** A: Shutterstock.com / TTstudio; B: Shutterstock.com / Eszter Szadeczky-Kardoss; **S. 31** Strand: stock.adobe.com / Nick Hawkes / nickos; Karte: Shutterstock.com / Art Berry; **S. 33** unten re.: Shutterstock / Dyek Marina; unten li.: Shutterstock.com / Vector FX; oben: stock.adobe.com / pxl.store; **S. 34** Theo: Shutterstock.com / paulaphoto; Darja: Shutterstock.com / Damir Khabirov; **S. 35** Cornelsen / Anja Poehlmann; **S. 36** Mitte re.: Cornelsen / Chocolate Films; unten re.: stock.adobe.com / cartoon-IT; **S. 37** Mitte li.: Shutterstock.com / I Wei Huang; unten li.: mauritius images / alamy stock photo / Alex Segre; oben re.: Shutterstock.com / Monkey Business Images; Mitte re.: mauritius images / Vantage; **S. 39 unten (drei Grafiken)**: Shutterstock.com / Mizanur Rahman razu; **S. 41** B: stock.adobe.com / Jaroslav Moravcik; C: stock.adobe.com / Denis Feldmann; D: stock.adobe.com / I-Wei Huang; A: Imago Stock&People GmbH / Loop Images / Peter Noyce / LOOP IMAGES PNE991430\r\n\r; **S. 44** Emojis: Shutterstock.com / Magnos Weber; Rosie: Cornelsen / Chocolate Films; Mitte: Shutterstock.com / Monkey Business Images; oben re.: stock.adobe.com / Nicola; **S. 45** Emojis: Shutterstock.com / Magnos Weber; unten li.: stock.adobe.com / Kaspars; Omar: Cornelsen / Chocolate Films; Familie: Shutterstock.com / Spotmatik Ltd; **S. 46** B: Shutterstock.com / Kite_rin; A: Shutterstock.com / Andrey Arkusha; C: Shutterstock.com / Cast Of Thousands; D: Shutterstock.com / insta_photos; **S. 47** Shutterstock.com / Pixel-Shot; **S. 48** Emojis: Shutterstock.com / Magnos Weber; **S. 50** Cornelsen / Chocolate Films; **S. 51** Emojis: Shutterstock.com / Magnos Weber; unten: Shutterstock.com / LightField Studios; **S. 52** oben: Shutterstock.com / sitthiphong; **S. 53** Shutterstock.com / Ververidis Vasilis; **S. 54** unten: Digital Learning Ass. Ltd.; oben: mauritius images / alamy stock photo / Jeffrey Mayer; **S. 55** oben: Shutterstock.com / sitthiphong; **S. 56** unten re.: Shutterstock.com / Alexsey t17; kämpfen: Shutterstock.com / VectorSun58; tanzen: Shutterstock.com / Illizium; Basketball: Shutterstock.com / Great_Kit; Fußball: Shutterstock.com / Great_Kit; rennen: Shutterstock.com; Skateboard: Shutterstock.com / my_design; Karten: Shutterstock.com / popicon; Controller: Shutterstock.com / Hasebalcon; Würfel: Shutterstock.com / popicon; schwimmen: Shutterstock.com / Makkuro GL; **S. 57** Emojis: Shutterstock.com / Magnos Weber; Omar: Cornelsen /

Chocolate Films; Trent: Shutterstock.com / Alexsey t17; Pokal: Shutterstock.com / JosepPerianes; **S. 59** Interfilm Berlin Management; **S. 60** Kind 2: Shutterstock.com / Khosro; Kind 3: Shutterstock.com / Max Topchii; Kind 5: stock.adobe.com / Jelena Ivanovic; Kind 1: Shutterstock.com / Marian Fil; Kind 4: Shutterstock.com / Diversity Studio; **S. 61** Shutterstock.com / BearFotos; **S. 62** 1, 2, 4, 6: Shutterstock.com / Denis Cristo; 3, 5: Shutterstock.com / Lemberg Vector studio; **S. 63** Emojis: Shutterstock.com / Magnos Weber; oben re.: Shutterstock.com / tommaso79; **S. 64** 2: Shutterstock.com / Gleb Usovich; 1: Shutterstock.com / Daniel Hoz; 3: Shutterstock.com / chomplearn; 4 Shutterstock.com / Kaentian Street; **S. 65** Cornelsen / Personen: Chocolate Films, Hintergrund: Shutterstock.com / Ian Reay; **S. 67** C: stock.adobe.com / David Matthew Lyons; A: mauritius images / alamy stock photo / Matthew Wilkinson; D: mauritius images / robertharding; B: mauritius images / alamy stock photo / CBW; **S. 69** stock.adobe.com / fizkes; **S. 71** Mitte: stock.adobe.com / 1STunningART; **S. 72** oben li.: Cornelsen / Chocolate Films; A: stock.adobe.com / Sergii Figurnyi; C: stock.adobe.com / moofushi; B: mauritius images / alamy stock photo / Nicola Campbell; **S. 73** E: stock.adobe.com / Apostolis Giontzis; F: mauritius images / Destinations; D: stock.adobe.com / Fun Altitude; oben li.: stock.adobe.com / Richie Chan; **S. 74** Imago Stock & People GmbH / imagebroker / RolandxMarske; **S. 75** unten: Shutterstock.com / Moving Moment; oben: stock.adobe.com / mauritius images / VisualEyze; **S. 76** oben: stock.adobe.com / G3D Studio; Mitte: Cornelsen / Personen: Chocolate Films, Hintergrund: stock.adobe.com / avtk; **S. 77** unten: stock.adobe.com / olizabet; **S. 78** 4: Shutterstock.com / Vito Horak; 2: mauritius images / alamy stock photo / Simon Price; 3: Shutterstock.com / coka; 5: stock.adobe.com / Duncan Andison; 1: stock.adobe.com / EpicStockMedia; 6: stock.adobe.com / Ellis Travel Photography / Matthew Williams; **S. 79** unten: Cornelsen / Chocolate Films; oben: Cornelsen / Chocolate Films; **S. 80** Shutterstock.com / BearFotos; **S. 83** unten: Shutterstock.com / gonzagon; oben: Shutterstock.com / STEKLO; **S. 86** oben: Cornelsen / Chocolate Films; **S. 87** 3: Digital Learning Ass. Ltd.; 2: Digital Learning Ass. Ltd.; oben: Digital Learning Ass. Ltd.; 1: Digital Learning Ass. Ltd.; **S. 88** 1. Mitte li.: stock.adobe.com / Adam; 1. li.: stock.adobe.com / pict rider; 1. re.: Shutterstock.com / Volurol; oben re.: Shutterstock.com / Lubomira08; 1. Mitte re.: stock.adobe.com / May Thawtar; **S. 90** oben re.: stock.adobe.com / lovelyday12; oben li.: stock.adobe.com / davidionut; **S. 91** b) oben Mi.: stock.adobe.com / andreusK; b) oben li.: Shutterstock.com / Lukasz Z; oben re.: Shutterstock.com / Vaclav Sonnek; b) unten li.: stock.adobe.com / Pawel Gubernat; b) unten Mi.: stock.adobe.com / alexandrum01; oben li.: Shutterstock.com / eurobanks; b) oben re.: stock.adobe.com / AdobeTim82; b) unten re.: stock.adobe.com / POPROTSKIY_ALEXEY / Alex Photo; **S. 92** B: stock.adobe.com / Magdalena Bujak; A: Shutterstock.com / Helen Hotson; **S. 93** mauritius images / alamy stock photo / stephanie hager; **S. 94** oben re.: Cornelsen / Chocolate Films; oben li.: Shutterstock.com / Marti Bug Catcher; unten: stock.adobe.com / design / exclusive; **S. 95** oben re.: mauritius images / Roger parkes / Alamy Stock Photos; Kekse: Shutterstock.com / Moving Moment; **S. 96** Shutterstock.com / Sudowoodo; **S. 97** unten li.: Shutterstock.com / Loch Earn; unten re.: mauritius images / robertharding; oben: mauritius images / alamy stock photo / Philip Hills; **S. 99** unten re.: mauritius images / alamy stock photo / GFC Collection; oben re.: Shutterstock.com / Lukassek; **S. 102** B: Shutterstock.com / Richard Whitcombe; C: stock.adobe.com / wavebreak3; oben re.: Cornelsen / Chocolate Films; D: stock.adobe.com / Sebastien, A. mauritius images / alamy stock photo / StockimoNews / Lancashire Images; **S. 103** re.: stock.adobe.com / Huebi; li.: Shutterstock.com / Peter Hermes Furian; **S. 104** StockFood GmbH / Look / Pompe, Ingolf; Emojis: Shutterstock.com / Yefym Turkin; **S. 105** stock.adobe.com / Richard Whitcombe; **S. 106** Digital Learning Ass. Ltd.; Digital Learning Ass. Ltd.; Digital Learning Ass. Ltd.; Digital Learning Ass. Ltd.; **S. 107** stock.adobe.com / studioshot; **S. 108** f: stock.adobe.com / Etka; a: Shutterstock.com / VIEW17; b: Shutterstock.com / IRgraphic; e: Shutterstock.com / GetThis; d: Shutterstock.com / pnDl; c: Shutterstock.com / Pixelr Studios; Dylan: Cornelsen / Chocolate Films; Owen: Cornelsen / Chocolate Films; **S. 109** mauritius images / Westend61; **S. 110** unten re.: Shutterstock.com / Roman3dArt; unten li.: Shutterstock.com / izabel.l; Emojis: Shutterstock.com / Yefym Turkin; **S. 111** E: Shutterstock.com / Raura7; B: stock.adobe.com / Sergey; Owen: Cornelsen / Chocolate Films; A: stock.adobe.com / Belozersky; C: stock.adobe.com / 4luck; F: Shutterstock.com / Cosmic_Design; D: Shutterstock.com / Yandi Rs; **S. 112** Shutterstock.com / LightField Studios; **S. 113** Shutterstock.com / stockfour; **S. 114** Dylan: Cornelsen / Chocolate Films; Emojis: Shutterstock.com / Yefym Turkin; Cornelsen / Person re.: Chocolate Films, Wagen + Hintergrund: mauritius images / PHILIP SMITH / Alamy; **S. 115** Dylan, Owen: Cornelsen / Chocolate Films; Emojis: Shutterstock.com / Yefym Turkin; unten li.: stock.adobe.com / Krakenimages.com; oben li.: Cornelsen / Person: Chocolate Films, Hintergrund: Shutterstock.com / muroPhotographer; oben re.: Cornelsen / Person: Chocolate Films, Hintergrund: Shutterstock.com / muroPhotographer; **S. 116** 4 e: Shutterstock.com / sore88; 4 c: Shutterstock.com / Dreamerdesign; 4 d: Shutterstock.com / Leremy; 4 b: Shutterstock.com / koblizeek; 4 f: Shutterstock.com / Rawpixel Ltd.; 4:a: Shutterstock.com / daddy.icon; **S. 117** oben: Shutterstock.com / gritsalak karalak; unten: Digital Learning Ass. Ltd.; **S. 118** stock.adobe.com / Krakenimages.com; **S. 119** stock.adobe.com / Tyler Olson; **S. 120** oben: stock.adobe.com / Colin & Linda McKie; unten: stock.adobe.com / JoeE Jackson; Mitte: Shutterstock.com / Tomas Marek; **S. 121** rechts: stock.adobe.com / Krakenimages.com; Emojis: Shutterstock.com / Yefym Turkin; links: Cornelsen / Chocolate Films; **S. 122** B: Shutterstock.com / Stu Porter; D: Shutterstock.com / Vtmila; C: Shutterstock.com / gowithstock; A: Shutterstock.com / icemanphotos; E: Shutterstock.com / Teodor Lazarev; **S. 123** Shutterstock.com / Terelyuk; **S. 124** unten: Shutterstock.com /

stockfour; oben: mauritius images / Westend61; **S. 125** Mitte: stock.adobe.com / David; oben: stock.adobe.com / postywood1; unten: stock.adobe.com / Eddie Cloud; **S. 127** oben: stock.adobe.com / Jackie Davies; unten: stock. adobe.com / Alexey Fedorenko; **S. 128** A: Shutterstock.com / lazyllama; B: Shutterstock.com / Gorodenkoff; F: Shutterstock.com / CHIARI VFX; C: Shutterstock.com / Roman Samborskyi; E: Shutterstock.com / Ayesha kanwal; D: Shutterstock.com / guteksk7; **S. 130** A: mauritius images / Hemis.fr; oben: stock.adobe.com / Peter Hermes Furian; C: mauritius images / SagaPhoto; B: stock.adobe.com / aitormmfoto; Jack: Cornelsen / Chocolate Films; **S. 131** D: stock.adobe.com / Eugene Remizov; Orla: Cornelsen / Chocolate Films; E: mauritius images / alamy stock photo / Striking Images – Tourism Ireland; F: mauritius images / Rene Mattes; **S. 132** A: mauritius images / Loop Images / Extramural Activity; B: stock.adobe.com / hunterbliss; D: mauritius images / John Warburton-Lee; C: mauritius images / alamy stock photo / Jane Sweeney; **S. 133** stock.adobe.com / BCFC; **S. 134** Interfilm Berlin Management; **S. 135** A: stock.adobe.com / triocean; B: stock.adobe.com / brizmaker; D: stock.adobe.com / bit24; C: Shutterstock.com / Ihor Khobta; E: stock.adobe.com / ti_to_tito; **S. 136** Shutterstock.com / Duncan Andison; **S. 140** oben: stock.adobe.com / Maayan; Flaggen: Shutterstock.com / ONYXprj; **S. 141** oben rechts: Ungermeyer; Mitte rechts: Ungermeyer; Mitte rechts: Cornelsen; **S. 142** Shutterstock.com / Illerlok_xolms; **S. 149** Shutterstock. com / Iakov Filimonov; **S. 152** Shutterstock.com / fizkes; **S. 167** Shutterstock.com / Laurie Barr; **S. 168** car park: stock.adobe.com / Zoe; traffic light: stock.adobe.com / alice_photo; zebra crossing: Shutterstock.com / Claudio Divizia; block of flats: stock.adobe.com / bzyxx; petrol station: stock.adobe.com / Carolyn Franks; oben re.: Shutterstock.com / Barbara Sauder; roundabout: stock.adobe.com / Sampajano-Anizza; office building: stock. adobe.com / william87; skyscraper: stock.adobe.com / Rich Lindie; **S. 169** Emojis: stock.adobe.com / jehafo; oben: mauritius images / Maskot; **S. 170** cotton: Shutterstock.com / Gemenacom; rubber: Shutterstock.com / Nataliia K; silk: Shutterstock.com / Jag_cz; leather: Shutterstock.com / In Green; plain: Shutterstock.com / RooftopStudio-Bangkok; polyester: Shutterstock.com / Anastasiia Horova; canvas: Shutterstock.com / Preto Perola; colourful: Shutterstock.com / VLADIMIR VK; striped: Shutterstock.com / Sandratsky Dmitriy; wool: stock.adobe.com / Kapaw-tord; metal: Shutterstock.com / Jan Dix; patterned: stock.adobe.com / Dmitry Naumov; checked: Shutterstock. com / hidesy; flowery: Shutterstock.com / NJMSTOCK; dark: Shutterstock.com / RooftopStudioBangkok; light: Shutterstock.com / Africa Studio; dotted: Shutterstock.com / pornpawit; **S. 171** Emojis: Shutterstock.com / Yefym Turkin; oben: stock.adobe.com / Maryna; **S. 173** handball: Shutterstock.com / Focus and Blur; gymnastics: Shutterstock.com / BearFotos; ice skating: stock.adobe.com / petunyia; canoeing: Shutterstock.com / Kzenon; boxing: Shutterstock.com / PeopleImages.com – Yuri A; archery: Shutterstock.com / VicVic Liu; rowing: Shutter-stock.com / videoTD; volleyball: Shutterstock.com / Monkey Business Images; rugby: Shutterstock.com / wave-breakmedia; scuba diving: Shutterstock.com / Jukkis; judo: stock.adobe.com / JackF; athletics: Shutterstock.com / Jacob Lund; **S. 174** frog: Shutterstock.com / Dinda Yulianto; bee: Shutterstock.com / Feng Lu; deer: Shutterstock. com / Radek Karko; fox: Shutterstock.com / Sandra Standbridge; valley: stock.adobe.com / Tomasz Zajda; butterfly: Shutterstock.com / CHAINFOTO24; mushroom: Shutterstock.com / romvo; coast: stock.adobe.com / Gordon Fahey; grass: Shutterstock.com / SHUTTER TOP; corn: Shutterstock.com / ABCDstock; wave: stock.adobe.com / NorthShoreSurfPhotos; rocks: stock.adobe.com / pamela_d_mcadams; **S. 175** oben Mi.: stock.adobe.com / Michael Conrad; Mitte Mi.: stock.adobe.com / cceliaphoto; unten li.: stock.adobe.com / M·H; oben links: stock. adobe.com / motorradcbr; unten links: stock.adobe.com / Leonid Andronov; unten Mitte: stock.adobe.com / WernerHilpert; Mitte links: stock.adobe.com / M. Schoenfeld; oben rechts: stock.adobe.com / Sina Ettmer; Mitte rechts: stock.adobe.com / Ralf; **S. 176** von ob. nach un.: stock.adobe.com / Dilip; stock.adobe.com / atScene; stock. adobe.com / martialred; stock.adobe.com / manstock007; Shutterstock.com / Arafat Uddin; Shutterstock.com / Great_Kit; stock.adobe.com / North; stock.adobe.com / anisa; stock.adobe.com / KR Studio; stock.adobe.com / yoyonpujiono; stock.adobe.com / iconin Ja; stock.adobe.com / martialred **S. 185** canal: stock.adobe.com / EMrpize; compas: Shutterstock.com / Aldiki Gustiyan; skyscrapers: stock.adobe.com / Elnur Amikishiyev; bagpipes: stock. adobe.com / mipan; **S. 186** Mitte: stock.adobe.com / Elenarts; unten: Shutterstock.com / Monkik; oben: stock. adobe.com / serkat Photography; **S. 187** unten: Shutterstock.com / Rvector; oben: Shutterstock.com / Sonyaudina; **S. 188** umbrella: stock.adobe.com / jantima14; London Eye: stock.adobe.com / Photocreo Bednarek; Säule: stock. adobe.com / TimurD; Schrift: stock.adobe.com / milavas; roundabout: stock.adobe.com / Harald Schindler; **S. 189** orange juice: Shutterstock.com / Digital Genetics; chickpeas: stock.adobe.com / Diana Taliun; unten rechts: Shutterstock.com / worradirek; cucumber: stock.adobe.com / sommai; **S. 191** oben: stock.adobe.com / andreusK; unten: Shutterstock.com / Patra.K; **S. 193** unten: stock.adobe.com / Africa Studio; oben: stock.adobe.com / Nata-liia; Mitte: stock.adobe.com / Tarzhanova; **S. 195** unten: Shutterstock.com / Flat vectors; oben: stock.adobe.com / Mak; Mitte: Shutterstock.com / Peera_stockfoto; **S. 196** stock.adobe.com / Roman; **S. 197** oben: stock.adobe.com / koft; unten: stock.adobe.com / dekART; **S. 198** Shutterstock.com / wavebreakmedia; **S. 199** unten: Shutterstock. com / arsa35; oben li.: Shutterstock.com / Syda Productions; oben re.: Shutterstock.com / Nerthuz; **S. 200** Shutterstock.com / Popartic; **S. 201** oben: stock.adobe.com / dwi; unten: Shutterstock.com / sirtravelalot; **S. 202** stock.adobe.com / Enrico Ferraresi; **S. 203** unten: Shutterstock.com / Quang Ho; Mitte: Shutterstock.com / Dim Dimich; oben: stock.adobe.com / Creaturart; **S. 204** oben: stock.adobe.com / David Peperkamp; unten: Shutterstock.com / Denis Belitsky; **S. 205** Shutterstock.com / lynx_v; **S. 206** unten: Shutterstock.com / photomaster; oben: Shutterstock.com / rogelson; **S. 207** unten: Shutterstock.com / Macrovector; Mitte: stock.adobe.com / lightgirl; **S. 208** Mitte: stock.adobe.com / pcruciatti; unten: stock.adobe.com / Matthew Gilbert; oben: Shutterstock.com / New Africa; **S. 212** unten: stock.adobe.com / New Africa; oben: stock.adobe.com / Africa Studio; **S. 213** Shutterstock.com / Federico Rostagno; **S. 214** oben: Shutterstock.com / Vydrin; unten: Shutterstock.com / Yulia Davidovich; **S. 237** Shutterstock.com / HitToon

Textquellen
S. 36: *All in this together:* Zaina / *https://www.museumoflondon.org.uk/discover/languages-london*

Datenquellen
S. 36: Die Karte basiert auf Daten (Census 2021) des Office for National Statistics in London, *https://www.ons.gov.uk datasets/TS024/editions/2021/versions/1#version-history* (Zugriff: 16.08.2023);
S. 112: Die statistischen Daten in Text A basieren auf Informationen von *https://cybercrew.uk/blog/cyberbullying-statistics-uk/* (Zugriff: 09.11.2023) und *https://www.mayoclinic.org/healthy-lifestyle/tween-and-teen-health/in-depth/teens-and-social-media-use/art-20474437#:~:text=Social%20media%20is%20a%20big,media%20use%20have%20on%20teens%3F* (Zugriff: 9.11.2023)

continent / country / region	adjective	person	people
Afghanistan [æf'gænɪstɑːn] *Afghanistan*	Afghan ['æfgæn]	an Afghan	the Afghans
Albania [æl'beɪniə] *Albanien*	Albanian [æl'beɪniən]	an Albanian	the Albanians
America [ə'merɪkə] *Amerika*	American	an American	the Americans
Asia ['eɪʒə] *Asien*	Asian ['eɪʒn]	an Asian	the Asians
Austria ['ɒstriə] *Österreich*	Austrian ['ɒstriən]	an Austrian	the Austrians
Bangladesh [bæŋglə'deʃ] *Bangladesch*	Bangladeshi [bæŋglə'deʃi]	a Bangladeshi	the Bangladeshis
Caribbean [kærɪ'biːən] *die Karibik*	Caribbean	a Carib ['kærɪb]	the Caribs
China ['tʃaɪnə] *China*	Chinese [tʃaɪ'niːz]	a Chinese	the Chinese
Cuba ['kjuːbə] *Kuba*	Cuban	a Cuban	the Cubans
Czechia, the Czech Republic [tʃek rɪ'pʌblɪk] *Tschechien, die Tschechische Republik*	Czech [tʃek]	a Czech	the Czechs
Denmark ['denmɑːk] *Dänemark*	Danish ['deɪnɪʃ]	a Dane [deɪn]	the Danes
England ['ɪŋglənd] *England*	English ['ɪŋglɪʃ]	an Englishman / -woman	the English
Europe ['jʊərəp] *Europa*	European [ˌjʊərə'piːən]	a European	the Europeans
France [frɑːns] *Frankreich*	French [frentʃ]	a Frenchman / -woman	the French
Germany ['dʒɜːməni] *Deutschland*	German ['dʒɜːmən]	a German	the Germans
Great Britain ['brɪtn] *Großbritannien*	British ['brɪtɪʃ]	a Briton ['brɪtn]	the British
India ['ɪndiə] *Indien*	Indian ['ɪndiən]	an Indian	the Indians
Ireland ['aɪələnd] *Irland*	Irish ['aɪrɪʃ]	an Irishman / -woman	the Irish
Italy ['ɪtəli] *Italien*	Italian [ɪ'tæliən]	an Italian	the Italians
Jamaica [dʒə'meɪkə] *Jamaika*	Jamaican [dʒə'meɪkən]	a Jamaican	the Jamaicans
Japan [dʒə'pæn] *Japan*	Japanese [dʒæpə'niːz]	a Japanese	the Japanese
Kenya ['kenjə] *Kenia*	Kenyan ['kenjən]	a Kenyan	the Kenyans
Latin America [lætɪn ə'merɪkə] *Lateinamerika*	Latin American [lætɪn ə'merɪkən]	a Latin American	the Latin Americans
Lebanon ['lebənən] *der Libanon*	Lebanese [lebə'niːz]	a Lebanese	the Lebanese
Lithuania [lɪθju'eɪniə] *Litauen*	Lithuanian [lɪθju'eɪniən]	a Lithuanian	the Lithuanians
Mexico ['meksɪkəʊ] *Mexiko*	Mexican ['meksɪkən]	a Mexican	the Mexicans
Nepal [nə'pɔːl] *Nepal*	Nepalese [nepə'liːz]	a Nepalese	the Nepalese
the Netherlands ['neðələndz] *die Niederlande, Holland*	Dutch [dʌtʃ]	a Dutchman / -woman	the Dutch
Nigeria [naɪ'dʒɪəriə] *Nigeria*	Nigerian	a Nigerian	the Nigerians
Pakistan [pɑːkɪ'stɑːn] *Pakistan*	Pakistani [pɑːkɪ'stɑːni]	a Pakistani	the Pakistanis
Poland ['pəʊlənd] *Polen*	Polish ['pəʊlɪʃ]	a Pole [pəʊl]	the Poles
Portugal ['pɔːtʃʊgl] *Portugal*	Portuguese [pɔːtʃu'giːz]	a Portuguese	the Portuguese
Puerto Rico [pwɜːtə 'riːkəʊ] *Puerto Rico*	Puerto Rican	a Puerto Rican	the Puerto Ricans
Russia ['rʌʃə] *Russland*	Russian ['rʌʃn]	a Russian	the Russians
Scotland ['skɒtlənd] *Schottland*	Scottish ['skɒtɪʃ]	a Scot [skɒt]	the Scots
South Africa [saʊθ 'æfrɪkə] *Südafrika*	South African	a South African	the South Africans
South America [saʊθ ə'merɪkə] *Südamerika*	South American [saʊθ ə'merɪkən]	a South American	the South Americans
Spain [speɪn] *Spanien*	Spanish ['spænɪʃ]	Spaniard ['spænjəd]	the Spanish / the Spaniards
Turkey ['tɜːki]; Türkiye *die Türkei*	Turkish ['tɜːkɪʃ]	a Turk [tɜːk]	the Turks
the United Kingdom (the UK) [juˌnaɪtɪd 'kɪŋdəm, ˌjuː'keɪ] *das Vereinigte Königreich*	British ['brɪtɪʃ]	a Briton ['brɪtn]	the British
Ukraine [juː'kreɪn] die Ukraine	Ukrainian	a Ukrainian	the Ukrainians
Wales [weɪlz] Wales	Welsh [welʃ]	a Welshman / -woman	the Welsh